WALKING

WEST

Noëlle Sickels

St. Martin's Press
New York

Design by Ellen R. Sasahara

Map by Marion Dies and Terry Wilson

Library of Congress Cataloging-in-Publication Data

Sickels, Noëlle
  Walking west / Noëlle Sickels.
      p.   cm.
  ISBN 0-312-13208-5
  1. Overland journeys to the Pacific—Fiction. 2. Frontier and pioneer life—West (U.S.)—Fiction. 3. Women pioneers—West (U.S.)—Fiction. I.Title.
  PS3569.I269W34   1995
  813'.54—dc20   95-15456
                                                            CIP

First Edition: July 1995

10   9   8   7   6   5   4   3   2   1

Published by arrangement with Ariadne Press, Rockville, MD 20853

for Marilyn
without whom, so much less

Acknowledgments

THOUGH WRITING is a profoundly solitary activity, it is one that can be made easier or more difficult by the interpersonal relationships of the writer outside her workroom. I am fortunate in having a cluster of people who support me and my writing in various ways. Many heartfelt thanks belong to:

Victor Parra and Jude Parra-Sickels, who graciously leave me alone at my desk for many, many hours and who tolerate my distracted state of mind at those times when I've left my desk but not my story; Brian McDonnell, inveterate alchemist, who got *Walking West* its first reading at a publisher; Marilyn Monaco-Han, who will talk books and writing into the wee hours; Tom McGovern, who punctuates the family's progress with meals and photographs; my writing group, Jacqueline de Angelis, Lynette Prucha, and Terry Wolverton, who manage to bestow the right combination of praise and challenge; Carol Hoover of Ariadne Press, whose interest in the first draft of *Walking West* encouraged me to plunge into the second; Tom Epley of The Potomac Literary Agency, who has been my long-distance shepherd and champion; Hope Dellon and Jenny Notz of St. Martin's Press, who shed on my manuscript careful, intelligent, ardent attention; and Bertha "Snooky" Sickels, my mother, who was not alive to read one word of *Walking West,* but who long ago imparted to me her passionate attachment to language and books. I wish to acknowledge, too, the nineteenth-century women and men whose diaries, letters, and reminiscences of westward migration were the backbone of my research for *Walking West.*

The Muller Party

Council Bluffs, Iowa
Spring 1852

Alice Muller, *33*
Henry Muller, *38*
Sarah Muller, *14*
Hank Muller, *9*

Faith Muller, *22*   Jerusha Muller Hall, *35*
John Muller, *26*   Royal Hall, *35*
Elizabeth Muller, *3*   Flinder Hall, *16*
                            Ellen Hall, *11*
                            Gideon Hall, *5*

Helen Bowen, *19*
Derrick Bowen, *20*

Jack Webster, *22*   Bailey Jeffers, *35*
Reed Bennett, *19*

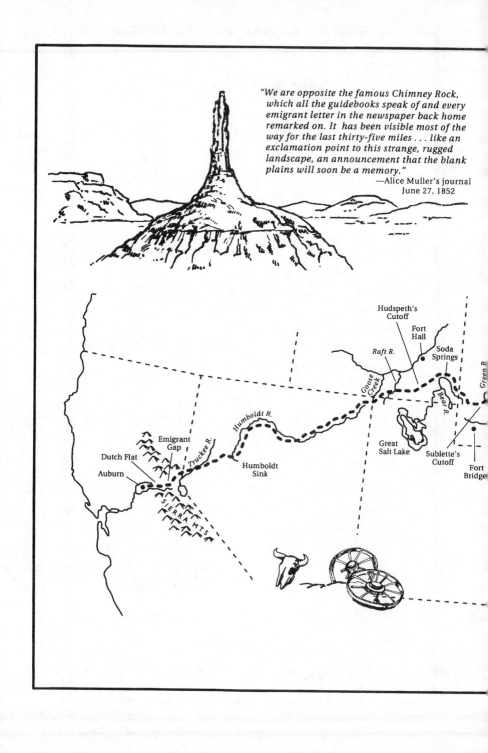

"We are opposite the famous Chimney Rock, which all the guidebooks speak of and every emigrant letter in the newspaper back home remarked on. It has been visible most of the way for the last thirty-five miles . . . like an exclamation point to this strange, rugged landscape, an announcement that the blank plains will soon be a memory."

—Alice Muller's journal
June 27, 1852

The Route
of the
Muller Party
May – November 1852

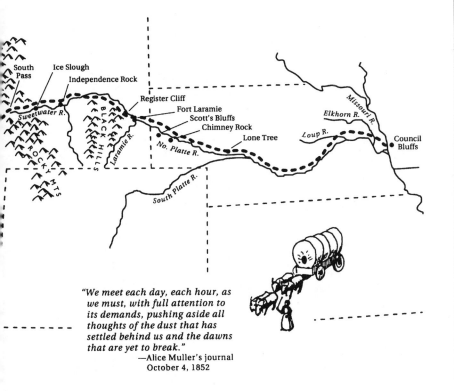

South Pass

Ice Slough

Independence Rock

Sweetwater R.

Register Cliff

Fort Laramie

Scott's Bluffs

Chimney Rock

Lone Tree

No. Platte R.

BLACK HILLS

Laramie R.

ROCKY MTS

South Platte R.

Missouri R.

Elkhorn R.

Loup R.

Council Bluffs

"We meet each day, each hour, as we must, with full attention to its demands, pushing aside all thoughts of the dust that has settled behind us and the dawns that are yet to break."
—Alice Muller's journal
October 4, 1852

Chapter 1

BREAK OF DAY," Alice Muller said to herself as she stood at the kitchen window and poured a second cup of coffee.

Alice had arisen in the dark. Today dawn did indeed seem to break in upon her while she worked. Alice was aware of no slow graying, only the end of the last night and the start of the first day, as if this morning had no time for a sentimental entry.

Through the window, Alice could see Henry in the yard loading the big wagon. Yesterday he had half-loaded the supply wagon they'd be sharing with the Halls and taken it over to their farm.

She finished her coffee, wiped out the tin cup and the coffeepot with a cloth, and tucked them into a wooden box on the floor. It was the last kitchen utensil to be packed. Already inside were a Dutch oven, a camp kettle, the rest of the tinware, a rolling pin, a bread pan, a frying pan, and a milk can. These few things and an open fire were to be her kitchen for the next six or seven months. Alice lifted her eyebrows in resignation.

She had stopped arguing months ago. If you could call arguing Henry's silent forbearance of her repeated comparisons of the virtues of their well-groomed Indiana farm to the uncertainties of California. She finally saw that good sense and wifely pleas were poor opponents to the alluring tales of western lands Henry had been accumulating from newspapers. Ideas built slowly in Henry, like stalagmites, but once established, they were unshakable. More impulsive men had been making the overland journey to the free land and gold fields of the far West for several years, but it was only now, in the spring of 1852, that Henry had determined the time was right for him.

"It will be the end to hard winters," Henry had said to her. "And we can hold far more land, and richer, by what everyone says, than here. It'll be a better, healthier life for the children, more prosperous, now and later. For us, too. And think of the sights we'll see!"

It would not be Alice's first move. When she married, she was transplanted from her parents' Philadelphia town house to the farm in western Pennsylvania Henry had newly cut from a generous corner of his father's land. That move, though a significant change, was one every young woman was expected to make without hesitation or, at least, without outward regrets, and Alice was determined to be a good wife from the outset.

They spent four years in the little cabin in the woods; Sarah was born there. Alice never got used to the darkness; Henry had not put in enough windows, nor razed enough trees. It always appeared, inside that house, to be five o'clock on a cloudy evening. Alice sometimes thought that Sarah's quiet, in-turning nature came of having been a baby and a toddler in that dim cabin and shaded yard.

Henry had never been truly content there, either. The farm remained in his mind his father's land, and though Henry was on cordial terms with his father, it seemed to Alice that Henry was somehow distrustful, even disapproving, of the old man. In any case, Henry was not comfortable being beholden to anyone. So he gave their farm to a younger brother who was planning to marry, and they set out for Indiana, along with another of Henry's brothers, sixteen-year-old John.

John had been living with them since he was fourteen, and before that he was at their place nearly every evening for supper, after his chores at his father's place were done. Alice helped him with his schoolwork. He would have got none of that at home. His father was illiterate, and among the motherless crowd of brothers and sisters, none had patience for John's slow ways. In truth, it was Henry and not Alice who drew John, but Alice didn't mind. The ease and joviality between the brothers was a pleasure to be around. They were of such like minds, at times one could finish the other's thought.

Henry had told Alice they must leave Pennsylvania before more babies came. Henry believed bringing forth children on a piece of land was a way to claim it and a way it claimed you. Alice was not sorry to go.

Alice built a most agreeable life in Indiana; she had friends, and she was always busy. The new house was more airy. There were many fewer trees. It was what the Pennsylvania cabin had never fully felt, her own true home. It was here that, in the course of time, John married and set up his own household. Meanwhile, there were three more babies, though only the boy had lived past six months.

"Hank, go tell your pa the grub box is ready to be attached to the side of the wagon," Alice called to her son, who was sitting at the doorway weaving a straw hat. He had already made one for himself and another for his father and was now fashioning one for his cousin Gideon. He put down his work and stepped out into the yard, his bare feet making no sound as he ran toward the wagon in the advancing April sunshine.

Alice surveyed her house. Despite some disarray from packing, it looked quite ordinary. Most of the furniture was in place and would stay so. The cast-iron stove was warm from breakfast. The beds were bare of blankets and ticks, but curtains still hung at the windows. Hank's wooden toys, carved by Henry on long winter evenings by the fire, were jumbled in a corner. A pretty English-made sewing basket sent by an aunt in Philadelphia lay in the seat of the rocking chair.

Alice began moving quickly around the house collecting various articles and carrying them to the rocker. In one armload she deposited an ivory-handled brush and mirror set, a daguerreotype of her parents, and a lace bonnet trimmed with pink silk rosebuds. In a second armload she deposited the family Bible and some other books and several folded paper packets of flower seeds. She was carrying a roll of three yards of white flax cloth and a roll of two yards of flax she had dyed red with ripe pokeberries when Henry entered the house.

Before he could speak, Alice began talking at him rapidly.

"I know we can't take anything bulky like Grandma's oak washstand or the old cradle or the rocking chair, but surely, Henry, you can find a place for these few things. You know how I worked to sun-bleach that white flax. It'll make a fine Sunday shirt for you or maybe a start to Sarah's hope chest. The red'll be a blouse for me. You like me in bright colors.

"The other things may seem foolish to you, but I simply cannot part with them. Different reasons, each, and some you'd laugh at, no doubt, but tightly set nonetheless."

Henry walked to the rocker. Alice stood behind it and watched him as his eyes roved over the objects in the chair's seat. His tanned, weather-lined face rarely gave a clue to the workings of his mind, even to Alice, who had been studying it for sixteen years. He was not a secretive or passionless man, but a man who craved simple answers and was willing to wait for them.

"Space'd be better used for trading goods or extra rations," he said tentatively, not yet looking up.

Alice did not move or speak. She knew he had not yet come to a decision.

"But," he finally said, smiling at her, "after such a speech, I can't see how to deny you. I'll bring in a box from the barn. Best finish up smartly. The others will be down at the crossroads soon."

Henry had succeeded in assembling a party of fellow emigrants from the neighborhood. There was John, of course, and his family; Henry and John's sister, Jerusha Hall, and her family; and the newlywed Bowens. A modest outfit, but Henry had heard that large wagon trains often became unwieldy or disharmonious on the trail and ended up breaking into smaller units anyway. Henry trusted his own resources to meet any eventuality the now well-worn road could present.

When Henry returned from the barn, Alice was rubbing the rippled glass of the windows with watered-down vinegar.

"That's no thing to be doing now," he said, setting the box inside the doorway.

"Henry, this is my house, and I'll leave it clean and respectable."

Alice rubbed more vigorously, not, he could see, to hasten the chore, but to stay further protests from him. He lingered in the doorway watching her; her vitality always impressed him. When she'd finished the windows, she took up a broom and began sweeping, moving in a pale cloud of dust motes ever closer to where he stood, as if she were gathering to his feet all their years together in that snug house. When she came up beside him, he reached out and grabbed the broom handle to stop her a moment. He felt as if he'd cut in on a dance.

"Say, girlie," he said, using the name he never spoke before others, "I'm figuring on tying that rocker to the back of the wagon last thing. How's that?"

Alice nodded at him and turned away abruptly. She carried the broom back to its customary corner and sloshed the vinegar water out the side window. She heard Henry's boots clump down the two wooden steps into the yard. Only then did she lift her apron to her face to pat away the tears.

A MONTH LATER, Alice was drying her sudsy hands on the same apron while, out of hearing range, she watched Henry shake hands with two young men. In the solidity of the hand-clasps and the slight head nods that accompanied them, she recognized the signs of an agreement.

Alice wondered if Henry had managed to find some honest tradesmen at last. Their small party had been camping outside Council Bluffs for a week, waiting a turn to ferry their five wagons and their animals across the Missouri River.

Wedged into a ravine, Council Bluffs was a rude town of

mostly log buildings along a gullied main street, with more than its share of profiteers. In her one walk through it, Alice had been unsettled by the high prices being asked for everything from flour and salt to wagons and draft animals, though Henry, who had gotten a good price for the farm and had been studying emigrants' guides for two winters running, was neither surprised nor dismayed. Still, Alice was glad they had outfitted themselves at home and needed only minor replenishments and some blacksmithing services.

Equally unsettling were the amount of gambling and the number of drunken men in the streets. There was no civil authority. Avoiding the town, as Alice and the other women did, was no guarantee of peace, either. Some emigrants had spent the latter part of the winter camped here, getting their outfits together, waiting to be joined by friends and relatives from other states, sitting out the wet weather until there'd be less mud and better grazing on the prairie. Boredom and idleness lured many men to cards and liquor, and these diversions, in turn, could lead to arguments, fights, and even shootings.

A woman in an adjacent river-bottom camp told Alice how one Sabbath a band of Mormons had broken up a dance among the Gentiles, as they called them; but she held that the saintly Mormons were as shrewd shavers in trade as anyone and that dealing with them in business did not guarantee you would not be Yankeed. She said, too, that though the Mormon bands were aimed for the Great Salt Lake, where Mormons had headed every spring since 1847, they would accept Gentiles to passenger over the plains with them as long as there were no arguments on religion. Of course, she continued, she wondered who would want to travel with them. Leastways, she said, it wouldn't likely be folks from Ohio, Missouri, or Illinois, who hated and feared Mormons and had driven them out of their states.

Council Bluffs was the Mullers' first stop of any duration, but Alice would always remember it as a place of movement. At any time of day she could turn in any direction and see people walking, men loading and unloading wagons, women cooking and washing, animals and wagons lumbering toward the flatboats, children running alongside.

At night, campfires flickered on all sides. The sounds of banjos, fiddles, and singing overlaid the cries of sleepy babies. The periodic bray of a mule broke into the lowing of the oxen.

The air itself was alive. Food aromas from neighboring cook pots mingled with stinging barnyard scents, and breezes off the river brought in the wet smell of spring.

Alice watched Henry and the young men part. Henry strode over to where she was draping wet laundry around the wagon. They had encountered spring snows and heavy rains crossing Iowa, and much of their clothing had become mud-sodden.

Henry pulled his pipe and a leather tobacco pouch from a pocket. He hit the pipe against the side of the wagon.

"Well, those boys have had themselves some adventure already, and not even really on the prairie yet," he said in an admiring tone.

"Are they tradesmen?" Alice asked.

"No. They hope to be prospectors. Had all they needed loaded on a steamer in St. Louis bound for Independence, but the boat blew up and sank."

"How horrible," Alice exclaimed. Yet what a relief, in a way, she thought. She would have preferred to be a victim of a God-sent catastrophe rather than a participant in the plodding destruction of her home, in which her house had been sold, many of her belongings given away, and the rest packed up and buried in the depths of the wagons. If one is to be unmoored, better at once and with the opportunity for loud grieving.

"They weren't aboard, luckily, but following in another riverboat," Henry continued. "They said a hundred thirty-five were killed."

"What were you shaking on?" Alice inquired.

"Oh," Henry said, as if it had slipped his mind, "on them joining our party. I'd talked to the one fellow earlier and was just now meeting the other. They'll help with the work in exchange for sharing our food and our company."

"But, Henry," Alice protested, "do we have the money and the space for more provisions?"

"We must make do," Henry said firmly. "I feel the need of more men in our party. Surely you can't object to two extra pairs of strong arms. I'm sure Jerusha will welcome relief from driving those oxen on the supply wagon."

Alice frowned. Two extra appetites to satisfy, she thought, and those arms won't be easing any of my chores. Alice was used to hard work, and she did not think of her lot as unfair, but she did not like added tasks to be cloaked as boons.

"Well, I hope they're not carousers," she said, wishing she had observed them more carefully.

"Two footloose, healthy young fellows sober at midday in Council Bluffs? That speaks for their characters a bit, now, don't it, girlie?" Henry teased. "And one of them plays the mouth organ."

Alice bent to the bucket at her feet, wrung out a pair of socks, and spread them to dry on the iron tire of a wheel.

"So," she retorted, "if the other one juggles, we can hire them out for campfire entertainments."

Henry chuckled. He tamped down the tobacco in his pipe and leaned over the low-burning campfire to light a spill. Sucking deeply on the lit pipe, he leaned back against the wagon box and exhaled fruity clouds of smoke in a long, relaxed sigh.

Disagreements between them were often settled in this in-direct fashion. Just as they reached the brink of conflict, Alice would turn back, as if she had looked over the edge and de-cided it was not worth it to go on. Now she gave a coarsely woven linsey-woolsey shirt an extra tight twist to squeeze out the cold, gray water, and added her own, quieter sigh to Henry's. Shaking the shirt out in front of her, she looked over the encampment and noticed her brother-in-law approach-ing.

Royal Hall's bright orange hair and beard were easily spotted at a distance. Trotting on either side of him were two boys, Roy's five-year-old son Gideon, also orange-haired, and Alice and Henry's nine-year-old Hank, both wearing straw hats. Holding Gideon's hand was his eleven-year-old sister Ellen. She, too, was a redhead, but her hair was darker than her father's, like rust or red clay.

"Webster and Bennett meet up with you yet?" Roy asked Henry in greeting.

"Sure did. I was just telling Alice about them."

"How about Miss Jeffers?"

"Who?"

"Miss Jeffers," Hank interrupted. "She's a schoolmarm, not as pretty as Miss Thompson back home . . ."

"But she gave us licorice," Gideon added in her defense.

"They ate it all right away, but I'm saving mine," Ellen said, cocking her head toward the boys hopping up and down in front of Alice.

"Hush, children," Alice scolded. "You boys go gather me some kindling, and, Ellen, look in your ma's wagon for any clothes need washing before I dump this bucket."

Ellen extracted a licorice stick from the pocket of her gingham dress and bit off a piece before walking away. The boys, glad to be set loose from the adults, ran toward the river. Roy's hounds, Rouser and Old Smith, who had been dozing under the wagon, shuddered awake and loped after them. Alice watched the four of them weaving between wagons and leaping over boxes and around the groups of littler children sitting in the dirt.

She tried to see with their eyes for a moment. If the trip so far had seemed to the children like a long picnic, which was what Sarah had said, this encampment, with its hundreds of wagons and thousands of emigrants, must have the feel for them of a grand fairground.

The number of wagons was matched by the variety of people. There were farm folk like themselves, some herding large numbers of cows and chickens and sheep, and many single men, some still boyish and wide-eyed, others more seasoned and gruffer. In town, occasional cavalrymen and infantrymen could be spotted, and Mormons. The Mormon men, who favored the Upper Ferry ten miles north, were ordinary enough to look at, but they always provoked clucking speculation on the number of wives and children they might claim.

Hank had been thrilled to report he had seen three Omaha Indians wrapped in red blankets perched on the opposite riverbank early one morning. Another day, he had spent an enraptured hour watching two Indian marksmen shooting arrows at nickels thrown up in the air by emigrants.

A party of freedmen had passed one afternoon. Alice had studied them as their mule-drawn wagon rattled by; they stared straight ahead, their dark faces frozen into a neutral expression Alice could not confidently ascribe to any emotion, though it did seem closer to anger than anything else. When the little girl with them, her head bristling with short, tight braids tied with strips of red muslin, looked directly at her, Alice had smiled and nodded at her, but the child had only regarded her impassively and then turned away.

Alice could not imagine what these people's lives had been like, what they had endured to get onto the road they now traveled, what they expected to find in the future. She felt a little bit afraid of them, of their self-possession and the acquaintanceship she assumed they had with bravery.

Gideon and Hank and the dogs disappeared from sight around a tent, and Alice turned her attention to Henry and Roy.

"So Miss Jeffers is looking to join a party bound for California," Roy was saying. "And, of course, she'd prefer a party as has women in it."

"Could she pay?" Henry asked.

"Don't know, but I should hope she expects to," Roy answered.

"If she's a teacher," put in Alice, "she might fit in some lessons for the children."

"Lessons are all well and good," Henry said, drawing deeply on his pipe and squinting through the smoke, "but lessons won't get us across the prairie or through the mountains. She'll have to pay."

Roy took out his pocket watch.

"She was to meet us at the ferry landing at two o'clock if she didn't find a place with another party," he said.

"Let's go then," said Henry jovially.

Alice watched the two men winding their way through the encampment as their sons had, though more decorously. This is a great fairground to them, too, she thought, complete with appraisals and negotiations. She shook her head with a mixture of amusement and irritation.

But these reactions were fleeting, edged out by the drowsy, leaden feeling that had overtaken her almost every afternoon at this time in the past week. She had come almost to look forward to it, for when the heaviness settled upon her she had no energy to spare for remorse over what she'd left behind nor for worry over what lay ahead. While it lasted she existed only in the thick present, peacefully stranded.

Alice sat down in the rocking chair. I'll fix some hyson tea in a bit, she excused herself. But when she laid her head back, she quickly fell asleep.

A half hour later the shouts of Hank and Gideon pulled her awake. When she opened her eyes, she saw Helen Bowen smiling down at her. Helen's smile was always a surprise because it seemed to hold her face together and make some sense of it. Without a smile, Helen's features looked mismatched and comical. One eye was noticeably smaller than the other, and one corner of her mouth dipped down sharply. Her nose was too large, but the youthful roundness of her cheeks and throat forgave it, and Helen so intrigued onlookers with the range of her facial expressions that she was often mistaken as comely.

Alice had enjoyed watching Helen's changeable face during the weeks crossing Iowa. She herself was pretty in a traditional way. People had always praised her slanted blue eyes, her even teeth, her delicately shaped mouth and nose, and many times she'd had herself compared to a cameo. Alice never bothered about her prettiness, thinking her looks rather uninteresting, though she was vain about her hands, which were finely shaped and fashionably creamy-skinned.

It took no small amount of effort to keep them soft and manicured in the midst of farm life, but she accomplished it through the use of work gloves and imported lotions. Jerusha had always been suspicious of Alice's hands, convinced Alice must be stinting somehow in her duties as a wife and mother, but Jerusha had never been able to find hard proof of it. She had come, finally, to conclude not that her suspicions were ill founded, but that Henry was far too lenient and easily satisfied. Hands like that had no place on a respectable married woman.

Alice returned Helen's smile, though weakly, for she felt fatigued and vaguely unwell despite her nap.

"Good news," Helen declared, raising her thick eyebrows. "We cross tomorrow."

"COME ON, THEN, let's go find a game of monte," Jack Webster said, giving his cousin's arm an encouraging squeeze.

Reed Bennett did not move or return Jack's broad smile. Reed had seen that same smile worked on others, chiefly hesitant or aggrieved women. He himself was swayed by it at times, though less and less frequently as the years went on. Once, Reed watched Jack's special smile save him from a knife-wielding drunk who thought Jack had cheated him at cards.

The smile seemed to say, "I know I'm a trouble to you, and where you are probably right and I am probably wrong, indulge me just this once anyway. I promise you'll be happier for it. I'll see to that."

But this was too big a matter to allow Jack to have his way. At least not so easily. Reed would not let himself be rounded into a card game as if he were too dumb to see he was being handled.

"You shoulda told me," he said, frowning and shrugging off Jack's hand.

"It didn't seem like you'd mind so much."

"We're partners."

"Yes, yes, partners. No cause to doubt that."

"Partners decide together."

Jack's smile faded. He looked down at the ground, then frowned up into the sky, as if he were judging what turn the weather might take.

"And I never woulda agreed to signing on to a party full-freighted with women and their broods. You shoulda told me about them," Reed added, hoping now he'd got the dead-wood on Jack.

Reed was uneasy with Jack's gaze off him. It made him feel like he wasn't there. Jack's attention had a habit of wandering away from a person even when that person was right before him and wanting his attention badly. Actually, Reed knew, it was just when a person most wanted Jack's attention that it was likely to ramble. Reed had never known anyone to con-quer Jack in this—not Jack's mother, who had raised both boys, nor Jack's first woman, the crazy Widow Larkin, nor any woman after, nor any man either, though the men, of course, mostly did not care as long as Jack worked and sported fairly, which he did. But Reed cared. And school himself as he might, he could not stop caring.

"Look, Reed," Jack finally said, still staring up and speak-ing as if he were describing something he saw in the blue distance, "where there's women, there'll be good food, clean clothes, soft voices. The journey's hard enough."

"I've no need of such things."

Jack slowly lowered and turned his head, seeming to scan the horizon behind Reed. When his eyes met Reed's, a gent-ler version of that smile broke out again.

"Those folks need us, Reed. They're so appreciative, they're taking us on for free, remember. We should have paid a hundred dollars. Each."

"That candies it some," Reed conceded.

"And to soothe your fitful impressions of women, I'm going to take some of that money we saved on our passage and buy you the handsomest whore in Council Bluffs."

Reed shoved his hat deeper onto his head to hide a blush. If Jack knew which was the handsomest whore in town, it was a sure bet he'd been to her himself already and might do again. Reed didn't mind that Jack might have preceded him—it wouldn't be the first time—but he didn't like Jack to follow him. You never knew what a woman might tell, especially with a charmer like Jack in her bed.

"Don't want the handsomest," Reed grumbled. "Handsome women expect admiration. Even whores."

Jack laughed loudly. "But, Reed, admiring a woman can be a very pleasant thing."

Jack stretched his arm across his cousin's shoulders and steered him toward the hotel saloon several yards away. Jaunty piano tunes and sporadic shouts of merriment sallied from the open windows.

"Never mind, Reed, old boy. We'll get you a gal that knows her business and won't expect nothing from you but some silver dollars."

SEATED ON A small wooden stool opposite the Council Bluffs City Hotel, Bailey Jeffers had been watching Jack and Reed argue, and now she watched them stroll into the hotel together. She hadn't heard any of their discussion and hadn't cared to. They were just one facet of the scene she'd been trying for the past half hour to capture with charcoal on paper. She was making a series of rough sketches to develop later into a pen-and-ink drawing.

The two men, off to one side as they'd been, had made a good compositional foil to the group of five other men crouched over a dice game and a whiskey bottle just beside the hotel's front entrance. Bailey worked quickly, knowing her subjects could move away at any time. A steady stream of wagons and pedestrians crossed from right to left and left to right across her line of vision, and they and their dust obscured her view, making her task more challenging.

But Bailey Jeffers was not afraid of a challenge. If anything, she was afraid of not having challenges, even obstacles, in life. Orphaned at an early age, unmarried, and now about to embark on an arduous journey with a band of strangers, Bailey was more at home with struggle than with peace and ease. Most people, she was aware, craved contentment, but she did not trust contentment, maybe because she never expected to achieve it herself. In its place, she aimed for experiences, as many as a woman alone could collect, which too often meant merely observing or listening to the experiences of others. It was the desire to see for herself that had brought her by steamboat from St. Louis to Council Bluffs to sign on to a wagon train to California.

Reed and Jack interested Bailey not only because they balanced the drawing overall, but also because the two of them visually balanced each other so well. They appeared to be about the same age, and their builds were similar, lean, with the singular muscularity of youth, but there the likeness ended.

The one who was doing most of the talking was startlingly good-looking, with hair as black as an Indian's, a full mouth sensuous enough to be envied by an actress, and a dashing white scar slicing across one black eyebrow to save the face from a boring wooden perfection. The other, more glum man, in contrast, was pallid and somehow worn down. His hair, though longer than the dark man's, was thinner. Lanky, light brown wisps hung well below his collar; when the breeze lifted them, his neck showed an unnatural whiteness. Some sort of scarring, Bailey thought—burns perhaps. The skin on the backs of his hands had clearly suffered burning. The man's face was freckled, his features regular enough, but not appealing. He wore a scraggly beard and had no eyebrows.

When the men entered the hotel, Bailey closed her sketchbook and stood up. She stretched her arms above her head; her limbs and back were cramped from sitting on the low stool hunched over her work so long. From the corner of her eye she caught the disapproving glare of a fat woman passing in a mule-drawn wagon; the woman poked the man beside her sharply in his ribs when his gaze lingered on Bailey's gracefully arching figure.

Sighing, Bailey turned her back on the estimable couple and picked up her stool. She began the long walk back to her little tent to pack up. Henry Muller had said he'd send his brother John with a wheelbarrow that evening to convey her belongings to their camp.

FLINDER HALL liked walking through the jumble of camp-sites with her uncle. John Muller, though ten years her senior, was only twenty-six, and so could easily be mistaken for her husband. She had no romantic interest in him at all; her wish to have passersby, especially men, think of her as John's wife was a purely tactical one.

In the short time at Council Bluffs, Flinder had seen more men and more kinds of men than she had in all her years at home. The way so many of them looked at her, some full on, some furtively, alarmed her, but it also fascinated her. She almost wished she could find one with a friendly enough face that she could ask him what the looks really meant. But even Flinder, whose father often upbraided her for being too bold, knew that such an inquiry was impossible. Now, however, in John's company, on the way to fetch the schoolmarm, she felt undisturbed by the attention she drew, and she openly watched the men watching her.

Back in Indiana, her mother, Jerusha, had actively dis-couraged any interest paid to Flinder by the few eligible young men living near their farm. Flinder hadn't minded. Though she was already of marriageable age and fully ex-pected to be someone's wife someday, she was in no rush to marry. Every woman she knew was married, and she had never seen one of them lift her long skirts to run across a meadow or sit in a chair for even an hour without a baby in her lap or her hands busy with something.

"You'd best keep your eyes on your path," John said when Flinder stumbled into an anvil beside someone's wagon.

"I am," she replied, embarrassed.

John's pace had quickened, and Flinder had to trot now and then to keep up with his long-legged strides.

"I guess it's only natural. My Faith was only a year more than you when we wed. Still, you want to be cautious, Flin, where you set your gaze. A girl that looks like you do courts trouble."

"What do you mean, Uncle John?" she said, feeling both wronged and flattered by his remarks.

John steered his wheelbarrow in a wide arc past an open area where two men were training a three-yoke team of six oxen to work together. They had wisely yoked the youngest steers between the two leaders and the two wheelers. Even so, it was a hard task, but not so heartrending as breaking mules, which would kick, bite, and strike with their forefeet. It seemed only unbroken mules were available along the Missouri, and some emigrants, especially the city men, hired Mexicans to break the long ears into harness. Yesterday John had seen a man foolish enough to try to ride a mule thrown hell, west, and crooked. John was glad he and the other men in the Muller party had worked their teams at home.

Three men were watching the efforts of the ox handlers and calling out words of advice. John scowled at one who shifted position to watch Flinder go by, and the gawker quickly turned away.

John had grimaced at the man because he thought it his duty to do so, but he did not really blame him for his hungering stare. Flinder Hall's smooth, pink-cheeked face was framed by soft auburn curls that had pulled free of the ribbon loosely binding her thick, wavy hair at the base of her neck. Her eyes were a velvety brown with flecks of yellow, thickly lashed, and arched over by dark eyebrows that looked drawn on, so lyrical was their curve. She had what was politely called good carriage, which meant a full bosom and erect posture. That her movements were as lively and innocently free as a child's only added to the allure of her well-favored body. And John knew many of these men, traveling alone, had already been some weeks away from their wives and sweethearts and faced many months more without the prospect of a woman's company.

John's thoughts turned then to his pregnant wife and her blooming, full body. As he watched Faith last night in the simple act of slipping her chemise over her head, a longing had welled up in him that he had not felt in many weeks. She was a lovely study in contrasts, her delicate frame supporting the bulk of the baby inside her; her girlish face, as timid as a mourning dove's, floating above the startling assertion of her enlarged, blue-veined breasts. He had reached out and stroked her round, impossibly hard belly, and she had laughed at him, at the awe in his face, and then stroked her belly herself, as if it were not a part of her, looking over at him with a distracted smile. John had fallen asleep in her arms, beneath the itchy cowl of unspent desire.

"Just be cautious is all," he finally replied hoarsely to his niece.

Flinder sighed and carefully looked straight ahead or down at the ground for the rest of the walk. She wondered if, when she was a grown, married woman, people would answer her questions more fully. Then she remembered how her father had simply walked into the kitchen one afternoon while her mother was kneading bread dough and announced he'd sold the farm and they'd be leaving for California in two months. At least in the case of her parents, marriage did not seem to guarantee any more information than childhood. Flinder guessed it was up to her to find out things on her own.

Chapter 2

ALICE LAY in the wagon pretending to sleep. Here at Council Bluffs she had been sleeping inside rather than on the ground beside the wagon in order to gain a little privacy in the rambunctious camp. She could tell from the voices outside that everyone else was already up. She wished the cook fire were not so close to her wagon. The smell of bacon fat was nauseating.

She stared up at the arching double thickness of canvas supported five feet overhead by six hickory bows. The bed of the wagon was also hickory, well seasoned, and measured ten feet by four feet with straight, three-foot-high sides. Henry had worked months building it and fitting it with hinged pine provisions bins. Alice felt as if she were lying in a box, like a baby in its cradle. But she did not feel safe, as a baby would. This wagon was not just her bed, it was her whole world now, and all the home she'd have for a long time.

Alice hoped the wagon proved as sturdy as it looked; the road had not really tested it yet. She hoped, too, that she'd find it in herself to be sturdy. Only she could make again the home she'd lost. Only she could fashion a sense of home on the journey. Because only she knew how or saw the need.

The wagon creaked as someone climbed onto the rear apron. Alice sat up and saw the stout head and shoulders of Henry's sister Jerusha. Her ruddy face showed concern.

"Are you ailing?" she asked.

Though Jerusha was only two years older than Alice, Jerusha's greater size and her naturally meddlesome disposition, nurtured by her position as eldest girl in a family of nine, inclined her maternally towards her sister-in-law.

"No, no," answered Alice. "I guess it's just thoughts of home are still heavy on me."

Alice had fallen asleep the night before wondering if the new woman on the place would keep up the rock garden she had carefully laid out and tended over so many seasons, putting aside the last hour of light each summer's day to weed and thin and to cultivate the soil. She thought, too, of the day lily border along the picket fence around the small graveyard on the hill behind the house, and the ring of marigolds she used to plant each spring in front of the two little headstones of her babies.

A friend had promised to check the grave sites for her and keep them groomed, but how long could Alice really expect her friend, with a large family of her own, to do that—two years, three? Alice had photographs of both babies in their funeral gowns. The pure marvel of those still, dreamy images would have to do in place of the quiet summer evenings gardening on the windswept hill.

Jerusha considered Alice's answer a moment, then bent down her fleshy frame and stepped completely into the wagon. She smoothed a shawl over her ample bosom and looked hard at Alice.

"I've been watching you, Alice, this last week," she said at last. "Off your food, sluggish in the afternoons . . . You might have told me you were expecting."

Alice suddenly felt guilty and afraid, like a criminal who has been caught red-handed and knows what her fate must be, and, like an apprehended wrongdoer, her first impulse was to contradict the plain truth.

"Jerusha, you do look for worries. Isn't it enough John's Faith is six months along and will have to birth her babe God knows where on this journey?" Alice was annoyed to find her voice quavered.

"What is it, Alice? Is Henry unawares? No need to be so sly. Had he known, it wouldn't have stopped him coming."

Jerusha, who had nursed her own mother through several

unwanted birthings, was well aware of men's indifference to the sometimes heavy toll of motherhood. Even though she set Henry, her favorite brother, apart from other men as superior in virtue and sympathy, in this care she was sure he must be as blind as any other of his sex. After all, he hadn't to this day ever admitted the real cause of their mother's death, though he had been old enough at the time to guess it.

Alice slipped the quilt up to her chin when she felt the corners of her mouth pulling downward and her throat tightening. She didn't have it in her to evade Jerusha any longer.

"There now, no crying after spilt milk." Jerusha gently withdrew the quilt. "It's not like it's your first. Nor Faith's either, come to that. When do you figure?"

The factual question calmed Alice a little. "Late November, I guess," she replied with a steadier voice. "Maybe middle December."

"Well, then," Jerusha said cheerfully, patting Alice's knee, "yours'll be born in California in your new house on a proper bed. So set the best foot forward. The men won't take kindly to an unborn babe losing them their place at the river."

INDEED, THE MEN were so excited about the crossing, none of them had noticed Alice's late rising. Eating a wedge of cornbread Jerusha had saved her from breakfast, Alice walked behind the Bowens' wagon, the last in their line. Alice had succeeded in checking her tears during her talk with Jerusha, but she could feel them still clutching at her throat and chest. She pushed them down with hard swallows of the dry bread and tried to corral her mind's commotion by watching the sway of the wagon ahead. She found no soothing rhythm there, however; the Bowens' wagon lurched and tottered and shivered as if Alice's tumbling thoughts were driving it.

Derrick Bowen had approached Henry at church about a month before their departure and asked to partake in their proposed journey; Henry, pleased to bolster his preference of not joining a larger company in Missouri, eagerly agreed.

Derrick and his new bride, Helen, had been the first to arrive at the crossroads meeting place, and they greeted each subsequent family with bright shouts and eager waves. Their stage of life, Alice had thought, looking at their zealous smiles, is a better time to undertake this trip, when there're fewer memories and ties to be left behind and every day seems to start fresh anyway.

During the month it had taken the little band to cross from Indiana to the Missouri River, Alice had noticed that neither cold weather nor muddy roads nor the discomforts of living always outdoors had dampened the festive spirits of the young couple. Alice could still picture the two of them crouched together under an umbrella for more than an hour keeping the rain off a Dutch oven buried in the embers of the supper fire. They had looked like two children trading secrets.

"This is no weather for baking," Jerusha had lectured when she saw what Helen was up to.

"But today is Derrick's birthday," Helen had insisted, blithely beating the first dimpling raindrops into the cake batter. "Today he turns twenty and no other."

It was Helen who was driving the jerking wagon that Alice was following down to the banks of the Missouri. Derrick Bowen had chosen mules over oxen, reasoning that mules were faster than oxen, had less tender feet, and endured summer heat better. But they were notoriously stubborn, and Helen was new to driving. Derrick had said Helen must learn to handle the team because there might be times on the trail when he'd be needed with the other men for some important task. Back home, a woman rarely, if ever, had to drive a wagon.

When the wagons were lining up to head for the river, Derrick had assured Helen she was ready to drive alone, and with a boyish whoop and a slap to his horse's rump, he had ridden ahead to be beside the first wagon. She could see his straight back bobbing beside Henry Muller's wagon whenever she glanced up from the vexatious mules.

Helen would have liked to be up ahead, too. She and Derrick had taken several rides during their brief courtship, and she'd always been proud of his fine set as a horseman. At the least, she wished he'd come back and help her, but she did not dare call out to him or even send word by one of the boys trotting alongside the wagons.

Helen was still learning the ways of her marriage. She and Derrick had been wed only a week before their departure, and they had spent that week in her parents' small house. They'd slept on a cornhusk-filled mattress thrown down each night in the kitchen and taken up before first light each morning so that her mother could stoke up the stove for breakfast.

In the beginning on the road, their first time really on their own, really married, Helen had been confused. Derrick treated her almost as a stranger by day. He stayed near the other men in the party as much as possible. When Derrick drove the wagon, he expected Helen to sit beside him silently.

"A man needs to think," he'd say.

Soon Helen chose instead to walk with Sarah or with Flinder. With the girls, only a few years her junior, Helen could abandon for a while the puzzling job of being a wife. They were easy together and seemed never to run out of things to talk about—friends back home, the passing scenery, the look of other emigrants they encountered. Sometimes they even sang as they strode along. The journey became then what Helen had expected it to be—a lark.

At night Derrick was a different person. He pulled her to him gluttonously, as if they had been forcibly parted for weeks. Then he lay back and talked about the day's travel and what yet lay ahead. He asked her if she had noticed the same things in the places they'd passed that he had, and he imagined aloud again and again what the plains would be like, and the desert and mountains and finally California.

Some nights he'd turn to her a second time, but more gently, and brush her hair back from her face when he kissed her, and as he entered her, murmur river and creek names from the maps he'd studied back in Indiana. Missouri, Wolf

Creek, Buffalo Creek, Loup, Big Nemeha, Elkhorn, Little Sandy, Platte. It did not matter to him that he, and indeed, no traveler west, would encounter all of them on a single route. The mere existence of the waterways enchanted him, the sinuous, mysterious movements and stretch of them, the way they reached out into the vast, open territories west of the states like fingers groping across an unfamiliar room in the dark.

"Those streams have slid for centuries through lands no white man trod," he'd said once to Helen. "And now we will tread there and master them, the rivers and the land both."

And he'd shaped his hands to her hips and guided her to him again. Deer Creek, Laramie, Kansas River, Big Vermilion, Big Blue, Green. On such nights, Helen herself began to feel like a river, wide and rolling, and the love of a husband began to seem a stunning pleasure.

The line of wagons stopped. Alice walked to the lead wagon at the river's edge and looked across the broad backs of the oxen at Henry and Sarah. She was just pondering how similar their profiles were, with long, straight noses and high cheekbones, when Sarah suddenly screamed and clasped her hands together beneath her chin in a childish gesture of fright that Alice hadn't seen in years.

Alice looked quickly in the direction of Sarah's horrified stare. Shouts and other screams came from the river and from both shores. In midstream, a flatboat that had been overloaded was canting dangerously. The three small wagons on board listed toward the lower side of the flatboat. The men were rowing furiously to reach the landing, but crossing the strong current was slowing them.

Alice pressed her hand firmly against her flat belly. So far, her pregnancy had inspired only fears for herself. Now these feelings were swept aside like leaves in a flood. Watching the desperate struggle in the water, Alice felt a surge of protectiveness towards the baby she had acknowledged only an hour ago.

The flatboat was nearing the opposite shore at last. Then, as if the river everyone called Old Muddy had its own watery intelligence and a mean sense of humor as well, the boat hit an underwater snag. Seven men, three women, and all their belongings toppled into the river. The crash panicked their animals, who had been swimming behind tethered to the boat. One horse and an ox broke free of their tethers and were carried off downstream. Two men at the landing jumped into the river to help the unlucky passengers.

Alice kept watching until the last sodden person, who had grabbed hold of a swimming horse's tail, was pulled up onto the bank, and the disaster appeared done. She wanted to remember it clearly, as clearly as she remembered her friends' voices across the quilt frame or the feel of the wood floor of her house beneath her bare feet when she rose in the night to tend a sick child. Since she could not spare her unformed baby this journey, she decided, she'd store up for him all she saw and heard on the road west, the family's course through the days and nights of this shifting time.

"We'll bide together," Alice whispered to her baby. "Every mile."

"Mrs. Muller?" An unfamiliar female voice pulled Alice out of herself.

Alice turned her head and met the frank gaze of a tall, square-shouldered woman with dark eyes and an olive complexion. The woman extended a broad hand with ink-stained fingertips. Alice shifted her left hand to her belly so that she could put out her right hand to be shaken.

"Bailey Jeffers," said the dark woman. "I believe you're the only one of the party I've not met yet."

Alice nodded and smiled politely.

"Not an auspicious start," the newcomer said, tilting her head toward the river. "But a necessary sobering for some of us perhaps," she added.

Alice nodded again and peered thoughtfully at the woman. Bailey Jeffers did not look like a person who needed sobering. She was watching the far riverbank where a cow was being pulled up out of the water. Her expression was calm and serious. Alice could easily picture her, erect and businesslike, in a schoolroom. What manner of woman was this, she wondered, who would be drawn without the prompting of a husband's will to an undertaking of such indefinite outcome?

The wagons moved forward to the ferry landing, and the work of unharnessing the stock was begun. The wagons were rolled onto the flatboats and the wheels locked. Under the anxious stares of onlookers on both shores, loading was accomplished with only a few shouted directions among the men. Other loadings that morning, prior to the accident, had been accompanied by more banter.

The women and children sat on the floors of the rafts. Alice motioned to Sarah and Hank, settling one on either side of her. Hank, probably wanting to appear brave, wiggled away when she laid her hand on his arm, but Sarah clasped her other hand firmly, and Alice drew as much comfort from the girl's touch as she gave. It had always been so with Sarah, her daylight companion in the years in the woods, the child who had witnessed the arrival of all the other children and the departures of two of them and who had seemed, despite her tender years, to keep the solemnity of those events even better than Henry.

Bailey Jeffers was on the first boat with Alice's family. The single woman sat with her eyes fixed on the pulley overhead which attached the boat to a guide rope stretched across the river. Her hands were folded in her lap on top of a gutta-percha bag that contained a flat, rectangular object; the bag hung from a thick silken rope wrapped several times around her waist.

Alice had never been on a boat of any kind. She disliked the insubstantial feel of it. It was as if she had fallen from a tree and been halted in midair by some unknown force. This physical experience of dizzying buoyancy meshed unpleasantly with the emotional realities Alice had been working months to forget. To be a piece of flotsam, in fact or in fancy, was extremely disquieting. Alice tried to push out of her mind the awareness that this was only the first river crossing. Ribboned across their plotted path like gauntlets, five other rivers waited to be forded or ferried over in the weeks ahead.

The men began rowing. The river rushed against the boat's side, pushing it downstream in spite of the guide rope. Alice pressed her hands hard against the boat's damp bottom. Its solid feel did not reassure her.

The river was all around them now, red–brown and noisy. It was like a living thing, a rampant animal heedless of anything in its path. Alice was grateful for its muddiness. She didn't want to see beneath the choppy surface, where she imagined smashed wagons lay tangled with dead trees and worse.

She looked towards Henry, who was partly hidden from her view by the corner of a wagon. She could see only his head, which was pointed to the approaching shoreline, and at intervals one rigidly muscled arm. Briefly her trepidation was blunted by his display of strength and determination. He had raised the buildings on their land; he had assembled the stalwart wagons. He would bring them across this torrent and across the continent, too. She had to believe that or give in to resentment.

In the past, Alice's faith in Henry would have come forth spontaneously. Now she spun it deliberately, as when at her spinning wheel she coaxed tufts of combed wool between her fingers into twisted strands of thread strong enough to weave together into warm and useful cloth. More than once during the last days in Indiana, Alice had wondered, before she could stop herself from thinking it, what lay under the years of her marriage if she could remain so displeased with her beloved husband over a decision it was his right to make, a decision that should bring greater prosperity to both them and their children. She held fast to the promise of California Henry had laid before her, but it did not quell the anguish of leaving her home, could not still her worry over the dangers of the journey.

Suddenly Alice found she wanted Henry to know about the coming baby. Somehow, she felt, his knowing would wrap the child in an extra layer of safety, like a husk around her womb. She would tell him tonight.

Finally they reached the bank and were towed upstream to the landing. It needed two more boats to get the rest of the group over. As each boat landed, the passengers climbed out and, after unloading, set themselves to face the river and watch the next crossing. There they stood without speaking or moving, as if they were at a graveside. Even the children were subdued. Sucking her thumb, Elizabeth Muller, Faith and John's child, sat on the ground with one chubby arm wrapped around her mother's ankle; Faith, in turn, held fast to John, who crooked his arm to accommodate her grasp as if he were escorting her into a formal dining room. Alice, glancing at them, was reminded of the game Hank used to play of balancing wooden figures against one another to make them stand upright.

From horseback, Derrick and Roy and the two new men, Bennett and Webster, swam their stock across—thirty-two oxen, eight mules, a milch cow, and another horse. The men left their reins slack to make the swimming easier for their mounts. The two dogs needed no herding, but paddled along exuberantly beside the riders. After passing the river's mid-point, as if it were a set signal, the four men began to show some enthusiasm for their task, shouting at the animals more loudly and more often than strictly necessary, waving their hats in the air.

Once ashore, their high spirits increased and infected the rest of the group. The reharnessing of the oxen and mules to the five wagons was accomplished quickly. Each wagon was loaded with about two thousand pounds and used six draft animals; four could manage it, but it was harder work for the beasts, and on such a long journey, they'd wear out sooner. The extra oxen and mules, two per wagon, were driven as loose stock.

No one looked back as they ascended the bluffs and left the river. Relief drove them forward without a stop until the noon halt. Even then they paused only long enough for bread, cold coffee, and eggs that had been hard-boiled the day before. Both far ahead and to the rear all day they could see the swaying white tops of rolling wagons. Farther on, they knew, as companies varied in their pace and the trail diverged into cutoffs and alternate routes, the migration would string out more, and they'd feel, and be, on their own in the wilderness. Despite the proximity of so many other emigrants, however, they had set up a system of night guard duty. They were, after all, in Indian territory and treading, too, on the range of wolves and coyotes, any of whom might skulk up and stampede the stock.

That night, around the supper fires outside the ring of wagons, with the children bedded down and the animals corralled, the men genially debated how many miles they had covered during the day. They were well set into the first section of their long trek; from the Missouri River to the South Pass of the Rocky Mountains, they could expect the going to be good, with acceptable grazing and water and a flat natural road along benchlands and river bottoms. They congratulated themselves on the safe river crossing that morning and the proper packing of their wagons.

This was the shakedown segment of the journey for emigrants just starting out in wagons from one of the jumping-off places along the Missouri. Weak equipment broke and was repaired; people and animals hunkered down to trail life; loads were repacked. The Muller party had passed several wagons that day that had been too heavy. The owners had had to stop and transfer goods from boxes and barrels to sacks and leave behind trunks and chests and bulky furniture.

One wagon they passed had overturned under its ungainly weight. A man and woman were climbing in and out of it unloading. Their train had moved on without them, expecting them to catch up at the night's stopping place. Three small girls stood glumly next to a rear wheel; each time the woman exited the wagon with something and carried it a short distance from the wagon to set it down, the girls clutched her full skirts and tripped along with her until she shook them free to enter the wagon again. Alice averted her eyes when the young wife paused in her labors to look up at her accusingly.

Alice could not share the men's rejoicing at the day's accomplishments when she thought of that look. She sat now in her rocker across the campfire from them and lifted her attention away from their crowing conversation. Her hands were busy slipping buckshot into skirt hems to keep them from blowing over her and Sarah's heads on windy days. The call of distant coyotes spoke more distinctly to her than the masculine voices, which had subsided to a low-pitched hum.

When no more could be made of the day's events, the men drifted apart. Jack Webster and Reed Bennett settled beside Alice's wagon to mend harnesses with Henry. Alice watched the softening firelight flutter over the three faces. Though Henry's dark beard was flecked with gray and his eyes nested in deep wrinkles, his face glowed, making him appear almost as youthful as the two men across the fire from him. It was the journey yeasting up in him, Alice knew. Since they'd left Indiana, Henry's step had assumed the spring of a younger man's and his laughter had come quickly and freely, like a creek flushed with May runoff.

Comparing the three men before her, Alice decided she favored her husband's forthright, sharp features best. Jack's face was comely, but too perfect—his character could not be read in it. Reed's face, for all its ordinariness, had a menacing quality. Perhaps it came from the way his curiously smooth forehead, unbroken by eyebrows, loomed over his small eyes or from the knowledge that the hair that hung forward over his shoulders grew only from the top of his scalp because no hair could grow from the large burn scar that covered the back of his head. Alice knew it was unfair to judge either man by his appearance, but she resolved to be wary of both of them all the same.

Alice looked over at the other fire. Jerusha was dressing three freshly killed chickens bought yesterday in Council Bluffs; cooking them tonight would mean less work and time needed at tomorrow's nooning. Jerusha's husband, Royal, and Henry's brother John were sharpening knives and axes. The Bowens, as usual, had retired to their wagon early. Pretending it made little difference to him, Derrick had volunteered for the late watch on guard duty, which amused the other men. John's wife, Faith, was also in bed, asleep with three-year-old Elizabeth in a tent near the Halls' fire.

Between the fires on a rug next to her small tent sat Bailey Jeffers. She had a book open on her lap. Her hand was moving swiftly over the exposed pages, but not in a regular enough pattern to be writing. A lantern stood on a rock at her right side. Alice filled a clean tin cup with coffee from a pot keeping hot at the edge of the fire and walked over to her.

"I thought you might use some coffee, Miss Jeffers," Alice said after she had stood beside her for a minute or two without being acknowledged. "The evening is turning chill."

"I hadn't noticed."

Alice watched the woman look up at the Halls' campfire and down at her book several times more, then stepped behind her to see the drawing she was making. Reproduced in charcoal on the page were the two men sitting cross-legged on the ground with glinting knives in their hands and Jerusha bent like a wagon bow over a cook pot. Behind them was a wagon, its linseed-oiled osnaburg top ghostly with shadows.

"Why, it's so true to life," Alice exclaimed.

"Yes, I'm afraid so," Bailey answered, putting a few more strokes of charcoal on one of the men's shirts.

Alice studied the figures at the fire. "It's a scene that's homely in its way," she said, almost to herself, "but there's a lonesome air to it, too."

Bailey put down her charcoal stick and turned around to look at Alice in surprise. "That's just the feeling I'm trying to seize on," she said.

"Well, I shall leave you to trying." Alice set the cup of coffee on the rock beside the lantern.

Bailey watched Alice walk away. She realized she'd been a little rude. It was a bad leaning of hers, born of not being often in the company of others. She knew how to speak instructively to children, how to speak soothingly or with concern to parents, and how to speak deferentially to employers, but she was not experienced in the language of friendship or even casual companionship.

"Mrs. Muller," she called out. Alice turned.

"Thank you." Bailey lifted up the cup.

Alice smiled and waved her hand dismissively.

May 26, 1852

I begin this diary all aware of my shortfall as a writer. I had thought to send it later to Mother. She'll miss my letters over these many months. But now I am thinking it may serve more important ends. Pure memory's an untrustworthy thing, and I want the events of this time to survive all of a piece because I wish my new child to know what went before him in this life, in my life.

Henry is much taken with history-making and says we are all doing it. But that grand notion does not help me grab hold of this journey as I must if we are to come through it hale and hearty—for which I'll work and pray and work some more. Perhaps, with the aid of this humble diary, I can catch the simple acts of our true days and nights like a prism catches sunlight and bends it into colors you can see and name. Then, won't it be fine, later, to open these pages and point up what really passed on such a day or at such a turn in the road?

I told Henry of the child tonight, and a grin splayed over his features as if I had brought him a wonderful gift all free of any trouble. Then he clasped me so tight to him, it was like the gift echoed back again to me.

I mark this as the true start of our journey, for though we've already traveled some, it's been through tame lands much like home. Now, across the Missouri, we are truly set in the wilderness. The hills are green enough, but no trees or homesteads break the long, featureless view of unnumbered ridges and gullies.

We have met other parties on the road, but each group is marked off from every other. The Mormons, especially, keep to their own. Though they are not in the majority on the trail, they are noticeable by the man-pulled handcarts so many of them use instead of teams and wagons.

So independent are we from our fellows on the road, we didn't even stop to help a family with an overturned wagon, as we surely would have in Indiana. No one did. Our men are as neighborly as any, but they agreed there must be no delays if we are to meet good weather in the far-off mountains and make our supplies last. And though none said it, I know there is the fear that those who tarry too long in one place are prey to Indians. So I did not try to persuade them. I only wish I could harden my heart as readily as I hold my tongue.

Helen Bowen remarked on the beauty of the sunset tonight and the wideness of the sky. Flinder and my Sarah fell in with her on that. Yet it is a beauty too large for my tastes, too empty of comfort and shelter.

It grieved me not to aid those people, especially as the woman looked so discouraged.

Chapter 3

FAITH MULLER pressed the heels of her hands into her aching lower back. She twisted in her hard seat to look enviously at little Elizabeth, who was sleeping soundly inside the wagon on a small feather tick laid atop two double-sewn canvas sacks of flour. John, whistling "The Arkansas Traveler," walked beside the middle yoke of oxen, his back as straight as a soldier's. She envied him, too.

Both Elizabeth and John shone with robust good health and a steady stream of optimistic energy. They were at ease anywhere, like cats that can fit themselves to the oddest corners and ledges and then descend into unconcerned and graceful sleep. Faith, on the other hand, was frail and nervous, and had been all her life. Yet it was she, the weakest one, who bore the heaviest physical burden.

Faith's mother, Emeline, had fretted and cried something awful when they left Indiana. She would have done so in any event, since it was likely she'd never again meet her daughter, but Faith's condition crowned Emeline's grief. Faith was the only child of Emeline's who had survived infancy; four babies had died before her, and two after, the last nearly carrying Emeline along with him. This history left Emeline with an unnatural (her neighbors thought) fear of babies and a naturally excessive concern for her daughter's always-precarious health.

Faith could not help but absorb some of her mother's canon that without Emeline's proximity and protection, she was sure to come to harm. That she was in physical peril from the twin afflictions of pregnancy and the journey, she firmly believed, even though, more than halfway through her pregnancy, she had experienced only the average and expected discomforts, and despite the fact that Elizabeth's birth had been quick and astoundingly uncomplicated.

Off to the right beside the line of wagons, Faith saw Alice and Jerusha walking together. The prairie grass lapping around them, big bluestem and sandreed, almost reached their waists. They strode along with their heads turned towards one another in conversation. The parted grass closed behind them seamlessly, leaving no sign of their passing.

Though within Faith's sight were all of the Muller party, plus the thirty-five wagons of a train ahead of them, something in the way the prairie grass whispered shut behind the two women made her feel desperately alone. Faith feared being alone more than anything else, for it seemed to her that a connection to other, stronger people was the only way she could hold on to her own life's thread.

"Like it could swallow them whole," she said to herself about the swaying grasses.

"What's that?" John called up to her, breaking off his whistling. He fell back so that he was walking alongside the wagon and they could converse more easily.

"Oh, nothing." She'd been unaware she'd spoken aloud.

"If we camp early enough tonight," John said, unconcerned, "me and Derrick's going hunting. Some rabbit stew would set well, now, wouldn't it?"

"Don't go too far," Faith said, looking out anxiously across the billowing grass as featureless and alien as a sea.

"Only as far as it takes." John grinned.

John's relaxed view of life was a bulwark to Faith and helped her take delight where she would otherwise have shrunk back and demurred, but it also made her fret more than she would have had he shown a splash of apprehension himself now and then. She supposed that's what came of his being the baby of his family, every path beaten down before him by older brothers and sisters.

"But you will be careful?" she said.

"Except for your circumstances, I'd take you with me, it's such an innocent errand," he answered. "Rabbit-hunting, Faith, not lion-snaring."

"Well, then," she said, resolving not to pick at him further, "see you find enough rabbits that Lizzie and I shall both have fur trim on our coats to surprise the Californians next winter."

"And you may trim my coat as well." John smiled up at her.

Faith turned again to check on Elizabeth. The child had rolled from her side onto her back, but she was still soundly asleep. Her straight, blunt-cut bangs were stuck to her forehead with sweat, and a dirty smear across one cheek traced the path her plump hand had taken rubbing her runny nose. Faith had given up trying to keep Elizabeth clean weeks ago, and the girl seemed no worse for it. Still, Faith felt the grime to be a reproach to her; her own mother would never have let her go about dirty for fear of disease, to say nothing of propriety's sake.

Faith wished Emeline were along to help her with Elizabeth. It was so much harder a job now than it had been at home. Elizabeth was a constant trouble to Faith on the road. Either she was alarming Faith by running out of sight after Gideon Hall and Hank Muller, or she was exasperating her by dawdling along picking up pebbles and wildflowers and poking at insects on the ground, or she was begging to be carried. Sarah and Helen spelled Faith with the carrying sometimes, as did Flinder when she wasn't driving the supply wagon, but no one could spell her with the worrying. Faith could not imagine how she would manage when she had a new baby to bundle, too.

"I believe I'll walk a spell," Faith said, turning back to John. She knew Elizabeth would be up soon and probably fussing because of the bad sunburn she'd got on her arms yesterday. Best to take the chance now to stretch a bit. With a loud "whoa," John halted the oxen to let her down.

"Let me know when Lizzie wakes," she called as he

snapped his long-handled whip over the oxen to start them up again.

John was a good husband, treating Faith with almost as much care as her mother had, seeming, in fact, to prize her delicateness and fearfulness, but he had little interest in tending to Elizabeth, especially when she was irritable. This indifference had always puzzled Faith, for John was otherwise kind and responsible. Perhaps, she'd thought, he'll show more interest when Elizabeth is older; some men just didn't take to small children, whose reason had its own map and whose needs were so constant and physical. Yes, she had decided, in only a few more years John's attentions would turn; she was sure of it.

Faith was glad to be off the wagon. She took long steps, swinging her arms and enjoying the pulling sensations in her thighs and buttocks. Her ominous feeling about the prairie lessened. The green grass studded with wildflowers and rippling in a soft May breeze really was quite pretty in its way.

When she felt her baby kicking, she patted her belly and decided her sudden fear had been due to her condition. She remembered when she was carrying Elizabeth how easily her emotions had been stirred. Corn seedlings and cocoons inspired an awe that brought tears to her eyes, and a runt piglet evoked a tender pity that was inexplicable in a farm-bred woman.

Faith heard giggling and found herself suddenly flanked by her two teenaged nieces.

"Tell us your opinion, Aunt Faith," demanded Flinder Hall playfully. "Isn't our Mr. Webster the handsomest man you've seen?"

"*Our* Mr. Webster? You'd better not let your mother hear such talk," Faith answered.

The reproof was hollow because Faith thought the question harmless and normal, but she knew Jerusha's disapproval would be sincere. Jerusha shielded Flinder from men as a mother bear shields her cub from ravening wolves. Faith thought it, at best, a waste of time, since it was inevitable some man some time must be let to get at Flinder. At worst, Jerusha's attitude had sinister undertones that Faith did not understand. It seemed to Faith that at times Jerusha had subtly encouraged Flinder to charm a man or had in some quiet fashion exhibited the young woman to him before she stepped between them with arms crossed and a threatening frown.

"Come on, Aunt Faith," Flinder coaxed, "Uncle John won't hear you."

Faith could not suppress a smile. She rolled her eyes at Flinder and shook her head at Sarah.

"This is all Flin's notion," Sarah said defensively. "It's of no interest to me."

Faith knew this was probably true. The cousins were an odd pair, different in so many ways and yet loyally and affectionately attached to each other. As if reflecting their dissimilar natures, their looks were a study in contrasts. Sarah at fourteen was almost as tall as sixteen-year-old Flinder, but she was long-boned and thin, like her father, and there was something in the tight construction of her body that told you she'd never achieve Flinder's voluptuousness, even as a full-grown woman, even, Faith suspected, as a mother.

Sarah wore her blondish hair in braids, like a younger child, and one was always coming undone. This errant braid and her usually serious expression gave her a waif's air that was at the same time appealing and disconcerting. Her gap-toothed smile appeared rarely; her wide-set brown eyes were as alert as a startled fawn's. Faith noticed that all the days outdoors had multiplied Sarah's freckles despite the deep brim of her sunbonnet.

"I can only answer," said Faith at last to Flinder, who was skipping backwards in front of her waiting to hear her opinion, "that I hold my own husband to be the handsomest man hereabouts. And I remind you girls of what my mother told me at your age: Handsome is as handsome does."

Flinder frowned. If she'd wanted a platitude, she could

have gone to Jerusha. But the frown flitted off her beautiful face as quickly as it had formed.

"Well," she countered, laughing, "not having been handsomely done as yet, I must stick for now to surface appearances."

Faith was earnestly shocked. "Shoo, you shameless thing!"

Still grinning, Flinder lifted her skirts and ran off. Faith glimpsed a frivolous band of blue ribbon near the hem of the first skirt.

When Flinder reached her father's wagon, she called up to five-year-old Gideon and raised her arms to him. The boy immediately jumped off to her despite a shout from Jerusha, who was walking along on the opposite side of the moving wagon. His feet barely cleared the wheel.

Flinder was knocked a few steps backward by the impact of Gideon's body. Her foot struck an uneven place and she toppled to the ground with the boy, whose arms were wrapped around her neck. Brother and sister were lost to sight in the tall grass, but the sound of their laughter said they were all right.

Just then Jack Webster galloped past Faith and Sarah and pulled his horse up short beside the place Flinder and Gideon had fallen. In one graceful motion, he was off his mount and bowing at the waist with one hand extended deep into the grass while the other held his reins.

When he straightened again and lifted his hand, Flinder was attached to it. She rose up out of the grass like an actress entering a stage through a trapdoor. Gideon scrambled up behind her, using the back of her skirts as a handhold. Jack was on his horse and away again before Flinder had finished resettling her sunbonnet. He touched his fingers to his hat as he passed Jerusha, as if she had done him a favor.

"You know," Faith said to Sarah, "for handsome manners, he'd get my mother's vote, sure."

★   ★   ★

39

"THERE IT IS," Henry said, pointing to the swollen Elkhorn River. Alice felt her heart quicken. Another crossing.

Henry stopped the team and unhitched the oxen, tying them to the wheels so that they would not walk off with the wagon. The other men followed suit and gathered together loosely beside Henry's wagon to select a passage.

Reed, stepping rapidly over the river bottom, tested for quicksand and marked the firmest ground with sharp sticks. When the water had reached the middle of Reed's chest, Jack tossed him a fishing line. Reed swam across the river with the end of the line clamped in his mouth; the line trailed behind him, uncoiling from Jack's hand. A strong swimmer, Reed let the current track him obliquely downstream, as it would do the wagons and the fearful animals. Again, with lively stepping through the opposite shallows, he found and marked the best exit ground.

Jack tied a long, heavy rope to his end of the fishing line and waved to his cousin. Reed pulled the rope across and fastened it to a wagon axle an earlier emigrant party had left staked in the ground. Then, deciding he had done his part, he lay down on the warm sand to dry off and wait until the other men had made and loaded a ferry and a couple of them had crossed over to help him pull it.

"We'll need the tightest wagon box for making our ferry," Henry said to the assembled men, who had been watching Reed's work anxiously.

"Mine's of well-seasoned white oak and near waterproof, I'd say," Roy volunteered.

The men moved off to inspect Roy's wagon, though Roy insisted it was unnecessary. He had had the running gear made to order by a wagonwright, as was common, but he had built the wagon box himself, so he knew its full merits. The men circled the wagon anyway and, their ears filled with Roy's self-praises, agreed soon enough that it was suitable. The whole party set to work unloading and dismantling all the wagons.

Sarah made a paste from candle wax and ashes, and she and

Hank and Ellen used it to fill the few cracks in Roy's wagon box, caused, Roy declared, by the wood's exposure to hot sun and rough wear on the journey. For extra waterproofing, Henry wrapped the box with rawhides while Roy attached Reed's rope to one end and another long rope to the other end so that it could be pulled back and forth across the river. The wagon pieces and contents would be ferried over in the makeshift boat little by little, then the women and children. The animals would have to be swum across.

Flinder went to help Sarah unload the supply wagon shared by their two families. Jack vaulted into the wagon before either girl could climb in and began handing goods out to them.

Jack's full-cut linen shirt was unbuttoned to the middle of his chest, and when he bent over to pass something down, it fell away from his sweating body, exposing a lean, muscled torso. Once Flinder saw a tuft of black hairs curling above his belt. The sight made her uneasy, almost as if she had seen an open wound. She wanted to avoid seeing it again, but every time she took something from him, she found her eyes searching for another glimpse of that dark growth. Gradually her unease shifted into something else, something with a strange tinge of pleasure to it.

She recalled watching a twister in that way back home once. The black tube of wind had shimmied across the horizon, a good distance from the farm yet. It was still safe to stand and watch its terrible dance. She had been fearful and fascinated at the same time.

She had wanted the funnel cloud to dissipate out there far from her home, but she had felt, too, a small, wild yearning for it to come closer so she could really see it and its power, hear its roar, feel it suck at her clothes and rake her hair. The twister never had reached the farm. She had forgotten her strange curiosity about it until just now.

"What are you dreaming on, girl?" her mother's voice cut in.

Flinder hadn't realized she had been standing still, facing

out toward the bright prairie since she'd put down her last load.

When she turned toward the wagon, it was empty. Jack was squatting beside it, working on removing a wheel.

"Go see if Faith needs a hand." Jerusha gave Flinder a little shove. "Doing nothing is doing ill."

HOURS LATER, all belongings and wagon parts, as well as the women and children, had been ferried to the other side of the river, and the men were driving the animals into the river to swim across. The women began rummaging through their jumbled goods so that they could prepare some lunch. The younger children were cranky with hunger, and everyone else was hot and weary.

Faith sat nursing Elizabeth in the shade of a high bluff. The little girl whimpered and squirmed. Faith figured her milk was beginning to dry up because of her pregnancy.

"Ah, Lizzie," she said, stroking the child's head, "you can't stay my baby for always. I allow it's almost as sad a puzzle to me as it is to you."

Faith looked up from Elizabeth to peer at the river, where the men were having difficulties with three oxen, the only stock left to send over. Each time the men forced the oxen into the swift-flowing water, the frightened beasts swam stupidly in a tight circle, trying to climb up on one another's backs. Then, despite the men's shouts and the cracks of their long whips, the oxen would break their circuit and turn back toward land, lumbering up through the mud onto the shore they had just left. Finally the men decided to lead the recalcitrant animals across one by one by means of the cordelle they had used for the ferry.

Faith saw John enter the river upstream with one of the oxen. The heavy tow rope had been looped around the ox's horns, and John was holding on to it like a leash. On the shore in front of Faith, Derrick, his feet planted wide apart, tugged on the other end of the rope to guide the animal. The ox was being tractable, swimming along beside John like a pet dog, but in midstream, it balked and tried to turn back. John held fast, and Derrick jerked the line. The ox cooperated and swam forward a few more yards. Suddenly, with a rending bellow, it swung its head violently to the side, slamming against John. He sank out of sight.

Derrick, pulled off balance by the frenzied ox, fell facedown in the sand; his grip on the rope was defeated. The ox lost its feet in the current and was swept downstream past any possible landing place.

Faith leapt up. With Elizabeth slung under her arm like a sack, she ran to the edge of the water.

"John! John!" she screamed.

Elizabeth wailed and kicked to be set down, but Faith only tightened her grip, as if by holding fast to the struggling child, she could help John break the surface of the river and return to hard ground.

Derrick scrambled into the water; Henry and Jack had already jumped in from the opposite bank and were swimming strongly to where John had gone down. At the spot, the three men dived beneath the water. Again and again they came up gasping and alone. They separated, diving in a circular pattern that widened out from where John had sunk.

Now Alice and Jerusha were next to Faith on the riverbank. Jerusha pried Elizabeth away from her. Faith vaguely noticed the retreating noise of the girl's crying as Jerusha carried her off. Faith felt Alice's arm around her waist and heard soft, shushing sounds in her ear. Faith had not stopped calling John's name. Her throat was sore with the dear, raw syllable.

Suddenly Faith felt rigidity abandon her body like the snapping of a taut rope. The sunlit river darkened, and the ground threw heat up against her so thickly, she could barely breathe or do more than whisper John's name once more. The last recognizable sight as she collapsed limply into Alice's arms was Henry coming in with slow strokes, towing the body behind him.

May 31, 1852

We lost John today to drowning. Faith, of course, is laid low.

Henry is mourning as for a son. John was the baby of the family. His mother died of childbed fever. Jerusha said as how Henry, twelve then, took on the baby, like boys will do sometimes with orphaned raccoons. She was busy doing her duty with the other six children, so let the boys, eldest and youngest, be, impractical though some of Henry's notions were. He'd take the little one, Jerusha said, from his cradle to see the full moon or out among the stalks to hear the corn grow on hot July nights. I never knew him to be so fanciful with our babies.

John, at sixteen, came with us from Pennsylvania to Indiana. There was never any query but he'd come on this venture, too. Now Henry walks impatiently up and down this little stretch of beach as if, should he wait long enough, John will again be pulling his wagon into line behind ours.

All in our party tasted the loss keenly. Young Derrick Bowen felt that much that he stood an hour or more staring into the river. Helen could not move him. When she tried, he pushed her from him and kicked viciously at the sand at the water's edge and cursed the river, as if it were a person that had wronged him.

We have passed eight graves since Council Bluffs, all with boards naming them as cholera or measles victims. Emigrants who have headed west to escape cholera epidemics in the states are finding no haven on the trail, where the disease follows as silent and unshakable as a shadow. On a morn of heavy fog, we passed four men digging a grave for a comrade who had sickened and died in one day. With the corpse beside them on the ground, the scene was like an etching meant to impart some stern lesson to the viewer. What, I cannot think.

It only caused me to look at the side boards of our wagons and wonder when they might serve as a coffin for one of us. Too soon have I met my answer, though in truth, I would still say too soon if it should be the journey's final day.

We corralled the animals over John's burial spot so the newly dug earth would be tamped down and protected from the digging of ranging coyotes. It's said Indians sometimes resurrect bodies for their clothes, so we settled on letting the place go unmarked, without even a bunch of flowers to show our feelings. My heart aches for Faith, who cried bitterly to go and leave her husband on the empty prairie, to part with that grave which she shall never see more.

Chapter 4

R EED BENNETT frowned into the hot wind. It had been blowing strongly all afternoon. The wagon canvasses repeatedly billowed and collapsed, making loud slapping noises that had drummed a fierce headache into him. It didn't help that Elizabeth, frightened by the sound, was whining inconsolably on her mother's lap right behind him.

If he were on horseback, he thought grumpily, he could ride out away from the wagons and their dust and noise and find some ease for his head. It'd even be sport to ride hard in a high wind like this across the naked plain, with the wildness in the air matching the free feel of solid horseflesh at full gallop. But no, he was tethered to a wagon as surely as an ox because the young widow, Mrs. Muller, couldn't manage her team in such weather.

He cast a glance back over his shoulder at Faith; it didn't seem to him that the woman had likely ever been able to manage anything, as skinny and sickly-looking as she was, even being big with child. Reed generally favored wiry women, when he had any use for women at all, but this one—he shook his head—this one had an air about her that one good thump would separate her soul from her body for good and all. Still, he mused, she might be tougher than she appeared. And lonely, too, with her man gone. He had to admit the appeal of that quiver of apprehension playing in her eyes from time to time. Usually he had to work to get a woman to look like that.

Before Reed could follow this interesting train of thought further, a sudden gust of wind lifted his hat from his head and sent it flying to the ground. With a hearty curse, he thrust the bullwhack at Faith so she could take over the oxen. In the process, he knocked the hard handle against Elizabeth's head and transformed her whining into outraged crying. With another curse, he sprinted away from the wagon and began chasing his hat, which was rolling quickly along. They were in short-grass prairie now, and, in addition, the passage of many wagons before theirs had flattened a wide swale, so there was nothing to impede the hat's merry escape.

The Muller party had struck the Coast of Nebraska, as the wide table of the Platte River valley was called, after fording the Loup River. Reed, who had once seen the Atlantic Ocean, thought it a fitting name, as the vast flatness of the sandhill-edged valley did resemble a seashore, and the yellow river, though only a few feet deep in most places, was so broad, it had the appearance of an inland sea. Derrick Bowen, who was always spouting some useless fact or other, as if he were a tourist on a jaunt and not a man in the wilderness, had said that Nebraska meant "flat water" in Indian, and Platte meant the same in French.

Hank was near the hat's path. With a happy shout, he entered the chase from a different angle and caught the hat before Reed reached it.

"Thanks, boy," Reed panted, taking the hat from Hank's outstretched hand.

"I put my hat in the wagon since the wind took up," Hank said.

Reed nodded. He didn't like to be without his hat at any time because of the burn scars on the back of his scalp. The injured skin was sensitive to the sun, and besides, he felt shamed by the stares aimed at him from behind when his head was uncovered, even though the scars had not been gained shamefully, but were, in fact, evidence of the one brave act of his life.

Reed beat his hat against his thigh to clean off the dust and loose bits of dry, brown grass. He looked ahead toward Faith's wagon and saw it was moving steadily, with her walking beside the lead oxen. He watched her raise the bullwhack and crack the long lash over the heads of the oxen to keep them moving. He had underestimated her, which strangely gladdened him. No need to rush back just yet. The sun was lowering anyway, and most likely they'd be stopping soon to let the animals graze before dark.

A walk with a boy would not be as invigorating as a ride on his horse, but it was better than shuffling beside a mewling girl-child. Reed could see that Faith had Elizabeth by the hand and that the child was straining so to be free that her small body leaned away from her mother at a forty-five-degree angle to the ground; Reed was sure she must be setting up a steady stream of complaint.

When he noticed Hank had shifted into a walk-trot to keep up with him, Reed was flattered. He remembered how he had hied through the woods after Jack when they were boys. Jack, at ten, had seemed so sure and strong to Reed, newly orphaned at seven by his mother's death and his father's desertion. Reed felt he still hadn't quite caught up with Jack, who effortlessly surpassed him in everything from horsemanship to charm. But envy did not diminish Reed's need for Jack's friendship. And envy was counterbalanced by the cold fact, known as well to his admirable cousin as to himself, that but for Reed, Jack would not be alive today—or, if alive, not as handsome.

Feeling expansive, Reed put his hand on Hank's shoulder and addressed him with the condescending cheer adults reserve for conversations with children.

"Well, boy, you figure on getting yourself some of that California gold?"

"My father says there's more than one kind of riches in California," Hank answered, adding helpfully when Reed did not respond, "He means farmland. But when I'm of age, I'm going to take to the gold fields. If there's any left."

Reed laughed at the seriousness and worry in the boy's voice.

"There's always adventure and prizes to be had somewhere

if a man has the gumption to go after them. My pa was a trapper, a real mountain man. Didn't hold with houses and farming."

"Ma says adventures are mostly mud and sweat. She says adventures are not a man's true measure."

"Measures," Reed snorted. Women were always taking a man's measure, and usually coming up short. "That's just how mothers think," he continued gruffly. "Women are made to stay put."

The lead wagon had curved off the road onto the prairie to begin the formation of a U-shaped corral, the signal that they would camp there that night. It was a likely spot, far enough from the river to spare them some from mosquitoes and with good grass for feed. Without a farewell to Hank, Reed returned to Faith's wagon to unhitch the oxen. They'd be driven to an island in the Platte for the night or let graze awhile and then herded inside the makeshift corral, fenced in by each wagon's tongue being chained to the rear wheel of the neighboring wagon. The horses and mules were picketed outside the corral. The men had given up the habit of guard duty; the loss of sleep was too costly.

Hank watched the man go. Despite his strange appearance, Mr. Bennett, and his partner Mr. Webster, seemed to Hank almost like the knights of the Round Table in the stories his mother had read him. They were on a quest, maybe not for something holy and not in the service of a king, but a quest just the same. It set them apart from other men of his acquaintance, all farmers or merchants, all predictable and careworn. This journey was the first thing Hank had known his father to do with any spark of glory in it. As for his mother, Hank figured Mr. Bennett must be right about her. What could she know of the thrills in store for a boy with gumption?

Hank considered his future. He'd do things when he was grown, he decided, go places, find gold or silver or something, be a man people eyed in the street. Adventures and prizes, like Mr. Bennett said. Hank's parents were fine, he knew, and he had no objections against them. For all he admired Mr. Bennett and Mr. Webster, he'd not want either one for a father. But as companions, as dreamers who could look at the same scene as his folks and find something different in it, something exciting, well, now, that would be just perfect.

Hank headed for his family's wagons. He knew his mother would be looking for him to make that long walk to the Platte to fetch water. They were following along the river, but a mile away from it. Many emigrants chose to get their water from the two-to-four-foot-deep seep wells dug by earlier passersby. Alice insisted on river water, even though it had to be boiled to kill the wiggle-tails and poured through a cloth to filter out the silt. Jerusha preferred to settle out the silt by adding alum to her water; she grumbled that every pail of water held a pint of mud.

Hank grabbed two buckets from the side of the wagon and headed for the river, pretending the whole way that he was slinking through the territory of Indians on the warpath and that he was carrying a vital message that must make it to the fort in time or all there would perish and lose their scalps in the bargain.

THE WIND was fiercer now. Supper was a sorry affair, consisting of crackers spread with the solidified bacon drippings from breakfast, picked beets, buttermilk, and dried apple slices, all well doused with sand by the wind. The women had not dared to make fires.

While they ate, the wind pushed at darkening clouds, piling them hugely on top of one another with astonishing speed. The eastern sky still showed some sunlight and wisps of white clouds, but on the western horizon, denser, murkier clouds had dropped a slate blue curtain to the earth, and it was advancing towards them. Thunder rumbled from the gloomy distance. After several muffled rolls, the thunder sounded loudly directly overhead, and the sky was split by sharp trails of lightning.

The oxen swayed and bellowed, lifting their thick heads heavenward as if questioning what affliction would befall them next. The mules and horses were skittish, too. Their ears twitched, and their large, soft nostrils flared. The men deserted their unappetizing dinners to picket the stock. But the storm was too quick for them. Only the five horses had been hobbled when a lightning bolt struck the ground so close, the air was saturated with the bitter smell of electricity. The cattle and mules, as if they were one beast and not forty, turned in unison and fled in a mad rush, leaving the stumbling horses screaming out in their wake. Rouser and Old Smith, barking wildly, chased around the wagons in mad circles.

Derrick and Roy ran after the stampeding animals a short distance, though it was obviously of no use. Suddenly an odd, clattering noise filled the air, as if scores of mules were kicking their hooves against a barn wall, and in the next instant, hailstones ranging in size from walnuts to hen's eggs pounded down, bouncing wildly in every direction as they struck the ground and the wagons. Everyone scrambled into or under the wagons, which shook and rocked in the furious wind. Elizabeth and Gideon would not stop shrieking, but they could barely be heard over the din of the hail, the howling of the dogs, and the terrified neighing of the unsheltered horses.

After an interminable fifteen minutes, the hail ceded its assault to rain, and the wind lessened, as if nature were catching its breath. In the relative lull, the party emerged into the rain to tend to the cuts on the horses' backs and prepare for the night. Sarah had the idea of saving some hailstones so that they might have ice water to drink on the morrow. She and Hank quickly filled several buckets and kettles.

Henry put some goods that could stand a soaking underneath the wagon to make room inside for Alice and the children. He crawled under there, too, with an India rubber sheet hung from the top rail of the wagon box to shield him from the slanting rain.

Roy had refused to make similar arrangements for his family, insisting that people dried out quicker and with less damage than foodstuffs and belongings. No one wanted to argue with him; he was nursing a nasty lump on his forehead from the hail and scowling across the plains in a fruitless attempt to spot the strayed animals. He seemed to take both calamities as personal affronts. He and Jerusha and Gideon bedded down under their wagon; Gideon, still sniveling and with an eye that would be black the next day, nestled tremulously against his mother's pillowy bosom. Flinder and Ellen were in their tent, as usual. Jack Webster had dug ditches around it and around Bailey Jeffers's tent to channel the rainwater away. This courtesy had raised him in Jerusha's opinion and lowered him in Roy's.

ALICE LAY AWAKE listening to the steady fall of the rain on the wagon top. She had to keep her knees bent to allow room for Hank and Sarah, who were jumbled together crosswise below her feet on top of two packing crates. Large drops were falling in several places from the soaked canvas. Alice was glad she had wrapped her books and her other special items in an India rubber sheet and stowed them beneath the wagon's false floor. When she thought about unpacking them in California and arranging them in her new house, the dampness of her bedclothes did not seem as discouraging. This time would pass. She would be able to reconstruct her home.

She looked down at her children, so soundly asleep, they had not moved in an hour. Hank lay on his back, his arms and legs flung wide, one hand propped against Sarah's hip. When he was awake, Hank often reminded Alice of a good-naturedly irrepressible puppy; now, even in repose, he suggested exuberance. Sarah, in contrast, lay curled on her side with her back to her brother, her knees drawn up and her hands tucked between them.

One open child, one closed. And yet, that wasn't really so. Sarah, for all her pensiveness, could turn to Alice and expose her heart with the sudden and simple clarity of the moon appearing from behind a cloud and spreading a path to its face across a dark lake, while the workings of Hank's mind, why he cried or raged or shrugged things off, remained largely a mystery that deepened with each passing year. Alice sighed and rolled over, shifting the position of her feet to get them out from under a bad leak.

Flinder could not fall asleep inside the humid, stuffy tent. Her younger sister, Ellen, was snoring, but that was not the cause of her wakefulness. Flinder had always liked storms. She had never before been so thoroughly in the midst of one. It was a different experience from watching through a farm-house window.

Flinder sat up and parted the tent flap just enough to allow her face to be out in the weather. She closed her eyes and smiled as the cold, hard rain pelted her cheeks and forehead. A particularly bright flash of lightning startled her eyes open. The resounding crash that followed made her jump. She laughed aloud at herself.

A few yards away Flinder saw the half-faced camp Reed had constructed as protection for Jack and himself. It was merely two upright forked poles with another pole across them resting in the forks. A gutta-percha cloth was attached to the cross pole, stretched at an angle on the windward side, and pegged to the ground. Flinder could not make out the figures of the two men in the dark, but she saw a bead of light at the lit end of a cigarette.

Feeling suddenly shy, Flinder withdrew into the tent and lay down. She wiped her wet face with her hands, then dried her hands by running them down the front of her damp shift. She held very still so as not to disturb Ellen, who had shifted and moaned when her sister had lain down.

Flinder thought about her hands, still moist with rainwater. She could feel the trail her hands had made down her body because of the way the cloth stuck to her skin.

She thought of Jack Webster's hands rolling that cigarette. She had watched him do it many times after meals. She shut her eyes and saw his callused, stained fingers cradling the cigarette paper and gently spreading the little curls of tobacco along the creased paper. She saw his thumb rolling the paper into a thin twist. She saw him draw his tongue slowly along its length to seal it.

Flinder had never before been so interested in the everyday actions of a man. Often she'd spy on Jack from a distance as he rode his horse out ahead to scout a camping place or a site for nooning. She'd fall back when he was driving Faith's oxen so she could watch the shape of his back and his legs while he walked. She carried her food away from him, the better to observe him eating.

Conversely, whenever he happened to be near her, she could not bring herself to look at him. If circumstances forced her to speak to him, the first few sentences sounded tinny and hollow to her, as if she'd got water in her ears, and then, under Jack's undivided attention, words flowed out of her like sap from a sugar maple; she could fairly taste their sweetness.

Was this love? There was some heat and confusion and a strange weakness to it that she had never been led to believe would be part of it. But if not love, what? For that matter, if love, what next?

Flinder turned onto her side with a long sigh. She could hear the storm abating, though it was still raining. She laid her arm over her sister's waist, and driving Jack Webster and his cigarette out of her mind, she dropped quickly to sleep. As her father had said, with bone-weariness for a pillow, the hard ground was soon soft enough. Of course, before he went to bed, he'd had a shot of whiskey extended with molasses to restore his spirits and smooth his rest; "skull varnish," Jerusha called it.

★　★　★

THE NEXT DAY dawned clear, though the mud and deep puddles all around soon soaked everyone's feet and weighted down the hems of the women's skirts. Poor Bailey emerged from her tent as wet as if she'd slept in the river. A stream of runoff had got in despite Jack's ditch. Alice offered her a damp dress—no one had any truly dry clothes available as all the wagons had leaked—but Bailey declined it, saying she'd let her dress dry on her back.

Right after breakfast, the men rode off in search of the draft animals, Henry on John's bay mare that he had favored so. No one had ridden the horse since John's drowning, though she was tame enough that even Gideon or Elizabeth would have been safe on her. Henry had leaned forward and stroked the mare's neck affectionately before riding out, an unusual gesture for him.

Rounding the stock promised to be a tedious chore, and the men might even have to lay by and return the following day if the animals had traveled far, but Roy was in a holiday mood. He actually pinched Jerusha playfully while she was packing his saddlebags with hardtack, smoked ham, and dried apples. Jerusha, blushing deeply, looked quickly around to see who had noticed. Alice and Helen, packing other saddlebags nearby, kindly averted their eyes.

Flinder was just passing at the moment of the pinch. She stopped to grin and giggle at her parents. Roy returned her grin, and grabbing the girl roughly around the waist, he pulled her to him and kissed her cheek with a loud smack.

"For luck," he said, releasing her.

It had been the briefest contact, but Flinder could still feel the span of his thick fingers along her ribs, his coarse beard against her face. She was embarrassed that her father had done this, especially in front of other people. Then she felt ashamed to begrudge him so simple a thing as a kiss on the cheek. Finally, she felt simply ashamed; she sensed, in a muddled sort of way, that it had something to do with her watching Jack Webster and how that made her feel. She wished she were anywhere but there, squirming inwardly under her father's gleeful regard.

"Get a gunnysack and search out some prairie coal," Jerusha ordered the girl. She never would say buffalo chips or droppings. Flinder ran to obey.

"Take Ellen, and don't go too far," Roy called after her. "We don't want to have to go hunting you after we're done finding the other strays."

Flinder knew he was thinking about the lost woman they had encountered a week ago, yet she felt his call as another part of the gruff kiss, a kind of claiming of her, a reminder of his dominion over her. She wanted to shout back that she'd go where she pleased, but that wasn't really what she meant to say, and in any case, she couldn't say anything. What did she have to rebuke him with? A father had kissed his daughter. That's all. Yet because of that kiss, Flinder suddenly felt that she was no longer his daughter, but something else entirely. Or, rather, that she was something else as well as a daughter. She knew, as she had never known before, that she was a woman and that other people knew it, too. She saw that a woman could not be as free as a girl. Uncle John had been right. She had to be cautious. But she still didn't understand all that that might signify.

THE LOST WOMAN, wild-eyed and still carrying a sack of buffalo chips, had stumbled into the campfire's circle of light one night last week. She held a limp, scrawny two-year-old boy on her hip. Either he was feebleminded or dazed from their adventure, for he never spoke or perked up, even when Sarah gave him her piece of peach pie, though he did it justice.

The woman said she'd wandered fifteen miles by her reckoning since losing sight of her train two days earlier while out collecting fuel. There were no landmarks on the prairie to aid her in finding her way. She'd caught a fish with her bare hands and eaten it raw, chewing up pieces for the boy like a mother bird. He was still suckling, so she had that for him, too.

But it was the fear more than the hunger that had preyed upon her. Her train, like the Mullers', had seen few Indians since leaving Missouri, only a couple of Oto and Pawnee family groups interested in trading beaded moccasins for metal utensils and calico shirts, but she was as well versed as every emigrant in the tales of white women carried off and "insulted" by lusty braves. Even at the Mullers' campfire, she started at every hoof stomp and kept standing up to look out with wide, searching eyes into the darkness beyond the circle of wagons.

Alice brought her a basin of water to wash her face in. That had calmed her more than the telling of her tale and the eating of a hot meal. She calmed down so much, in fact, that she ceased answering their questions and only dreamily rocked her boy back and forth on her lap, for all the world as if they were still friendless and alone out on the prairie. Alice laid a piece of canvas on the ground behind them, and Jerusha lowered the bedraggled pair to it as if she were baptizing them in a river. They were instantly asleep.

"Will she be all right, Ma?" Flinder had asked Jerusha.

"Nothing dries sooner than tears," the older woman answered.

They had overtaken the lost woman's train the next afternoon. A tall, skinny man whose gangly arms and legs stuck out of his clothes ran to greet her, looking no less worried for finding her alive and reasonably well. Eight sallow-faced children clattered behind him, each one managing to find a hold on their mother's skirt, the littlest ones stretching up their thin arms to try to touch her face.

Flinder was struck with the notion that should the lost woman dare to lean down into this welcoming brood, they'd eat her alive with their love and longing. The woman, however, stayed wisely erect, giving each child in turn a pat and a smile, at the same time disengaging their clutching fists from her clothing and handing over the boy, still remarkably unmoved, to a girl of about thirteen.

She leaned her head against her husband's bony shoulder, though it did not appear to provide a very comfortable perch, and walked in this awkward posture, amid an eddy of babbling children, toward their wagon. The train had already started up again. Last in a broad line of wagons three abreast and ten long, they'd be eating everyone else's dust the rest of the day. Flinder wondered if the woman wouldn't miss the clear air and solitude of the prairie just a little, and if, in each retelling of her story over the years, she'd drop out a bit more of the terror and come to find some of the wondrousness of it.

June 15, 1852

The men are out overnight rounding up the stampeded stock. We can see the fires of a neighboring pack train, which is a comfort, and far off across the Platte, fires from the south road, too. Jerusha marched over to the packers earlier to alert them we were women and children alone should any trouble occur; she said they took the information with little interest, but she relies on their Christian consciences to see us through. How she spied out the condition of either their Christianity or their consciences, I cannot think.

I confess some relief at the men's absence. I am not so used to their constant company. At home, I saw Henry in the evenings, other men on Sundays. My hands were busy with the house, the hens and cows, the kitchen garden, the flower gardens, the children, all the year's round of sewing and weaving and cooking and preserving. There was time enough for daydreaming, too, and keeping my own counsel.

Now, though many of my chores are the same as at home, they are performed under much altered circumstances. I find myself either cluttered up with people or left too much in my own thoughts, which carry me sometimes to unexpected places.

Faith awoke again last night with that same nightmare she's had several times since John's passing. It's got so that I listen in my sleep for her waking shout like I used to listen for the whimpers of my children when they were little.

Faith can never quite tell it all, but the scene that assaults her most strongly is that of her standing next to a wagon pinning up her hair in front of a looking glass that leans against the running gear. She feels a man come up behind her quiet-like. He slides his hands up her arms and squeezes her shoulders. She is so pleased, thinking it is John, for in the dream she knows he is dead. She closes her eyes and stays still, thinking that should she turn to see him, he would vanish. But the urge to look on him once more is so powerful, she opens her eyes to peek at him in the glass.

What she sees is a monster; he is shaped like a man, but his face has no features, and his hands are thick and stained like old leather. She tries to call out, but she cannot find her voice, nor can she move away from him. She is caught like that, watching him holding her, for many minutes, until at last she wrenches a sound from her throat and wakes herself up.

I sat with her last night after the dream until she fell asleep again. A small frown never left her face, even when she was resting soundly.

Chapter 5

ALICE OPENED her eyes and saw nothing but sky. She had slept out on the ground last night despite Jerusha's observation that it was not quite proper to do so with all the men gone.

It was very early. No one else was awake. Alice sat up and looked around her. The pack train was gone, having left before first light. Perhaps it had been their exit that had called her from sleep, though she hadn't noticed any noises. How easily Indians could have slipped in, she thought, but somehow the idea didn't frighten her.

She was vaguely aware that her equanimity had something to do with the sky. She stood up and looked at it again. In just those few moments between her two looks, it had changed. Alice had begun to notice in recent days how quickly and unobtrusively the vast skies over the prairie passed through dramatic changes.

Now the horizon, which she could see in almost full circle sixty or more miles away, was ringed with globules of clouds that looked like popcorn. From these frothed edges a huge, beaming blueness curved extravagantly over the wide Platte valley, and larger clouds, with flat bottoms and tall, foamy heads, scudded across it in slow-moving flotillas. These clouds were impossibly white above, their leveled-off underbellies slate or sapphire.

Alice shivered a little in her nightdress, for the dewy morning air was cool, but she did not consider retrieving a shawl from the wagon. Instead, she walked away from the circle of wagons, her eyes still raised to the glorious sky. She dropped her glance now and then to keep from stumbling into a prickly pear cactus, but otherwise the sky alone held her attention. She felt as if time and even place were draining away from her in an almost physical sense, and she surrendered to the emptying, which was, in an odd way, a filling up, a happiness.

Without thinking about what she was doing, Alice spread her arms wide and lifted them high. She spun slowly, as if she were dancing, her head thrown back so that she could see no piece of earth, only the magnificent vault above her. She felt a stirring in the center of her being, in a part of her so walled off from everyday life, she was barely aware of its existence. Even now, its nature was hidden from her, like the tangled undergrowth of an abandoned, cloistered garden, but it occurred to her that while she was busy each day pouring herself into this and that, some deep vitality lay untouched and unmoved. A tremor of fear seeded her mysterious mood. Something had come and gone just beyond her reach.

The barking of the dogs, followed by a thrum of hoofbeats, completed the interruption. Alice quickly lowered her arms and turned. Lumbering across the plain were the lost cattle and mules, with the five mounted men posting at the edges of the herd like floats on a seine. Henry was near the first oxen; he indicated he'd seen her by waving his hat.

Alice hurried to the wagon to make herself presentable, calling out to rouse the other women, who were, every one, lying abed much later than usual.

"THEY WERE ALL interlarded with some buffalo, maybe eighty all told," Derrick was saying excitedly around mouthfuls of bacon biscuits as he squatted beside the breakfast fire. "We had the devil of a time separating them without sparking another stampede."

Helen stood beside Derrick as he related his story to the women and children. She laid her hand on his shoulder, and he patted it absentmindedly. An indulgent smile translated the rebus of her features into a message of contentment. The sweetness would be on him tonight, she knew, and there'd be soft touches and the mutual recitation of plans and daydreams. It was always so after a day when Derrick had broken away from the constant hard toil to hunt or fish or ride to another camp and share a smoke with the men there.

"Worse than a stampede taking our stock off again," Derrick continued, "those buffalo could have charged us, maybe gored our horses or unseated us and trampled us underfoot."

Helen winced at the image of bloody wounds and broken bodies that Derrick's words evoked. But Derrick leaned forward as he spoke, obviously atingle from the danger that had grazed him. He looked eagerly into the faces of the children grouped around him to satisfy himself that they had fully grasped the intimacy of his acquaintance with peril.

"How'd you do it?" asked Hank, wide-eyed. "How'd you get our cattle and mules back?"

"Mostly just followed and waited till they parted company on their own," Henry answered for Derrick. "It's too hard on horses to be running after buffalo."

"Well," put in Roy, "there was that one big bull that me and Reed scared off."

"And he took our cow with him, now, didn't he?" Henry countered.

"We shall miss that cow," said Alice.

The women were in the habit of using the evening's milk at supper each night, and putting the morning's milk into a lidded tin jug. All day long the milk jostled in a moving wagon, and by afternoon they were treated to fresh-churned butter and buttermilk. Now they'd have to rely more on preserved butter; there was little of that, and it was too tedious a process to be done en route. Fresh butter had to be boiled thoroughly, all the while having the top scum skimmed off; eventually a clear oil was left, which was then soldered into tin canisters.

"We must take the fat with the lean," Jerusha said, coming to Roy's defense, not out of loyalty but to forestall his temper.

"What'd they look like, the buffalo?" asked Ellen. She'd seen a sketch of the massive beasts in one of her uncle Henry's guidebooks, and though she was a firm believer in such beings as fairies and mermaids, the brutish buffalo were almost too strange to credit with reality.

"Big," intoned Derrick with emphasis. "Bigger than oxen, and savage-looking, with high humped shoulders and great dark manes like lions, and sharp black horns. Their eyes glared bloodshot with wickedness."

"You'll get to see them for yourself in a day or two," Henry told Ellen. "Where the river forks to north and south is when their true range begins. We'll like meet hundreds and hundreds of them beyond there."

"Thousands," Derrick said with authority.

"We'd best catch up and roll," Roy said, wiping his hands on his blue flannel shirt. It was unbuttoned, showing a soiled cotton undershirt beneath it. "As it is, we won't make more than ten or twelve miles today."

Derrick rose and followed Roy toward the mules and oxen. Hank went along to help, in the hopes of hearing more about the men's adventure. The women and older girls began packing up. They had completely unloaded the wagons the day before to dry things out from the rains. None of the wagon tops was really completely waterproof.

Jack and Reed lingered by the breakfast fire, Reed drinking coffee and Jack softly playing "Sweet Betsy from Pike" on his mouth organ. Faith sat there, too, brushing and braiding Elizabeth's knotted hair. Gideon sat beside them in the dirt, patiently waiting for his playmate. Alice was folding blankets only a few feet away; Henry paused next to her.

"You were a sight this morning," he said cheerily.

Alarm spread hotly through Alice. She glanced at the group at the fire, who were not turned their way, but who were easily within earshot. Looking back at Henry, she saw he was ready to continue speaking. She felt as if she were watching from the other side of a room as a precious crystal vase tumbled from a mantelpiece toward certain destruction on the stone hearth below. Nothing she could do would divert its fall.

"What's a man to think," Henry went on in an amused tone, "when he finds his wife frolicking in the midst of the cold prairie in her nightgown?"

Alice walked around to the other side of the wagon to gather up clothing that had been spread to air on low-growing sage bushes. She tried hard not to care that Henry was invading the private moment of her morning. Its intensity had been gradually leaking from her grasp anyway all through the preparation of breakfast. Suddenly she felt drawn to explain herself.

"I thought I went out to look at the sky," she began, fumbling through her mind for the right words. "Then, when I did, everything was so quiet, so still. I felt like I was waiting."

"Waiting?" Henry had caught her seriousness and was trying to understand it. "For our return?"

"No, no, not that kind of waiting." Alice was annoyed. She should not have attempted to put this experience into words. She was killing what little traces of it were left to her.

"It was like waiting to be born," she said triumphantly, feeling she had hit upon a close description. But her elation evaporated when she saw Henry's puzzled expression.

"To me," he said, "you looked lonely out there."

"Alone. But not lonely." Alice thought of how, for her, loneliness was more likely to present itself when she was with other people, even people she cared about, than when she was by herself. She turned again, like a lagging child, to the collecting of clothing.

"Well, girlie," said Henry, reinstating his earlier lightness, "carrying babies always did make you dreamy."

Henry left to pursue some chore, and Alice lifted her gaze to the sky. Now deepened to hyacinth blue, it still spread grandly over the earth, and her heart flashed briefly with excitement at the archipelago of voluptuous clouds floating across it, but she could not recapture the morning's swelling expectancy.

She looked then at Henry walking away. His form seemed to thicken before her eyes, his familiar gait take on a plodding, spiritless quality. She felt as if she were observing a stranger. And as if, in feeling thus, she were betraying him.

THE AUTUMN she was seventeen, Alice was sent from Philadelphia to her mother's brother's farm in western Pennsylvania to tend her aunt, recently given to fits of apoplexy, and to keep house for her uncle until his wife was well enough to resume her duties. Alice had been keeping up a lively correspondence with this aunt for several years, so she was pleased to help out, and she was young enough and romantic enough to relish a temporary taste of a different kind of life and to think the contrast would make her a more worldly person.

Alice hoped, too, that her absence from the city for some months would finally prompt Charles to propose marriage; she knew her parents would not tolerate his attentions to her much longer if he did not. Her parents held the opposite hope for her visit and would have liked nothing better than to see the disreputable actor (in their view, there was no other kind) disappear.

Alice wrote Charles from the farm once a week. She'd have liked to write more often, but that did not seem a sophisticated thing to do, and sophistication was important to Charles. At first, he wrote one letter to every three of hers. He had a gift for description. Alice could almost hear the swish of faille gowns over cobblestones, could almost smell the roasting chestnuts and the dewy gardenia corsages of street vendors.

Then the letters came less frequently. Charles was touring in *A School for Scandal*. It was during this lull that Alice met Henry at a harvest dinner at a neighbor's house.

The face of the young farmer was handsome in a rough, unfinished kind of way, and his muscular build in its homemade clothing made Alice aware of the reality and foreignness of a man's body as she had never been before.

She was surprised to find him charming as well, though, of course, not in Charles's urbane style. Henry asked her about her childhood and about city life. In turn, he told her about his love of farming and the land, how a man's land and what he could wrest from it tied him to other men who lived far away from him, to men who had gone before him and to those who would follow. He seemed, too, to revel in the physical work of farming—the dark, living look of good soil breaking under the plow, the late summer smell of a barn loft filled with new-mown hay, the ache in his arms from chopping wood or digging fence-post holes. Alice, who had a small garden in Philadelphia, understood these pleasures though she had never known them.

Henry asked Alice's permission to visit her in her uncle's house. Amused, she agreed. So began a Sunday afternoon ritual that stretched effortlessly across four months.

Alice began to skip her letter to Charles some weeks. There seemed so little to tell him. Her life on the farm was busy, but quiet and simple. She was rather enjoying it, but she could not think how to convey that to Charles. She did not mention Henry in her letters; nor did she mention Charles to Henry. She constructed the idea that each man occupied a different shelf in her affections, and, like jars of pickled vegetables, could stand side by side and not corrupt each other's flavors. Charles was her beau, Henry her friend. There was no dishonor in liking them both.

One snowy Sunday, Alice was surprised to find herself keenly disappointed when Henry did not arrive at the usual time. She poked angrily at the logs in the parlor fireplace when her uncle pointed out that it was not practical weather for calling on folks, especially when the caller was on foot. Henry's parents' farm was five miles away. Alice thought to herself that practicality had no place in romance. Then she sternly told herself this was not a romance.

She sat for an hour by a window with a book of Byron's poems. She even read a stanza or two, but mostly she let it lie open on her lap while she watched the calmly falling snow and settled into her feelings. She remembered how often she felt unsure of herself around Charles's friends, and sometimes around Charles himself, how superfluous to them all. She thought about Henry's sincerity and steadiness, his unassuming beauty, and she knew suddenly that with Henry she need never fear the loss of love.

He came at last, red-cheeked, snowy-lashed, and sheepishly cheerful. His arms were filled with holly boughs which he had brought her, he said, because they were the only things he had seen on his long walk as pretty as the memory of her face.

Henry had never before been so openly flattering. Alice was not sure how to react. Considering how to respond to Henry was new to Alice; her vigil next to the drafty window had impressed upon her how much she wanted his admiration. She took the holly from him and arranged it in a large Canton ware tureen on a small table beside the front door.

They went into the parlor then. Alice's uncle had fallen asleep in his chair next to the fireplace, and the fire had died down. Henry added wood with careful movements so as not to wake the dozing older man.

As Alice watched Henry, she felt a desire to touch him. His posture pulled his cambric shirt taut across his back, and she imagined if she laid her hand there, she would feel hard muscles and body heat. Her hands were lightly clasped together in front of her. She unclasped them and extended her fingers out, but she made no true reach for him.

Henry straightened up and faced her. They stood looking at each other without speaking for a moment. A loud snore from the chair made them both smile, and taking Alice by the hand, Henry led her to the window on the other side of the room. He'd taken her hand on other occasions, to help her down icy steps, to guide her across a dark porch. But even that time they had danced on Christmas, Alice had not felt the shocking closeness of his flesh that she felt now.

"It's a different kind of evening," he whispered, releasing her hand and looking out the window at the darkening sky.

"So it seems to me as well," she said as quietly, looking at the side of his face. Again she felt the desire to touch him. She could smell tobacco and bay rum on him.

"Miss Alice . . ." he said, turning toward her. His eyes sparkled as if he had a fever.

"Yes?" Alice felt dizzy beneath his gaze.

"It was a slow walk to get here today."

"I thought you had decided not to come."

"Oh, I'd never do that," he said, dismayed. "It was only the weather delayed me."

Henry lifted his hand to one of the window quarrels and rested it lightly on the uneven glass, as if he were reading the strength of the swirling snowstorm through his fingertips. All the while he continued to regard Alice with those glittering eyes.

"Truthfully," he said, "my own thoughts slowed me as much as the snow."

"What could have made you lag on such a cold day?"

"You."

Alice turned to peer out the window. If I look into his eyes another moment, she thought, I shall surely do something to disgrace myself. But when Henry took both her hands in his and stepped nearer to her, she had no choice but to look at him again.

"I want you to be my wife," he said. Then, as if caught off guard by his own boldness, he added in a rush, "If you will. If I may. If your aunt and uncle—"

Alice lifted two fingers to Henry's lips to silence him. His mouth was warm and soft. It was the most intimate gesture that had ever passed between them, but it did not satisfy the longing she'd had throughout this visit to touch him. On the contrary, she found the longing had increased.

"I will," she said, her fingers still pressed to his lips. "You may."

Henry gave a loud shout that startled the oblivious uncle awake and made Alice laugh with pleasure. With their arms around each other's waists they told their news, first to the uncle, and then, after Alice had propped her up and helped her into a bed jacket, to the aunt. Alice marveled at how natural and easy Henry's body felt beside hers.

The rest of the evening was spent as they had always spent their Sundays. Henry stayed to supper and afterwards whittled a deer with grand antlers for his favorite brother, John, while Alice read aloud to him.

Alice's uncle, swept along by family pride and male sentimentality, took Henry home by sleigh. Alice, with only a thin ornamental shawl to shield her from the still-falling snow, stood outside watching them leave until the retreating sleigh was only a small, dark interruption on the pale horizon. Even then, she stood a few more moments contemplating the white fields and the dense, snow-outlined woods, the setting she had just adopted as her own. The city was already becoming a memory; Charles was already a phantom.

Charles took the news of the engagement in a manly enough fashion; in fact, Alice thought she detected a wash of relief under his chagrined expression. He gave her a pair of white kid gloves as a parting gift; he had always praised her lovely hands.

Alice still had the kid gloves. She had never worn them, but she had moved them from Pennsylvania to Indiana, and now was taking them from Indiana to California. She did not miss Charles or wish she had chosen differently. Alice loved and relied on Henry. She loved their children. She derived deep satisfaction from the cycles of creation that were her work on the farm, the circles of activity in which she was every link. She only wanted a reminder, she told herself, that she had had a choice, that she could have been another kind of woman if she had wished to.

But alone under the gaping morning sky of the broad prairie, she had begun to suspect that perhaps she had not lived her chosen life as full-heartedly as she could have. On the journey, life was stripped down, like a shorn sheep. Its skeleton was visible, as were the way the muscles tied the skeleton together and the vulnerable pink thinness of the skin. Alice was seeing ripples under that skin she had never noticed before.

AFTER SUPPER, Flinder took a basket and walked to the river to search for berry bushes. The Platte, wide and shallow, reflected the topaz sky of early evening. Flocks of swallows swooped and darted above the water; piping killdeer skittered across the mudflats. The open plain stretched far out from the river to distant sandhills, like rust-colored snowdrifts in the changing light.

The Platte extended in a twisted path one thousand miles westward; emigrants to Oregon and California followed along both sides of it for several hundred miles. Many complained about its sandy bottom, which made fording tricky, and its muddiness, which made the drinking water unpalatable. Jerusha said it was so dirty, you had to chew it. But Flinder thought the meandering river with its islands like scattered emeralds was simply beautiful.

Flinder spotted lamb's-tongue and wild horseradish near the river's edge. She slogged her way across a marshy place and picked some leaves from both plants. Walking on, she came across a cluster of red currant bushes. The fruit was bitter, but when stewed with plenty of sugar, it made suitable pie filling or fritter topping. Flinder set down her basket, squatted in the middle of the bushes, and picked currants, turning her head from side to side to scan for ripe ones and humming "Beautiful Dreamer."

"Ah, a fellow explorer."

The male voice so startled Flinder, she let out a small scream. When she looked in the voice's direction, she found Jack Webster. Angry with herself for her ridiculous squeal, she quickly shifted her anger to Jack.

"Good evening, Mr. Webster," she said sharply, standing up in order to appear more dignified. "I'd have taken you for a lurking redskin, but a redskin would probably hold it unmanly to frighten a woman just for the sport of it."

70

Jack said nothing in answer. They stood for a moment staring at each other across the bushes. Then he shook his head and broke into free, hearty laughter. After a few seconds, Flinder began laughing, too.

"Well, now, Miss Hall," Jack said, stepping forward and holding the bushes aside with his boot so that Flinder could walk out of the thicket more easily. "I'd as soon learn about manliness from you as from anyone."

Flinder hoped the twilight hid her blush. This man had the uncanny ability to make Flinder feel both older and younger than she was at the same time. He treated her as if she were wise in the ways of men and women, and his attitude was infectious, so that she did, indeed, sense in herself an intuition about how to answer him, how to move in his presence, when to hold his gaze and when to release it. But this intuition was often overlaid or obliterated by a sudden blankness of mind and childish embarrassment.

"I'm looking for berries," she said, trying to steer the talk to a more ordinary topic. She instantly judged it a stupid remark.

"Getting dark for that," Jack answered. He seemed to be enjoying her discomfort.

"Yes, you're right," she said, annoyance restoring her composure. "I'll be getting back then."

"If you come upriver a mite with me, I'll show you something." Now it was Jack who sounded like a child, a little boy aching to show off a prize and thereby earn a friend.

Flinder looked past Jack to the wagons grouped in a semicircle. The stock was grazing nearby. Tents had been pitched. She could see figures moving about. She couldn't make out their faces, but by concentrating on their shapes and how they moved, she could identify them.

The sight pulled at her, just as when, on cold winter nights back home, she'd slowly cross the frozen yard with heavy pails full of fresh milk and see Jerusha busy in the kitchen through the lighted window. The known quantity of the encampment lured her all the more because she felt that in some way she could never return to it again, would never again be that girl carrying milk into her mother's house.

Flinder took two halting steps in the direction of the wagons. Jack laid his hand on her forearm and spoke softly to her.

"No tricks, Miss Hall. It's something I've found."

Flinder paused, then turned away from the wagons. She almost expected that if she looked back, they'd be gone. But she didn't look back. She followed Jack, who had begun walking upstream along the river's sandy edge.

They stayed single file like that for ten minutes. Pinks and golds were bleeding into the sky now; the red sun had set behind a bank of purple clouds. The ground was sliced with brown shadows.

Jack stopped and knelt down in the sand. Flinder knelt facing him, and after his lead, looked to the ground between them. Nestled in the sand was a clutch of eggs.

"Turtle's eggs," he said. "Good as hen's eggs for cakemaking, I've heard."

"Then you shall have a cake. We all shall," Flinder said, delighted.

She carefully placed the five eggs in her basket. Jack retrieved one egg from her and set it back on the sand. In the near-darkness it almost glowed.

"For mama turtle," he said, shrugging to discount his tenderness. He stood up and began walking back to camp.

Flinder rose, brushed the sand from her skirt, and hurried after Jack. He stopped to wait for her, and they strolled on slowly, side by side.

"You're a different kind of girl," Jack said after they'd gone a bit without speaking.

"Why, what do you mean?" said Flinder, though she, too, felt she was different—different from Sarah, who was more cautious, different from her mother, who, for all her bluster, bowed to her husband's wishes in everything, different from her aunt Alice, who always seemed to be thinking more than she was saying. Flinder was headstrong and impulsive, traits she'd not seen in other girls and women. Jerusha implied she'd grow out of them. Flinder was beginning to think, however, that they were here to stay, and that it was a more important task to find how she might live and hold on to them than to learn to curb them.

"You aren't fearful," Jack replied.

"I can be," Flinder said, "but I don't like to let it rule me."

"Do you have a beau?"

"No." The answer seemed to put her in a poor light. "But I never wanted one before," she added.

"Before?"

"I just never wanted one."

"Well, when you do come to want one, you'll have your pick, I'll warrant."

"Am I to thank you for that?" Flinder said.

Jack laughed. "No thanks needed for plain facts. Only keep me in mind, Miss Hall, when you get around to the picking."

"If you mean what you say," Flinder answered, "then you'd best start calling me by my Christian name."

"To be honest, I sometimes don't mean what I say." Jack's expression, what she could see of it in the dusky light, was suddenly serious. His voice, too, had lost its jolly, teasing quality.

"I'm not sure people would want me around as much if I wasn't always sweet-talking them and joking," he continued. "But there's something about you makes me think I could tell you the truth and it would be all right."

"Then tell me this," Flinder said. She had to suppress a smile at Jack's worried frown. "Will you call me Flinder?"

"Yes, I will." He grinned. "I'll probably wear your name out with calling."

June 18, 1852

We are at the Forks of the Platte, though with all the islands in the river, it is hard to say exactly where the division lies.

We've come now four hundred some miles from the Missouri River.

We saw a large train cross over from the south road today. The river was high enough to get into the wagon beds, but low enough to ford, so to keep the contents dry, they had raised the beds with blocks of wood.

Two wagons suffered broken axles in the crossing, but the train's captain told Henry it was still a worthy decision. Cholera is raging on the south road, and they crossed in hopes of escaping it, having heard that the Council Bluffs road is not so hard hit by the epidemic. (Yet we have gained news of cholera deaths in almost every company we've met.) No one knows how to ward off the "great destroyer," as it's called. Each step farther west, however, is a step away from it, as they say its reign ends after Fort Laramie when the trail climbs into the mountains.

I spoke with a Tennessee woman from the train that crossed today who said they'd scarcely been out of sight of gravediggers since Independence and that in one place the dead lay in a row of fifty. In another place, where graves were left too shallow, they were confronted with the horrible sight of bones, bits of clothing and fouled bedding, and even hands and feet left scattered about by wolves. They have picked up many orphaned children, including an infant that this woman carries every night to other camps in search of nursing mothers willing to share their milk.

They left behind the two families with the broken axles to make their repairs and overtake the main group later. They wield time as a weapon, it seems, hoping to outrun the disease.

Time here is measured in miles instead of hours. Days are for passing through, not using up. The land is so much the same and the animals so slow-footed, it appears to the senses we are not moving at all; we have only our reason and our tired bodies to assure us we are. It affects the soul, this dissipation of time and distance into boundaryless corridors through which we march, one foot before the other over and over. It puts to question the shape of our normal lives. Are we always, anywhere, in our plans and in our associations, striving only to keep ourselves safe?

Chapter 6

JACK AND REED had been riding about an hour when Jack suddenly pulled up and dismounted. Reed scanned the prairie on all sides, but could spot no game. Since setting out that morning, they had encountered only a few delicate-limbed pronghorn antelope, far too fleet to waste throwing bullets at, and a town of a hundred or more yipping prairie dogs, also too quick for them, and by all accounts unpalatable anyway.

The absence of suitable targets irritated Reed, who was, to begin with, not in the best of moods. When he saw why Jack had stopped, his sense of tribulation was compounded almost beyond endurance. Jack was picking wildflowers.

"Jack!" he shouted in genuine horror.

Jack straightened up, spun around, and sprang for the Sharps carbine slung over his saddle pommel. If Reed hadn't been so disgusted, he would have laughed at Jack, with his frightened expression and his fistful of yellow umbels, purple locoweed, and brown and gold sunflowers.

"What? What?" Jack was saying, his rifle slid halfway out of its leather sling. Finding no obvious danger, he jammed the gun back and marched around his horse to face his cousin.

"Why'd you shout like that?" he demanded. "I thought you'd spied a war party or a rattler or something."

"What are you doing with them flowers?" Reed accused.

Jack looked at the forgotten flowers clutched in his fist. Some of the sunflowers' long stalks were broken, and the blooms hung down forlornly. He carefully extricated these from the rest and threw them away, retaining one stem to twist around the bouquet as a binding. Then he stuffed the stems of the bundled flowers into his belt.

Reed dismounted and walked up to Jack.

"They're for her, ain't they?" he said angrily.

Jack didn't answer, but only took out his bandanna and blew his nose.

"Never knew you to need flowers before," Reed teased, controlling his anger enough to try a new tactic. "Guess virgins is a little fussier than widows and whores."

The hard slam of Jack's hands against Reed's chest came so fast that Reed was sprawled on his back in the dirt before he fully understood what had happened. Strangely, the bitter fury that had welled up at the sight of Jack picking flowers fled in the wake of Jack's blow. Now Reed felt only astonishment and wariness.

He took a good look at his cousin's face before attempting to rise. He saw a threat there, but he also saw remorse and embarrassment. He stored away the observations; it would not do to forget any of them. Propping himself up on one elbow, Reed extended his other hand to Jack. With only the briefest of hesitations, Jack grasped it and pulled him to his feet. Reed noted the hesitation, too.

"You know this delay's got me broody," Reed said by way of apology.

Reed had already done a lot of complaining about the two-day break Henry Muller had ordered to rest the animals and make wagon repairs. The women were using the time to bake and do laundry; Reed persisted in blaming them for the halt.

"You fret over things too much," Jack said, leaving the topic of Flinder Hall untouched, as Reed had counted on him doing.

"One of us has got to keep his mind on business. We came out here to find gold, remember? Can't begin to do that until we get ourselves to the gold fields, the quicker the better. And traveling with women just ain't quick."

"Now, Reed, the women have kept step as well as any man."

"Maybe." Reed frowned out over the prairie. He could feel the thread of his argument slipping away from him, and he suspected this was a crucial point at which to stay in control of it.

Reed had noticed a difference in Jack lately, the kind of difference he had seen in other men just before they started thinking that curtains and babies might hold some delights after all. It was a difference that was more apparent to an onlooker, it seemed, than it was to the man it was happening to, which meant that Jack was still ripe for saving.

Reed had never had to save Jack from a woman before; he wasn't sure how to do it. Other times, Reed had simply waited out Jack's infatuations. Jack always moved on eventually. In fact, it was usually Jack who set them to roaming again, with a twitching kind of energy, sometimes interrupting Reed in the middle of a meal or rousing him from a fast sleep to saddle up.

Reed figured he could strike it rich on his own, if it came to that, though part of him didn't really believe it. But it wouldn't be the same if Jack wasn't there. Nothing would. Reed was too used to the form of Jack beside him on horseback or across a table, too used to the sound of his snoring, too used even to the waits and to the feel of winning when a wait was over.

"It's not just them," Reed said at last. "It's all the wagons and trappings needed when there's females and brats along. That's what slows us."

"I'd like to be moving faster, too, but what can we do about it?" Jack answered.

Reed knew Jack was agreeing with him only to get him to lay off his belly-aching and that Jack did not mean his question as a real question, but Reed recognized an opportunity when he saw one, and he took it.

"When we get to Fort Laramie, I bet we could hitch up with a stag company of packers. Then we'd move along smartly. Probably save a month off the trip."

"I don't know. These folks would miss us."

"It's what I aim to do." This was a gamble. Reed had never before suggested that he and Jack go their separate ways. He suspected that their long partnership was due as much to Jack's laziness as to his own dogged loyalty. If dissolution loomed, would Jack make an effort to stop it?

"You're that unsatisfied?" Jack said. The surprise and concern in Jack's voice encouraged Reed. He nodded emphatically in reply.

"You'd go on alone?"

"I wouldn't want to, Jack. You know that."

Jack took off his hat and wiped his sleeve across his sweaty brow. Reed could not bear to watch Jack's face as he studied the situation. He looked away; a bald eagle was gliding in indolent circles high above the prairie. The Indians would say that was a sign, most likely, Reed thought, but being an unimaginative man, he could not guess whether it boded well or ill. He was too unimaginative even to make a wish in his favor.

"The fort's still two weeks off, maybe more," Jack said after a long pause. "If you set yourself honestly to being a part of this company until then and still you find you want to leave, I'll ride out with you."

"Well, sure, Jack. That's fair. Like you say, maybe I haven't tried enough to like these people and to be likable."

Reed extended his right hand to Jack. Jack looked at the hand a moment before grasping it. Reed would have liked the handclasp to be heartier, but it was sufficient. Jack would keep his word.

"Reed, I don't make this promise lightly."

"Hell, Jack, you don't make any promises usually," Reed scoffed genially, trying to prick Jack's sober demeanor.

"If you call me on this," Jack continued, "I'll count us even at last."

For the second time that day Jack had astonished Reed. Though Reed had agreed to try to fit in with the Muller party, he fully intended to part from them at Laramie and take Jack with him. But he'd thought it would cost him no more than a couple of weeks' playacting. Now Jack had just informed him it would be more dear than that. Reed would have to spend the one coin he had kept from Jack all these years. He would have to acknowledge the debt from that long-ago night had been paid.

THE BOYS HAD CLIMBED into their beds at the usual time. Everything had been quite ordinary, from Jack's mother's check behind their ears after they'd washed up to her call as she blew out the lanterns in the main room one by one and the dancing shadows on the cabin walls blended into the night's blackness.

"Good night, sweet dreams, and God bless you," she'd called from her little alcove across the cabin from theirs. Same as every night. Sometimes Reed made faces when she said it, crossing his eyes and sticking out his tongue, crooking his fingers to look like grizzly bear paws. Jack always punched him in the arm for doing it. Jack was sentimental even then.

The motherly words comforted Jack. But she was not Reed's mother, only his aunt, and he was determined to have none of her comfort. Her existence was the reason Reed was not living in the wilderness with his father, like a real man. If she hadn't been around to take him on when his mother died, his father would have had to keep him. Then he'd know more now than Jack did about hunting and trapping and Indians. Jack's father was a mountain man, too, but he came home every once in a while for spells to hang on his woman and fatten up. Reed's father, Reed told Jack proudly, was a *real* mountain man because he didn't ever come home.

But that night, Reed had not made unseen faces at his aunt, and later on, he was glad he hadn't because, despite his gruff aloofness from her and her soft ways, Reed had a grudging appreciation for this woman who had brought him into her home without hesitation and without reproach to his father.

Jack, of course, was her favorite. It was only natural, Reed told himself; he'd be a fool to expect otherwise. He never could have stood all that petting, anyway. His own mother had been a worn-down, almost mute person who was always tired, but who never rested.

Reed couldn't say what exactly awoke him. He just rolled onto his back and opened his eyes and found himself alertly awake. At first he didn't know what was different; he only knew that something was not right. It was the light. There was too much light. Then he smelled the smoke, too.

"Jack! Jack!" he yelled, bounding out of bed and running to the doorway of their tiny room. Their beds were simply mattresses on two wooden shelves attached to the walls where they met at a right angle. The cousins slept with their heads nearly touching.

From the doorway Reed saw that the half of the cabin opposite theirs was a mass of flames. The heat made him wince. He could not see through the flames to the front door, nor could he see his aunt's room. He wanted to believe that she had got out before the fire grew so fierce, but he knew she'd never have left without them.

"Mama!" Jack screamed behind him.

Jack was sitting up in bed. The fire's light reached from behind Reed and lit Jack's face redly; his eyes glittered. Reed had the impression Jack was not seeing him, though he was staring right at him.

Reed ran to the small window. The forest outside was ablaze, but the fire hadn't yet reached that side of the cabin. Grabbing a footstool, Reed smashed out the glass. Intense heat and a roaring noise rushed in through the opening, as if the fire outside were lunging forward to find the fire inside, like a mother wild to retrieve a lost child.

Jack was still fixed on the other room. No recognizable feature or piece of furniture was visible. Only fire. Leaping, ravenous fire, writhing its way towards them. Now black smoke curled down from the rafters of the ceiling and invaded their alcove. Reed doubled up choking. Jack was coughing, too, but his attention did not swerve.

Reed climbed onto Jack's bed, grasped his shoulders, and shook him. Jack was frighteningly limp.

"Jack, we've got to get out," Reed shouted between coughs.

Reed jumped down to the floor, pulling on the older boy's hand. To Reed's relief, Jack followed without protest, though he did twist his head around to keep the interior of the cabin in view. Reed clambered out the window with some difficulty. He had to keep his smarting eyes closed, and he was afraid to let go of Jack, so his climbing was awkward. He slashed his forearm on a shard of glass still wedged into the window frame. Jack tumbled out after Reed, having gotten through the window more by Reed's frantic tugging than by his own efforts.

Once outside, Jack seemed finally to come to life. He gazed around them in terror, but he held his body taut, like a deer in the moment before it flees the hunter, and his face, for all its alarm, showed calculation, too.

"The creek!" he yelled at Reed. The boys were standing side by side, but the snapping, sucking voice of the fire pushed between them like a physical wall.

Access to the well-worn creek trail was blocked by a flaming fallen tree. Jack pointed to a small break in the fire several yards to the north of the trail. They'd have to push their way through some thick undergrowth to get to the creek that way, but they had no choice. Crazily Reed thought about the poison ivy woven through the thick brush and how cross his aunt would be if they came up with rashes all over their legs.

Jack struck out running for the gap in the fire, and Reed dashed close behind him. Both boys held their arms across their foreheads to protect their faces from the heat. It did little good. They darted and fell in an irregular route down the hill toward the creek, detouring around patches of burning bushes. In some places they found a wide, fire-free avenue, in others, a horrifyingly narrow corridor between flaming columns that used to be trees. At one point, they stopped, stupefied, when a squirrel, its tail ablaze, flew screeching across their path.

Finally the creek materialized, yellow and orange reflections shuddering across its black water. Jack burst ahead, tripped over a root, and sprawled flat out on the pebbly beach. Just at that moment, Reed heard at his back the unmistakable crack of a large limb breaking loose. He flung himself on top of Jack, and the end of the torch that had been a branch swept his back, setting his hair and his nightshirt on fire.

The pain was so complete and so startling, Reed did not at first register it as pain. He thought for an instant that he must be about to die, and a sudden stillness enveloped him during which he was conscious not of the devouring forest around him, but only of the searing reality of the back of his body from the top of his head to his waist and the hard shape of Jack's angular body beneath him. In the next instant, he cried out and rolled over and over, pebbles piercing his raw, burned skin until he hit the icy creek, whose relief was really only the replacement of one pain with another.

They stayed in the creek until dawn. By then the fire had spent itself in that part of the forest. Jack hiked to a neighbor's four miles away to get someone to doctor Reed. The fire had missed their place.

Reed healed, thanks to liberal applications of an ointment of hog's grease and chalk, though he was badly scarred on his back, arms, and scalp. Jack built a new, smaller cabin on the same spot. He found a few bits in the ashes that looked like bones, so he buried them and made a headstone for his mother over them. The boys were fourteen and seventeen then, able, their few neighbors concluded, to live on their own. When Jack's father came home six months later, he found them getting along well enough. They set the table with game and fish mostly. The Widow Larkin, who had taken poor, motherless, handsome Jack to her ample bosom and elsewhere, provided bread and pies regularly.

Jack's father was visibly diminished by the loss of his wife, like a man who's been stooped by old age. The boys' survival gave him insufficient solace. He decided to stay put at last, as if by finally settling down, which his wife had always hoped he'd do, he could somehow make up to her the long, lonely years and her gruesome, solitary death. Reed and Jack found the man doleful company. So when the attentions of the Widow Larkin passed from pleasant initiations to petulant demands, and Jack proposed that they strike off together to see the world and make their fortunes, Reed readily assented.

The world they'd seen so far was only their own country, but that was marvel enough, vast and varied, peopled with everyone from preachers to Indian chiefs, storekeepers' wives to soiled doves. They'd yet to make a real fortune, but they got along, and they'd had some high times, mainly from the fruits of Jack's poker playing. And through it all, the hellish night in the woods, never spoken of between them, spread beneath them like the net under a trapeze artist, making mistakes and slips of attention forgivable, keeping disaster at bay.

FLINDER AND SARAH were almost through with their families' laundry. The girls worked together, Flinder soaping the clothes in a tub, Sarah rinsing them in the river and wringing them out. Ellen appeared at intervals to carry wet clothes back to camp and spread them on the ground to dry in the hot sun.

Bailey Jeffers, with less washing to do, had finished her chore and was sketching the girls at their task. The boys had gathered extra fuel last night so that the wash water could be heated. Normally they needed five bushels of buffalo chips just to cook supper and breakfast. Not to waste a good fire, Alice had carried two Dutch ovens to the riverside and was slowly feeding the fire to bake light bread. It was only at rare stopovers like this that the women had opportunity to knead yeast dough; otherwise they relied on hardtack, crackers, biscuits, or fried cornmeal as breadstuffs.

The flow of the Platte was split, as usual, by several small islands supporting scraggly willows, poplars, and cotton-woods. The river's spring floods carried away seeds from its shores, and seedlings were burned out in the autumn prairie fires or broken down by foraging buffalo, so there was no timber on the prairie. This made the tall cedar the women now worked beneath a marvel. It was the first tree they'd seen in two hundred miles, and that last lone tree, a giant cotton-wood, had been the only one sighted since leaving Missouri.

Alice resisted an urge to embrace the tree. She didn't want to appear foolish before the others. She recalled how she'd disliked the thick forest around their cabin in Pennsylvania, the feeling of captivity it had evoked. She'd much preferred the open setting of their second home, in Indiana, with just two shade trees close to the house and small, contained stands of woods at the edges of the fields. It seemed, paradoxically, a more intimate place, a place more amenable to the nourish-ment of a community than the dense woodlands that cut peo-ple off from one another. But here, on the prairie, the absence of trees was too extreme. It was monotonous at best, desolate and heartless at worst, offering no shelter from rain or wind or sun, sure to defeat even the most optimistic soul with its sheer limitlessness. The wide sky continued to intrigue Alice, but she missed the hospitality of trees.

"We're done," Sarah declared, rubbing her wet hands on her skirt. "Do you need us to sit for more drawings, Miss Jeffers?"

"No, I've got enough studies here to work something up, I think."

"You girls turn the clothes Ellen's spread when you get to camp, in case she hasn't thought to," Alice said. "Then your time's your own unless Jerusha or Faith needs you."

Together Flinder and Sarah dumped the wash water and carried the tub with its last load of wet laundry towards the wagons. Alice lifted the oven's lid to check on the bread and clucked her tongue in annoyance to find the edges browning darkly while the center was still obviously undercooked.

"We shall have slightly burned bread again, I'm afraid," she said to Bailey. "I haven't yet mastered baking on an open fire."

Bailey's head remained bent over her sketchpad. Alice was not surprised her remark had drawn no response. The single woman, despite the smallness of the group, had remained politely apart. She did her share of communal chores, but no more. She walked alone. At meals and rest stops, she invariably pulled out her sketchpad and offered only small contributions to the general conversation active around her. No one knew more about her now than they had at Council Bluffs.

The men gave little thought to her, but the women often wondered among themselves about her. It was Jerusha's contention that Miss Jeffers either held a superior opinion of herself or had some shameful secret in her past; whichever the case, Jerusha summed up, such company was not missed. Alice could not harden herself so, or perhaps, as Jerusha accused, she was simply too curious. She stared at the woman, willing her to look her way, but soon realized she must speak directly to get her attention.

"How did you come to take up drawing?"

Bailey looked up quickly, as if a gun had been shot close by. Her eyes were unguarded for only a moment, but it was long enough for Alice, who had been waiting for just such a chance, to catch a gleam of remoteness so thorough, she could have been looking into the eyes of a blind person. Alice felt that this remoteness was at once this woman's strength and her curse, and that while it did not seem to forbid the offer of a bridge, it would require the offer to be sincere and forbearing.

"It seems like a great pleasure for you," Alice added.

Bailey glanced down at her pad and nodded. When she looked at Alice again, it was with a meditative expression. Alice felt that she was being examined, as one might examine the face of a child to see if he was lying or the color of soil to see if it would respond well to cultivation. Alice could not imagine how she should present herself under such scrutiny, so she simply let her features rest easy and took the opportunity to study Bailey in return.

What she saw was a plain woman with a boyish figure and large, capable hands who could by no means be called beautiful, but whose face was nevertheless arresting. It was, perhaps, her eyes that did it, large and dark, with the merest upward slant to them and a mixed expression of expectancy and skepticism. Alice felt that Miss Jeffers would not be likely to avert her eyes from any scene or person until she had seen all she wanted, no matter how alarming or embarrassing the sight might be. They were like magnets, those eyes, or lures.

"Yes, drawing does please me," Bailey said at last. "We had to study it at normal school, but I practiced it more than required. Some of my teachers despaired I should never learn enough natural science or arithmetic." She smiled at the memory.

"You carry your materials always with you, I've seen," said Alice, referring to the perennial bag slung around Bailey's waist.

"In the beginning, I used to draw only at the end of a tiring day in the schoolhouse. It was soothing. Then it crept up on me, and I found I could go nowhere without my pad and pens, and I had no shyness at all about drawing in front of anyone. Just as I'd have no shyness at drinking water before someone if I were thirsty."

Alice considered this. She had no similar compulsions in her life. Her gardening was the closest experience she could connect to what Bailey was describing. It certainly pleased and soothed her and claimed her energy even when she had little left. And now the journal. That was more near to Bailey's drawing. It had begun as a testament for the new baby, almost a long letter to the child, but it had not held that shape. Imperceptibly it had changed into something personal for Alice herself.

Sometimes she'd catch it changing right under her hand as the careful description of a small event or a landscape feature would slide into a recounting of ideas and feelings she was not aware she possessed until she saw them form into words at the tip of her pen. Then she felt in fuller possession not only of the unsuspected ideas, but of the original event or place as well. In this way, Alice had the impression she was making two journeys, the trek across the continent and a foray into her innermost heart.

"It's like taking hold of something inside, isn't it?" Alice said softly.

Bailey did not reply, but her expression showed agreement. Despite that, Alice felt a little awkward, as if she'd said something improper.

"And will you teach school in California?" she said in a more conversational tone.

"No. Teaching suits me in its way, because I have no family, and it is a respectable way to keep myself, but it is a little too respectable, I fear."

"Too respectable?" Alice shuddered to think how Jerusha would react to such a comment, or most anyone, for that matter.

Bailey laughed. "I mean nothing scandalous, I assure you, Mrs. Muller."

"I hadn't thought of scandal. It's only that respectability is not usually a source of complaint."

"Not aloud anyway." Again Bailey smiled.

"Do you mean schoolteaching is tedious?"

"It can be that at times. But what I mean is that teachers, especially female teachers, as models to children and in the community at large, are expected to be better than the average person, more refined, at peace with their position. They are not expected to stride unaccompanied through the countryside nor to sketch unshirted young farmers haying or mothers nursing their infants or watchers at a deathbed. They are not expected to want to see new places and go among wild animals and naked Indians."

Bailey stopped suddenly, as if someone had checked her speech with a cautioning wag of a finger. Alice had never heard her say so much at one time, and certainly not with such passion. How did a woman get such yearnings? Alice remembered some such notions from girlhood. She remembered being especially stirred by the story of Joan of Arc, though the saint's fiery end was certainly not enviable. Once Alice's attention was called by her mother to suitors, however, her vague dreams of an independent life lapsed, seeming as unattainable as the ambition to converse with kings and lead an army.

Listening to Bailey, Alice felt again, ever so faintly, the long-ago promptings toward an existence beyond hearth and family, so that although she could not imagine such desires holding any strong sway over herself, she could understand their predominance in another woman, especially a woman without a husband.

"I wondered," Alice said after an interval of silence during which she lifted the ovens off the fire and Bailey picked up her pencil again, "what had prompted you to go west alone. But for Henry's strong wishes, I would have much rather stayed in Indiana. The other women, excepting Helen, who's young and on her wedding trip, feel that way, too."

"I couldn't bear the hardships of this journey if it hadn't come of my own choosing," Bailey said.

Alice wondered if this was a judgment against her on Bailey's part. She was not used to looking at her life evaluatively, nor to having anyone else do so.

"To link my life with Henry's was when my choosing happened."

"Yes, I see that," Bailey replied gently, reassuring Alice that no judgment was intended. "My way of claiming a life is different from that. It always has been. I think the West will be a fair place for me. For us all, I hope."

June 27, 1852

We are opposite the famous Chimney Rock, which all the guidebooks speak of and every emigrant letter in the newspaper back home remarked on. It has been visible most of the way for the last thirty-five miles, a persistent curiosity for days. We will be able to see it behind us for that far as well, it's said. Though yesterday we came abreast the commanding, immense monolith called the Court House, off beyond the south-side trail, the Chimney is the more stirring landmark, like an exclamation point to this strange, rugged landscape, an announcement that the blank plains will soon be a memory. The land is changing, getting drier and rising up into castellated bluffs and great, sand-colored rock formations. I have never seen their like.

Derrick, who is a lover of geography, says we are across the one hundredth meridian and that this is the true look of the West, though he has had to view it from inside his wagon the past two days, being weak with the flux, an inflammation of the bowels few plains travelers elude. Indeed, most of our party have been visited by this summer complaint, though none so strongly that they needed to ride.

Helen's become quite the mule skinner, giving Derrick as even a ride as the terrain will allow. The ruts from buffalo trails to the river are laid out like washboards in some places, which gives the wagons a hard jarring. Helen has had to master, too, the efficient stopping and starting of their team, as the wants of nature call Derrick out the wagon so often.

Roy, who grumbles at stops almost as loudly as Mr. Bennett, surprised us by wishing to take time to wade across the river and visit the Chimney. Mr. Bennett, Mr. Webster, and Henry accompanied him, as did Bailey, who has seemed more one of us since the respite at the Lone Tree. The children clamored to go, too. In the end, they took Flinder and Sarah because they were old enough to keep up and watch out for themselves. I compensated the ones left behind with the spyglass, through which we got a good view of the Chimney and of our band of friends hiking to it.

It seems Flinder occasioned a flurry of excitement almost to equal the landmark when she revealed she wore a pair of her father's corduroy trousers under her skirts to make climbing *easier. Bailey declared she wished she'd thought of it herself; she and Sarah had to content themselves with observing the tall column of buff yellow clay from the top of its cone-shaped base, though from Bailey's sketches, that was quite high. (The whole solitary formation, like an upside-down funnel, stands about five hundred feet above the river.)*

Bailey depicts wagons below as small as cradles along the snaking Platte, and the sweep of the horizon is grand, giving off eastward to the massive Court House and Jail Rocks and westward to the majestic buttes and badlands of Scott's Bluffs, which we shall reach in two days' time or so.

Flinder and the men achieved somewhat higher than Bailey and Sarah, surmounting the area between the cone and the pillar, but, of course, no one can scale the spire itself. Legend says a Sioux brave, promised a pony by his chief, attained the summit, but fell to his death. The chief then wrapped the brave with his belongings, killed the longed-for pony, and placed it under the brave's burial scaffold for his use in the afterlife. I pity the pony, sacrificed by no fault of its own, but the notion that our possessions are so much a part of us we need them even after death touches me. I have seen along our route many abandoned belongings, and I cringe at them almost as mournfully as I do the makeshift graves we also encounter. I shall guard my possessions, the fretwork on which I shall hang our life in its new setting. I may be transplanted, but I do not wish to change.

Roy stood on Mr. Webster's shoulders to carve his name, the year, and "Indiana" in the Chimney's soft stone wall, squeezing the words, he said, between a James Evans from 1850 and a Captain Smith from 1845.

Sarah brought back a broken seashell. It is odd to think of this land having been once underwater. Sarah says Derrick may have the shell. With dulcet shrewdness, she saw how stung he was at missing the expedition. How generous to give up her little treasure to try to soothe his disappointment. Even if she were not my daughter, I should admire her.

I shall take the shell to Derrick now, along with a large cup of blackberry root tea to ease his stomach, for I do not want to miss the next chapter of David Copperfield, *Mr. Dickens's new book, that Bailey has taken to reading aloud every evening before retiring.*

Chapter 7

S ARAH," Alice said just past dawn next day, "go call Helen to breakfast. It may be she was up late nursing Derrick and has slept in."

Sarah skipped to the Bowens's wagon and stopped a few feet from it. She called Helen, but not too loudly for fear of disturbing Derrick. When Helen did not answer, Sarah raised her voice and even ventured to knock on the side board of the wagon. Still no reply. Thinking it would be impolite to intrude further, Sarah went to get her mother.

Alice looked cautiously into the narrow wagon. Derrick and Helen lay unmoving side by side. A low moan came from Helen. When Alice stepped on the footboard and leaned over the spring seat, a putrid odor of vomit and feces hung over the Bowens. Alice held one hand over her nose and mouth to block out the foul smells. She gently shook Helen's arm and then Derrick's and quickly withdrew.

Pulling Sarah with her, Alice backed away from the gruesome wagon. Last night she hadn't been sure. She'd hoped it was only dysentery. There'd been no cold sweats, no vomiting, no sore throat. Now Derrick was dead, and Helen's life was draining away rapidly.

"Ma, what is it?" Sarah asked fearfully.

"Cholera."

"But Helen said it was the flux."

"They can look alike at the start."

"Oh, Ma, Ellen had the flux bad last night. Flinder was bringing her in and out the tent all night. She complained her throat hurt, too."

"Lord help us." Alice felt panic alight on her like some dark, sharp-clawed bird of prey.

She had tried throughout the journey to protect her family by every means she could. She aired their bedding, she fed them regularly and well, she rubbed them with turpentine to ward off mosquitoes. She was, by these measures, arming against no particular ailment, but, rather, making the only concrete gestures available to her to protest the broad threats to safety and peace the dislocations of traveling had thrown up around her. Now here was a powerful, specific enemy with which to grapple, and Alice was afraid.

The scourge of cholera had boiled through the whole country in 1849. Four families in the Mullers' small congregation in Indiana had lost members to the mysterious, terrifying disease. Alice knew that although victims could linger for days, as Derrick had, the more usual course was much swifter. A strong man could be struck suddenly and be dead in a matter of a few agonizing hours.

Dread massed in the pit of Alice's stomach and thickened her tongue. Though her mind buzzed with disconnected thoughts like bursts of shot, her body felt cold and heavy, as if she were made of marble. Desperate to act, she was seized with a sense of futility. Recovery from cholera was possible, but it was never clear which played the saving role: the pitifully small array of remedies, prayer, or pure luck.

"Ma?" Sarah's voice quivered. She sounded like a much younger child.

Alice looked into Sarah's worried face. The girl was near tears. It came to Alice that Sarah needed her now in an almost primitive way, as a young animal needs its mother to shield it from impending harm with her own body, her own life. Alice had never thought of the self-reliant Sarah as requiring such blunt protection; indeed, she would have expected Sarah to recognize that there could be no perfect certainty in this world, to disbelieve it even if it were offered to her. Yet here she stood, lips trembling, entreaty in her eyes, a child after all, a child with knowledge she didn't want. As thwarted as Alice felt, she knew she must dredge up from out of her own fear at least a semblance of purposeful reaction to the killer in their midst.

"You tend to breakfast for the boys," Alice directed, calming both Sarah and herself by turning to practical matters. "Be sure Jerusha knows about Ellen. If we doctor her soon enough, we may save her. I must counsel with your father."

Sarah nodded and turned to go, swiveled back to give her mother a quick, hard embrace, and then ran off. Alice headed for the river, where Henry and Roy had gone to fetch two wheels they'd let soak overnight. A couple of felloes on each wheel had shrunk in the hot, dry air of the plains; consequently, the iron tires were loose, and a wheel with a loose tire was useless. Hot-riveting was the best solution, but without a smithy available, soaking the wheels to swell them would have to do.

Alice met Henry and Roy on their way back from the river. Alice noticed sweat stains on their shirts. The day was going to be very hot again.

"We've trouble," she began.

The men stopped to listen, their faces tight and ready.

"The Bowens are down with cholera. Derrick's gone already, and Helen nearly so."

"We've got to burn their wagon and move on at once," Roy declared.

"Let's set to Derrick's grave right away," Henry added. "There'll be no time to make a coffin."

"Helen can't travel," Alice objected.

"Then she must be left," Roy said angrily. "If someone wishes, they may stay to watch her and overtake us later."

"Royal," Alice said gently, "I'm not certain, but it appears your Ellen may be sick with it, too."

"Ellen?" he said, as if he couldn't recall who she was.

"Better go see to your family," Henry told him. "I'll tend to the business of the Bowens."

Deflated, Roy walked off without another word, his shoulders bowed like a man come in from a long day's plowing.

"The child," Alice said, watching Roy trudge away. "It's too cruel."

"Can anything be done?" Henry asked Alice. "I'll ride out to some other trains and look for a doctor, if you think it useful."

Alice was touched by Henry's willingness to help, which went against his impulse to flee, but in a corner of her heart, she wanted to blame him for the cholera. Though she had agreed to it, the decision to make this journey had been Henry's, had been the fruit of his dreams of adventure and his aspirations to a better life for them and their children. She shared Henry's hopes for the new life in California, but unlike him, she had feared the rigors of getting there would take an extravagant toll. Her concern, dismissed as overly sensitive by Henry and Roy in Indiana, now held the shape of stark reality. She was ashamed to notice in herself a bitter satisfaction.

"We can do the same for Ellen as a doctor would," she answered. "It may be too late anyway."

"Come on, then. Let's pack up."

"Henry, it may be of little difference to Helen, she is so near the end, but Ellen . . . I'm sure Jerusha will not want to subject her to the miseries of lying sick with cholera in a moving wagon. Would you leave your sister and her family to suffer this calamity alone?"

"Ellen will live or she won't, Alice. We must consider the healthy ones above the ailing."

Alice knew he was right. Even before he spoke, her inclination to stand by the Halls was losing the battle with her instinct to spare her own family. She felt a sudden partnership with Henry in this horrible crisis. Her swallowed rebukes evaporated.

Alice wrapped her arms tightly around Henry's waist and pressed the side of her face against his chest, wanting the reassurance of his strength. He smelled of tobacco and stale sweat and sawdust, acrid, familiar smells.

He put his hands on top of her head and dug his fingers through her hair to her scalp, which was gritty with road dust.

He massaged her head and neck and shoulders. After a few minutes, he put his hands on her hips and separated her from him.

"There's hard things need doing this day, girlie. You must school in now."

They returned to camp without further conversation and set about the usual morning tasks of packing with the solemn vigor of fugitives.

A HERD OF GRAZING BUFFALO was slowly passing the Muller camp, not even glancing aside at the small group of wagons and the people rushing to and fro. There were thousands of the tremendous beasts. The Bowens's wagon was locked within the herd. Henry, finding Helen dead after his return from the river with Alice, had had the wagon pulled about a mile away from camp, where it sat unnaturally alone, as terse a sign as a grave marker, which, in essence, it was. Its dirty canvas top stood out whitely against the heaving brown drove. Occasionally the wagon would be jostled into eerie vibration, as if someone inside were shaking it, trying to get out.

The herd stretched ten miles on the other side of the Bowens's wagon. The men paused nervously in their work from time to time to check the herd, watching for any warning sign that the mass of huge animals might be about to make a thundering run to the river. The camp was right in their path.

Jerusha, too, sitting beside her sick daughter, glanced at the herd from time to time. Though it was not yet midmorning, it was already hotter than it had been at noon on other days. It seemed to Jerusha that the heat emanated from the Bowens's wagon, as if it were the bonfire Roy had wished to make it.

Ellen lay in the shade cast by her parents' wagon, though it was not any cooler there than in the sun, only less bright. Jerusha had tied a slat bonnet on the girl to screen her face from the floating dust churned up by the buffaloes' hooves. She knew that Ellen was probably past noticing such fine points of comfort, but fine points were all Jerusha had left to offer.

An hour before, she had stopped giving Ellen laudanum and peppermint water and had told Faith not to bother making any more mustard plasters. Ellen had begun vomiting, and Jerusha knew that that symptom meant all hope was gone. Now she could only watch and wait and try to ease her daughter's passing. She held Ellen in her lap and rocked her like a baby when the stomach cramps hit her. The girl was sleeping lightly when Roy and Flinder approached.

Roy squatted beside his failing daughter. She seemed to him already gone. He could barely recollect the bony feel of her on his lap or the way her skin and hair smelled after a bath, the citrus scents of lemon and bergamot, the vestiges of lavender. He did not touch her, but only stared at her, as if expecting her at any moment to open her eyes and tell him something. Or, better, to ask for something, something within his power to give her. For Ellen's plight left Roy feeling, above all else, helpless and useless, unmanned.

"Let Flinder watch awhile," Roy said at last to Jerusha. "Come refresh yourself."

Flinder held out a plate of beans, rice, and fried eggs. Alice had bought eggs that morning from an enterprising woman on a passing train who had several crates of live chickens tied to the sides of her wagon.

"No. I'll stay," Jerusha answered, brushing a fly off Ellen's clammy cheek.

"Come now, I say." Roy pulled gently but insistently on Jerusha's arm.

Jerusha stood up and listlessly accepted the plate of food. Flinder took her place, cooing a greeting to Ellen. Roy walked Jerusha just outside the circle of wagons on the side away from the buffalo and stopped. He watched her eat a few mouthfuls before he spoke.

"Bennett and Webster are digging the graves for Derrick and Helen," he said.

"I saw Mr. Bennett with a shovel." Jerusha was still eating, but with obvious disinterest.

"It's been suggested they dig a third one, too," he continued. "For the saving of time."

The fork halted halfway to Jerusha's mouth, and all signs of weariness and sorrow fled her features.

"Who has dared utter such inhuman thoughts? And you, you repeat them to the mother of a dying child, your child!"

Roy straightened up, as if squaring off for an arduous physical task.

"It's my duty to tell you that, as she is my child, I have consented to the idea."

"A father's right. A husband's duty." Jerusha's voice was a tight, angry whisper. "What of a Christian's duty to trust in the Lord?"

"Jerusha, you yourself called her a dying child. We must move on the moment we can to save others."

Jerusha looked away from her husband, fixing her gaze out over the dark, rippling sea of the buffalo herd. Roy could not see Jerusha's face, which in profile was hidden by her sunbonnet.

Roy thought absurdly of a pet box turtle he'd had as a boy. Despite years of being handled, it had never failed to pull into its shell whenever he put his face close to its head. Roy had never felt its breath.

Jerusha turned, and Roy caught a flash of pink skin and brown hair as she bent her head and stared down at her plate. He had to lean toward her to hear her.

"Can any words unbend you?" she said.

"No."

Jerusha looked at him then, her eyes filled with reproach, and handed him the plate of half-eaten food.

"I'm going back to Ellen now. When next you see me away from the wagon, it will be finished."

Roy watched her walk away from him. A good farmer knew when to let his draft animals have their heads and when to rein them in, and a wise husband knew when to let his woman take the last word. Besides, looking into Jerusha's face just now, Roy had recalled how perfectly her pointed chin was replicated in Ellen, and the tragic fact of the child's death suddenly visited him as a real and personal loss.

When Jerusha returned to Ellen, she saw that Flinder had taken off her sister's bonnet, washed her face, and neatly plaited her long dark red hair into one thick braid at the side of her head. Ellen was still, eyes closed; from time to time her breath came fast and she rubbed her hands over her belly, like a woman with birth pangs, but she had left off groaning. Flinder, sitting on the ground beside her sister's pallet, was crying in long, silent gulps.

"Come now, girl," Jerusha said softly to her older daughter. "Take yourself off somewhere and collect yourself. Our Ellen wouldn't want to think she was the cause of such grief."

"Oh, Ma!" Flinder stood up and reached for her mother. The girl's body felt strong and vital in the tired woman's arms. Jerusha did not want to let go, yet at the same time, Flinder's bloom served to underscore Ellen's frailness, and Jerusha, at first comforted by Flinder's embrace, next became woestricken by it.

"Go along now," Jerusha said, wiping the tears off Flinder's cheeks.

"I can stay with you. I'll be all right."

"No, no. I know misery is supposed to love company, but I think I'm better alone now. If you want to be of use, go console your brother. And help Faith with her loading. All this has ignited her grief for John."

Flinder nodded. "I love you," she said to Ellen, stooping to kiss her forehead. Then she strode off quickly, as if pursued.

Jerusha settled herself down beside Ellen to wait, and while she sat there, she thought about love. She wondered if Ellen had gotten enough. Love, which had eluded Jerusha in her parents' home and in her husband's bed, was something she had only truly begun to understand when she'd become a mother.

Jerusha's brothers and sisters had been burdens to her. Her mother had borne nine children in twelve years and had died by her own hand when John, the last one, was three days old. Jerusha buried the empty bottles of laudanum behind the smokehouse under the light of a full moon. She told no one, though she always believed Henry knew. She held her father accountable. A light sleeper, Jerusha had heard her mother plead with him time and again, after there were six little ones in the house, not to inflict her with any more babies. Jerusha was unforgiving against her mother as well, for her desperate act had snared her daughter, at eleven, into the very life she had found so intolerable.

Henry was the only person for whom Jerusha felt deep affection. Her one older sibling, he required from her only the getting of his meals and the laundering and mending of his clothes, and he took on unasked much of the care of the infant John. Henry was stiff with their father, a cold, self-contained man, and did not question Jerusha's unspecified grudge against him.

Jerusha had thought at first that Royal Hall was like Henry. Because Roy was laconic, she assumed him gentle. Because he was physically strong and decisive, she believed he could afford to be generous. When she learned later he was not all she had presumed, her disappointment was short-lived. He was, after all, what she expected, in general, a man to be, and marriage was the arrangement she had always thought it to be. It was better, she told herself, to bend the neck than bruise the forehead.

The children had helped Jerusha in her effort to make a long harvest of a little corn. There had been four so far. In a very real sense, Roy had been the father of Jerusha's love, and however much else she counted against him, she was always beholden to him for that.

How she had doted on Flinder as a baby! She was drunk with love for her. That the pleasure was so unexpected added to its richness. Each new child had been a new intoxication, though none as consuming as the first.

Roy hadn't been much comfort when the second baby died that one hard winter. Maybe he would have felt more if it had been a son. And now Ellen, dreamy-eyed Ellen, almost out of childhood, but destined to be stayed there forever.

The two favorites left, Flinder hers and Gideon Roy's. Hard as it was, she was secretly glad that Roy was acting to spare them. Roy always was a man to take charge. She was glad she didn't need to. He had released her to spend all her care this morning on Ellen.

"Ma," Ellen said hoarsely.

"Yes, Ellie, I'm right here."

"Am I going to die, Ma? Am I?"

"Do you feel it, child?"

"I do, Ma. It hurts so, and yet I don't care. I'm awful weary."

"You'll be going to a better place than this world, my dear." Jerusha truly believed this, but she found it was no solace. If she could have arm-wrestled God for the prize of keeping her daughter alive, she would have rushed to the contest without hesitation.

"I'm afraid. Hold my hand, I'm afraid."

Jerusha took Ellen's cool hand in her own callused one.

"Close your eyes, child."

"No, no. I don't want to be alone in the dark."

"Well, then, let's look at the clouds, and you can let your eyes drop shut just when you feel like. Remember how you and Flinder used to read the clouds on summer days at home?"

Ellen nodded weakly.

"There, see that big one to the left? It looks to me like a spinning top."

"Or a dromedary. And a prince upon its back," Ellen whispered.

"Flinder always said you were best at this game. What about that one there?" Jerusha pointed to a large, barmy formation directly above them.

"A grand lady in a ball gown. With furbelows."

While Jerusha was studying the cloud to pick out Ellen's lady in it, she felt the girl's fingers go slack in her hand. She looked down to find Ellen's eyes still open, but glazed and empty. Overhead the clouds pulled apart and re-formed into new shapes, unnamed and undreamed on.

June 28, 1852

Our niece Ellen died soon enough this morning that we were able to all pull out together. It would have torn my heart to leave the Halls behind, even though they themselves saw the need of it. We countenanced a small delay when Jerusha, beside herself with terror that Ellen's grave was not deep enough to keep it from being violated by wild animals, threw herself into the hole and began digging it out with her bare hands. Roy quickly removed her, and Mr. Webster, without being asked, set to with a spade and dug until she was satisfied.

It is a sore trial to see young people meet death. Such early ends hold no sense. We are cheated not only of who they were to us, but also of who they might have yet been. I wonder how many children Helen and Derrick might have had and what kind of home they would have built together. I wonder what sort of woman Ellen would have matured into; she was such a shy, fanciful child. Can the Eden of California ever be reckoned as worth costs like these?

We are all watchful of one another, trying to detect the first signs of physical weakness. I search my body carefully with my mind, not wishing the twinges of pregnancy to hide the beginnings of something more worrisome.

We did not burn the Bowens's wagon on account of the buffalo surrounding it, but we wrote a note on a rag and posted it on a stick to warn away passersby. How soon shall that rag be tattered by rain or blanched by sun? I cannot help but consider our frail selves as little better defended than that forlorn bit of cloth against the forces of nature and disease set here around us.

Chapter 8

FLINDER WAS walking fast a good distance in front of the little line of wagons. She wanted them out of her sight for a while. Her arms still ached from carrying river rocks yesterday to cover Ellen's grave to protect it from wolves. She willed the pain to last, the final hard proof that her sister had existed, a reality that Flinder was frightened to find already felt fictitious.

She heard the clump of hooves in back of her. Reed Bennett came up beside her leading the string of mules Derrick had picked so carefully.

"Mules step quicker than oxen," he said, explaining his intrusion on her.

Flinder's pace clearly expressed a desire to be alone, but Reed did not want to pass up this chance to speak to her privately. He had even declined a buffalo hunt with Jack for it.

"It's a shame about your little sister. I guess you'll miss her."

"Yes, I will."

Flinder answered automatically, in the same mechanical way that she was walking. Reed's presence was annoying, but easy to ignore. The environment, of which he was no more than an animate piece, was mere backdrop, false and muted in comparison to her sharp sorrow. His voice came to her as just another noise, like the droning mosquitoes or the rattling wagons.

"Me and Jack, we're cousins, but we're like to brothers. It'd be hard to lose him."

Flinder made no reply, and Reed wondered how he could move further into the topic of Jack. He had not planned exactly what he was going to say. He'd thought only that if he ever had the opportunity of getting Flinder's ear, he ought to plant some doubts in her about Jack's suitability as a beau. Jack would find his promise easier to keep if the young lady was discouraging to his attentions.

"Yeah, me and Jack has traveled a long way together. Death is about the onliest thing that would be likely to split us."

Still Flinder did not speak, nor even look at him. Her indifference affronted him. Now what had begun as a strategy to wean Flinder away from Jack festered into a wish to topple her from her haughty self-regard. Reed sensed that he was of no account to her, but he knew he had the power to wound her heart, and with the cunning of the runt of a litter, he determined to do so.

"Old Jack, now, he's quite a charmer, as I know you've noticed. Yes, a real champion with the ladies. And some might say that him and me would be broke up by a marrying preacher some one of these days, but I know better."

Flinder flashed a quick look at Reed. He was pleased to see interest in her eyes; he saw, too, the struggle in her to suppress any open show of that interest.

"See, with Jack, women are a game, like cards. He's a good poker player because he can hide how he feels about what he's got in his hand and get the other players to put more and more into the pot even against their good sense. And he can do the same with women."

"I don't see why, Mr. Bennett," Flinder said crisply, "you are telling all this to me. It seems, for one thing, disloyal to your cousin. And even if it were of some interest to me, you show great indelicacy to bring it to me now in my grief over my sister, who I held alive on my lap only yesterday morning."

"Just so, Miss Hall. I don't wish to see your grief added to by my cousin's frivolousness. I know he's honeying up to you, and I know he's brought you to thinking fondly of him."

"How can you know what I think on anything?" Flinder demanded angrily.

"Why, 'cause Jack himself told me, of course. Jack always tells me of his progress with a woman; it's part of his pleasure in it, maybe even his chief pleasure. Yes, I've heard many stories over the years, but you won't be wanting the details, I'm sure."

Reed watched Flinder closely. Had he gone too far? If he painted Jack too blackly, Reed knew Flinder might dismiss his talk as unbelievable. Exaggeration was a better tool for this job than outright lies. Jack was a flirt and a seducer, but he was not as calculating and heartless as Reed was implying. And certainly in the case of Flinder, Jack was not following his usual pattern. He was, in fact, in the midst of the one true courtship of his life. Reed hoped Flinder had not recognized this.

"He spoke to you about me?"

Reed was gratified by the outrage and pain in Flinder's voice.

"Don't feel too harsh about it, Miss Hall. It's just his way. You're a pretty woman, and a pretty woman to Jack Webster is like a red flag to a young bull. He's got to have a go at it."

Flinder stopped and took a deep breath. Reed saw tears fill her eyes, then recede. He had to admire her self-control. For an instant, he wanted to pull her to him and force her by his sympathy to let the tears come. It would be a fine thing, he thought, to have a proud beauty like Miss Flinder Hall heaving with sobs against him.

"I'm going to my mother now. She needs my company. Thank you, Mr. Bennett, for your advice. May I ask you not to repeat this conversation, especially not to your cousin?"

"You can depend on me, Miss Hall."

"And I wish you to never speak to me on the subject again, either."

Reed concurred by making what he considered a chivalrous bow. He had hit his mark, stirring Flinder's emotions as deeply as Jack had, and who was to say which was the more satisfying conquest? Indeed, Reed counted his success more delightful than the physical caresses of such a troublesomely outspoken female could ever be.

BAILEY BUCKED herself up and set out to intercept Jerusha, who was walking alone. Everyone except the team drivers were staying far off to the side of the lumbering wagons, which today were sending up intolerable clouds of dust as thick as fog.

Bailey had a drawing of Ellen she wanted to give to Jerusha. It showed the girl peering dreamily into the campfire, her head leaning against Flinder's shoulder. A subtle smile shaped her mouth; it was a moment of true contentment.

Bailey had never given anyone one of her drawings before. She had left boxes of them in storage with the school supervisor she'd last worked under, planning to send for them later. Many of them she threw away or painted over. Now here she was, about to offer a drawing to the person who had been the least welcoming to her on this journey.

The cholera deaths had alarmed Bailey, for some of the same reasons they had alarmed the others, and for some of her own. When she saw that the group had been prepared to abandon Helen to die alone, her own aloneness took on a whole new meaning. She had always looked out for herself, had taken pride in doing so, but now independence appeared not to be always an advantage.

Since her talk with Alice at the Lone Tree, Bailey had been easing more into the social circle of her traveling companions. She did not possess all the skills of the farmwives, and she had paid for her passage, so she did not expect to bear equal responsibility for the daily work, but she found herself wanting to contribute to the group welfare. Amazingly, she found herself desirous of being one of them. That was how she had hit upon the idea of reading aloud at night. But she had so far refrained from any direct expression of her growing feelings about these people.

Now she wanted to let Jerusha know that she was sorry about Ellen's death and that she cared about them all. Unable to summon adequate words, especially before so critical a listener, Bailey had decided to make a present to Jerusha of Ellen's portrait.

"Mrs. Hall?" Bailey said tentatively, aware she might be interrupting heavy thoughts.

"Miss Jeffers." Jerusha nodded, a look of surprise flitting across her face.

Bailey noticed how red Jerusha's eyes were. She suspected the redness was more from crying than from the dust that the wind occasionally threw their way. The evidence of such raw emotion embarrassed her a little. Her next impulse was to wish she could pull out her sketchpad and copy the strong lines of Jerusha's grieving face.

"I don't wish to intrude," Bailey said. "I wanted you to have this, if you'd like."

Bailey held out the drawing wrapped in a wrinkled piece of brown paper. Jerusha unwrapped it slowly, as if she were suspicious of what she would find. She stopped walking when the picture was exposed. She held it in both her hands, studying it as intensely as if it were a map in a foreign language and she were hopelessly lost.

Bailey wondered if she had been too hasty in giving Jerusha the drawing. Perhaps she should have waited for more time to pass. Perhaps, coming this soon after the child's death, the gift was more of a cruelty than a kindness. Inwardly she berated herself for her sometimes faulty sense of when to say what to whom.

Finally Jerusha carefully rewrapped the drawing in its brown paper and turned to Bailey.

"It's just my Ellen. Just like her," Jerusha said in a raspy whisper.

"I'm glad you think so," said Bailey, relieved.

"Thank you, Miss Jeffers."

"You're very welcome, Mrs. Hall."

ROY WAS NOT overly impressed by Bailey's gift. When Jerusha showed it to him, he agreed it was a good likeness, but he saw no cause to treat it as reverently as his wife was doing.

"Have you no feelings?" Jerusha demanded when Roy laid the drawing aside carelessly and she almost stepped on it. She was arranging buffalo robes as their mattress in the wagon.

Tonight Gideon was bedded down outside on the ground with Sarah, Hank, and Elizabeth, eagerly awaiting the meteor shower promised by Bailey's almanac. How readily, Jerusha had thought, children can turn from one thing to another, giving themselves wholeheartedly to each event. She, on the other hand, felt like a peddler bearing a loaded sack she must carry everywhere and never set down for more than a few moments at a stretch, so that every new step was weighted by what had been collected in steps in the past.

"Of course I have feelings," Roy countered testily, pulling off his boots. "But one must be master of one's feelings, and not the other way round."

"I shall never master my sadness over Ellen, only my showing of it."

"Ellen won't be brought back because you are sad."

"Even so, as I loved her, I am sad, and I am not ashamed of it. On the contrary, I should be ashamed not to be sad."

Roy let this go unremarked, though it seemed uncomfortably close to a scolding. Jerusha was, after all, in mourning and not guarding her tongue as she ought. Even in the best of times, she could be a woman of cutting words. They both lay down in their clothes and arranged blankets over themselves.

"You do know, Jerusha, that Ellen's passing grieved me, too."

"Yes, Royal. I misspoke myself. But you were so cold about Miss Jeffers's lovely drawing."

"It doesn't do, Jerusha, to dwell on sadness or on what's past changing. You must put such things out of your mind. That drawing will not help you do that."

"That drawing will help me in my grief over Ellen more than you and your hard advice ever will."

Jerusha turned her back to Roy. He knew it was no use continuing to speak to her. As long as it didn't interfere with Jerusha's duties as a wife and mother, he guessed it didn't really matter to him if she chose to torment herself. He couldn't understand why she insisted on holding on to bad feelings as if they were gold coins. To his way of thinking, you either did something to rid yourself of them right quick or you ignored them.

Jerusha, and all women for that matter, were a mystery to Roy, and not one he was particularly interested in solving. He'd have liked to be able to read her a little better, if only for his own convenience, but he accepted it as natural that he couldn't. Since his will always prevailed, usually without much output of energy on his part—he'd only had to strike Jerusha two or three times in all their years together—he called himself a satisfied husband. Her compliance was sufficient; he didn't look for sweetness in it.

Still, since leaving Indiana, Roy had often felt, in his wife's presence, like a worm on a hook. For the first time, Royal Hall found himself wanting admiration from Jerusha. He wanted her to see him as a man among men, a conqueror of the wild, open land.

Looking at the back of Jerusha's stout frame set so steadfastly against him, Roy thought how maybe what he really wanted was not her admiration, but her dismissal of him. Better no wife than one whose mind follows its own tracks in spite of her dutiful actions.

Roy thought about the ride he'd taken that day near sunset in hopes of shedding the melancholy occasioned by Ellen's death. All the previous day, badlands rising up in the south along the river had captivated the attention of the Muller party. The chain of high sandstone buttes and sculpted hills was a delightful spectacle after a month on the monotonous prairie, even to the eyes of the newly bereaved group. Then today, the imposing formations of Scott's Bluffs had loomed up majestically.

Roy had felt his spirits lift as soon as he was out of earshot of the wagons and riding southwest toward Scott's Bluffs, to which the chain of lesser mounds proceeded like country hamlets leading to a grand city. The main bluff rose massively above the river badlands like some huge, ruined palace, the shadows of its many folds intensely blue in the waning light, the rock faces on which the setting sun shone glowing golden. Black and white magpies flew overhead, squawking loudly; their tails, longer than their bodies, streamed out behind them like the trains of bombazine gowns. Somewhere in the pine woodlands on the bluffs, a great horned owl hooted seven times.

Roy had never beheld a landscape so beautiful. If his daughter had to be left somewhere, better within a day's journey of such splendor than on the bland, bleached prairie. He would tell Jerusha, he'd thought, that having died near here, Ellen was certain of being close to heaven.

But he hadn't told Jerusha. She'd been too full of the drawing from Miss Jeffers and too cross with him. As he mulled over the sights of his ride and the exultation they had bred in him, he decided he would never tell her. It had been as grand a feeling as it had, he thought, because he had experienced it alone, as a man should do all the important things in life. He turned on his side, his back to his wife's back, careful not to lean against her. Sleep came quickly. He dreamed about his horse.

June 29, 1852

We are camped in sight of Laramie Peak, far to the west, a mountain standing beyond Fort Laramie, where we expect to arrive in a few days' time. The high, darksome Peak warns of more difficult travel ahead, where our way will continue up-

ward, but not on so wide and gentle a slope as we have known along the Platte.

We passed to the north of Scott's Bluffs, a monumental range of beetling sandstone hills formed like citadels, mausoleums, and American Gibraltars spiced with stunted trees— Rocky Mountain juniper and ponderosa pines, Bailey says.

Though Jerusha thought it disrespectful to our recent dead, Mr. Webster went hunting and brought down a buffalo cow. He ran her a good ways from us, and as he was alone, he could carry back only the hump and the tongue, but we got some juicy steaks from it, and Faith and I jerked the rest. Our wagons look like they're wearing fringes front to back with all the strips of meat hanging down over strings to dry. We boiled the buffalo grease for our wheel bearings, as we've spent our store-bought grease.

The work was somewhat awkward for Faith, whose belly is so big now, with the baby only a month or a little more away, but she seemed to relish it. Perhaps, as it did for me, the chore eased the hollowness over Ellen and the Bowens. Life turns on small things.

Like in the case of Hiram Scott, the fur trader for whom Scott's Bluffs are named. He died of starvation nearby in 1828. His tragedy began with one accident. Scott, ill, was traveling with two comrades when their bullboat capsized and they lost all their weapons and supplies. The two healthy men, promising to return, left Scott behind in order to overtake a company of trappers three days' journey ahead of them. But when they met the trappers, they said nothing of Scott. No one went to his rescue. The next summer, the group passed by the bluffs again and found Scott's bones; the desperate man had dragged himself sixty miles before finally expiring.

Had the bullboat remained steady, would the men have kept with Scott and brought him through? Did Scott trust their words and only slowly, through the long days alone, realize his abandonment, or did he suspect from the first their selfish intent? Then, too, there is a version of the story that says Scott, knowing he was dying, urged his companions to leave him and save themselves. *Betrayal or nobility: No one knows which was the true author of Scott's fate. Certainly this land seems able to draw out either from men.*

Each event of our journey, whether ill or glad, drops into me like pearls of wheat onto a threshing floor. As they accumulate, I find myself more and more separated from the ground of the old life and myself in it. Yet I have come to believe this is as it must and should be.

I remember twin cats in Philadelphia who were kept always indoors to save them from the crowds and traffic on the streets. One day when my mother was sweeping, they escaped out the open door and were missing for two days. My brother found one on the next block; it had been run down by a diligence. The other came home muddy-pawed and hungry, but safe.

That cat was never content indoors again. She cried at the windows and darted forward at the sound of the key in the latch and managed to get out and return unharmed so many times, I finally allowed her to come and go as she pleased. She lived to die of old age.

I must be like my wily cat. I have entered a wider and different world whether I like it or not, and I must find in myself the means to thrive in it.

Chapter 9

THE DAYS continued bright and hot under vast blue skies studded with massive, brilliantly white clouds. Most afternoons, along some part of the horizon, the sky darkened for a couple of hours, and long, forked bolts of lightning leapt to earth. The nights were cool, for the trail, though seemingly on flat prairie, had in fact been imperceptibly rising. The heat had browned much of the blue grama and buffalo grass, but the stock ate it anyway, accepting dumbly what the people had to philosophize to learn—that on this journey you used what was given, turned your shoulder to what was needed, and kept on.

Faith's nightmares had stopped, though the heaviness of her pregnancy, now in its eighth month, kept her restless at night. She could find no truly comfortable position and slept in spurts. Between the periods of sleep, she lay awake for twenty or thirty minutes at a time, awkwardly turning from side to side, often staring scratchy-eyed up at the wagon bows.

One night Faith found sleep especially elusive and the wagon especially confining, so she wrapped a quilt around her shoulders and climbed outside to stretch. It was the time of the new moon, and the prairie breathed darkness. She waited for her eyes to adjust, then began to pace slowly. She couldn't pick out anything that was more than a few yards away.

The burials of Ellen Hall and the Bowens had occurred only two days prior, and since then Faith had found her mind repeatedly turning to John and the look of the place where they had laid him. Now, stretching her cramped legs, she recalled different small events of their life together. The way he loved gingerbread and doughnuts made with rose water. The argument they'd had over naming Elizabeth (he'd wanted Ardeth or Bella). The long trek they made through snowy woods to find the perfect fir tree for their first Christmas.

Having rounded the space inside the circle of wagons, Faith stopped at her own and leaned against it, still reminiscing. There was a crunch of footsteps just behind her. She stiffened but did not turn; the scene felt alarmingly familiar.

The quilt was pulled off her shoulders; two hands grasped her at the elbows and began a firm, slow slide up her arms. Thick fingers encircled her throat, briefly stroked it, then slid back down to her elbows. The man stepped in closer, pressing his body against her.

Faith's heart was pounding with fear. She grabbed the hands before they could begin to move again. Horrified, she found, as she had expected she would, that they did not have the texture of normal skin. She felt utterly defeated. The tenant of her dream, the faceless leather-man, had stepped into her real life.

She released the hands and stoically submitted to their explorations, up and down her arms, across her breasts, over her swollen belly and down under it. The thin cotton of her nightdress was a meaningless barrier between the awful hands and her trembling body. Then the man grasped her upper arms tightly and thrust his pelvis rhythmically against her buttocks, panting loudly in her left ear. Near the end, he crooked one arm around her neck to turn her and hold her close, and she beheld the pleasure-twisted face of Reed Bennett. He used his other hand briskly on himself, roughly pulling her hand against him in time to feel the pulsing explosion of his wetness.

Throughout, Faith had managed only a few whimpers. Unlike in the dream, no strangled scream had finally burst forth to release her. She was not freed from her agony until Reed let go of her and left. She was struck at how jauntily he walked, like a man who had no fear of retribution. His awful confidence was as frightening as what he'd done to her. He was obviously relying on her silence. And silent she knew she would be, not to suit him, but because she was a woman without a husband to defend her, because she had not cried out at the start, and because she had dreamed this, had maybe somehow called it to her.

Only when Reed had thoroughly disappeared into the darkness at the other end of the small camp did Faith begin to cry. Squatting, she retrieved the quilt from the ground and stuffed a corner of it in her mouth to muffle her sobs. In an attempt to erase Reed's defilement, she rubbed her hand in the dirt until it was raw and bloody. The burning pain calmed her, but she still found herself unable to reenter the wagon. The idea of lying down beside her child seemed horrible to her, as if she had been changed in some way that made her unfit for the company of innocence.

It was the leaking of an orange and lavender dawn across the eastern sky that finally sent Faith into the wagon. She did not want to be found sitting sprawled in the dirt by anyone, not even by the rising sun. Before the onslaught of the coming day, Faith sought the sheltering shadows of the wagon, like a wounded dog retreating beneath a porch to lick itself well.

DIRECTLY AFTER BREAKFAST, Henry and Reed went to retrieve the stock. They had had to drive them several miles last night before they found good grazing; a recent prairie fire had burned off all the grass near the road. Roy had spent the night guarding them. The day's traveling would have a late start.

It was just as well. The women's chores were taking longer this morning, left, as they were, to Bailey, Alice, and Sarah. Allowances for inactivity were still being made for Jerusha and Flinder, and Faith was inexplicably lackadaisical today. She'd been the last to arise, had sat staring out over the prairie while the coffee beside her bubbled over and burned, and later had stood listlessly wiping one plate while Sarah cleaned and packed away all the others. At last, complaining of a sick headache, Faith had climbed into her wagon to lie down again.

Though the group was too small for Flinder to completely avoid Jack, she had managed in the two days since Reed's poisonous words to dodge all situations in which they might be alone together. She remained largely quiet when he joined her family during meals, as had become his habit, and was stiffly polite when she did speak.

The others, noticing Flinder's odd manner, put it down to grief over Ellen. Reed, making a more accurate assignment of the source of her reserve, observed the subdued young woman with the complacence of a cat who has rounded a mouse into an inescapable corner. His satisfaction was enriched by knowing that Jack was bewildered by Flinder's behavior. There was time enough before the fort, Reed figured, for bewilderment to turn to frustration and then to anger and retreat.

But Flinder was not as single-minded as she appeared. She did not, in fact, know what to do, and she had no one to whom to turn for advice. Early on, she had confided her attraction to the dashing Mr. Webster to Sarah, but that had been in the spirit of excited, girlish fancies. She felt far beyond such lighthearted games now. Her attachment to Jack had deepened into something wonderfully and unnervingly new, and part of the delight was that Jack, too, seemed a wide-eyed explorer in this fresh landscape of the heart. The threat introduced by Reed exposed Flinder to another set of new feelings, ones she felt she must navigate on her own.

She could not ignore what Reed had said. She had no evidence to discredit him. On the contrary, Reed must know his cousin's habits and history better than anyone, and despite her accusation that he was being disloyal by speaking to her about Jack, Flinder knew he was devoted to him. Jack had told her about the fire.

Still, Flinder's affections stubbornly rallied to Jack. Where she expected to find in herself repulsion and fury, she discovered only a wounded confusion and a wild hope that somehow everything would be righted. This last she pushed down whenever she noticed it surfacing, like a grim housewife drowning a sack of surplus kittens.

"Flin," Gideon said, flouncing onto his daydreaming sister's lap. "Take me to see the dog town. Mother says I mustn't go alone in case of the rattlesnakes."

Flinder shifted her legs to accommodate Gideon's weight and laid her arm loosely around his waist, but she did not answer him. The boy was used to distracted adults. Jerusha had taught him children were to be seen, not heard. But, really, they all seemed to be unusually impenetrable today, and that was so inconvenient when they were camped in the suburbs of the biggest dog town they'd passed so far, covering acres and acres.

Gideon tugged on Flinder's earlobe to get her attention.

"Will you take me?" he repeated.

Flinder looked into the earnest face of her little brother. She had to smile at his supplicant expression. She decided she could feel gloomy over Jack just as well while visiting the dog town as sitting in camp. She set Gideon on his feet and stood up.

"Now, you mustn't run and shout or we'll not see any prairie dogs, you know," she said. "And you might trip in one of their holes."

Gideon nodded solemnly. Flinder instantly regretted her strict words, which sounded like her mother's. Gideon was an overly serious child as it was, liking Bible stories over penny dreadfuls. Flinder usually thought it her task to jolly him up. Suddenly she felt terribly annoyed by the burden of her muddy thoughts.

"Maybe we'll see some burrowing owls, too, Gideon," she said encouragingly. "We must watch for the porches they make outside the prairie dog burrows. Can you imagine, a porch of cow dung? And they line the burrows with it, too, and share the abode not only with the dogs, but with snakes as well. What unparticular creatures!"

Gideon laughed at his sister's exaggerated display of disgust, and Flinder, laughing with him, felt uncomplicatedly happy. Life was too marvelous and too various, she thought, to dwell for long on its stern demands. Flinder had never been one to hesitate to pluck a rose for fear of its thorns.

Flinder took Gideon's hand and walked over to where Jerusha and Alice were sitting, even though nearby them Jack was driving wedges under a tire. Alice was in her rocker, which she laboriously untied from the back of the wagon in every camp; she was mending a pair of pants. Jerusha sat on a low stool beside her. Flinder saw she was cutting apart one of Ellen's dresses, probably to fashion a shirt for Gideon, who had made an unexpected growth spurt since leaving Indiana. Sarah sat cross-legged in the dirt, practicing penmanship in her journal. Elizabeth was napping with her head on Sarah's lap.

"We're going to the dog town," Flinder announced.

"Don't be long," Alice warned. "We'll be striking camp soon."

Jerusha looked worriedly at her children. Though they would not be out of her sight, the idea of them leaving the camp clenched at her stomach.

"Mr. Webster," she called. "Will you accompany Flinder and Gideon? Indians, you know."

"Oh, Ma," said Flinder. "There's no need of that. I declare, the worst we've suffered from Indians is the scares from all the horrible stories about them."

"They're lazy, unclothed beggars. We've seen that," Jerusha protested, referring to some Pawnees who had followed them for two days near the Loup River and had asked repeatedly for sugar and coffee. Bailey had told Jerusha that Indians held it a mark of friendship and politeness that strangers traveling through their lands should proffer small gifts, but Jerusha countered Bailey's explanation by insisting that begging was a

119

depraved activity and only a small step away from thievery.

"I'm glad to go along," Jack said, putting down his mallet. "I'd be interested to see the prairie dogs, too."

"You may find your interest is not rewarded," Flinder said.

"I shall risk it."

"Well," Flinder said loudly, "who else wants to go? Sarah? Hank?"

"Good idea," Jerusha approved. "There's strength in numbers."

Hank, who had been playing marbles a few yards away, jumped up. Rouser and Old Smith got up, too, sniffing hopefully at Hank's side, but he sternly ordered them away and they slumped dejectedly to the ground again.

Sarah looked thoughtfully at Flinder's cross face and at Jack's anxious one. "I'm staying," she said.

Flinder turned abruptly and strode quickly out of camp. She held tightly to Gideon's hand, though she knew he longed to be off with Hank, who had run ahead. Jack stayed beside her no matter how she varied her pace, so she finally fell into a more natural rhythm of walking.

"Flinder," he said, "I've missed your company these last days."

"We are always in each other's company."

"I mean your particular company. Oh, you know what I mean."

"Do I? I wonder if one can ever truly know what another person means."

They walked on, both staring in front of them. Flinder was electrically aware of the physical space between them, which seemed to have assumed as much substance as a living being.

"Gideon," Jack said, forcing his voice to be offhand, "how old are you?"

"Five. Nearly six."

"I sure would like to see how fast a nearly-six-year-old boy can run." Jack pulled out a pocket watch. "Shall I time you running up to where Hank is? You don't really need to hold your sister's hand, do you?"

"No, sir," said Gideon manfully. He jerked his hand out of Flinder's. She frowned, but she did not attempt to catch at him.

Jack lifted the watch dramatically in the air, and Gideon crouched down as he had seen the men do in relay races at the county fair back home.

Both man and boy looked at Flinder for permission to continue.

"Give him his chance," Jack said quietly.

Flinder looked at each of them in turn, sighed, and nodded yes. Jack swung his arm down with a flourish; Gideon, after a minor stumble, sped away, his arms and legs pumping up and down wildly. Jack laughed heartily at the sight.

"Thank you," he said to Flinder when they had resumed walking.

"You are used to getting your way, I suppose," Flinder answered.

"No, ma'am. Not always."

"But enough of the time."

"Enough, yes. Up to now."

Jack stooped to pick up a clod of dried mud. He flung it out across the prairie and watched its path as if it were of absorbing interest. Flinder took the opportunity to sneak a quick peek at him. His black hair gleamed in the sun. His beard stubble and a rip in the elbow of his butternut shirt made him look uncared for and vulnerable, while the tight muscles evident under his close-fitting clothing and the confident grace of his movements implied he would provide caring as well as take it.

"And now?" Flinder dared to prompt.

"Now," Jack said, turning a serious face to her, "there's you, and what used to pass for enough is not enough anymore."

"So what you want now is more than enough?" Flinder found she could not restrain herself from teasing him.

"What I want, Flinder Hall, is your true affection. And for you to accept mine in return."

A slow, mischievous smile unfurled across Jack's features.

"Because I figure more than enough is exactly what you are," he said.

Flinder felt filled to bursting with every emotion she had ever known. If she had found herself, in the next moment, to be crying or laughing, neither would have surprised her. She could never have brought herself to ask Jack directly about Reed's allegations, and so she had believed they would creep between her and Jack like a fast-growing vine, choking out any tendrils they sent to each other and finally filling the space with an impassable tangle. But here was Jack, cutting through the weeds with a declaration as simple and honest as a scythe. Flinder, ever an optimist, endowed him again with her complete trust, and Jack, who had not even known how perilous his position was, greeted the animation in her face with the grin of a pampered child on his birthday.

"Mr. Webster!" Gideon's voice came from a distance. He was standing next to Hank and waving his arms.

"Time for us to run," Jack said.

Flinder lifted the edge of her skirt with one hand to make running easier. Impulsively Jack grabbed her other hand and squeezed it fondly. When he started to release it, Flinder held on, and they ran like that, hand in hand, towards the excited boys, who turned and dashed hollering ahead, like gypsy dogs before a galloping fire wagon.

"LOOK THERE," Alice said, coming up beside Henry.

She pointed to a crude cross of hickory marking a solitary grave. Though the north side of the Platte had fewer cholera deaths, it equaled the south in accidents, so graves were a common sight, marked by scrap-wood headboards or sometimes by elk horns or iron wheel rims. Roy had a datebook in which he recorded their daily mileage; next to his notation, Jerusha entered the number of graves observed each day.

Alice usually did not call Henry's attention to the graves they passed, but this one was unusual. The most common headboard inscription was a name and date; sometimes cause of death and place of origin were also noted. On this marker had been carved simply the word WOMAN. The vertical part of the cross had been cut very long, so that the crosspiece and its epithet were poised high above the dry prairie. The disproportion of the two pieces of wood gave the impression of an arm thrusting out of the land to bear up a talisman.

Adding to the eerie singularity of the grave was a skinny mongrel sitting atop the upturned earth. He was watching the Muller wagons lumber by with the mournful eyes unique to his species, periodically lifting his head to howl piteously.

"I suppose," said Henry, prodding the lead oxen with a long driving stick, "that those who buried her didn't know her name."

"It's strange to think that her dog may be the only living being who remembers who she was," Alice said.

Hank ran up to his mother, his cousin Gideon close on his heels.

"Ma, can we take the dog these moldy biscuits? Sarah said you meant to cut them down for bread pudding. The dog can have my portion," said Hank, holding out two crumbling biscuits.

"Mine, too," joined in Gideon, pulling another biscuit from his pocket.

"He looks near starved," Hank added.

The Mullers had left Hank's collie with neighbors in Indiana because she was too old to make the journey. Alice suspected this accentuated the boy's sympathy for the dog on the grave. Still, their food supply was not so bounteous that biscuits could be squandered on a stray dog.

"He must go hunting if he's hungry," Alice said. "Or decide to follow a new master from some passing train."

"But he won't leave the grave," Hank said. "We already tried to coax him."

"Bread pudding is your father's favorite dessert."

"I believe I can forgo it this once," said Henry. "Such faithfulness as that dog shows should be rewarded."

"All right," said Alice to the boys. "Ask Sarah to give you the rest of the biscuits. But nothing more."

After the boys had run off to their small adventure, Alice walked beside Henry in silence. She'd been surprised by his response to Hank's notion. Henry was a good-hearted, generous man, but he was not sentimental, especially about animals. A lifelong farmer, he respected his animals and took good care of them, but it was because they were his partners in work, not because he held them in any special tenderness. She wondered if it was the grave, and not the dog, that had inspired his empathy. They had four graves of their own at their backs, and as informal leader of their little band, Henry might be feeling some responsibility for them.

"Do you regret we left no headboards for John and the others?" she said tentatively. "I know we buried them unmarked to keep their remains safe, but it did seem forgetful of us to leave them in foreign places without even their names to claim the spots."

"Why bother to mark a grave that will lie miserably untended and that no one who knew the person shall ever visit?"

Alice was taken aback by the uncharacteristic dejection in her husband's voice.

"Henry, their deaths were no fault of yours. You could not have protected them any better than you did."

"Yes, girlie, I know, and that is what plagues me so."

Alice was baffled at how to respond. Despite her own domestic competencies and the touted moral superiority of women, Alice had always accepted the idea that she needed protection in the larger world and that Henry was it. Henry, too, operated on the assumption that he could and would unfailingly guide the family through every physical and economic challenge. Even in the face of obstacles beyond his sphere, like a late spring freeze or a price slump, Henry never lost his basic belief in his own capabilities and position. He always looked ahead, past troubles, with confidence.

Now he appeared to be recognizing his limits and the consequences of them. To see her protector doubt himself was disconcerting to Alice, but at the same time, she felt a small swell within her, as when a stream that has been pent up into a pond is sluiced into a millrace and flows with gurgling energy to power the mill wheel and turn the heavy grindstone. Alice stepped closer to Henry and wrapped her arms around his free arm. The feel of his hard muscles through the blue drilling of his shirtsleeve was a simple, reliable enjoyment to her.

Henry looked at Alice and was buoyed by the open pleasure in her face. He ducked down over her mouth and delivered an amorous kiss, pulling away with a broad grin at his own brassy immodesty.

July 1, 1852

Today we ferried successfully across the Platte and are camped, with many others, one and a half miles from Fort Laramie. It was our first ferrying since the Elkhorn, as we were able to ford the Loup River in spite of its quicksand, and all were relieved when it was done. The south siders must use a jerry-built toll bridge (for a high fee) or ferry over the Laramie River to the fort; it is questionable which river is the wilder, both being swollen with melted snows from the Black Hills and the Rocky Mountains.

Some on the Council Bluffs road, mostly the Mormons, do not cross to the fort, but we need to use the blacksmith and the post office. Supplies and fresh stock can be got here, too, and perhaps as important as practical matters, it will be a breath of civilization after our long, monotonous weeks on the prairie. We will stay two days, though grass is scarce, and the stock may need to be driven ahead and then brought back.

There are considerable numbers of Sioux and some Arapaho and Cheyenne camped nearby along the Laramie River. We passed an Indian village on the move yesterday, the men astride ponies, the women walking with papooses strapped to cradleboards on their backs. All their belongings were tied to travois

125

pulled by dogs or horses. I do not know which group, emigrants or Indians, is more curious about the pageant presented by the other.

Everyone in our party is affected by the excitement of the fort. The children are incited by the presence of all the Indians and soldiers. The men anticipate buying, selling, trading. We women look for brighter foodstuffs and some tale swapping with other emigrants.

I am surprised, therefore, to find that tempers are short. Our timid Faith barks at every small inconvenience, the bustle and noise around us appearing to discomfit and even alarm her. Then again, at other times, she slips so deeply into her own thoughts that she does not seem to notice the commotion, even ignoring Elizabeth calling at her knee. Mr. Webster has got quiet and is curt with Mr. Bennett, who, for his part, despite a cheerful demeanor, is crisp and edgy in his speech. His cheerfulness has a forced ring, as if he suspects it will not last. Roy snaps at the children and at Jerusha for no good reason. He and Henry are sobered, I know, to consider that though we have now accomplished a full one third of our journey, it was the easiest leg. The trail gets harder from here on, and we face it with our freshness spent.

On the prairie, feelings had to be guarded. With the elements against us, we dared not be against one another, even in minor ways, and we had to pocket fears and frustrations as best we could. Now, amidst the closest thing to a town we have seen and will see in two thousand miles, we let our worries and our hopes run free, and both fray us. What a strange effect for civilization to have!

Chapter 10

ORT LARAMIE sat on a peninsula between the North Platte and Laramie Rivers. Black, snowcapped Laramie Peak loomed in the western distance. Forty-five miles away, the Peak was the only local source of wood, so most of the fort buildings were made of adobe. There weren't many buildings yet, as the army had just taken over the fort in 1849 from the American Fur Company. The twelve-foot-high adobe walls of old Fort John were still standing, but they were propped up with timbers; the dilapidated structure was in use as a storehouse and a hospital. The enlisted men were living in tents and cooking and eating outdoors.

The officers had fine quarters, however. Old Bedlam, a long, two-story frame building, faced the broad parade ground. Spacious porches fronted both lower and upper floors. The shutters on the wide windows were folded open, and the wood exterior had been painted a gleaming white. All in all, Old Bedlam gave the impression of a "real" house, something the emigrants hadn't seen in six hundred miles.

Though not a man much interested in houses, Reed had chosen Old Bedlam as the place to meet Jack and give him the news. He sat on the steps and watched the criss-crossing flows of emigrants, infantrymen, and Indians. Every person appeared set on a course. Reed grinned. He, too, felt full of purpose. The optimism with which he had set out months ago and which had been muffled and eroded by the company of the Mullers and their friends was reborn in him.

Reed pulled out the gold pocketwatch Jack had given him on his eighteenth birthday. It was his proudest possession. Engraved on the back in curly script was the phrase *auld lang syne.*

Reed didn't know that the watch had been given to Jack by a married lady with a husband three times her age. The ambiguous inscription referred to a set of experiences quite different from the boyhood comradeship it always reminded Reed of.

The watch marked Jack as thirty minutes overdue, but Reed did not yet feel impatient. Jack was often late, and this morning he had gone to try to get them a couple of Indian ponies. A transaction like that could take some time.

Reed reclined against the edges of the steps, propping his elbows on the top one. His upper body rested in the shade of the porch, and his legs stretched out into the sun. His mind turned again, as it kept doing in idle moments, to Faith. Though Reed had sometimes treated women roughly, he had never taken one against her will before. In fact, he had never taken a woman without paying her for it, if not in hard cash, then at least in hard liquor.

Reed knew he ought to feel some guilt for what he'd done to Faith, but he couldn't find any in him. He was aware that he could be harshly punished by the Muller men for his transgression—they'd passed a grave marker several weeks back with the grim inscription: "William Wilkerson, 19, killed by a man for making too free with his daughter." But as each hour passed with no accusing word from Faith, he relaxed more and more.

He'd even begun to think that the fierce embrace under the moonless sky the night before last had been his just deserts. Hadn't he helped the widow with her animals and her wagon? Hadn't the Muller party interfered with his and Jack's progress to the gold fields? Didn't women—free women—always turn away from him like they were too delicate to make his acquaintance? Women were meant for men's pleasure and service, anyway, and deep down they must know it as well as he did. Whores knew it. Faith knew it. That's why she hadn't fought; that's why she hadn't told. She knew her place, and what's more, she probably even liked it. Even so, the sooner he was away from her and all the rest of them, the better.

"Reed!" Jack was waving from a short distance away. Reed descended the steps to meet him.

"Any luck?" Reed said.

"I got us two fine ponies. Had to give a bit more than I had reckoned on, but if I'm any judge of horses, they'll be worth it. You can come with me later to fetch them."

"Sure, sure," Reed said briskly; he was eager to tell his story. "I've been making a deal of my own this morning."

"Oh?" Jack, distracted by his growling stomach, showed only mild interest. "Let's head back to camp for some victuals, and you can tell me about it."

Reed stepped in front of Jack to block his way. "I don't want to talk about it in camp."

"You know I listen better with a meal in me," Jack said.

When Reed did not move, Jack sighed and sat down on the barracks' steps. Reed remained standing. He put one foot up on the bottom step, and resting his forearms on his raised knee, he leaned over Jack.

"Remember our talk a while back about leaving the Mullers? And you asked me to give it till we reached Fort Laramie?"

Jack nodded apprehensively. Reed could tell Jack knew what was coming next.

"Well, I'm here to tell you those folks still don't set right with me. What's more, I've found us a place with some prospectors leaving first thing tomorrow."

Jack stared hard into Reed's pleased expression. Reed saw several emotions rapidly follow one another across the handsome face. Reed wasn't sure what kind of reaction he had expected from Jack. Perhaps, somewhere deep inside, he had hoped for a whoop of elation and a backslap of congratulations. Instead, there was this silent parade of disbelief, anger, and confusion.

"You've given this honest consideration?" Jack sounded suspicious.

Reed nodded, arranging his face into what felt like sincerity. He thought he spied resignation settling over Jack's features.

Jack looked away from Reed in the direction of the emigrant camps. He rubbed his palms on his thighs and stood up.

"I still want those victuals," he said.

"We're agreed?" Reed asked anxiously. A resigned yes was still a yes, but Reed wanted to hear Jack say it.

When Jack turned to face him, Reed was startled by the fury in his eyes. He saw the muscles over Jack's jaws tighten and twitch.

"We shook on it, didn't we?" Jack spit out. Reed saw this was all he'd get right now, and he knew better than to push.

Anyway, Jack had walked off before Reed could say anything more. Reed headed for the sutler's store to buy some whiskey. Deeming it prudent to stay clear of the Muller camp for a few hours at least, he thought he might pay a visit down the road to the girls at the "hog ranch" that a soldier had told him about. After tomorrow, there'd be no more women for quite a while.

JACK DIDN'T KNOW if he was pleased or sorry when he found the two things he sought together. Flinder was rolling out piecrust on a smooth board on her lap and giving an occasional stir to the stew bubbling on the cook fire beside her. No one else was about.

Jack stopped some distance from her before she was aware of him. He enjoyed observing her efficient movements and the relaxed, absorbed look on her face. The sunlight picked out copper highlights in her hair. A smudge of flour on one cheek called attention to its downiness. She seemed, at that moment, perfect to him, her beauty as nourishing and matter-of-fact as the food she tended. He would remember her like this, he knew.

When he noticed the subtle shift of her breasts beneath the pale green cotton of her blouse as she leaned over the stewpot, he felt an uncharacteristic embarrassment. He was not unused to ignoring propriety if it suited him, but he had a strong sense of fairness, even in matters of seduction, and he felt that his admiration of Flinder, now and like this, was not fair to her.

He coughed and began walking forward again. Flinder, who had just lifted the crust over the pie tin, looked up. They nodded to each other, and she turned her attention to fitting the crust into the tin. Jack squatted beside the fire so that, even though Flinder was seated on a stool, her head was above his. He had an urge to knock her work away and lie across her lap, to beg for kisses and loving touches he had just relinquished the right to request.

"Stew ready?" he asked instead.

"Meant to be saved for supper," she said, her eyes still trained on her fingers as they pinched the dough around the rim of the pie tin.

"Maybe I'd best move off a ways, then. It's awful hard on a hungry man to smell such a meal and have to wait on tasting any."

Flinder stood up and put the pie tin down on the stool.

"If you want some, why don't you just come out straight and ask for it?" she said in mock exasperation.

Without giving him time to reply, she walked to the side of her parents' wagon, opened the grub box, and extracted a tin plate, a spoon, and three biscuits left from breakfast. Returning to the fire, she handed Jack the plate and ladled a generous helping of stew over the biscuits.

She sat down again. While he ate, Jack watched her spoon a syrupy mixture of apples and raisins into the pie shell, then set the filled pie carefully on the ground, take the board on her lap once more, and begin to roll out the top crust. It seemed to Jack, knowing they were soon to part, that he would never tire of watching her. All her ordinary actions, in the context of the looming separation, appeared to him poignant and nearly miraculous. He had to get on with telling her before the spell of the scene stole all his sense.

"I know you make a fine pie, Miss Flinder," he said at last, "but a body does tire of apples."

"Yes, I know. But Pa got some long sweet at the fort, so this pie'll have a newer flavor."

"Molasses is tasty, but for real pleasure to the tongue, none can match French chocolate."

"Chocolate?" Flinder laughed. "And where would that be found out here?"

Jack put down his plate and reached into his vest pocket. He pulled out a small, chunky object wrapped in purple paper. Unfolding the paper, he extended to Flinder a thick piece of milk chocolate that was melting around the edges. Though he was clearly offering it to her, she made no move to take it.

"I got it special for you," he urged in a soft voice.

Flinder put out her hand, and he placed the paper and the chocolate on it. She lifted it near her nose and inhaled its rich aroma.

"Thank you." She smiled.

Jack winced under her smile the way he would have winced under another woman's tears.

"I'm only sorry to have to tell you it's by way of a good-bye token," he said quickly. "I wanted you to know—even before your uncle or your father—that me and Reed are splitting off on our own."

Flinder's smile disappeared. Jack felt like a murderer.

"There's no call for you to single me out, sir, for good-byes or gifts," she said tartly.

"For my part there is," he said, adding in a cajoling tone, "and I thought for your part, too."

"You truly are the presumptuous man!"

Flinder's voice was quavering, and since she was looking down at her lap, Jack was not sure if her emotion was anger or sadness. Carefully he brushed the curve of her right shoulder with his fingertips.

"Flinder," he said, "it won't be for good. I swear I'll come find you in California and be a proper suitor, as you deserve."

Flinder stood up so suddenly, the rolling pin and the board with the flat circle of dough stuck to it tumbled from her lap, glanced off Jack's boots, and landed in the dirt.

"And do you think you might ever know what I deserve?" she shouted.

Flinder hurled the chocolate and its wrapper into the fire, where it blazed up with a burnt, sweet smell. She turned her back on Jack and the unfinished pie and ran out of the cluster of wagons. He watched her jostle through some passersby and angle around a line of tethered mules. Just before he lost sight of her, he saw her bend her head and lift both hands to her face.

MEANWHILE, across the Laramie, Bailey was trying hard not to make the baby in her drawing look like a piglet, though it was undeniably the homeliest infant she had ever seen. Bailey did not like to prettify her work, but Colleen O'Sullivan, the proud mother, was watching over Bailey's shoulder, and the drawing, after all, was meant to be a gift to her for having let Bailey spend a good part of the day sketching her and her six children.

As soon as Bailey saw Soapsuds Row from the fort side of the river, she knew she wanted to visit it with her sketchpad. Bailey preferred human models to landscapes or still lifes, and she especially favored people engaged in the activities of their everyday lives. Bailey was sure the double line of laundresses' tents, with their garden plots behind them and their fatso stoves and steaming laundry vats in front, would present her with a wealth of subjects, so she had given a Sioux ferryman her pocket mirror in exchange for being taken across the river in his canoe.

"Oh, Miss Jeffers, my mister will be so pleased with that drawing," Colleen O'Sullivan was saying. "A photographing man come through last year, and though it was dear, we got a picture of all the children—just a sixth-plate size—but Seamus here wasn't born then."

As if responding to the mention of his name, little Seamus began to squirm and squeal, his chubby fists punching at the air in spasms. His already pink face reddened with effort, and his open mouth rooted intently towards his mother's full breasts.

Mrs. O'Sullivan smiled benevolently at him, and Bailey wondered, not for the first time, how most mothers were able to surrender their bodies and their attentions so liberally to babies and young children. They let themselves be climbed over and sucked on; they hoisted children on their hips while they worked, held them on their laps while they rested, and tolerated the little ones' saliva, tears, blood, mucus, and excrement as thoughtlessly as a river plain accepts silt.

Bailey had never known her own mother, though as a child, fleeting impressions too vague to be called memories used to haunt the last minutes of every day before she dozed off. As she dipped into the edges of sleep, a process she always fought against, believing her sleep to be a dangerously unguarded time, Bailey would imagine the hypnotic stroking of a cool hand smoothing her hair back from her brow over and over, and through a haze she would see, when she could force her lids to lift one more time, a woman's high-necked white blouse and heavy coils of light brown hair above a pale, indistinct face.

Contrary to lurid popular novels, the orphanage had not been an unkind home. But the matrons who operated it concentrated more on hygiene and efficiency than on human warmth. Friendships were not forbidden, but they were not encouraged, either. It was felt that orphans, especially girls, must learn to be content with as little as possible, both materially and emotionally, and must learn to rely on themselves.

With this training, Bailey turned out a thrifty, neat housekeeper and a bit of a social recluse. From what she'd seen, she suspected she'd have made a passable frontier wife, but she feared she'd have been an indifferent mother. Teaching had suited her; she liked books and had a lively curiosity about the world, but she did not make pets of her students, and she related to their parents in a businesslike manner. She was essentially friendless. It was a familiar state.

On this journey, Bailey had been thrown into intimate company with others as she never had before. In the beginning, she recoiled from it, using her sketchpad to keep a distance between her and her companions. But she was growing accustomed to the constant intermingling. As she got to know her subjects, her drawings were, more and more, invested with emotion. Bailey did not associate these two developments as cause and effect. She recognized only that her style of drawing was changing—deepening, becoming both more challenging and more satisfying. Her feelings about her avocation were changing, too. The activity of drawing had always been a joy to Bailey, but it had also always been overlaid with the taint of self-indulgence. Now her work had broken free of guilt and timidity and apology. For the first time, Bailey truly respected her art.

"I'll just take him in the tent, miss," Mrs. O'Sullivan said when Seamus's rooting grew more insistent.

Bailey retrieved some earlier sketches from the portfolio at her feet. She shuffled through them until she came to the one of the two oldest O'Sullivan daughters at the laundry tubs. Bailey set to work filling in details of the background. Some of the laundresses had two tents, one for sleeping quarters and one for a kitchen, but the O'Sullivan setup was more usual. One large tent held foodstuffs, cookware, clothing, belongings, and cots for the whole family.

Bailey was adding the chickens scratching in the dirt and the two hogs asleep in the tent's shade to her drawing when she spotted the eldest O'Sullivan, Erin, coming from the garden. She had a basket over her arm with a few small tomatoes and a cabbage in it. Mrs. O'Sullivan had told Bailey the garden was hard to keep because the grasshoppers were so destructive.

"Erin, have you time to sit and let me finish the portrait I began earlier?" Bailey asked.

"Yes, miss, I guess so," Erin said listlessly. It was just this dulled, almost aged quality that Bailey wanted to capture in her drawing of the girl.

Erin sat on the ground near Bailey. Behind her, Soapsuds Row, perpendicular to the river, pointed to the gathering of buildings and tents that was Fort Laramie. Women down the Row were stirring vats of wet clothes with sticks or stoking stoves to heat water. Children were everywhere; most laundresses had at least seven. Soldiers came and went with bags of laundry. Bailey heard a bugle call from the fort. She'd been hearing them throughout the day.

"The man who's to be my husband is a bugler," Erin said. "He blows thirty calls a day."

"When will you be married?" Bailey asked.

"We've got to wait for the commander's permission," Erin replied, sounding in no hurry.

"Are you looking forward to it?"

Erin shrugged and squinted into the sun.

"You'll get your own tent then, I suppose," Bailey said.

"Oh, I shall have that anyway," Erin said. "I am old enough now to take a contract with the army as a laundress. I'll sign with my man's company, so if he's transferred, I'll move, too."

Bailey studied the girl's inexpressive face and her slouching posture. She was probably no more than fourteen or fifteen, but she showed no youthful energy. She did not seem an appealing mate, but Bailey knew that here, where women were scarce, it was likely Erin had her pick of suitors. Mrs. O'Sullivan had said that though most laundresses arrived as soldiers' wives, sometimes a trail widow was hired on and that these women rarely stayed single longer than three weeks.

"Wouldn't you like to move on from here someday, Erin?" Bailey asked, looking for a topic that might liven up the girl. Bailey knew the army contracted laundresses for a minimum of five years. She could not imagine that five years of washing clothes and linens would be a welcome prospect for a young woman, even a young woman in love and wishing to follow her husband, which, in any case, Erin did not seem to be.

"Maybe. But we get good pay, you know." Here a brief spark lit her eyes. "A dollar a man per month, and we each take care of nineteen men. Why, my father only gets thirteen dollars a month."

Mrs. O'Sullivan, buttoning the front of her calico dress, emerged from the tent without Seamus, who was presumably asleep and dreaming of milk and his mother's warm, freckled skin. She joined Bailey and Erin, summarily sending her daughter to punch down bread dough that was ready to be shaped into loaves.

"Erin's no beauty, but she's a good girl," Mrs. O'Sullivan said, glancing at Bailey's portrait of her daughter. "She looks a mite tired there."

"Yes, I expect she is," Bailey said, though she speculated she and Mrs. O'Sullivan were referring to different kinds of tiredness.

"Sometimes," said the laundress, staring meditatively at the drawing, "things go easier for a woman if she gives in to the tiredness and thinks no more of it than she does the shape of her nose or the spelling of her name."

Bailey was moved by Mrs. O'Sullivan's remark, and she felt a little ashamed of her earlier assumption that the woman did not see or did not care that resignation and withered expectations had lodged in her daughter at such a young age.

"Will you be wanting to go to the Sioux encampment, Miss Jeffers?" Mrs. O'Sullivan said, shaking off her moment of melancholy.

"I'd thought of it," Bailey answered. "We haven't seen many Indians on the trail. Certainly not so many together as they are here."

"Why, for the treaty council last year there were ten thousand of them here—Sioux, Arapaho, Snake, Crow. Now there's usually four hundred or so a day come to the fort to get their annuity. And there's a number stay here pretty regular to trade. I call two or three of the squaws friends. I'll take you to meet them tomorrow evening after supper, if you'd like."

"Oh, yes, I'd like that very much, thank you."

"My mister, he still thinks of them as savages. It's his being a soldier, I guess. But I admire them. Those squaws are good mothers, and they do beautiful handwork with beads and quills. One of them doctored my Liam when a snake bit him; she saved the leg the fort surgeon had said would have to come off."

"Can I bring them anything?" Bailey said.

"You might take some cloth if you've got it. Or shirts."

"Do they speak English?"

"A little. And I've got a few of their words. Your drawings will help, but usually we do fine with pointing and miming. Like I tell my mister, half of communicating is just wanting hard enough to understand the other person. I don't know, though—he still don't seem to get it."

Mrs. O'Sullivan shrugged, as if classing her husband's denseness with the shape of her nose and other immutable things better left unlamented.

July 2, 1852

It is just after sunset, but still light enough to see this page. I have come to the banks of the Laramie to write. There is no truly private spot hereabouts—the bustle is as fervid as in Council Bluffs—but at least I am away from the consternation in our camp. I should, by rights, be at Henry's side, but I am too angry to be a soothing influence on him. Soothing now would be an insult to the honest feelings of each of us, anyway, so I shirk my wifely duty and tend instead to my own thoughts. The river's steady gurgle calms me and lets me be alone in spirit if not in place.

The consternation comes from the announcement of Mr. Webster and Mr. Bennett that they are leaving tomorrow morning. It appears our homely outfit is hobbling them. Henry and

Roy are worried over our low complement of men, but not wishing to be Yankeed again, they have not suggested we look for replacements for the fickle fellows.

Henry thinks Sarah can handle the stock if Hank helps, too. John's horse continues as the madrina, or bell mare, and the eight mules follow her docilely enough. Roy's horse can be attached by her halter to a stout rope between two wagons and so guided along. We will only have three loose oxen. To get four fresh ones, Henry had to trade eight of ours and Derrick's horse; subtracting the ox lost at the Elkhorn, we are left with twenty-seven.

I pity Flinder. She took to her tent early, without supper. I agree with Jerusha that Flinder is well rid of a man whose promises are just so much chin music, but I know the girl's affections are badly bruised, and she probably does not yet look at the departure as lucky.

This seems to be a place for changes of heart. We met some folks today who have had enough of westering and are turning back to the states. I felt Henry watching on me while they spoke to us of their plans. A piece of me did envy them, I confess, but I was that surprised to find that a bigger, heartier piece of me was satisfied to stay set on our course.

There're things in life just can't be undone, or shouldn't be. As we've paid so dearly, we must go on or mock the hopes and hardiness that propelled us this far. The road has already visited on me much of what I had feared before setting out, and I have kept steady. Perhaps worse is to come; I hope not. But I feel a strength alive in me that is marrow-deep and as sure as blood.

The light is failing now, and the night chill is creeping in. Tails of smoke from hundreds of campfires rise into a gossamer cloud over the river. I am ready to return to my family and my friends.

Chapter 11

ALICE WAS NOT the only one who felt a need to escape the camp for a while after Webster and Bennett had delivered their news and the Muller party had indulged in railing against it among themselves. Royal Hall, who had set out to walk off his anger and worry, found himself, after a half hour of vigorous striding, next to three tepees on the edge of the Indian encampment.

Roy had come out without his rifle, and though he wore a bowie knife as always, he felt nervous alone in the vicinity of such a multitude of Indians. Darkness had fallen while he walked, and he could no longer see the fort.

Four men and a woman were squatted or seated around a fire in front of the tepees. Smoke wound out of the tops of the tepees, indicating additional fires inside.

The men had looked up when they heard Roy's approach, then turned their gazes back to the fire or to various interrupted tasks. Now only the young squaw nursing her baby still stared at him. For all his nervousness, Roy remained standing there, unable to look away from the woman.

The squaw was beautiful; her dark, elliptical eyes reflected the firelight, her black braids shone like polished obsidian, her lips rested in her serene face like some rare, ripe fruit. The infant nuzzled blissfully against her; Roy could see the lower curve of her milk-tight breast under the baby's chin. He watched, mesmerized, as the baby lovingly stroked the free breast, occasionally pushing up the woman's blouse to reveal glimpses of a dark, erect nipple and smooth, round flesh the color of maple syrup.

The squaw stood up, and with her child still attached to her breast, she entered one of the tepees. Her supple deerskin skirt pulled tautly across her buttocks and thighs as she bent to lift the small buffalo hide over the doorway. In a rush of desire, Roy imagined following her into the tepee; he visualized finding her waiting there for him, the baby set aside, her loose clothing discarded, her skin silken and warm, her soft fruit-mouth open, and her generous breasts, her hard, muscular legs, all of her, his and his alone. So taken was he with this vision, Roy actually took a few steps forward.

"Bonsoir, monsieur." A man's voice from the fireside broke Roy's reverie.

Roy had thought the people at the fire were Indians. Now, on closer inspection, he saw that the men, though dressed like Indians and clean-shaven, were white. He realized they must be trappers or fur traders. He'd seen two or three at the fort, greasy-haired, full-bearded men in fringed buckskins. There was a cautious alertness in their postures and movements as Roy had seen in wild creatures that had just caught the scent of humans nearby.

"Evening," Roy replied, nodding at the men.

Again the men shifted their attention away from Roy. Two of them were cleaning buffalo guns. The man who had spoken held a chunk of meat on a forked stick in the flames. On his outstretched wrist Roy saw a bracelet of shells and teeth. The fourth man, reawakening Roy's fantasy, word-lessly left his friends and entered the tepee of the beautiful squaw.

Though he had not been invited, Roy moved in closer as if to warm himself by the fire. He found he was keenly curious about these men and the life he supposed they led, free of the concerns of laws, money, or politics, moving on when they wanted, working or not as they pleased, their only duties to their guns, their dogs, and their horses. He wondered what such freedom must be like. He was sure they must be as happy as lords.

There was a good bit of envy buried in Roy's curiosity, and

not just because of the woman. Envy lay, too, beneath his disgust with Webster and Bennett, though it was obscure to him. He knew only that as stunnèd and infuriated as he had been by their desertion, he felt as well a twinge of admiration for their sovereignty. They lived obliged to no one, reliant on no one.

"Guess you fellas have seen a lot of this country," Roy said companionably.

The meat cooker nodded.

"A lot of changes, too, I guess." With a wave of his hand, Roy broadly indicated the fort and the sprawl of emigrant camps.

"We used to take more beaver pelts," said one of the rifle cleaners. "Now they mostly want buffalo robes."

"And we don't have the big summer rendezvous in the Rockies like we used to," said the meat cooker.

"Still," said Roy, anxious to hold on to his romantic impressions, "it must be a grand life."

"Mister," said the meat cooker, extracting his snack from the fire and biting into it, "there's more real pleasure in one year in the mountains than in a whole lifetime in a settlement."

Roy grinned, appeased and disconsolate at the same time. His grin felt put on, like a separate thing and not a real part of his face. It seemed to him he must look foolish to these men, standing jovially by their fire in his homespun farmer's garb and his settler's smile. He resented them for what he fancied was their disdainful judgment, and he inwardly cursed as unnatural their free-ranging ways and their pairings with exotic beauties. He turned abruptly and left the little group without saying good-bye. He wouldn't give them further topics to laugh over by treating them with good manners.

FLINDER AND SARAH lay on their backs looking up at the sloping canvas of their tent. They were still keeping open Ellen's accustomed space between them. Even on the first night, when they had wept in one another's arms, the girls had rolled apart as their breaths lengthened and their tear-burned eyelids drooped.

"I went with Hank to the Indian camp today," Sarah said.

"Um," Flinder answered absently.

"We saw some squaws painting pictures of deer on a tepee. You know, I counted twenty buffalo hides sewn together in that tepee cover, and the skins had all been dressed so they were perfectly white."

"Did Uncle Henry know you went over there?" Flinder said.

Adult supervision on the journey had been more lax than at home, but Flinder knew an unescorted visit to the Indians would have been considered beyond even these looser limits.

"We slipped off when they were all fussing about Mr. Webster and Mr. Bennett," Sarah replied.

"What were they saying?" asked Flinder with greater interest.

"Oh, your mother said that's what comes of buying a pig in a poke. And the others held how it was dishonorable of Mr. Webster and Mr. Bennett and how back home a man felt bound to carry through on his intentions."

"But we're not back home anymore," Flinder observed curtly.

"Still," insisted Sarah, "we've got to follow the same strictures."

"That's what folks would have you believe, but I get to wondering sometimes."

"Well, I expect we'll have to when we're back among houses and neighbors. Won't we?"

"I don't know."

Flinder really did not know. Until Jack's promise to come to her in California, Flinder had given little specific consideration to what life in her new home would be like. She saw now that she had been assuming it would be simply a resumption of the life of Indiana and that this assumption might be wrong. The new demands and opportunities of the trail might not prove temporary conditions after all.

Flinder thought about the things she and the other women had learned to do on the trail, like handling teams and driving wagons, pitching tents, yoking and unyoking oxen. She got a secret thrill out of having the power to set a wagon going by cracking the long bullwhip. She thought of the ladies she'd seen in split skirts riding horses or mules astride instead of sidesaddle and the women marching along in bloomers. Flinder herself had known the strange feel of trousers at Chimney Rock. Long, full skirts let the women curtain one another off for privacy on the wide-open plains, but Flinder remembered the exhilaration of stretching her legs and climbing in pants.

"Flinder," Sarah said timidly. "Shall you miss him?"

Flinder swallowed before she answered.

"There will be a difference to the days now," she said, turning on her side and putting her back to Sarah to forestall further questions. She heard Sarah sigh and shift position.

"Good night, Flin."

"Good night." Flinder reached behind her and placed her hand on the cool, empty space between her and her cousin. Sarah extended her arm and laid her hand on top of Flinder's, curling her fingers gently around it.

FLINDER SWAM IN AND OUT of sleep all night. Each time she awoke, fragments of dreams floated through her drowsy mind. Just before dawn she dreamed she was watching Ellen open a small yellow box tied with red grosgrain ribbon. Inside was a single pink pearl hung from a finely twisted cord of white silk.

Ellen held it up to admire, then carefully rewrapped it, saying, "I shall save this to wear on my wedding day." Flinder grabbed her sister's shoulders and shook her violently.

Suddenly fully awake, Flinder sat up, her heart still pounding.

"She never had such a jewel. Nor a wedding day," she whispered to herself when her heart had quieted.

She knew she would not fall asleep again if she lay down, so she put on her linsey-woolsey dress and crept out of the tent.

This was a time of day Flinder had always favored. She liked the dewy tentativeness of the light and the tepid electricity of the air. She liked, too, being abroad while others slept. The proximity of sleepers made Flinder feel both safe and adventurous. She was more aware of being alive. It was as if the world had been created just for her.

This day, her aliveness spoke to her as sorrow. Every breath of air she took in seemed to lay a weight on her chest. The paling apricot sky and the sharp Black Hills outlined against it were, of course, always indifferent to human joys or pain, but today their unconcern with her plight impressed her as cruel. She was alone with her emotions. Not that she really wanted to share them with anyone, not even with unfeeling Nature. There was only one person to whom she might show herself, and she could not imagine how she might ever trust to let that happen now.

A horse's whinny close by caused Flinder to turn from her contemplation of the hills. Reed and Jack were leading their new Indian ponies from behind the supply wagon. When Jack spied Flinder, he spoke a few words to Reed, who frowned in her direction and mounted. His horse loped toward the fort. Jack took off his hat, and still leading his horse, he walked over to her.

"Good day, Miss Flinder. I didn't count on seeing you this morning."

"I didn't plan it so. I'm sorry, sir, if it discomforts you." Flinder did not want to retreat before him, so she resumed instead her study of the hills.

"Oh, I'm much gladdened to see you. It allows me to renew my promise. I *will* come when you've settled in California. You can tell your folks so, too."

"I won't be telling anyone," Flinder replied icily. "And I won't be watching for you."

"But would you welcome me?"

Jack touched Flinder's elbow with the tips of his fingers. It was the only part of her body that felt real to her then. She turned and stared into his eyes. She could not misread the longing she found there. Why did he have to be so handsome and sound so piteously sincere? Why did his words, the instant he uttered them, strike her as the very words she had been wanting to hear from him?

"I can't say that I'd welcome you," Flinder stalled, frantically searching her mind to discover what indeed she did feel about this man and the possibility of his return. "I might. I expect I wouldn't regret meeting again."

Flinder lowered her head after this admission. Her pride would not let her show him more. She looked at her moccasined feet facing his booted feet in the dust. Nervously she began winding and unwinding a strand of hair around the fingers of her right hand. Jack took off one leather glove and lifted his hand, but before he could touch her, she took a step backwards.

"Would you give me a lock?" he asked.

"I'll give you no tokens and make no pledges," she said, facing him squarely again.

"You'd send me away empty?"

"No one's sending you."

"You're an exacting woman, Flinder Hall."

Jack's name was shouted from a short way off, and both Jack and Flinder turned to see Reed and three other men on horseback. One man held a line to a string of four heavily burdened pack mules. Boxy rawhide fardels for holding supplies hung at each animal's sides, and their backs were loaded with goods wrapped lumpily in blankets. With wide scoops of his arm, Reed motioned Jack to hurry along. Flinder felt her throat thicken, as if her heart had risen to fill it. Seeing Reed reminded Flinder of the warnings he had made about Jack and how she had let her affection for Jack override Reed's hard words. Now Jack was turning his back on her loyalty and leaving with the traitorous Reed, and he did not even know that Reed had slandered him and that she had kept faith with their mutual endearment anyway.

Jack moved toward his horse, grasped the saddle horn, and hesitated, looking mournfully at Flinder. Seized by a frightening urgency, Flinder stepped closer to him. In the cool morning air she could feel the moist heat from the horse's body and smell its animal pungency. She was acutely aware, too, of the heat and shape and weight of her own body and the proximity of Jack's. She was brimming with a wild kind of caution.

"If you'll take no meaning from it," she said quickly, "you can kiss me."

"Can't no one wrestle down another's meaning in a kiss," he answered gently, adding with a smile, "Thinking don't usually play much part in kissing anyway."

"Jack!" came another shout from Reed.

Flinder moved away from Jack's horse so that he could mount. His little speech had given her enough time to be embarrassed by her boldness. Jack put his foot in a stirrup and swung his leg up and over the horse's back. As soon as he was seated, however, he reversed the motions and dismounted. Dropping the reins to the ground, he took hold of Flinder's wrist and led her quickly to the other side of a wagon where they were out of sight of the waiting men.

"You still willing?" There was no hint of a smile now. His eyes, full of yearning, moved swiftly, cataloging every feature of her face. Flinder nodded.

He pulled her against him. Surprised by the overwhelming firmness and reality of his embrace, Flinder lifted her arms and laid her hands on the front of his shoulders. He pressed his mouth onto hers and slowly tightened his arms around her so that her breasts flattened softly against him.

She felt him lean his hips forward toward her body, and though, in alarm, she first tilted her own hips away from him, she noticed under the alarm a desire to feel more of him against more of her, so that as his lips continued to play over hers and the hard feel of his hand against the small of her back petitioned her forward, she eased her body fully against him, and what had begun as alarm distilled into a tiny pulse that quivered within her like a firefly in a jar. Flinder heard a moan, and she honestly did not know if it had come from her or from Jack.

It was she who ended it. Jack smiled at her and kissed the palms of both her hands. In three or four quick strides, he reached his horse. He waved before galloping off, but his smile was gone, his face tense, his arm stiff in its farewell gesture.

Flinder could not bear to watch him ride out of sight. Though, like yesterday, she felt sad, this sadness was sweetened by the lingering loose happiness his kiss had stirred in her body, and watching him go, she feared, would rob her of that. She turned to the breakfast chores, all the while whispering to herself, as she used to do when preparing a recitation for school, learning by heart the last conversation with Jack, storing it away safely and accurately. No matter what the future brought, she would possess the moments of this morning, and though her experience was still slight, she was already wise enough to know that the moments, in turn, would possess her and would inform other similar moments for years to come.

July 3, 1852

Flinder did bravely on breakfast, so there was little work left when I arose, and I have the luxury of writing now while I am fresh rather than at day's end.

We have unloaded, aired, and repacked all four wagons with an eye to lightening, as we are about to begin the long upgrade to the Rockies. Roy made Jerusha discard a heavy oak dresser, though it had been her mother's and of special meaning to her. I surrendered some books and a mattress. Our various neighbors have jettisoned bellows, chisels, a gold-washer, a pig of lead, tents, harness, cooking stoves, winter clothing, and grindstones.

Henry used wood from a dilapidated, abandoned wagon—there are countless ones about—to construct pack saddles for the Bowens's mules. The two horses are next to no good as pack animals; they are in worse shape than either the oxen or the mules because they cannot manage as well on the sparse, wild forage and need a steady supply of grain (which we do not have) to keep their full power.

Henry entered our party in the Fort Laramie emigrant register yesterday. A soldier scribe records the number of men, women, children, mules, oxen, horses, wagons, cows, and deaths for every company. Henry signed our names and places of origin in another ledger; he said his name was #34,166.

It appeared for a while today we must subtract one member of our party from the register, as Elizabeth wandered off alone, and it took Faith, Flinder, Sarah, and me, all scouting in different directions, two hours to uncover her at last, contentedly at play with some other children a good mile from our wagons. Faith was heartily relieved to find her and clutched the child to her as if she'd been stolen, though it was her own neglect that allowed Elizabeth to stray. Indeed, if it were not for my Sarah keeping an eye out, Elizabeth would not have been fed properly nor tucked to bed in good time the past few days, Faith has been that distracted. Henry thinks perhaps her mourning for John has been enlivened here because she has had to write home about his death. Henry, too, had to send that sad message to family in Pennsylvania, and there were many sighs from him over the writing of it. But it does not make him forgetful of the present, as it seems to do Faith.

Roy has heard from the post surgeon that old Senator Clay is gravely ill in Washington. It was his compromise that brought California into the Union a free state, as the Californians had wished, and managed to stave off civil war. The question is not done, however, I fear; when we left Indiana, Congress and others were still wrangling over balancing slave and free states and what might be done about slavery in the territories.

I will go to the sutler's store once more today. We have already laid in hominy and farina, vinegar, cocoa, preserves of quinces and of cranberries, potatoes, onions, brined pork and sugar-cured ham, macaroni, and ginger. The children all have Indian moccasins, for their shoes are fair worn-out with walking. We've replaced the wagon jack and grease bucket we lost *traveling on a rough track after dark one night. So my visit to the store today will be just to savor it once more before returning to the road. I have promised myself to spend a few coins frivolously.*

It is amusing how the store captivates me. It is a great deal less tidy and less hospitable than the town stores in Indiana, and it holds nothing out of the ordinary by way of goods. But the patrons! Every sort of American is there: lonely soldiers barely into their manhood; farmers and city men, both out of their element; strong-smelling old-time trappers; women in every shape, many pregnant, and most in much torn and mended skirts; wild-haired children running loose. And the Indians: tall and bronzed, the men with bared chests and legs, the Sioux by far the handsomest. The beadwork on their women's clothes is quite accomplished. Among this throng I can sense for the first time that we are going to a new place and that the life of no one I see is likely to stay completely the same, neither in outward show nor in the heart's knowledge.

Chapter 12

ALICE FELT time-wealthy. Supper had been planned and set by, the wagons were packed and ready for an early departure next morning, and it was only early afternoon. She and Sarah had washed their hair in the Laramie's clear, icy waters, finishing with a borax rinse. Sarah had even managed to douse Elizabeth in the river for a much-needed scrub.

"Shall we take a last walk to the fort?" Alice said to Sarah as she was buttoning up the back of Elizabeth's smock.

In Indiana, Alice had liked to walk out with Sarah in the summer twilight, feeling the humidity begin to lift off a little and an evening breeze start to stir. Sometimes they'd talk over the small events of the day or the week and the thoughts they might have provoked. Other times, they didn't speak, except to note a passing bird or butterfly, for Sarah was not a chatty child and knew how to keep a companionable silence. This had been a summer of walking, but there was no leisure to it; now, during the pause in their incessant progress that this layover afforded, Alice found she missed those genial rambles with her daughter.

"Me, too, me, too," Elizabeth chirped. "I want to go, too."

"No," Alice said. "You must stay by your mama for now. Come, we'll tell her we're leaving."

Elizabeth scowled at Alice, as if calculating the chances of further protest proving effective. But after a moment, with a sigh and a visible droop of her shoulders, she took Alice's outstretched hand and let herself be led to her wagon.

Alice peered into the back of the wagon and saw Faith sitting inside knitting.

"The light is dim for such close work," Alice said to her.

"It suffices," Faith answered, looking up.

"Well, I've brought you Lizzie, as Sarah and I are leaving camp for a while, and there's no one to mind her out here."

Faith rested her hands in her lap, her fingers holding the strands of yarn in place along the needles. Alice expected her to put the work aside and climb out. Elizabeth would be a much easier charge playing outside than cramped into the wagon.

"Lift her in, then," Faith said.

Alice hoisted the little girl up, and she scrambled to Faith's side.

"I've had a bath, Mama," Elizabeth said importantly. "And it was so cold, so cold, but I didn't even cry once."

Faith returned to her knitting. Unperturbed by her mother's seeming disinterest, Elizabeth settled into a long story about the bath—the women washing clothes next to her, the greasy feel of the soap, her goose bumps, the scary back-float Sarah made her do to wash her hair. Alice chuckled, remembering her children at Elizabeth's age, so impressed with themselves and so easily amazed at the world and its multiple experiences.

"We shall bring you a sweet, Lizzie," she said in parting.

As Alice and Sarah strolled arm in arm across the parade ground, they spied some soldiers draping red, white, and blue bunting along the porch railings of Old Bedlam. They stopped to watch them work. The stone magazine and the store were already decked out.

"I'm sorry we shall miss the fort's Fourth celebration," Sarah said.

"Yes," agreed Alice. "but it's just as fitting to mark the day with miles as with schottisches."

"We mark every day with miles," Sarah said grumpily.

"Perhaps someone camped near us tomorrow night will have music," Alice offered.

"And we can join them?"

"It might mean more hiking."

"Oh, I won't mind that."

"Do you hope so much to dance, then?" Alice smiled at her.

Sarah unlinked her arm from her mother's and looked away from Old Bedlam as if she were ready to move on. A line of soldiers trotted by. When they had passed, Alice and Sarah began walking again.

"I don't know that I'd like to dance if it means I am getting to be grown-up," Sarah said cautiously.

"But you *are* getting to be grown-up," Alice said.

"I don't want to, Ma."

"My dear, what a notion. Why not?"

Alice studied Sarah's face. She could see that the girl was struggling with her thoughts, and that they were perplexing thoughts rock-ribbed with melancholy. Alice wished fervently that she could erase her daughter's apprehension, however natural it might be. She felt a different kind of powerlessness from that she had when facing the cholera scare, but one as profound in its own intricate way. If Sarah were ill or had cut her hand, Alice could act, could rally comfort and care, but there was no way to spare the girl sorrows of the heart.

"I just want to stop as I am," Sarah said at last, though she did not seem satisfied with her reply.

"Sometimes, Ma," she added quietly, "I even wish I could have stopped sooner and still be silly and unmistaken and ignorant. Like Hank or Gideon or even Elizabeth."

"They are not truly that way, Sarah, nor were you ever, really, as you will know if you think carefully on it. Children have their woes, too, and they only seem small when we get older and find new ones."

"I don't want new ones," Sarah said, her voice faltering.

Alice stopped and took Sarah's hand, turning the girl to face her. She tucked some loose strands of hair behind Sarah's ears and fought down the quaver she felt in her own throat.

"You shall make a fine, strong woman, Sarah," Alice said.

"I know this because you are fine and strong already. I cannot tell you that being grown-up does not bring its troubles—you would not believe me if I did—but it brings gratifications, too."

Sarah nodded, and Alice drew her close for a hug. They resumed their walk at a slower pace.

"Growing up is like leaving home, as we've done," Alice concluded. "We miss what we've left behind and the ending of ways we've known, but, slowly, new ways take their place, and we do keep some of the old ways within us, and by the time we are well settled in California, we will find we have made the change almost unawares and will look back on the past fondly, sometimes sadly, but without fruitless longing."

They kept across the broad parade ground without further conversation. They were still holding hands, and Alice could feel by Sarah's loosening grip and the freer swing of her arm that her mood had lightened.

"Isn't that Miss Jeffers?" Sarah said as they came up to the guardhouse.

Bailey, sitting on the edge of her low stool and resting her foot on loose sheafs on the ground to keep them from blowing away, was hard at work on a drawing. Alice and Sarah stopped to watch her. Appearing, line by line, under Bailey's pencil was a young soldier standing guard duty. His chin bristled with a few stray whiskers, but his sunburned cheeks were as hairless as a child's. A cartridge belt bunched his ill-fitting blue uniform jacket at the waist, and his broad-brimmed hat looked as if it had been rained on several times too often. Still, knowing he was Bailey's subject, the young man stood straight and held his carbine crisply against his shoulder. Bailey was working on his face, and Alice saw she had found the fatigue and loneliness in it.

"May we see what else you've done?" Alice asked.

"These all need more work," Bailey said, bending to pick up the papers under her foot.

Bailey stood up, and Alice and Sarah stepped in closer to look at the drawings.

In one, a gaunt-faced man with saucer eyes stood holding a wheelbarrow. He grasped the handles so tightly, his bony knuckles poked from his hands like spiny armor. He was poised for defense, as if he feared the wheelbarrow would be wrested from him at any moment.

"Those are all his belongings in that wheelbarrow," Bailey said. "He's pushing it to Oregon."

In another drawing two boys and a girl, all barefoot and wearing tattered and much-patched clothing, climbed over a wagon that had been stripped of its running gear. Bailey had frozen their play in such lively poses, they seemed to be still moving. Next was a study of two Indian women sewing buffalo hides together with rawhide thread. They wore elk-skin dresses and short capes ornamented with porcupine quills in geometric designs. In the last drawing, a stooped soldier just released from two weeks' solitary confinement in a tiny, windowless cell spread his arms wide and grimaced in the sunlight.

"The guard said this man was a repeat offender. Mill birds, they call them," Bailey explained to Alice, who was lingering over the haunting sketch. "Those cells are only five feet by two and a half feet, and just five feet tall."

"Like a grave," Alice said, shuddering. She handed the papers back to Bailey.

"Yes, I want to put that in his face," Bailey said. She shuffled through the drawings thoughtfully. "I want to put in all these faces what lies in back of the moment I've stopped them at."

"You're very brave," said Alice.

"Brave?" Bailey smiled.

"To search out such things."

"You know," said Bailey, "I don't search for them in any planned way. I just see them. It's like sitting in darkness in a strange room and staring; after a while you pick out the shapes of objects, or enough of their shapes to make a good guess at what they are."

"We're headed for the store. You may find some faces to see there," Alice suggested.

"Yes, I'm through here," Bailey said, picking up her stool. "Thank you," she called to the guard as they walked away. Confounded, the young man saluted her.

As Alice, Sarah, and Bailey recrossed the parade ground, they passed four soldiers polishing two field cannon. Ahead of them they saw the sutler's store. Emigrants were entering and exiting the two narrow doors in such a steady flow, they appeared to be dancing a reel. A half dozen Sioux braves stood outside observing the activity.

The directness of the braves' stares as the women walked by them caused Alice to feel uncomfortably conspicuous. She lifted her chin and straightened her back, steadfastly keeping her eyes on the store's doorway, but the more she ignored the stares, the more sharply aware of them she found herself. She felt no menace; the setting was too secure. Besides, in her few dealings with Indians on the trail, they had showed more curiosity about the emigrants than animosity. She had been patient, even amused, when they poked their noses into the backs of the wagons or picked up the lids of cook pots. But now she felt pinioned by their dark, appraising eyes.

Sarah and Bailey stepped into the store, but Alice's way was barred by two men coming out carrying a heavy sack of oats between them. In the few seconds she had to wait to gain entry, Alice was surprised to sense a blush spreading up her throat and face. She knew this feeling. It was then she realized that the braves were not discomfiting her because they were Indians, but because they were men, and although it was only a flash, it was the first time Alice had considered the Indians as in any way familiar or like ordinary people she knew. Everything she'd read or been told before the journey had painted Indians either as ferocious devils or as noble innocents. In her own encounters she had not yet passed beyond regarding them as natural curiosities, though she had been relieved at their general peaceableness and grateful for the antelope meat they'd brought in trade. Now, in her feminine fluster under the open regard of a group of men, Alice had engaged the Indians at last as fellow humans.

In the store's hum, Alice's attention was quickly pulled away from her fleeting insight. She noticed Bailey had located her stool in a corner from which she had a vantage of the whole scene. Sarah was wedged between a stout woman and a gangly youth at the long, crowded main counter, craning her neck to survey the contents of the shelves behind the counter. Alice went and stood beside Bailey and scanned the large room.

She took in the barrels of turnips and potatoes; the wooden bins of green coffee beans, yellow-white rice, speckled pinto beans, black-eyed peas, and pale limas; the firkins of raisins and figs. Two big green metal containers declared themselves in embossed silver letters to contain English breakfast tea and Chinese gunpowder tea.

On the tall shelves behind the counters sat such delicacies as black walnuts, vanilla extract, oyster catsup, Jamaican rum, sardines, Worcestershire sauce, Spanish olives, rose water, castile soap, canned salmon, and canned lobster. Copper pails gleamed beside homely cedar buckets and oak piggins. Bottles of sherry, claret, brandy, and whiskey perched on the highest shelves. Coffeepots, pans, camp kettles, and skillets hung from rods overhead. Every other kind of kitchen article was in evidence, too, including coffee mills, nutcrackers, and nutmeg graters.

Along one of the shorter walls were tools. Planes stood alongside augers, saws, horseshoe nails, and beaver traps. Pitchforks, shovels, and ramrods leaned against the wall. Coils of rope were piled up next to a variety of whips: ox lashes, drovers' whips, carriage whips, and whip stocks. Wagon needs were addressed by a supply of cruppers, tongue pins, kingbolts, yokes, chains, wagon covers, and bridle bits.

On the opposite wall were clothing and personal items. Hats, blankets, shirts, vests, coats, pants, and bolts of fabric filled the shelves. Much of this, Alice had been told, had been sent from the states as trading goods for the Indians. She spied a few books, mostly popular novels or songsters or biographies of military heroes. Bailey had purchased drawing paper here yesterday and had brought Alice a gift of a few sheets of blue letter paper.

"I think I shall do a portrait of that storekeep," Bailey said to Alice. "He looks to be in charge."

She pointed with her chin to a thin, sandy-haired man with elaborate sideburns who had just put a pair of wooden stirrups on the counter before a man. The storekeep was dapperly dressed in a white linen shirt and gray cheviot trousers, and he held a clay pipe tightly in his teeth while he scooted back and forth filling orders.

"Perhaps the tobacco smoke shields him from his customers' odors," Bailey said.

"You're not used to living indoors anymore," Alice laughed.

The store was thick with July heat, and the odor of unwashed bodies was strong. Alice concentrated on her sense of smell for a minute or two, and soon she was able to pick out the more pleasant aromas of cinnamon, ginger, nutmeg, mint, and pepper. Overlaying these was the sharp sting of new leather from the boots, saddles, and holsters crowded on the floor behind the counter just to Alice's left.

Alice patted Bailey's shoulder, which was bent over her drawing pad, and moved more deeply into the room. Some spools of ribbon caught her eye. She wound off a half yard of a narrow, dark blue velvet ribbon and cut it with a pair of shears tied to the side of the counter.

Absentmindedly stroking the ribbon with her thumb, Alice slowly considered a row of large glass jars holding sweets. There were peppermint sticks, hunks of chocolate, horehound drops, tiny macaroons, licorice, and strings of crystalline rock candy. Sarah came up beside Alice and slipped her arm around her mother's waist.

"Yes?" A brisk voice made Alice look down from the shelf of candies. The dapper clerk was facing her across the counter. His raised eyebrows and a short puff of smoke from his pipe implied there was no time to lose.

"I'll have this," Alice said, handing him the length of ribbon, "and a quarter pound of—what do you think, Sarah—macaroons?"

"Oh, yes," Sarah said enthusiastically. "Macaroons."

"Usually officers' wives buy those, or sometimes the homesick young enlistees on payday," said the clerk, as if objecting to her choice. Two more quick puffs of smoke seemed meant to encourage Alice to make up her mind quickly and in a manner more fitting to an emigrating farmwife.

"On second thought," said Alice, lifting her eyebrows in imitation of the dandified man, "I'll take a pound of the macaroons."

R OY CALLED EVERYONE before the sky even hinted at dawn. The goal for the day was Register Cliff, only thirteen miles away. The short haul would allow them to break in the four new oxen. The early start was not needed to cover the distance, but Roy had insisted on it. He wanted to shake off the sense of weight and sluggishness that had been gathering like dust on him throughout the stay at the fort.

In the cold darkness, Alice and Jerusha prepared a hearty breakfast of pancakes, bacon, beans, and coffee.

Elizabeth and Gideon were left to awaken on their own later. Dredging young children from sleep only made more work for the women in getting ready to move out.

Faith, too, was not disturbed. She usually made sure to clear up after supper in order to be able to sleep in a little in the mornings. She had not done so last night, but the women let her be anyway. In the past three days Faith had been of little help; she'd start on a task with a furious, undisciplined energy, then suddenly abandon it midway to retire into the wagon to rest. Jerusha and Alice had had to set their girls to finish or in some cases redo most of Faith's chores.

No one associated Reed Bennett with Faith's erratic behavior. In the excitement and activity of the arrival at the fort, no one had noticed the careful way Reed's eyes followed Faith's every move, nor the way she started at the sound of his voice as if she'd been struck. At any rate, he was no longer around. He and Jack had quit the Muller party just two days after Reed's assault on Faith.

Faith herself barely connected the changes in her with Reed. It was as if her dream, having split open to admit a real intruder, had also lengthened backwards in time so that her fearful anticipations of the journey, her leave-taking of her mother, John's drowning, and all the foreign sights and everyday discomforts had congealed into one endless siege against her. And though Reed was gone, she could not escape the sense of her life as a living nightmare. Her only relief came in diminishing her participation in it as much as possible, slighting even her maternal duties, waiting and still hoping for the release of waking up on the other side of the dream, if not restored to her former self, then at least freed of her present downtrodden one.

Nevertheless, when the jiggling wagon roused Faith from sleep as they left Fort Laramie, she was glad to hear Flinder instead of Reed shouting to the oxen pulling her wagon. Slowly she sat up, first resting the weight of her body on her forearms and elbows, then on the palms of her hands. It took two lurching attempts before she got onto her knees and was able to climb out onto the wagon seat.

As she did so, she inadvertently kicked her foot against Elizabeth's shoulder, but the child remained asleep. Faith was thankful for Elizabeth's sturdiness and her ability, like a young animal, to sleep unclouded in cheerless surroundings, to eat plain food without indigestion, to fold herself against Sarah or Flinder or one of the others when she wanted coddling and could not draw it out of Faith.

"Good morning," Flinder greeted her, falling back so that she was walking beside Faith's seat.

Faith nodded in reply, spreading her hands over her bulging abdomen and gasping audibly as the baby inside her pushed a foot or a fist under her rib cage with a sharp jab.

"It appears to be glad to be rolling again," Flinder said, cocking her head toward Faith's belly. "Must be a boy."

Faith managed a wan smile. The baby stilled, and Faith relaxed her shoulders.

"A boy," she said. "John would have liked that."

They kept on in silence for an hour, each absorbed in her own thoughts. The sun rose at their backs. Flinder occasionally cracked the whip over the oxen's heads to keep them aligned. The middle pair were new, but they were working in well with the others. Refreshed by their rest at the fort, all six pushed against their yokes at a steady pace.

Flinder thought later that perhaps it was the combination of the warm air, their daydreaming, and the oxen's lulling gait that caused her and Faith to miss the sounds of Elizabeth stirring inside the wagon. Whatever the reason, neither woman noticed the little girl until she was standing precariously at the front opening of the canvas. Before either of them could speak to her and before Faith's staying hands could reach her, the child, arms outstretched like a fledging, hopped out, missed her footing, and fell.

Flinder immediately yelled "Whoa," but stopping a moving wagon was always a clumsy affair, and this time it was too late. The front wheel of the fifteen-hundred-pound wagon had rolled over Elizabeth, and she lay motionless beneath the wagon box.

Flinder scrambled under the wagon. She was horrified at the unnatural way Elizabeth's legs angled away from her upper body, as if her waist marked a kind of dividing line. The child could have been a carelessly dropped rag doll except for the blood beginning to soak through her gingham dress.

Faith jumped off the wagon so quickly, she lost her balance when she landed and fell onto her side on the ground. Not bothering to get up, she dragged herself to her daughter's side and knelt over her. Reaching out towards the child, she withdrew her hands without touching her, as if she feared disturbing her. She repeated this same reaching and withdrawing over and over again.

Flinder put her arm around Faith's back to urge her out from under the wagon, but Faith pushed her away. Flinder ducked out and stood up to face the others, who had come running to the wagon. For an instant they looked like strangers to her, and she felt alone and frightened. Her hands began to tremble. She looked quickly from person to person. A portly woman with tears in her eyes opened her arms to Flinder. Flinder took one tottering step toward the woman. With a rush, she recognized her as Jerusha and gratefully entered her embrace.

Jerusha walked Flinder away from the doll-child in the dust. Flinder pressed one ear against Jerusha's bosom and covered her other ear with her own hand to close out the sound of Faith's screaming, which was so loud and so deep-throated, it seemed to be coming from the bowels of the earth.

Alice and Bailey pulled Faith, still screaming but otherwise not resisting, out from under the wagon. Henry crawled under and wrapped Elizabeth in a blanket. After he had laid the limp bundle gently in the wagon bed, he brushed the little girl's hair back from her face. She could have been sleeping, she looked so serene. A slight sunburn pinked her nose and cheeks.

Alice and Bailey led Faith to the back of the wagon. Bailey got into the wagon, and with her pulling and Alice pushing from behind, they helped Faith in and sat her down beside Elizabeth's body. Bailey laid one of Faith's hands on Elizabeth's chest. Her screaming suddenly stopped. She looked at Elizabeth with a stunned expression, as if she had just stepped out of bright sunlight into a dark root cellar. Still resting her hand on Elizabeth and staring at the child's round, placid face, Faith groped for Bailey and gripped her hand tightly when she found it.

Alice was about to climb into the wagon, too, when Henry put a restraining hand on her arm. He motioned her out of Faith's hearing.

"I'm going to take Elizabeth back to Fort Laramie for burial," he said.

"You mean you alone?" Alice asked.

Henry nodded. "I'll make better time on horseback alone. No need for us all to turn back. Roy can take the rest of you on to the Cliff. I'll join you tonight."

"Faith isn't likely to let her go so soon."

"You must convince her. It's for her sake, anyway. The child's grave will be kept in repair at the fort. It will be easier with Faith later to know that. I only wish we could have done as well for John and the others."

Alice suddenly felt a terrible sadness at Henry's leaving. She was ashamed of the feeling, knowing how small a thing a day's absence was compared to the permanent losses Faith and Jerusha had suffered. But she could not rule herself. She desperately wanted him at her side or at least within sight and sound, not traveling in the opposite direction from her.

She did not fear for his safety. She did not worry about the personal anguish with which this lonely errand might visit him. She only knew their separation felt wrong. Slowly, over the many miles, Alice had come to see the journey as a joint venture. It asked of her more than all her previous years of marriage had, and she was learning that a full-hearted answer was the only suitable one, both to the journey and to the marriage. Like a sleepwalker who awakes in an unexpected place, Alice felt new to herself and to her partnership with Henry. She did not understand the newness, but it intoxicated her with the feeling of being alive.

"Let me go with you," she said impulsively.

"Certainly not," he said.

Alice knew he was right. Her suggestion was impractical. Just uttering it had made her feel better, though, like saying "I love you" to someone who already knows it. She turned to look at Faith's wagon.

"I'll talk to her," she said.

"I'll be by with a horse in fifteen minutes."

★ ★ ★

ALICE WENT TO bed only after she had dozed off twice by the fire and singed the edge of her skirt. She had wanted to be awake when Henry returned.

Everyone else had retired hours ago. Alice had sat alone by the fire under the vast sky writing in her journal. Her entry complete, she had stared out into the night until she was dizzy with the struggle to keep her eyes open.

Her thoughts had skittered everywhere, jumping from Elizabeth to her own dead babies, from her Indiana garden to the Pennsylvania woods to Philadelphia's wharfs and alleys. She even thought of Charles, though try as she might, she could recall only certain unimportant occasions with him and could not summon up in any real way the emotional tone of their connection. This seemed odd to her, but she was not disturbed by it. That the memory of Charles did not tug nostalgically at her heart as it once had was, surprisingly, a relief.

Lying in the wagon, Alice continued to wait and listen for Henry. At first it was easy. The cotton lining of the quilt was cool against her skin, and the sleeping space felt too wide. Gradually, however, she fell asleep.

She didn't hear Henry enter the wagon and undress. She only noticed him when he crawled under the quilt and moved his feet to where the bedding had been warmed by her body. She was glad to have this simple gift for him, the heat of a living body.

She nestled against his shoulder. He sighed. They both lay still for several minutes. Alice assumed Henry had drifted to sleep. She herself was beginning to doze off again when Henry rolled onto his side, pulling away from her slightly.

Slowly he stroked her, traveling along the side of her body from her shoulder down to her knee, again and again, his hand shaping itself to her curves. Then his hand began sliding off her side to the front of her body as well. He traced the roundness of her breasts, and his fingertips tarried on her nipples.

Alice felt as if she were in a silken cocoon that Henry was unwinding thread by thread, drawing her deliciously toward the light.

She parted her thighs, and he slipped his hand between her legs. He moved his fingers back and forth and in circles, sometimes tugging gently at her. Over and over, he coaxed her body toward the limits of its pleasure, lingering in one tiny spot or with one rhythm, then changing his caress to hold her back yet a little while longer.

She rode on her sensations as if they were tangible objects, as if her body had sprouted new parts. The stronger the sensations became, the more deeply she dived into them, until there was no wagon, no night, no Henry, only her body, her body, and finally not even her body, but just the sensations and their glorious energy.

Alice lay on her back. Henry, propped up on one elbow, waited beside her silently. As her body quieted, she felt welling up in her a great affection for him and a desire to hold him solidly against her. She pulled at his arm, and he climbed on top of her.

She welcomed him into her body. She ran her hands down his hard back to his hard buttocks. She pressed her feet against his hard thighs. He held himself up from her because of the mild swell of her uterus. She lifted herself to him. She watched the play of passion across his face until he lowered his head beside hers and groaned in her ear.

She gave him a little push and he rolled off her. She sat up to smooth out the covers. When she lay down again, they arranged themselves so that her back was against his chest. He laid his arm over her waist and sprinkled a line of kisses across her shoulders. She felt linked to him and purged of the day's sorrows.

July 4, 1852

We have lost Elizabeth, our youngest member, to the accident of falling out the wagon. Faith is dumbstruck at what has befallen her. She will not speak.

I am frightened and ashamed to say I did not cry for long. At each death, it seems my grief is shorter-lived, as if my heart is growing a callus. I am not so dulled as Roy, however, who seems to remark the biggest happening of the day to be going over the ridge of Mexican Hill, which put our new oxen to the test. We had to rough-lock the wheels and slide down, the oxen stiffening their legs to brake the descent.

We are stopped at Register Cliff, where the river bends gently. Some neighboring campers fired thirteen volleys and had some fiddling to celebrate the date. We, of course, refrained, though I did give the children macaroons. Flinder, remembering how much Elizabeth always longed for sweets, would not take any.

A coarse-surfaced sandstone wall stands some 150 feet tall here. Mud-daubed swallows' nests cluster in the highest crevices, and scores of darting birds flit between the cliffs and the river. Covering the face of the cliff are names carved by others who have passed here before us. Hank found the name of our old neighbor Obidiah Stuart, who went gold-seeking in 1849. He had described its location in a letter to Henry.

I walked alongside the cliff looking at names for near a quarter mile at dusk. I ran my fingers in some deep-cut ones. What hopes and full hearts these scratchings signify. Did some think to ward off disappointment and ill luck by registering here? Perhaps even to cheat death? Whatever their fates, these souls were alive and hardy here, and what else may we ever face death with but life?

Chapter 13

THEY WERE THREE days out from Register Cliff, and still Faith hadn't spoken, except to insist each morning that her wagon be last in line. Now in the Black Hills, the way was strenuous for both animals and people; no one had the energy to draw Faith out. It was hard work going always up or down hills and crossing the numerous streams that fed into the Platte from higher up. The road was no longer following close along the river, as it had in the wide, flat prairie, though sometimes there was a view of the narrow gorges through which the Platte was cascading, or the sound of wild geese quacking along it.

On the first day, Faith had loosened the puckering string at the back of the wagon cover and sat mutely at the tailgate. With the intensity of a sailor's wife scanning the sea's horizon, she watched the landscape of hills and scrub timber scroll out behind the wagon like a roster of her trials. On her lap she held Elizabeth's frayed sunbonnet and a crude doll Sarah had made for the child out of dried grasses. She stayed put at the noon halt, and though she ate the fried bread and roasted mountain hen Alice brought her, she held her fierce stare and didn't once look down at the plate.

On the second day, Jerusha led Faith to the front of the wagon to sit on the seat. Faith made no protest. She looked ahead as steadily as she had looked behind, but her eyes had lost their fever-bright concentration. She did not return Flinder's timid "good morning," and Flinder could not bring herself to say anything more.

The silence between the two women—the stiff-backed

one being jolted in her seat as passively as a sack of grain and the younger one walking beside the overtaxed oxen and guiding them over the rough track with shouts and whip-cracks—was so sovereign that over the course of the long day it came to seem to Flinder like an actual sound. It entered her ears as fully as the clatter of the wagon, the lowing of the oxen, and the stray filaments of voices that floated to them from the other wagons. Gradually the silence became the loudest thing Flinder heard.

The third morning passed similarly. Now, however, the silence was not only audible to Flinder, but tangible. She felt it first along the side of her body that was next to the wagon. Her right shoulder sloped down, as if a heavy coil of rope lay on it.

Then the weight spread across her back and chest until her whole body was encased by the silence. The wagon was moving, but its complaining creaks and rattles were muffled. She felt stones tumble away beneath her feet, but she did not hear them knock against one another. It was only by a great effort of will that she managed to keep watch on the team. The snap of the whip came to her as from a distance. At last she drew the wagon to a halt and climbed onto the wagon seat beside Faith. Faith took no notice.

"I tried to stop in time, Aunt Faith. You must know that. I did all that I could."

Though Faith turned and looked at Flinder, she did not answer her. Flinder found no accusation in her aunt's eyes, but there was no forgiveness either. There seemed, in fact, to be nothing there at all. Flinder realized that Faith, too, was enclosed in silence, a silence more terrible and more tenacious than her own. Even from within her grief, Flinder knew at her core that her silence was a cloak she would manage to slough off, but Faith's silence, it came to her, had become skin.

Flinder stood up. Faith lifted her gaze to Flinder, but she still did not speak. Though pregnancy had swollen Faith's belly and breasts, and sorrow had aged her face, she appeared almost waiflike beside Flinder's straight, solid adolescent frame.

A sudden wind came up. The cedars and pitch pines around them swayed and rustled softly. Flinder lifted her hair; the chilled feel of the wind on the sweaty back of her neck filled her with a mysterious passion. She drew in a deep draft of cool air and exhaled shakily.

Sudden tears streamed from her eyes and down her face. Flinder dropped her arms to her sides and tilted her face to the sky. She had to close her eyes against the sun. Then she began to sing.

The song was as unexpected as the tears had been, and Flinder abandoned herself to it, singing more and more loudly until her voice lost its tremolo and she felt the heat of the sun on the roof of her mouth. Somewhere in the middle of the song, Faith slipped her hand into Flinder's and began singing along in a whispery cadence one beat behind Flinder.

When she reached the end of the song, Flinder began it again.

"One more river, there's one more river to cross," she sang out. Now and then a sob still broke through a word, but she kept on, undaunted, ebullient.

"Flinder Hall, what is this foolishness?" shouted Roy, who had come running when Gideon noticed Faith's stopped wagon.

His shout interrupted not only the song, but the consuming passion as well, and Flinder was as startled as if he had yanked her from a dream by dousing her with cold water as she slept. Still, a vibration, like that of a plucked harp string, reverberated within her, making her feel fired with strength. She sat down calmly, still holding Faith's hand. Looking toward the other wagons several hundred yards ahead, she saw Jerusha approaching with hurried steps.

Roy pulled hard on Flinder's skirt to get her attention. She frowned down at him.

"There's no cause for singing on this wagon, young lady. And, as far as I can see, no cause for stopping either," Roy said, surveying the wagon and the oxen for problems.

"Must everything have a reason?" A slightly plaintive note in her voice modulated the bite of disrespect.

Roy glared at Flinder. He seemed unsure how to react.

"Such questions are for preachers, not for farmers' daughters," he finally replied. "You'll rue it if this wagon stops again without a plain-faced cause."

He paced off toward the other wagons and motioned Jerusha to follow. She had been standing to one side observing Flinder and Faith curiously.

When Roy reached Faith's lead yoke of oxen, he stopped, as if he'd had an afterthought.

"Girl," he barked to his daughter, "you'd best keep in mind those who are aggrieved in this party, and hold back your joyful noises and sporting ways."

He turned his back on her and began walking away.

"Pa!" Flinder yelled defiantly, standing up and releasing Faith's hand. She was frightened, but also gratified, to see his back stiffen when he halted.

"Flinder," Jerusha hissed, stepping close to the wagon, "sit down."

Flinder ignored her mother. Roy turned slowly. The man and the girl regarded each other over the thick heads and broad backs of the patient oxen. Flinder was the center of a triptych, flanked by Faith's smooth, wounded vacancy and Jerusha's furrowed anxiety. She drew steadiness from one and alertness from the other. The boldness was her own, fueled by a furious trust in her emotions.

"Your words wrong me, Pa," Flinder declared. "I am not an unruly child. I am not a child at all any longer."

"You *are* a child," Roy countered angrily. "Your very actions bespeak it."

"Which actions, Pa? Singing? Killing Elizabeth? Kindling Jack Webster?" Flinder's voice got more shrill with each question, but her self-possession did not waver.

"You go too far," Roy said, his words choked with anguish and menace.

Roy strode forward purposefully, but before he reached the wheel yoke of oxen, Jerusha had gotten up on the wagon seat and placed her bulk between her daughter and her husband. Indeed, she'd moved so rapidly, she appeared to have leaped rather than climbed there. Flinder would not cower behind her mother; she faced her father squarely over Jerusha's shoulder. But she was wary enough of the vehemence of the situation to let her parents speak first.

"Get down, Jerusha," Roy ordered darkly.

"She's endured too much already to have her own father berate her," said Jerusha, holding her ground.

"She's disgraced me."

"Roy, she's your only daughter now."

"She's your only daughter, too, and you may have her."

Roy, mumbling an oath under his breath, stepped back from the wagon. It was clear by the set of his legs that he intended to return to his own wagon without further action, but he was hesitating.

In that suspended moment, Jerusha suddenly turned to Flinder and slapped her hard across the face. Just as suddenly, she turned away from the stunned girl and gathered her skirt in order to climb down from the wagon. Roy came forward to help her.

Flinder, her cheek stinging, stood very still, willing down tears. She knew she had won something here and that tears would diminish it. She felt consumed with stillness, as she had earlier felt consumed with silence and then with song.

Flinder caught Roy's eye briefly over the curve of her mother's back as Jerusha bent to descend. He looked tired, and his face was more lined than she remembered it. She wondered if she appeared at all different to him.

Flinder sat down and watched her parents depart. They walked side by side about five feet apart, apparently not speaking. Neither one turned back to look at her, but she didn't mind. If it were she walking away from them, she wouldn't have turned either.

NINE DAYS OUT from Fort Laramie, after more than one hundred miles of rugged hill country, the Muller party arrived at the northerly bend of the Platte where the river had to be crossed and at last left behind. Beyond the Platte, they would have to traverse a desertlike region fifty miles wide and pocked with poison springs before hitting the next riverside trail along the Sweetwater.

They stopped at the mouth of Deer Creek. Other emigrants were camped nearby along both the creek and the river, though the congestion was far less than at the early stages of the trek.

The Platte here was two hundred yards wide, deep and icy cold, with a swift, rolling current. A crude sign announced the Mormon ferry at Upper Crossing, a day's journey ahead. According to the notice, the Mormons also offered blacksmithing and teeth-cleaning services. A few other ferrying operations were in business between Upper Crossing and Deer Creek, run by companies who had stopped for a week or so to make some money by constructing cottonwood rafts and taking parties across at anywhere from three dollars to five dollars a wagon.

"Well, Henry," said Roy, excitedly rubbing his hands together over the fire, "first thing tomorrow, we'll caulk the wagons for floating them over the river, and by nightfall we'll be camped on the other side."

"I think we should wait for a ferry," Henry replied quietly.

"But that could be two or three days!" Roy sputtered.

"The animals could use the rest, as hard as we've been driving them."

"Ain't no fit grazing here, Henry. The sod's been picked at by hundreds of teams already."

Roy was still rubbing his hands together, but what had begun as a gesture of gleeful anticipation had taken on a nervous quality. Alice, beside Henry at the fire, watched Roy tug at his orange beard and stare pointedly into the flames as if he did not want to look squarely at Henry. She wondered if Roy did not trust himself to hold his temper, obviously on a short leash already, or if he feared the sensibleness of Henry's arguments would win him over once he met him eye to eye.

"We'll take advantage of the wait to drive our animals up the creek to find better feed," Henry continued reasonably. "Maybe even cut grass to carry. There'll be some barren miles between here and the Sweetwater River."

Roy was silent for a few minutes, and when he finally looked at Henry, it was with the gaze of a daydreamer; to Alice it seemed that Roy was peering through Henry. Then the muscles in Roy's face shifted ever so slightly, his expression first acknowledging Henry's presence, then tightening into distaste.

"Barren miles are the only kind ahead, far as I can see," Roy muttered.

Henry took a deep breath and let it out before speaking.

"Royal, this is one of the most dangerous places on the trail. Animals drown here every day. Men, too, sometimes. We'll wait for the ferry."

Roy stood up abruptly, spit into the fire, and strode away to his wagon.

"He wants soothing," Alice said, watching his angry departure.

"That's Jerusha's job, not mine," Henry answered, his voice gravelly with irritation.

"I suspect he's turned from her as he has from the rest of us."

"Turned?" Henry scuffed his boot toe in the dirt to bury some sparks that had flown out of the fire. "Don't put that much on it, Alice."

July 18, 1852

We started this morning at three o'clock and are now stopped for breakfast on the Sweetwater, which we gained after three hard days. I have just seen an otter glide into the stream. Inde-

173

pendence Rock lies in the near distance, looking as much like a huge whale as anything.

After ferrying the Platte, we headed directly over steep, sandy bluffs onto the heaviest road we have traveled yet. The animals and the wheels sank into the sand four inches. The dust churned up was mixed with the powdery, dried excrement of the cattle, mules, and horses who passed here before us, making breathing unpleasant. Strong winds added to our misery. One afternoon we were afflicted, too, by more mosquitoes and buffalo gnats than we've met before. Poor Gideon looked like he had measles, his face was so bitten.

We turned away from the Platte at Upper Ferry, and I felt I was leaving a loyal old acquaintance. As if in farewell, the ground along this part of the Platte was covered with little purple, pink, and white daisies. Except for Willow Spring, we found only bad water in crossing the broad valley leading to the Sweetwater. Blue-gray, dry sage bushes were the main vegetation, so our animals suffered from lack of water and poor grazing. Fortunately, we had the hay Roy and Henry cut to supplement their forage.

Mules have the sense to shun alkaline water, but oxen will indulge freely if not restrained. I have seen emigrants clubbing their oxen to keep them away from the poisonous pools. We passed more than one hundred dead oxen, bloody-nosed and bloated, some burst open and full of maggots. The smell in places was quite horrible. We didn't lose any oxen, but we did have three sicken. We doctored them with fat pork, tying it to stick ends and pushing it down their throats.

Besides the alkali pools, we passed many alkali flats— shining, white beds of what will be salt lakes in a more rainy season. Jerusha, on Bailey's assurance, scraped some of the snowy stuff up and was delighted to find it as good a rising agent for biscuits as saleratus. With such small diversions—the dry alkali, the view of the Sweetwater valley from Prospect Hill, some pretty green stones Sarah found—we comforted ourselves across this difficult leg. We are pleased to note, too, that there is no news of cholera since leaving the fort, as if the Black Hills had scoured it away.

Despite the hard pulling, we have not had to abandon any goods, as many others are still doing. We have seen, among other things, a sidesaddle, wagon tires, burnt wagons, a jack, boots, and stacks of bacon. Having lightened once already, a second round of deciding what to give up would befuddle and pain me.

Roy continues sour about what he considers our slow progress, and though he is not so bold to say so, I believe he resents Henry for curbing his zeal. To my mind, sixteen miles a day through such territory as we have just crossed is not indolence. Henry is wise to spare the oxen, for on this journey, we belong to them more than they belong to us.

Chapter 14

HENRY AND ROY stood on top of Independence Rock, almost two hundred feet above the valley floor. The climb up the smooth, sloping east face had been an easy one; all the women and children except Alice and Faith had managed it earlier. Now that group was on a mile-long tour around the base of the rock, so the men were alone, looking out meditatively across the vast, mountain-edged sage plain they had just finished crossing. Directly below, the Sweetwater curled through grassy banks past the massive landmark like a rivulet of molten silver. A constant, brisk wind at the summit added to the sensation of great height.

While Henry continued to stare out at the huge panorama of sky and land, Roy wandered around reading names. Here, as at Register Cliff and Chimney Rock, emigrants had carved into the rock or painted on it with axle grease or tar white or red lead. Nature, too, had subtly marked the rock with crusty patches of lichen that wiped the mottled granite with smears of lime green, rust, mustard yellow, and dark brown.

"Going to add your name?" Henry asked when Roy had circled around to him again.

"Naw I did the Chimney. How about you?"

"I don't think so. My mark will be on my land at the end of this journey."

A soft roll of thunder drew their attention. The sky far to the north was clotted with dark clouds. Gray curtains of rain hung down from them like a widow's cloak. Elsewhere the sky gleamed blue as a jay's back and was tufted with cottony clouds. The bad weather, moving southward, would pass them by.

"The end of this journey," Roy echoed thoughtfully.

"It shall have an end, Royal, though at times it feels not."

"Is that what you think of, Henry, while we walk and walk and push and pull those wagons every day—the end of the journey?"

"Well, of course," said Henry. "We must think of that. The better life we'll have, the fine new farms."

"The farms may be better," said Roy bitterly, "but they'll still be farms. And working them will mean the same sunup to sundown chores, over and over, as ever."

Henry looked at Roy in surprise.

"I could no more leave off farming than breathing," he replied. "Land is life, Royal—land and the things that grow and die and grow again in it under our hands. If a man doesn't see the wonder in that, he won't see the wonder in anything."

"But remember last winter in Indiana when we all talked of adventures, too?"

"In Indiana, adventures appeared to be as safe as sightseeing. And they were never to be our main purpose."

"John and Derrick were keen enough on them," Roy protested.

Henry turned up the collar of his pilot cloth coat against the insistent wind. He cleared his throat loudly before answering Roy.

"John and Derrick were young men. And they're both dead," he said tersely.

"But adventure is not just for young men, Henry. It's for any self-reliant man on the move, taking what he wants however he wishes and is able."

"Fool's gold, Roy, only fool's gold," Henry sighed.

"Are you calling me a fool, Henry Muller? Just because I'm not content with the same things you are?"

"No, Roy," Henry said patiently. He looked down, as if

studying the names scratched in the rock surface near his feet. The meek pose and a doleful note in Henry's voice assured Roy that no insult had been meant.

"It's I who played the fool, leading us all out here," Henry continued, still frowning down at the names. "I thought I could test myself—have an adventure, as you call it—with no harm done, and improve my holdings in the bargain. I thought I had strength and goodwill enough to surmount anything. As it is, I shall never forget what my dreaming has cost, and I shall look closely at any future dreams that might tempt me to leave again a good piece of land with my family whole and prospering on it."

As if embarrassed by his speechifying, Henry abruptly turned from Roy and began the long descent. Roy took a last glance at the sweeping vista. Scattered across the valley he saw moving yellow spots that were grazing antelope and a few black mounds that were buffalo. To the west, sharp mountains waited like short-tempered schoolmasters.

Roy felt enlarged by the view, as if all that lay around him were his own dominion. Henry's sour practicality, Jerusha's stiff-necked endurance, Flinder's rebelliousness—they all seemed petty annoyances not worth the attention of a man of vision. Even the deaths, which one by one had shocked and saddened him, felt here and now distant and impersonal, almost unbelievable, like newspaper stories of wars in foreign lands. Roy could feel the beat of his heart and the lick of the wind against his face. The idea of risking death had become more bracing than dreadful, enlivening Roy's quickened spirit all the more.

Roy soon caught up with Henry, who was walking slowly. Watching his brother-in-law's careful steps down the granite incline, Roy felt a sudden pitying tenderness toward him. Roy was reminded of the twinge of sorrow that had pricked his elation at setting off from Indiana when he had to say good-bye to his grandfather. The old fellow had been the only man in Roy's female-ridden childhood. His father had died when Roy was an infant. His mother and ten sisters had babied him long past the time he found it enjoyable, and he had never been able to prove his worth to his two brothers, many years older. They gave their hounds more attention and respect than they did Roy, and they were out of the crowded house before Roy was ten.

Wondering why he had thought of the leave-taking from his grandfather and why he felt separated from Henry, Roy realized it was Henry's cares he felt apart from. It was as if Roy were a convict newly freed from prison looking back through a barred window at a friend still inside. He could sympathize with his friend, but he could not regret his own release. Still, Roy was twitted by guilt.

"Henry," Roy said, wanting to give him some ease. "It was plain hard luck that did John and Derrick. Hell, things like that happen back home, too."

Henry stopped and turned to look at Roy. His eyes, a velvety brown, were as direct as a child's. And like a child's eyes, they seemed to be appealing to Roy to continue his soothing words. But Roy, who had spoken without a clear objective, had lost the vague impulse that had set him off, and he could think of nothing more to say. Henry must have realized that, because the openness and expectation faded from his eyes, and he turned again and began walking down the rock.

"We got work below," he said flatly.

THREE MILES FROM Independence Rock, the Sweetwater cut through Devil's Gate, where perpendicular granite walls rose four hundred feet above the river on either side. Fortunately, the Mullers did not have to take their wagons through this narrow gorge, but bypassed it over an easy hill a half mile to the south. The Sweetwater, though barely more than a broad stream, flowed through a wide valley of rolling hills between high mountain peaks and sharp ridges. The road was sandy in places, which slowed the wagons, and the river had to be forded a number of times, but generally the route was quite passable and supplied with good grass. It was hard to believe they were in the middle of the Rocky Mountains.

Alice was walking near the river with Flinder and Sarah looking for strawberries, huckleberries, and wild onions. She was thinking about the emigrants who had come in earlier years and how much more unsure and rugged their way had been. The first people through with wagons, in 1843 to Oregon and in 1844 to California, had had to smell their way west. In the ensuing years, new cutoffs were explored, trees cut, boulders pried aside, and even some steep areas leveled. There were small trading stations where provisions could be had, albeit at excessive prices. But the rivers are the same, Alice thought, and the plains and great rocks, and the chancy weather.

"Aunt Alice," Flinder said, interrupting her thoughts. "Were you ever parted from Uncle Henry? I mean, before you married."

Alice turned to her niece, whose cheeks showed an uncharacteristic blush. Flinder lowered her eyes from Alice's questioning look, ostensibly searching the ground for edible plants. Alice knew Flinder was really talking about her own separation from Jack, perhaps trying to determine whether or not to banish the young man from her thoughts.

"No, Flinder," Alice answered. "We've never been parted for more than a few days."

"Oh," Flinder said, disappointed.

"But I had another beau once," Alice offered. "And we were parted for months and months."

Flinder looked up with interest. So did Sarah. She knew her mother was referring to the mysterious Charles, whom her grandmother had alluded to once or twice as her mother's "other prospect," always implying that Henry had proved by far the superior man, even though he was a farmer. When Sarah asked Alice about her "other prospect," Alice had replied that Charles was a previous suitor whose company she had found pleasant, but who, in the end, had not shown the makings of a good husband. Sarah had been impressed by her mother's sensibleness. She wondered why Alice was bringing Charles up now.

"And when you parted, did you pledge to meet again?" Flinder asked.

"No, but we expected to."

"What happened?"

"Henry Muller happened," Alice laughed, though, of course, it had not been so simple.

"But suppose you had really wanted to meet this other beau again," Flinder persisted. "And he had felt the same. It could have happened like that, couldn't it?"

"Flinder, my dear, that is beyond answering. And if you are talking about Jack Webster, that, too, is beyond answering."

Flinder blushed again. Alice regarded her with sympathy.

"She found a letter from Mr. Webster at the post office," Sarah informed Alice.

Sarah was referring to a barrel at the base of Independence Rock on which someone had lettered POST OFFICE with tar. They had met such devices all along the trail, especially at landmarks and river crossings. Sometimes papers were affixed to boards, or messages were written on elk horns, rocks, cow or buffalo skulls and shoulder blades. Through this "prairie telegraph," people were able to leave advice and information for friends and relatives known to be coming along behind.

"Sarah!" Flinder scolded. "That's private."

"But you showed me, Flin."

Alice smiled at the girls. Sarah's interest in her cousin's experience with romance was understandable, as was Flinder's desire to share it with someone. Alice wondered if the erosion of innocence was always so poignant, or if she felt it so only because of her ties to these two girls on the trailing edge of childhood.

"May I ask what he wrote?" Alice said to Flinder.

"Only that he'd meet us in California, that I should look for him to come in the spring," Flinder replied in a carefully casual voice.

"Let me give you some advice, girls," Alice said, "though

you may not understand it until later on. Don't let today be only a bookmark between yesterday and tomorrow. For if you do, you may miss the love of your life, or even life itself."

The girls were listening, but Alice could tell it was only out of deference. No matter, she thought, for she was speaking as much to herself as to them, maybe more so. The journey had awakened Alice to the complexity of the present, which showed itself capable of the unexpected in ways both beautiful and horrible. She was beginning to realize that the present had always had this capacity, but that she had carefully turned from it, giving it only as much of her attention as was absolutely needed. She did not want to do that any longer.

As if to punctuate the conversation, a cold wind came up, and it began to rain lightly. Leaving the girls to devise more lighthearted exchanges, Alice headed for the wagon to get a shawl.

Walking quickly, Alice was not sure, but she thought she felt a ripple of soft thuds inside her. She stood still for a few minutes to let her body listen. Again came the unmistakable thrumming sensation.

She hadn't thought about the baby much lately. She had been very aware of the discomforts of the pregnancy, the occasional nausea and bouts of overwhelming sleepiness, the aching legs and swollen ankles, and in sudden moments she had experienced rushes of fear about where the coming labor would find her, but the baby as a distinct fact, as a new child, had not entered her mind since the Missouri River.

Now the tiny body had collided against its chamber, which was her body, and made itself known as someone apart from her aches and worries even as it was the source of them. The fluttery kicks said the baby was not her. It was, of course, something she already knew, but now she could truly inhabit the knowing. Alice felt rising in her again a bond with the stranger growing inside her, a bond that, though it did not diminish her cares, did strengthen her resolution to meet them.

She signaled to Henry as she came abreast of their wagon, and he called "whoa" to the oxen.

After she had retrieved her shawl and a woolen scarf for her head, Alice fell in step beside her husband.

"I hope the rain doesn't get any harder," she said, peering up at the ashen sky.

"You can hope till your heart bursts, but the moon doesn't heed the barking of dogs."

"Why, Henry, what a cold thing to say."

"It's only the truth. Better to face it than to hide from it behind futile wishes and gibberish."

"Gibberish! What is wrong with you? I make a passing remark on the weather, and you treat me as if I were a bothersome child or a half-wit."

"Your feelings are too tender," Henry said, dismissing her with no hint of apology.

"But that's what feelings are—tender. You'd know that if ever you uncovered your own."

Even in her anger, Alice knew this was not entirely fair. Alice relied on Henry's quietness and steadiness; it had attracted her to him from the beginning. Now she was upbraiding him for those qualities. Besides, he did, in fact, reveal his feelings to her often, though he was not a man at ease with words. She withheld corners of her heart from him at times, so why not allow him the same reserve?

They strode along in churned silence. The air between them seemed to shimmer like a mirage. Gradually Alice began to feel more sorrowful than angry. Earlier, when she'd been talking to the girls, Alice had realized that in the past several weeks she had actually fallen in love with her husband anew. Informed as it was by their years together and the upheavals of the journey, it was a more honest love than she had ever known.

Alice ventured a glance at Henry's face. Though he must have been aware of her doing so, he did not turn to her. She read in his furrowed brow not the annoyance that had been there a short while ago, but a sorrowing equal to her own. He was waiting for her to show him a way out of this impasse.

"Henry," she said quietly. "I've felt the baby move."

"First time?" he said.

"First time."

He looked at her and then at her belly, giving it an approving nod.

"You haven't said it, girlie, but I'd guess traveling now is not so easy on you."

The remark was Henry's peace offering to Alice, as Alice's news about the baby moving had been hers to him.

Henry had never expressed concern about any of Alice's previous pregnancies. He'd been a little nervous in the early months of the first one; Alice would catch him watching her with studious suspicion, as if he expected her at any moment to fall to the floor in a writhing fit. Alice had supposed then that Henry's worry stemmed from having seen his mother slowly fail through each pregnancy, always ending up lower in strength and spirit than she had begun, never fully regaining her health before the next pregnancy started.

But Henry had relaxed as Alice's pregnancy with Sarah progressed and she grew not weaker and more wan, but stronger and rosier. He took later pregnancies so much in stride, in fact, that she sometimes had to remind him in the latter months when she needed help lifting things or getting up out of chairs.

"You know," Alice said, "Jerusha said—and I thought she was correct—that had you known about the baby before we left Indiana, you wouldn't have put off going."

"No, I don't expect I would have. But I'm not of the same mind I was, and I'm wondering if we should have put it off. Or maybe even turned back. Now it's too late; we've come too far, and too much has happened. The only reasonable course lies in going on."

Here, then, Alice thought, was the root of Henry's bad temper. She watched him crack his whip twice in the air over the oxen's heads to encourage their pull across a patch of soft sand, and though his motions were purposeful and efficient, there was a rigidity to them, as if he were made of wood, not flesh and blood. Or as if he wished he were.

"It will be all right, Henry," Alice said, though they both knew there were no guarantees of that.

AFTER FIVE DAYS along the Sweetwater, the Mullers were traveling sixteen miles across a barren sandy plain dotted with sage and milky white alkaline ponds in order to avoid following a long northerly swoop of the river. They were still in the Rockies, though the broad Sweetwater valley belied it; the Wind River range, patched with snow, was visible to the northwest.

"Now, there's a curiosity," Henry called to Alice. "Must be Ice Slough."

Alice was in the wagon reading to Hank, who was suffering from an earache and a slight fever. Gideon was there, too, to keep Hank company and to escape walking for a bit. Alice put down the story paper, "Fanny Campbell," the tale of a woman pirate, and looked out to where Henry was pointing. She saw what appeared to be a marsh, an area about a mile long and a half mile wide covered with a medley of swamp grasses and sedges. The boys crawled forward to see, too, but Alice made Hank lie down again. He thumped onto his pillow with an exaggerated slam of his body and inaudible mutterings, obviously disgruntled to be left out of an excitement.

The party halted, and Gideon, delighted to be besting his cousin for once, jumped out of the wagon and ran after Henry and Roy, who were walking onto the bog with spades. After digging down through the tufted plants and muck about a foot, they hit not water, as would be expected in an ordinary marsh, but a six-inch-thick layer of ice.

Admonishing Hank to stay put, Alice joined the others, who had gathered around to see the men's strike. Even Faith showed an interest in the phenomenon, tentatively licking at a piece of ice Jerusha handed her. Jerusha had set herself up as

Faith's gadfly, keeping the still-retiring woman tied to all the group's activities. Jerusha looked forward to the arrival of Faith's baby, which she was sure would right her at last.

Henry and Roy used pickaxes to chop some chunks out of the ice to melt for drinking. Alice wrapped a piece of ice in her apron and took it to Hank. Gideon went with her, eager to lord over the older boy.

"Here," she said, handing Hank the ice in the apron. "Slide this over your brow and chest."

"Ice?" Hank said, amazement nudging aside his petulance.

"Yes, ice," Gideon emphasized with uplifted arms, as if he himself had produced it single-handedly out of thin air.

"How can ice keep here under the summer sun?"

"It's as when you lay straw over the ice blocks from the lake in our icehouse back home," Alice explained. "There must be a pond or spring beneath the grasses which freezes in winter. Then the turf blocks the sun enough to preserve the ice."

"It's God's gift to us in this desert," Gideon said.

"We'll see truer desert than this before it's done," Alice remarked, almost to herself.

"I shall come back here someday and dig up my own ice," Hank said, his peevishness returning.

"Come back? I think not," said Alice, amused that the boy would conceive such a plan.

"You don't know what I shall do," Hank answered crisply.

"I know you shall speak to me in a different voice than that, Hank Muller, no matter that you feel sick and deprived."

"Yes, ma'am," Hank mumbled, turning over on his side and closing his eyes to invite sleep.

Alice regretted her rebuke, though it had been deserved. Hank, at nine, was not as near to adulthood as fourteen-year-old Sarah, yet in the past year Alice had felt him moving steadily away from her, strutting away from her, it seemed at times. He did not climb into her lap anymore, nor ask for stories as often. He did not give her stories either, as he used to, of jaunts in the woods with his dog or of games and quarrels with other boys at school. She was sure she could feel him stiffen ever so slightly when she kissed him good night. He adroitly avoided her touch in public.

Last winter, Alice had carefully policed her actions toward Hank, had refrained from questions and caresses, had let him fumble through tasks alone without her help or advice. The restraint had made her feel hollow, and she had lived through a terrifying week when she'd thought that she did not love her son any longer and that that was exactly what he wanted. Then, just as suddenly as it had come upon her, the deadened feeling in her heart vanished. Of course she loved Hank, she'd thought when she looked out the window one day to see him racing across a shorn, frost-crusted field toward the house, and he loved her, but he would tread paths, in his mind and in the world, that she did not know, and that would keep them always apart. The only surprising thing about it was that it had come so young.

"Hank," Alice said now. "Do you want more of 'Fanny Campbell' to help you fall off to sleep?"

"Oh, let's do have more, Aunt Alice," said Gideon.

Hank did not open his eyes, only shrugged his shoulders and gave an almost imperceptible nod yes.

Alice found her place in the story paper and began to read. After a few paragraphs, Hank opened his eyes and shifted his position, stretching out one hand to rest it on his mother's knee. Alice resisted the urge to stroke his hand; the warm weight of it was portion enough.

Four miles on from Ice Slough, the Muller party made camp atop a steep bluff overlooking the willow-lined Sweetwater, which the road would rejoin the next day. The view encompassed the winding road on one side of the river and the numerous wagons, tents, cattle, and horses stretched along it, with clouds of dust floating behind those on the move. Distant noises rose to the bluff. In contrast, the other side of the river was empty of people and animals, even antelope or elk. The land spread out in silence and serenity, like a velvet skirt on a fat woman's lap.

FOUR DAYS LATER the river valley that had been laid out so prettily before them from their bluff-top campsite brought the Muller party to South Pass, which marked the Continental Divide and the halfway point of their journey. Here they had as many miles behind as in front of them, and more than one of them wondered privately whether they could count half the happenings of the journey as done, too.

South Pass, a wide, dry plateau, was not a dramatic-looking place, though it stood over seven thousand feet above sea level. To the north the mountains were timbered with pine and poplars, and the ravines were filled with snow. To the south, tan, rolling hills were dotted with dark bushes. The wind was strong and constant. Occasional forb meadows scattered the broad sage plain with green areas where pregnant and nursing elk, antelope, and mule deer ranged.

Henry, through a careful reading of Fremont, the famous explorer, determined the exact position of the Divide and called everyone to a halt. The small group of people gathered to hear his announcement about their significant location.

"We stand at the summit of the continent," he said. "The rivers we've followed so far all flowed eastward, back towards old associations. The next stream we meet will drain toward the Pacific."

He fell silent, seeming unsure of what else to say or do, but reluctant to disband them so quickly.

"We ought to celebrate, at least in some small way," Bailey said.

"We ought to pray," Gideon said.

Flinder frowned at her sober little brother. Then, smoothing her features, she extended her arms, taking up Sarah's hand on her right and Jerusha's on her left. Jerusha took

Faith's hand, and Sarah reached out for Alice. They, in turn, held out their free hands to others, and a rough circle formed.

"I'll lead the prayer," Flinder declared. Her voice was so sure and her face so cheerful, no one contradicted her.

"Dear Lord," she began. "Thank You for making this easy passageway through the mountains. Please draw close to You our loved ones, Ellen, Elizabeth, John, Helen, and Derrick, and watch over distant friends. And keep the rest of us well and together, as we need one another's help and comfort as much as we need Yours. Amen."

"And," amended Jerusha, "we are grateful to be in Your hands. Amen."

August 1, 1852

We are in the roughest mountain country yet, with high ridges, pine forests, and many streams. After South Pass, we chose Sublette's Cutoff to the Green River, following the Big Sandy a ways, then crossing a ten-mile desert area of no water and no grass. It was hard on the weaker oxen, and we woke up one morning to one dead. Now we have no oxen that are out of yoke. The very steep descent down the sandy bluffs to the Green River was difficult; a Mormon ferry took us over the Green for three dollars a wagon. Bailey found a herring fish fossil on the riverbank. We will rejoin the old trail, coming up from Fort Bridger, at the Bear River.

We have not lacked for human contacts. At Ham's Fork we encountered a Shoshone village of about fifty buffalo-hide tepees, though the range of the buffalo ended at South Pass. Another day we met a Mormon from Salt Lake City scavenging for abandoned iron articles. At Fontenelle Creek we found an unsavory camp of old mountaineers living in tents and skin lodges. Each seemed to have several wives, both squaws and white women, so there were plenty of children of varying color about. They were selling horses and Indian goods, though they appeared more interested in drinking whiskey and playing monte than in business. They were fine riders, though; we were treated to the show of a few of them racing hard over uneven ground after a runaway pony.

At Soda Springs, at the end of the Bear River valley, emigrants for Oregon, who so far have traveled the same route as ours, will split off northwest to Fort Hall. It occurred to me at South Pass, the dividing line of the continent, that this journey has been a collection of divisions. The children are growing, as children never stop doing, and that growth will eventually take them from us. The adults are sorting through the dreams and fears they set out with and measuring them against what they have really met. For me, though my vagabond thoughts still wander at times to the people and places I have left, my parting from them is now so complete that I imagine I'd look on them with judging (yet fond) eyes if I were to be among them again.

The dews are heavy and the nights very cold. I've pulled out our mittens and heavy coats. I feel the baby most every day. He reminds me that life beats in the present because it was seeded in the past, and he turns my heart to the future.

Chapter 15

WE SHALL FEAST tonight," said Henry, laying two ducks and a goose on the ground in front of Alice and Jerusha.

"I should say so," said Jerusha, lifting a string of speckled trout from the wagon tongue. "I traded a calico shirt of Roy's for these from a Snake Indian who passed by while you men were away."

"And the children found yellow and black currants and rhubarb," Alice added.

"This is a fine valley," said Henry.

The way through the Bear River valley was largely level; only in a couple of places did canyons force the trail away from the river and over hills. It was a luxuriant area of thick grass, flowers, rushing streams of clear, cold water, and abundant wildlife. For the first time, they were somewhere that looked to Alice as she had expected the mountains of the West to look. Henry had grown more cheerful on this leg; travel here was as restorative as rest in less hospitable places.

"We've even had baths," Alice exclaimed.

"I believe I'll take your lead, ladies," Henry said. "I've been questioning if I'm still myself under all this trail dust."

"There's a sheltered spot a few hundred yards upstream," Jerusha offered.

Alice gave Henry a towel and soap out of the wagon, and Jerusha went to her wagon to get the same supplies for Roy, whom she saw leaned against a nearby willow smoking. She figured he must be pouting over not having shot any fowl. She knew he would have been sure to accompany Henry on his delivery if even one of the dead birds had been his.

The men gone, Jerusha set about preparing the fish and the ducks and goose for cooking. Jerusha was still nettled by open-air meal-making, but the afternoon was so pretty, she was able to find some pleasure in the work today. She smiled at the sound of songbirds and the feel of a breeze over her face and her forearms. The camp was empty and quiet, a rare experience.

Bailey was off sketching on a rise that gave a good view of the valley, and she had convinced Faith to go with her. Faith had resumed being sociable, though she still slipped frequently into lengthy brown studies. The children were downstream looking for more currants.

Jerusha was so enjoying the solitude that she had been working ten minutes before she wondered why Alice was tarrying inside the wagon. Jerusha had been humming "Oh, Susannah" not six feet from Alice's wagon, so Alice must know she was there, and sense should tell her Jerusha needed help. A little perturbed, Jerusha wiped her hands on her apron and went to the wagon.

"Alice, you asleep?" she called.

"No," came the barely audible reply.

"Trying to sleep?"

"No."

"Good, on account I could use some help out here."

"Jerusha, I'm afraid."

Jerusha felt her heart stumble a beat. Her mother had used the very same words all those years ago when Jerusha had brought newborn John to her after the midwife had dried him and swaddled him in a blanket.

Jerusha touched the tiny sapphire earrings her mother had folded into her hand that same day she had said she was afraid. She gave her a pair of tiny rubies, too; both sets of earrings had been in Jerusha's mother's family for generations, passed to the eldest daughter on her twenty-first birthday. Jerusha had not wanted to tire her mother with questions when she was given them at the age of twelve; the questions could wait until her mother was stronger, Jerusha had thought. But her mother had lived only one more day after making the gift.

Jerusha's mother had rarely worn the earrings; Jerusha's father said pierced ears were wicked. But a week after the burial, Jerusha had gritted her teeth and pushed a sewing needle through her earlobes, and she had worn one pair or the other every day since. They were her only ornaments.

"Afraid?" Jerusha said, trying to marshal her composure. "Whatever can you mean, afraid?"

"I think the pains are on me."

Pain. Here was something Jerusha could combat. She climbed into the wagon.

Alice was lying curled on her side, legs drawn up, one hand under her cheek and the other hand on her belly. She reminded Jerusha of a sleeping child. Ellen came to mind, and again Jerusha's heart stumbled.

"What pains?" Jerusha whispered, though she already suspected the answer.

"It can't be, I know, but it feels like birthing pangs."

"Come and go regular?"

"Yes."

"Have you taken some whiskey to halt them?"

"Yes. It took no effect."

This was not a good sign, but Jerusha did not want to admit that a process had begun that neither of them could stop. And even if she had believed it, she was wise enough to know Alice was not ready to hear it yet.

"Well, it's not been long, has it?" Jerusha encouraged. "Most likely they'll pass. Just you stay quiet now."

"I thought maybe the cold water earlier . . ." Alice said.

"Yes, yes. You rest. I'll go on out. Supper'll just have to be late. Hunger is the best sauce, anyway."

Quiet, Alice thought after Jerusha had left, yes, I'll lie quiet, and the day is certainly quiet—I can hear bees droning—but will my body be quiet? There, again, another pull. It stops my breath, it fills me, stronger than the last one. How can I still it?

Tentatively Alice stretched out her legs as the contraction

193

subsided. She rearranged herself more comfortably, moving her body as carefully as if it were made of fine porcelain. When she felt another contraction gathering, she groaned, not from pain, though pain was there, but from a growing sense of helplessness. In every labor, Alice knew, the moment came when the mother had to surrender to the forces working within her, like a leaf in a current. But Alice refused to do that now because this was a labor that should not be; she set her will against it.

Her body quieted; for good, she let herself hope. She heard a metallic clatter as Jerusha tended to some task outside. She was about to call to her for a drink of water when another, stronger contraction began. Its mounting energy washed over her, making it impossible for her to speak. Her womb was gripped in a hard rush of pain, and in its center lodged a tiny spot of yielding softness. She closed her eyes. Her ears were deadened to all sounds except her own breathing and the moan that marked the contraction's peak.

Again the pain subsided. Her surroundings returned to her. Then another surge that pushed them away. A pause. And another surge. She felt her insides being pried open and her will being overridden.

She pulled a comb out of her hair and clenched it in her fist. The sharp little points of pain in her palm made the insistent tumult within her easier to bear.

She knew even as she fought the knowledge that this was not going to stop, that her baby would be born and would die before it even truly was a baby, that it would lie, a fantasy child, caught in her mind as if in amber, at times tugging at her as strongly as her flesh-and-blood children did. With the next pain, Alice felt warm liquids gushing from her and a powerful downward pressure pushing through her torso.

"Jerusha!"

Jerusha straightened up from the fire where she was brewing black cohosh tea for Alice. The anguished cry told her all she needed to know. She reached for the clean rags she had gotten from her wagon. She'd been saving them for Faith's labor.

"I was just fixing some black cohosh," she said as she entered Alice's wagon.

"It's too late for that," Alice said, throwing back the light blanket covering her so that Jerusha could see the blood on her dress.

Without a word, Jerusha set to work, helping Alice undress, clean herself, and put on a nightgown. She found the fetus and took it to the end of the wagon where the light was brighter, wiped it dry, and wrapped it in a small cloth. It was only seven inches from head to rump and weighed about a pound.

"It would have been a girl," Jerusha said gently as she handed the little bundle to Alice. Then she took the rags outside to rinse them.

Alice unfolded the cloth and looked with disbelief at the creature in her hand. The translucent skin was red and wrinkled and covered with downy hairs. The head was too big for the lean body. Alice touched her fingertip to the fused eyelids and the miniature fists, and traced the elegant curve of the spine. Rather than appearing new or unfinished, the tiny baby looked ancient and complete, with an integrity indecipherable by the grosser humans who had grown beyond it.

She must have a name, Alice decided, refolding the cloth around the fragile body as carefully as if it were a living baby who needed protecting from chills. A name is all I can give her now.

The wagon jiggled, and the canvas was yanked roughly open. Alice squinted as the sunlight fell full on her face. Henry stood looking in at her, as if the power of forward movement that had got him up on the wagon had been suddenly drained from him.

His hair was still wet from his bath. His clean shirt was unbuttoned. Despite his beard and his distressed expression,

195

he reminded Alice of a boy fresh from swimming, a boy in the midst of his last carefree summer.

That impression was brief, however. Tears blurred the boy out of her vision. She lifted one hand from her lap and raised it slowly to her face. As if cued, Henry entered the wagon and pulled her against him.

The canvas flapped closed behind him, and Henry was enveloped by the wet, slippery smells of birth. Alice's face felt hot against the cool skin of his chest.

"The baby . . ." Alice began.

"I know, I know." Henry rocked her gently.

He did not want her to talk. He himself had no words pressing to be said. Henry trusted silence more than he trusted speech. Words seemed to him like the strange tools of some obscure craft he had never learned.

He wanted right now to simply enfold Alice and stand witness to her sorrow. He wanted her to feel that his arms and his caring could contain what had happened to her and could make it something that had happened to him, too.

She leaned against him for what seemed to both of them a long time, though neither of them wished to disengage. Sometimes she wept softly. Sometimes he let out long, low-pitched sighs that were almost like chants.

They heard the others return to camp from their various outings. They heard Jerusha crossly shush each one, then a murmur of voices, and then quiet until the next arrival.

At last Alice sat up straighter and smoothed her hands over her face and tangled hair.

"I want her to have a name," she said.

"Is there one you favor?" Henry asked.

Alice shook her head. She lowered her gaze to her lap. Henry watched her gingerly lay one flattened hand on each of her thighs. The folded bundle still lay in the hollow her long nightgown made between her legs.

Henry stretched to one side of the wagon and pulled the Bible from its niche inside a small leather-covered trunk.

"Let's look in here," he said.

He turned the thin pages quickly, scanning the stories of the Old Testament for names. Finally he handed the book to Alice and pointed to the middle of the page. It was the Book of Ruth.

Alice shook her head again. Ruth had traveled into a strange country, it was true, but in this Ruth stood for duty and submission. What did the otherworldly being in the cloth on Alice's lap know of those? She had only known darkness and liquid and heat, the thumping of her mother's heart, the churning of her mother's gut, and the roll of her mother's gait.

"I want a name that suits," Alice said.

Henry shrugged. He took the Bible from her hands and replaced it in the trunk.

The loss of the baby saddened Henry, but only vaguely. He didn't share Alice's need to act in some way against it. The fact of the lost baby lay in his mind like a flecked stone at the bottom of a pond.

"How can you find a name for one who never was?" he said.

"She was. In my mind, she was."

"What was she?"

"A thought. A question. A fellow traveler."

"Then call her Pilgrim."

Alice looked into Henry's eyes as if she had just noticed him. Indeed, although she'd touched him and spoken with him, she'd felt alone. The blood still flowing from her was more real than he was. Henry, the noises outside, and the jumbled contents of the wagon had all seemed ghostlike in comparison to the clammy bulk of her body and the burden in her lap.

"Then call her Pilgrim," Henry had said, and because the name was right and because he had given it, Alice was no longer alone.

"Pilgrim," she said, nodding.

Alice took down the sewing bag hanging on a wagon bow near her and pulled a pair of scissors and the blue ribbon from

Fort Laramie out of it. She fingered the velvet a moment, then cut the ribbon in half and tied one piece of it around the baby's wrapped body.

With a quick movement, she handed the small bundle that would have been their daughter to Henry, who took it outside to bury it.

When he had left, she readied herself for sleep. She fixed a clean rag between her legs and wrapped the soiled one in a scrap of India-rubber blanket. She brushed out her hair and tied it loosely at the nape of her neck with the other half of the velvet ribbon. Finally, she took a quick swallow of whiskey and lay down.

These practical actions, taken after Henry's sitting with her, calmed her. She knew the heartache had been only temporarily dulled, but she was tired enough to accept the respite gratefully.

THE SMALL BAND lingered around the fire, which Jerusha kept stoking, delaying the dispersal to their separate sleeping quarters. Supper had been the feast anticipated, but minus the holiday spirits of the afternoon. Alice had eaten in her wagon, with Henry for company. To have both of them absent from the meal underlined the sad fact of the miscarriage and added to the group's dejection. There was a misshapen, indecorous feel to the gathering, as if they were seated at a long dining table and the two set places at either end, the places of the hosts, were vacant. When, at last, Henry joined them, there was a subtle rustle among them like bits of gravel sliding out from the depression of a footprint.

"How is Alice now?" Jerusha asked him.

"Setting to sleep," Henry said, handing the two empty plates he carried to Sarah, who had stood up to take them.

"Come, have some coffee," Jerusha said, pouring him a cup before he could refuse it.

Henry took it and sat down in Alice's rocker, which was positioned just beyond the reach of the firelight, where henna shadows diffused into the surrounding night. Faith watched Henry there, the pensiveness in his expression, the prayerful clasp of his big fingers around the tin cup, and despite his beard and his older age, she saw his brother John in him, John as he might have come to look as the years and the cares added up.

Faith felt a tremor pass through her. She pulled her shawl more tightly around her shoulders and stepped in closer to the fire. She concentrated on the dance of the low flames and twists of smoke over the greasewood sticks, but visions of John continued to dog her mind, John asleep beside her, John pulling stumps with Henry, the back of his shirt dark with sweat, John calling to her across the barnyard. Then, close behind him, Faith spied Lizzie peeping from around her father's long legs, as she sometimes had in true life when she felt shy before strangers. A brittle net of guilt pierced Faith's melancholy like boiling candy syrup poured into cold water. She looked quickly around at her companions, half-expecting to meet accusing fingers and blaming stares.

"And Ma is all right?" Sarah was asking her father.

"Of course she is," Jerusha interrupted. "She'll be fit as a fiddle in a day or two, mark my words."

"Though she keeps to herself, she is not alone," Henry said, reaching out to pet his daughter's shoulder. "That shall see her through."

"Faith," Jerusha said loudly. "Mind your skirt. It's too near the flames."

Faith, surprised at being addressed, stepped back obediently.

"You may have my seat," Bailey offered, getting up from her canvas camp chair. "I'm taking to my tent."

"You children must be off to bed now, too," Jerusha scolded, as if just aware of their presence. "Flin, settle Gideon in the wagon; Sarah, lay out the bedrolls for your brother and your father."

Everyone truckled into action, including Jerusha herself, who began lifting quilts and blankets off wagon wheels, where they had been set to air earlier in the day. When she handed two to Sarah, she gave the girl a firm kiss on the top of her head, then shooed her away, as if embarrassed at such a show of tenderness. Roy offered Henry his tobacco pouch, and both men filled and lit their pipes. Faith felt excluded from the scuttle of activity around her and the simple confidence underlying it.

"I shall make my good-nights, too, then," she said so softly that no one heard to respond. She was at her wagon before Jerusha noticed she'd left the fire.

"Sleep careful, now, Faith," she called.

Faith waved at her sister-in-law and climbed laboriously into the dark wagon. Her big belly would not let her do anything without care. If only her mind had some similar encumbrance so that it could not skate so often and so precipitously into dangerous recollections. Achingly sunny scenes from Elizabeth's three short years came unbidden to Faith almost daily, filling her with regret and confusion that such a vibrant being had fallen out of existence from beneath her very reach. And she was still infested from time to time, at night usually, by the sickening fondle of Reed's rough, unloving hands over her body, though she fought this memory hardest of all. Sometimes she was actually glad John was gone, so that he could not know her disgrace. She wished she could find a place of not-knowing, too.

August 13, 1852

Yesterday the day was bright and calm, the place lovely in ways only Nature can be lovely. Then, too, there are ways of disinterested cruelty that only Nature can contrive.

Yesterday Pilgrim was born along the Bear River a half day's journey before Soda Springs, where hot, effervescent waters boil and foam up out of the ground. Born and was left there. She shall never see this journal, as once I thought she would. She shall not sit on a hearth rug and hear the stories of our trip; instead, she has become one of the stories.

Today I am very weary and feel at once emptied and over-filled with emotion.

I am keeping to the wagon as a hermit might to a mountain fastness. I write of this time only to be able to reconstitute it later. Some small voice within me says that I shall want to, and though motherly grief claims it is a demon voice, I find it must be heeded.

Chapter 16

TWO NIGHTS later, Alice was wakened from a fitful sleep by her aching breasts. She slid a hand across her chest and felt two damp spots on her shift. Her breasts beneath the cloth were full of milk, round and hard as young melons.

She let out a long sigh. But Alice was weary of copious grieving. Too many times in the past two days, a bump in the road or the sound of a child's laugh outside or the flight of the moment of amnesia upon awakening had started her crying. Now she sat up and waited for her eyes to adjust to the darkness.

The wagon smelled of dried apples that still held some of the heat from the day. From her shift came the odor of sour milk. The scent of a baby, Alice recalled.

Henry turned in his sleep. His movement lifted a small cloud of fine powder up into Alice's face. Salty dust from the trail had invaded the wagon's interior and thinly coated its contents.

Alice had kept firmly to her self-imposed exile since the miscarriage, exiting the wagon only once when they were descending a defile so steep, the oxen trod ten feet below the level of the wagon wheels. Jerusha had locked arms with her as they walked, digging in their heels, stumbling and sliding, down the mountainside. Despite her feeling of disconnection from the scene, Alice did note how matter-of-fact they had all become with such descents; in the journey's early days smaller grades than this were considered great obstacles. Less than two weeks ahead, however, lay the drop into Goose Creek valley, which, by all accounts, was a frightful decline.

Now, in the night's silence, the wagon felt for the first time oppressively confining. Grabbing her boots and shawl, Alice scrambled out, taking no care to be slow or quiet. Henry, exhausted from a long day of twenty-nine miles, did not wake up.

The air outside was fresher than the air in the wagon. Alice drew a deep breath and wriggled her shoulders. She liked the feel of her body standing erect, though she was a little light-headed.

They were camped beside a brook in a small mountain valley, on their way to the Raft River via Hudspeth's Cutoff, a route pioneered by the gold-seekers of '49 in an effort to save miles by eliminating the main trail's northern jog to Fort Hall. It was Roy's urging that had put them on the cutoff, which made a more or less straight western push to the Raft River. Many California travelers continued to use the route through Fort Hall, dipping southwest from there along the Snake River to the Raft River, as there were differing opinions and reports on whether Hudspeth's Cutoff actually saved time or not. Other California-bound emigrants chose the course through Salt Lake City, despite the commonplace repugnance engendered by Mormons, because of the availability of provisions and fresh draft animals there and out of curiosity about the city in the desert with its fabled Tabernacle and the grand houses of Brigham Young, one for himself and one for his wives. But Roy had made a rough inventory of their supplies and convinced Henry they did not need to restock at Fort Hall or Salt Lake City.

"There may be a sameness to our fare," he'd declared, "but we won't starve."

Alice looked around her. By starlight, the wagons took on the appearance of boulders. It was unimaginable that they sheltered living beings or that they could actually move. A fear splashed over Alice that the wagons would, in fact, never move again.

"A foolish fancy," Alice chided herself.

She began walking toward the children's tents. She meant

to smooth their blankets. In truth, she wanted simply to look upon them for a few moments, to listen to them breathe. She needed this small ritual of watching sleeping children.

Alice was surprised to see a light and moving shadows in Flinder and Sarah's tent. Coming closer, she found the girls asleep in bedrolls on the ground several yards away. When Jerusha emerged from the tent, Alice went over to her.

"Jerusha?"

"Alice, what are you doing up?"

"I might ask the same."

Jerusha looked back over her shoulder at the lit tent. When she turned her face to Alice again, she seemed hesitant, almost apologetic.

"It's Faith's time," she answered, reaching out to pat Alice's forearm.

Alice felt a tingling in her nipples. Milk dripped from them. She laid her hand on the soft flesh over her abdomen. Only days ago, yet she could not summon up exactly how it had felt to be as Faith was now. How relentlessly forward–looking life is, she thought.

"How is she?" Alice said.

Jerusha's face took on a more businesslike expression.

"It's a slow one," she said. "The hardest pains aren't on her yet, though she's had them regular all day yesterday and all tonight. I was just off to sleep some. Miss Jeffers is spelling me. She's had no experience, but she was willing to sit. I told her to call me should Faith progress."

Alice stared at the tent.

"Go back to your wagon," Jerusha said, taking hold of Alice's elbow and attempting to turn her around with a gentle nudge. Alice would not move. She would not even look at Jerusha. Jerusha shrugged and walked away toward her own wagon.

Alice remained transfixed on the tent. Birth. The age-old drama was playing out again, and so near that Alice could be a part of it if she wished. A sharp, sweet sense of reminiscence tied Alice to Faith, who was repeating Alice's recent experience even as she was living one uniquely her own. Alice suddenly felt able at last to consider her turn over. It was Faith's time, as Jerusha had said, though she hadn't meant it in the same way Alice now did. She felt a muffled settling within her as when on a windless November day the last leaf drops soundlessly from an elm.

Alice returned to her wagon. Before going inside, she sat down beside the dead campfire and relieved herself of some milk.

Next morning she awoke to stillness. The two mornings after Pilgrim's birth, Alice had been awakened by the jerking forward of the moving wagon. All day she would drift in and out of light slumbers. The wagon bounced and rattled her even though the road was a good one, leading across a basin of lava formations and then up over hills and ridges.

After binding her full breasts tightly with a strip of cloth, Alice dressed and got out of the wagon. She could tell immediately by the sun that it was late morning. It seemed they were not going to travel today. She guessed Faith must be close to giving birth.

Henry was leaning against the wagon whittling. He put his knife and wood in his pocket and came to Alice. Shaping his hands along the curves of her jaw, he tilted her face slightly upward. He saw the circles under her eyes and the pallor beneath her sunbrowned skin, but he did not question her decision to be up and about.

"Welcome back, girlie," he said softly.

Alice laid her hands on top of his. She drew his hands away from her cheeks and clasped them firmly between her own. His hands were large and work-hardened, but she knew their capacity for secret delicacy. She found, now that it was over, that she had missed him during her private mourning.

Gideon and Hank, in the midst of a game of tag, ran by them shouting. Alice and Henry let go of each other's hands.

"What news of Faith?" Alice said.

"None since dawn when Jerusha told Roy we couldn't be moving her today."

"I'll just go see," Alice said.

Henry laid a restraining hand on her arm.

"None will blame you if you spare yourself," he said. "The other women can manage."

"Faith needs us all," Alice answered testily.

Henry let his hand drop.

"It's women's business, I know," he said. "I only meant . . ."

Alice, repentant, stepped closer to him and laid her hands on his chest.

"It's all right," she said. "I'm ready."

"Don't overreach yourself now," Henry said.

Nodding, she turned from him and walked slowly to the girls' tent. She paused a few moments before lifting the flap. Periodically she could hear short moans from Faith. She felt a small clutch in the pit of her stomach, but she took a deep breath and it passed. She would only be of use inside, she knew, if she could give herself over to the event, could read Faith's energy and help it flow strongly, and she did want very much to be of use right now. For both her sister-in-law and herself. After one more deep breath, she entered the tent.

Jerusha and Bailey were sitting beside a cot on which Faith, eyes closed, lay clenching and unclenching her fists. Bailey was wiping Faith's brow and throat with a wet cloth. The tent was humid with Faith's dampness.

Jerusha and Bailey looked up when Alice came in. Alice saw surprise in Bailey's face and approval in Jerusha's. Jerusha stood up and stepped out of the tent, motioning Alice and Bailey to follow.

"I'm worried," Jerusha said in a low voice. "She's much too feverish."

"How close is the baby?" Alice asked.

"I checked her a half hour ago. She was ready then. But she can't seem to bear down. Or she won't."

"Won't?" Bailey said.

"God helps them that helps themselves," explained Jerusha, "and it appears Faith has set her will against this birthing. She's got no fight in her."

"But surely her will or lack of fight can't stop the birth," Bailey said.

"Not forever," Jerusha said. "But it can slow things down a powerful lot, and sometimes taking too long leads to trouble. Bad trouble."

"If Faith won't fight," Alice said, "then we must do it for her."

She looked at Jerusha and Bailey hoping to meet an answering determination.

"All between the cradle and the coffin is uncertain," said Jerusha, "but you are right, Alice, that Faith must be taken in hand."

"If you tell me what must be done, I'll do it," Bailey said.

Alice nodded at both of them, and though she was worried about whether or not they could succeed in bringing Faith through, she could not repress a smile at their solidarity.

"Let's to it," Jerusha said.

The women reentered the tent, and Alice knelt beside the cot.

"Faith," she said loudly. "Look at me."

Faith groaned but did not open her eyes.

"Faith, it's Alice. Look at me."

Slowly Faith turned her face in Alice's direction. Slowly she opened her eyes. There was no recognition in them. She seemed to be looking through Alice to somewhere far away. Alice had seen that same cast to Faith's eyes in the days after Elizabeth's death, when Faith had stared from dawn until darkness at the horizon behind them, down the miles they had traveled away from Elizabeth's grave at Fort Laramie.

"Faith, your baby wants to come out. You must help it," Alice continued.

Faith's eyelids trembled. Her eyes large and round, like a frightened doe's, she looked back and forth from one woman to another.

"My baby's dead," she said at last.

Alice's heart leapt against her rib cage, and she looked at Jerusha in alarm.

"She means Elizabeth," Jerusha explained.

A series of quick images jittered across Alice's mind. Henry riding off with Elizabeth's body wrapped in a quilt and slung over his horse's rump; the hilltop graves in Indiana of her own dead babies; the blue velvet ribbon around Pilgrim's tiny shroud; the mound of rocks over Ellen. Standing up, she shook her head to clear it. Then she spread a blanket on the dirt floor.

"We're going to help you get up, Faith," Alice said.

Bailey and Jerusha each took an arm and coaxed Faith off the cot and into a squat on the blanket. Jerusha directed Bailey to kneel behind Faith so that Faith's buttocks could rest on Bailey's knees.

Alice laid her hand on Faith's belly. She felt it hardening into a contraction.

"Now you must push, Faith," she said firmly.

Faith looked at Alice, still as across a great distance, but with a glimmer of comprehension. With a loud, deep-pitched keen, she pushed.

"That's right, that's the way. You can do it," Alice said.

The pushing contraction faded, and Faith relaxed, leaning back against Bailey. Alice lifted a cup of heavily sweetened pennyroyal tea to Faith's lips. She took a few sips.

After several minutes, Faith spread her feet farther apart and began pushing again.

"Good, good," Alice encouraged.

Four pushes later, Jerusha declared she could see the water bag.

"Work's almost done, dearie," she said to Faith.

Jerusha went to a basin near the tent's doorway to wash her hands and forearms. When she returned, she sat on the ground in front of Faith. Her sleeves were pushed up and her plump arms were still wet.

Again and again, Faith lowered her chin to her chest and

pushed. Each time Jerusha shaped her hands into a circle and pressed gently against Faith's bulging skin. Between pushes Faith dozed, her face smooth, her arms limp at her sides.

No one spoke. The women breathed in rhythm with Faith, not by design, nor even in full awareness, but because Faith's power was drawing all their attention. She had become their pivot. Alice even grunted during Faith's pushes. No one heard her except herself.

Finally Faith gave a long, bellowing cry that spoke as much of amazement as of pain. Before her cry had ended she had cast the baby from her.

Clear liquid tinged with blood gushed over Jerusha's skirt as she caught the baby, whose head was encased in the silvery caul. Alice quickly leaned over, hooked her fingernail into the membrane, and peeled it back over the baby's face.

The infant, her fat body glistening and her limbs flailing, began to cry furiously. Her skin flushed from blue to pink. Alice passed Jerusha the linen swaddling cloth.

With Bailey's help, Faith climbed back onto the cot. She turned her back on them all and would not roll over even to make Jerusha's cleaning of her easier. It was as if the baby had gathered up the last vestiges of vibrant life in Faith and carried them off like so many eggs in a basket, leaving behind only a soft depression in the grass where they had lain.

August 16, 1852

Faith gave birth today to a girl. We have named her Hope. Faith refused to hold her. Even now, many hours later, Faith stays curled unto herself like a young fiddlehead fern. I have had to become the child's wet nurse until Faith comes around.

We all believe Faith's unnatural turning away from motherhood will not last. I heartily wish her well again in both body and spirit, but I will confide here that that wish does not dispel the comfort to me of an infant at my breast.

As Jerusha might say, I shall cut my coat according to my cloth. Pilgrim came too soon, but she readied my body for this baby. *The milk that urged more tears upon me and would have dried up in a few more days now nourishes Hope.*

She came to me. Faith carried her, and Jerusha caught her, but I called her forth. It's as if she'd been born twice, first out of Faith and then out of her caul. It's said such babies have good luck throughout life. A superstition, perhaps, but superstitions are the escorts of mystery and miracle, and I, for one, will not discount them.

Chapter 17

AITH SLEPT ALL day. Jerusha roused her twice for some food and to get her to change her lochia rags. Both times Alice brought her the baby, and though Faith looked at her new daughter and felt some of the wonder that any baby evokes, she did not want to hold her. It seemed strange to Faith that Hope should be here when John was not, that there should be a second child when she had failed the first. She did venture to trace two fingers along the baby's fat cheeks and chin, careful not to use the hand that Reed had sullied.

The weather being clear, the women set Faith up each night in the tent and had Flinder and Sarah sleep outside. Jerusha thought the extra comfort would lead Faith to accept Hope more readily than if she were housed in her wagon, where she lay all day on the move. Each evening Alice carried the baby into the tent, but each time, she emerged with Hope still in her arms and took the baby into her wagon to nurse. If Hope was asleep, Faith could manage to hold her, and she even began to look forward to the winsome fit of the tightly swaddled baby in the crook of her arms, but as soon as the child began to squirm or cry, Faith was seized with anxiety and quickly handed her back to Alice.

Just after sundown on the third day, as the light inside the tent honeyed and then grayed, Faith heard footsteps approach and stop outside. Alice had already made her daily call with Hope.

"Faith?" came Henry's voice through the canvas. "May I come in?"

"Yes," she answered, sitting up and smoothing her hair back away from her face.

Looking ill at ease, he came in and stood in the middle of the tent, pulling off his straw hat as if he were in someone's parlor.

"Alice said it would be all right to come," he explained.

"Yes, Henry, it is all right."

"Normally I wouldn't visit at a time like this, but as John isn't . . . John would have wanted me to make sure you were safe and looked after."

"I am," Faith said quietly.

Henry glanced around the tent, though there was nothing to see, only Faith's cot, and a pitcher of water and tin cup sitting on the ground.

"Do you recall," he said, looking at her face again, "at the Elkhorn, how I said you and the children would have a home with us as long as you wished it?"

Faith nodded.

"Well, I have thought on that some more. Especially with the new baby. And if you would prefer it, come spring, I'll take you and Hope to San Francisco and see you on a clipper ship back to the states, to your mother and your old friends. It's a long journey, but not as hard as this one maybe, and with a more looked-for destination."

Faith did not know how to answer this startling proposition. Her thoughts had been so much in the past in recent weeks, she had almost forgotten there was a future. She stared at Henry.

"That's what I've come to say," he concluded. "To put your mind at rest."

"To put my mind at rest."

Henry stepped nearer Faith's cot and knelt beside it, laying his arm across her back and nudging her head down onto his shoulder. It was then she realized that she had begun to cry. The feel of his man's body was a shock at first, but he kept so still and hummed so softly to her, as if she were a frightened child, that her instinct to recoil began to fade. Here was someone who felt John's loss as keenly as she did and who had found her Lizzie a proper resting place. Here was an unquestioning source of shelter.

When Henry did start to move, stroking her arm from her shoulder to her elbow and back again, Faith felt her initial alarm threaten to froth up and part her from his comfort, as if another set of hands had pushed Henry aside and were dunning her, covering her mouth and her nose to hamper her breath, hiding her eyes, cupping her ears.

The familiar despair billowed upward from the pit of her stomach, but close on its heels rode another, less well-known emotion. Faith was surprised to discover within her the sting of anger. It pumped through her so fiercely that her skin began to warm and prickle, as if she were covered with nettle rash. Desperately Faith resisted the urge to pull away from Henry and instead put her hand on top of his to stop its movement. He complied, spreading his fingers apart as Faith twined hers between them. She could feel his hard palm firm against her arm, and the coarse hairs and big knuckles of the back of his hand under hers. Faith felt as if she were a sapling in the midst of a roiling storm, with Henry's hand the earth in which her roots were sunk. Gradually the noise within her decreased, the anger pruning the despair.

"Faith?" Henry said, as her tears subsided and a rigidity crept into her back.

She did not answer him. When she lay down on the cot, he stood up, retrieving his hat from the floor.

"I'll send Alice again," he said. "With the baby."

"No."

The small tent felt crowded with ghosts demanding audience, and Faith found, for the first time, that she did not want to be released from them. Not even from Reed, whose scaly shadow seared the edges of her mind and stirred her gelatinous anger toward thick, silent hatred.

With a heavy sigh, Henry turned to go.

"Tomorrow, perhaps," she said to him before he exited, wanting to make some return for what he had brought her. "But not yet. Not yet."

HUDSPETH'S CUTOFF was presenting the Muller party with manageable passes, good grass, and sufficient streams, but the dust in places was a tribulation. The least breeze or footfall raised up the light, dry soil in great clouds that penetrated noses, eyes, and lungs. At times, a wagon only a few yards away was almost obscured.

On the afternoon of the fourth day after Hope's birth, Faith sat with Alice beside a creek. The baby, naked and gritty with dust, lay sleeping on Faith's lap.

Alice pressed a wet cloth into Faith's hand.

"Wipe her down," Alice urged quietly.

Nervously Faith began swabbing Hope. The baby kicked a little and rolled her head from side to side, coming by slow degrees out of her deep sleep, but she did not make a sound. Faith studied the little body as she worked on it, the tiny budlike toes, the fingernails like opalescent seashells, the soft, elastic skin. She wrapped a tip of the cloth around one finger and gently cleaned between the folds of fat at Hope's neck, elbows, wrists, and knees. Faith had not seen Hope naked before. The child was perfect, and Faith was awestruck by her.

Alice poured a small puddle of oil on Hope's chest. Faith hesitated, then began to spread it, massaging the baby's rounded limbs, which were curled up to her torso like sepals. Faith's hands warmed from the gentle friction, seeming to draw energy from the baby's body. Hope opened her eyes and gazed up at her mother with intent interest. Faith felt as if a pinpoint of light had appeared at the end of a long tunnel in which she'd been trapped for more days than she could remember.

Hope began to squall with her tinny newborn's voice. Faith touched the baby's cheek with her finger; Hope rooted eagerly towards the finger and began suckling it. In a few seconds, however, she rejected this substitute and started crying again. Alice stretched her arms toward the baby, but Faith, without thinking, snatched the child up and twisted around so that Alice could not reach her.

Holding Hope against her chest, Faith was reminded of her tender breasts; her milk had come in last night. Slowly she unbuttoned her blouse and shifted the baby, cradling her in her right arm. She leaned forward and lifted her breast carefully out of her chemise. Her movements had the inching deliberation of gestures in a dream. Hope, more animated than her mother, latched on to the proffered breast eagerly.

Faith winced at the pumping of the baby's hard gums. A minute later, she felt the pins-and-needles tingle in her nipples as her milk let down. Hope's frantic suckling calmed to a soft, sensual pace.

Breasts and hands. Hope had succeeded in calling back to life these two parts of her mother. The pinpoint of light was growing larger. Faith looked down at Hope's pink face. Enchanted and content, Hope had closed her eyes again. Elizabeth came to Faith's mind, how she had nursed in the same kind of peaceful ecstasy. Then she noticed the shape of Hope's nose and the widow's peak of her fuzzy, dark hairline, and she was reminded of John, from whom Hope had inherited these features.

Faith did not look up when Alice got to her feet. She was too engrossed in her baby and in all that was unfolding within her. She was only vaguely aware that Alice stood watching them for several minutes before leaving, biting at her lower lip and clutching her hands tightly together as if restraining herself from action. Ten minutes later, when Faith switched Hope to the other breast, she saw she was alone beside the creek, but she gave no thought to it. Ambushed by happiness, she was far too busy with thoughts of her own.

★   ★   ★

ALICE AND BAILEY stood beside the Raft River watching the children dangle baited strings in the narrow stream. The 134-mile long Hudspeth's Cutoff had brought them here along a route so southerly they had been able, from some bluffs, to see the Great Salt Lake, thirty miles away. The lake's dark, blue-green center was ringed by a wide expanse of salt, and high, black mountains rose beyond the white edging. Now they were on the old trail again, which had come down from Fort Hall. In a few days, at Steeple Rocks, the Salt Lake City trail would also meet this route.

"I wonder if the children will catch any freshwater lobsters," Alice said.

"If sheer determination counts, Flinder surely will," Bailey laughed.

Flinder had tucked the hem of her skirt into the waistband and was wading into the river. The skirt soon slipped its mooring, and the lower half of it dropped into the water. After a halfhearted attempt to hold it up with her hands, Flinder let it go and strolled through the shallows as unconcerned as if she were on dry land.

"They'll get your toes," the women heard Sarah shout to Flinder. Sarah, on the bank, was patiently tying rancid bacon onto strings for Gideon.

"Then I'll know they're there, anyway," Flinder called back.

"Your toes or the lobsters?"

"Both!"

"And there," said Bailey to Alice, "we have Flinder in a nutshell."

Alice smiled agreement at Bailey, but the smile quickly subsided. In the past several days, she had found it difficult to sustain lightheartedness for long. This made her feel out of step with the rest of the party, who were generally in good spirits. She knew her melancholy derived from Faith's claiming of Hope, and because she was ashamed to feel downcast over an event in which everyone else rejoiced, she had not told anyone of her feelings. Hiding her injured heart in this way added to her sense of separation from the group.

"I got one! I got one!" called Sarah elatedly, pulling up one of the lines she had fastened to a branch overhanging the river.

Bailey picked up a bucket from the ground near her and took it to Sarah. Hank and Gideon hurried from their fishing posts to see. Alice watched the flurry of excitement over the first crayfish from where she was.

"Alice," Faith's voice came from behind her.

In the clamor of the children, Alice had not heard Faith arrive. She turned to face her and found her, as Faith was always to be found lately, with Hope clasped lovingly in her arms. The sight still tugged at Alice, no matter how sternly she told herself it was how things were meant to be.

"Alice," Faith repeated. "I've been thinking. About how you helped me at the birthing and took care of my baby after."

"You would have done as much in my place," Alice said with a wave of her hand, hoping to stave off a lengthy speech of gratitude.

"I'd like to believe so, but I don't know that I would have had the strength of heart, not so soon after losing my own baby like you did Pilgrim."

Alice took a step away from Faith and turned to look out over the river. There was not much to see. It was quite a small river. But Alice did not trust herself to stay so close to Faith and Hope. She did not want to cry; she did not want to have to explain her tears.

"Faith," Alice said sincerely, turning back to her sister-in-law. "I'm just glad that you're well again."

"Yes, I'm well enough, but sometimes, Alice, I still feel . . . sort of broken inside. I think maybe you know a little what I mean."

Alice peered into Faith's eyes. A haunted look still flickered there, like a will-o'-the-wisp over a marsh. But Alice saw, too, a new serenity and strength in Faith's gaze, and a kind of wisdom. Had Faith's misfortunes attuned her more to the

217

subtle wounds others suffered? Certainly no one else, not even Henry, had seemed to notice Alice's recent sadness. Faith was right; Alice did feel "broken." What Faith did not know, Alice thought to herself, was that it was not just the loss of Pilgrim, but the loss of Hope, too, that had broken her.

Hope began to fuss. Faith jiggled her in her arms to quiet her. Alice felt a twinge in her breasts, as she often did when she heard Hope cry. It was an automatic response that would not go away until her milk was completely dried up.

"Ma!" came Hank's voice from upstream. "Look, Ma!" He set off towards Alice, water sloshing out of a bucket in his left hand. The bucket unbalanced him, so his progress was awkward, but he was coming on steadily. He would reach them in a few minutes.

Hope's crying had gotten harder. Clearly she was hungry.

"Alice," Faith said with put-on casualness. "Do you still have milk?"

"Yes, a little."

With one smooth extension of her arms, Faith held Hope out to Alice. The baby, red-faced and screaming, lay on her mother's outstretched hands like a gift. A gift, thought Alice, dizzy with the idea, a wondrous, essential gift. Fumbling with the buttons on her dress, Alice opened it up and roughly pulled off the cloth binding down her breasts to suppress their production of milk. Then, barely trusting her arms to bear up the miraculous weight, Alice took the baby from Faith.

"She is your baby, too," said Faith quietly.

When Hank arrived, he found his mother sitting on the grass nursing Hope, with Faith close beside them.

"Look, look," he said, holding out the bucket half-filled with wriggling crayfish, each four to six inches long.

"Let me see," said Faith.

Hank happily handed her the bucket. The others came up, and talking over one another, the children described all the pitfalls and excitement of lobster hunting.

During the lively report, Bailey stood quietly observing Faith and Alice. She wondered why Alice was nursing Hope.

Faith, tickling the children with questions and laughing over their bubbling responses, certainly did not appear to have slipped into melancholia again. As for Alice, she appeared positively beatific.

In all the currents of emotion and interchange within the small group of women and children, no one noticed Roy arrive. He stood to the side for a few moments, a rifle in one hand and a gunnysack in the other. He had gone hunting alone because Henry was down with dysentery.

Bailey finally nodded to him in greeting, but then she sat down and turned her attention to Hank and Sarah, who were boisterously digging among the crayfish to find the largest one.

"You all aren't the only providers, you know," Roy said loudly when it seemed no one was going to acknowledge him further.

"What's in the sack, Pa?" Gideon asked loyally.

"A bush fish," Roy answered in a tone of great significance.

The children looked at one another, puzzled.

"What kind of fish is that?" Hank said.

Roy set down his rifle and reached into the bag with dramatic slowness.

"This kind," he said triumphantly, holding up a huge, limp rattlesnake.

The boys ran over to Roy and gingerly petted the snake's cool skin.

"It's awful smooth," Gideon admired.

Roy brought the snake to the seated women for each to marvel at in turn. Sarah was captivated by the papery, ashen rattle.

Flinder, who was standing in a patch of sun behind Alice, had not come forward to view Roy's prize more closely. Looking pointedly at his daughter, Roy raised the snake to the height of his shoulders. It almost seemed he was about to throw it to her.

"Care to touch him, miss?" he said to her in a ragging voice thick with challenge.

Flinder glanced at the snake and at her father's smirking face. Then she looked down at her wet skirt and busily shook it out as if to help it dry. When she once more lifted her gaze to Roy, she still did not reply, deliberately making him wait. She felt again, as she had after his brusque kiss on the prairie and during the heated confrontation over Faith's stopped wagon, that she stood on new ground with her father, that he was a man whom she could judge like any other and that she was a woman whom he should not assume he knew. Roy, as static and resolute as a child in the game of statues, continued to hold up the snake.

"Is it heavy?" Flinder said at last.

In answer, Roy stepped around Alice and offered the snake to his daughter. Flinder put out her hands to receive it. Neither man nor girl looked at the reptile as it was transferred from one to the other. Instead, each watched the other's face, alert to any quail of hesitation or regret. They were careful, however, to avoid handling the snake's broad, triangular head, both knowing about the reflex action that made it possible for dead rattlesnakes to bite.

Once she held the snake, Flinder examined it thoroughly, hefting it in her hands as if she were evaluating it for purchase. The tan and brown scales gleamed in the sunlight and showed a greenish cast when Flinder tilted the thick body.

"I aim to make the skin into a band for my hat," Roy said when Flinder handed the snake back to him.

He replaced it in the sack and headed for camp, the boys at his heels with the bucket of crayfish. Flinder stared after him.

"A hat band," she said curtly to no one in particular. "Scant use for such terrible beauty."

ALICE LOOKED AHEAD anxiously as she walked next to Henry. Theirs was the lead wagon. They were ascending a ravine that would take them to the steep descent into Goose

Creek valley, a drop of two thousand feet over a rough, stony road. The valley seemed impossibly lower than where they were.

All around them were bare, gray hills. Scattered whirlwinds whipped dust across their path. The scenery was very different from that of the previous two days, when they had been among the City of Rocks, a valley filled with freakish formations of white marble resembling castles, Gothic spires, and domes. Alice had felt she would never tire of beholding the grand natural edifices.

But today, exhilaration had given way to foreboding when she saw the road they faced. She looked at Henry, whose eyes were set straight ahead. If he was worried, it did not show distinctly. He wore the pinched expression that had become habitual with him; it could denote anything from physical discomfort to reverie to vigilance. Though Henry's dysentery was gone, he was still plagued by occasional stomach cramps and a general weakness. He moved slowly and spoke only when necessary. Alice did not want to burden him with her fears.

Though she knew it was only a pause, Alice was relieved when Henry halted the wagons just after the road began dipping down. The small delay would give her a chance to marshal her courage.

Without speaking to her, Henry walked toward the end of the line of wagons. Last night Henry and Roy had taken a jug of haymaker's switchel to a neighboring camp to enlist some men to help in the difficult descent to Goose Creek. Alice expected they had stopped now to wait for them. She walked ahead a few yards and looked down the high divide. Shuddering, she spied far below the smashed remains of a wagon that had hurtled down the grade unchecked.

"Alice!" Henry called.

She hastened to where he stood. With him were the rest of their party and three strange men. At first Alice thought the men looked too old and thin to be of much use, but when she reached them she realized they were probably her age or younger. The journey had rendered them ragged, sun-drenched, and grave. It was hard to discern beneath the dirt and the dog-weary expressions the hopeful, brash young men they must have been at the expedition's start. Alice wondered how she and her companions appeared to fresh eyes. She knew they had not escaped the wearing down evident in every other party they encountered.

The look of the whole migration had altered in the months since leaving the Missouri. The route now was less congested, and the Mullers did not meet as many fellow travelers as they had before Fort Laramie, but they saw enough to note the changes. There were fewer riders because horses had wearied or been lost, and fewer loose oxen because their strength had waned and more were needed in yoke or because they had died on the wayside or been eaten. Some wagons had been shortened to make them lighter and more maneuverable, and overall there were many fewer wagons of any size. And the people reflected the state of their trains, grave, wizened, and tumbledown.

"We're all here now," Henry said to the three men.

"This'll be needing all of us, ma'am," one of the men said to Alice.

"Many hands make light work," Jerusha chimed in.

Without further explanation, the men disbursed like seeds blown from a pod.

"What wants doing?" Alice asked Jerusha.

"Nothing yet," Jerusha replied. "The men will fasten a long rope to the rear of each wagon and detach all but the wheel yoke of oxen, leaving them to guide the wagons down. We must all hold on to the rope to let the wagons go easy and not collide with the oxen."

Alice went to her wagon, where the men were chaining the rear wheels to keep them from turning. The muscles bulging in their arms as they worked would be as crucial to the success of the descent as the chains.

"All right," shouted Roy. "We're ready to take the first one down."

All the men except Henry lined up behind the wagon, each one gripping a section of rope. Henry was to lead the oxen. The women and children found themselves places along the rope behind the men. Alice was the last in line and so had a view of the backs of all the rest. She noticed how sinewy and lean they looked; even Jerusha's stoutness and the curve of Flinder's hips showed a certain tight rigor, and the forms of Hank and Sarah had evolved an unchildlike hardness.

Gideon stood several yards off with Rouser and Old Smith. Faith had bound Hope to Gideon's chest by winding a long shawl around them. The lump of the baby gave him the appearance of a rotund elf. Alice noticed his lips moving and wondered if he was praying. Her attention was jerked away from the boy when she felt the rope tense in her hands. She tightened her hold. The descent had begun.

Alice felt as if all existence had been condensed into one task, to hold back from runaway destruction this container of her past and her future. The coarse rope burned her hands. Her body sweat, and perspiration ran from her brow, washing salt and dirt into her eyes. Her ears caught and amplified the grunts of the others on the rope, Henry's occasional terse shouts, and the scramble of rocks as both people and oxen struggled for footholds. The wagon rattled and groaned as if aware of its peril.

Suddenly Alice was yanked forward and down. Bailey, who was directly in front of her, fell, and Alice tripped over her, keeping her balance but stepping on Bailey's leg in the process. Ahead, several others had also fallen. Flinder was on her knees off to one side. Hank was flat out on his stomach, sliding down the hill, face scraping along the stony ground; Alice saw by his upraised arms that he was still holding on to the rope.

"Hank, let go!" she shouted, but the boy either did not hear or would not listen.

One of the men who had come to help them was also flat out, but on his back, plowing his bootheels into the dirt as he was being pulled along.

"Dig in! Dig in!" he was yelling.

"Get back on the line!" Roy screamed at Flinder, who was already running to catch up. Alice felt Bailey bump into place behind her.

"Haw! Whoa!" came Henry's frantic admonitions to the oxen.

All the voices were shingled over by the racket of the careening wagon, the squealing of the two oxen, and the frenzied barking of the dogs, who had raced down the hill as soon as the wagon's speed increased.

Alice did not think she had any more strength left in her than that she'd already summoned, but somehow she kept on the rope and managed to shift her position so that she was leaning back against the down-pulling force, digging her heels into the sliding dirt as she had seen the man below doing. She cried out with the tremendous effort, and it was like the bracing, defiant cry of giving birth. All along the line, everyone else struggled to gain a similar footing, and one by one they succeeded. Even Hank managed to right himself and throw his slight weight backwards to oppose the momentum of the plummeting wagon. His body, slung from the rope, was almost parallel to the steeply sloping ground.

The wagon slowed some and slowed some more. The muscles in Alice's arms and legs quivered and threatened to fail, but she did not dare relax them even a little. After several yards, however, the wagon seemed in enough control that she did ease up a bit, walking now instead of sliding with her knees locked, bending her elbows and refitting her grip on the rope. Hank turned his head over his shoulder and leaned to the side to look up at her around the four people between them. His forehead, chin, and one cheek were scraped and bleeding, but he was smiling triumphantly.

Finally the wagon was down. Everyone dropped the rope and plopped down in the dirt where they were, sitting strung out behind one another like cranberries threaded up for a Christmas garland. Henry unyoked the oxen and came to squat beside Alice.

"You all right, girlie?" he said.

Alice looked up the hill to where the other three wagons waited to be brought down. She saw Gideon peering at them and rocking back and forth from foot to foot, probably to quiet Hope.

"You may ask me that later," she replied.

"Henry," Roy said, coming up to them with one of the extra men. "Mr. Calvert here had an idea I think we should try on the next wagon."

"Oh?"

"I was telling Mr. Hall," explained Mr. Calvert in a soft southern drawl, "if we hitch a couple of oxen behind the wagon, maybe they can help us hold it back."

"Our power is just too low, even with the added men," Roy insisted.

Henry nodded thoughtfully and stood up. The three men turned and began hiking up the hill. Alice got to her feet, too, as did the others. Trudging slowly uphill, Alice was able to read the steepness of the grade more closely than she had during the brutish work of the descent, and she marveled that anyone had ever gotten wagons down it in one piece.

Despite the addition of a pair of oxen at the back of the second wagon, Roy required everyone to apply themselves to the rope again. Alice began the descent clutched by apprehension, then moved, with the work, into a mindless state of animal exertion, capped by elation at the end when the job turned out so much calmer than the first. Mr. Calvert's idea had proved a good one. The oxen, unaccustomed to having their faces against the tailgate, pulled back from it and helped slow the wagon's tilting progress. For the final two wagons, Henry excused the women and children and hitched two pairs of oxen behind each wagon instead. The men still worked the rope, and Hank joined them, securing Alice's permission by allowing her to first wash his face with castile soap and honey and rub balm of Gilead ointment on his cuts.

When all the wagons were down, the women wanted to make a special lunch as a way of thanking the three men who had helped them, but it was difficult. Their stores were low. Alice wished they were still along the Raft River, where they had eaten plump marmots.

Still, the men were satisfied. There were no women in their party, so meals had been coarse affairs most days. They looked on Jerusha's potato bread as a delicacy, especially when Faith dug out a jar of pumpkin butter to spread on it.

While the women packed up after lunch, one of their guests drew a harmonica from his pocket and gave them a medley of tunes. He continued playing as he and his two friends walked uphill back to their own people.

The middle bars of "The Girl I Left Behind Me" were the last strains of his music the Muller party heard as they rolled on again through the bluff-lined valley of Goose Creek. Alice latched on to the fading song and sang it softly to its end as a lullaby for Hope.

August 30, 1852

We are arrived at the headwaters of the Humboldt River, after journeying five days through a dry, uninteresting country, which did, nevertheless, afford us small streams and sufficient, if nearly lifeless, grass. The oxen are looking gaunt, though they keep on faithfully.

The Humboldt is a brothy little waterway which shall lead us on the longest leg of our journey and point us to the mountains, the last barrier to our destination. Though it is a poor stream (some call it the Humbug River), it is, perhaps, the most vital one of all, for the country through which it will take us is little more than hot, dry wasteland, 365 miles of it.

Yesterday we were in Thousand Springs Valley, scattered through with springs both cool and warm. In one place, the hot waters were so numerous that clouds of steam rose from the wet turf over a good three acres. Jerusha declared we could boil eggs in one stream, and we would have, had we had any.

We found some sacks of sugar by the wayside today and took a little. Generally, there are fewer abandoned edibles on this part of the trail than heretofore. We must be frugal with our remaining food, though Henry contends we are stocked enough. There is little to hunt here—an occasional antelope and jackrabbits.

A backpacker is staying the night in our camp. I sometimes see such lone figures as he walking along out of dust's path during the day. They like to sleep near others for protection. Our man was with a train, but dissatisfied with its slow progress and free of family obligations, he decided to hike through on his own.

It is hard for me to fathom such a decision, nor the character of such a journey. I can stand my own company well enough— at times I even prefer it—but to forsake the society of others just when that society is the only kernel of steadfastness ready to one, that I do not understand.

A scrap of canvas overhead, some smoldering greasewood, and the odd bits of conversation shimmed between busyness and weariness are only shreds of home, perhaps, but I'd not forgo them even if my reward were fewer weeks on the trail.

Our minister was fond of saying we must accept what God gives us. This wilderness is God's, no doubt of it, and I'll endeavor to meet what He sends. But I must needs tinker a bit and gather around myself some of human-kindness, too.

Chapter 18

TRAVEL DOWN the Humboldt was monotonous. The surrounding land was arid, and except for the grass along the narrow river, there was little vegetation. More than at any other time on the journey, the Muller party experienced nerve-racking tedium. Almost without notice, they put one foot before the other, over and over, seeing every day the same sandy plains, the same hills dotted with scraggly, gray-green sagebrush, the same bare mountains.

Late one afternoon, after a week and a half of such travel, they spied up ahead a large camp of wagons. Two horsemen were riding out from the camp towards them. Roy, in the lead, called a halt to discover what news or request the horsemen might be bringing. Henry came up and stood beside Roy. Everyone else sat down in the shade beside the last wagon to rest. The day had been very hot.

The two riders, a weather-beaten, white-haired man with a bushy, yellowed mustache and a younger, dark-haired man who slouched in his saddle, soon overtook the waiting wagons.

"Good day," said the older man to Henry and Roy.

"Good day," replied Roy.

"I'm Sterling McGee, captain of that train over there," continued the man, pointing toward the camp. "And this is Levi Myers. We got a problem we could use your help with."

"What is it?" said Roy suspiciously. "We're a small company, as you can see. Only us two men. The rest are women and children."

"We need you men for a jury," McGee said.

"A jury?" said Henry.

"Myers here was traveling with five other men. Last night two of them got drunk and took to arguing, and this morning one of them shot the other one down in cold blood."

"Morgan and Pratt was always arguing," put in Myers. "Ever since we left Independence. Got worse since the Green River, though."

"Anyway," said McGee with a frown at Myers's interruption, "the four boys left held the culprit, and when we came upon them earlier they asked would we hold a trial. I saw your wagons in the distance and figured we should tap you for jurors, too, to make it a fair collection of strangers."

McGee sat ramrod-straight in his saddle. He kept a short rein on his horse, holding the animal's head up and turned to the right, ready to gallop. He seemed to think there was no question that Roy and Henry would agree to his request.

"How long would this take?" said Roy.

"Don't none of us want to waste any time," said McGee.

Roy looked at Henry, and Henry looked over his shoulder at the others sitting in the shade. They were not as large a group as McGee's, and at the moment they appeared rather bedraggled, but Henry was sure they were a match in spirit for any party on the trail. They deserved the most careful decisions he could muster.

"Did they think of taking the man on to California for trial?" Henry asked, turning back to the two visitors.

"The California courts have no say out here," snapped McGee. "If we don't do our own justice, no one will."

Henry and Roy exchanged glances again. Roy gave Henry a curt nod.

"Well, if you put it like that," Henry said to the impatient rider, "I expect it's our duty."

McGee and Myers took off for their camp without further discussion. While Roy turned the lead wagon aside to follow them, Henry went to explain the situation to the women.

"A trial?" said Alice. "But there's no judge, no jail. What can be the outcome of it?"

"That's to be seen," said Henry. "The matter is there's been a crime committed and some consequence must come of it."

"But the crime was not among us," said Bailey.

"All the same, we've been appealed to for help, and as I see it, we must take part," Henry answered.

"I fear," said Bailey with a bitter inflection to her voice, "that the criminal will not be the only one to feel the consequences of his act."

"Mr. McGee has assured us the delay will not be overly long," Henry said.

"I don't object to the time lost," Bailey said, "but to the right of the thing, the placement of ourselves in this sordid affair. No good can come of it."

"Obligation is not always clean or easy, Miss Jeffers, and in any case, it is Royal Hall and I who are placed in it, not you."

Bailey walked away, following the path Roy's wagon had taken. Henry felt no satisfaction in her silent acquiescence.

"Flinder," Jerusha called to her daughter, who was standing beside the oxen of their wagon. "Get those animals moving after your father."

Henry smiled gratefully at his sister. He could always depend on her to be uncritically loyal. Sometimes a man needed that, especially when he himself was secretly nagged by doubt.

It was only when he looked into Alice's eyes for a long moment before heading to his team that Henry let the worry that was in his heart pass across his face, delivering it to her as he might have done a torn piece of clothing that wanted mending.

Mrs. Sterling McGee took charge of the Muller women and children when they arrived at the camp. She was a feminine version of her authoritative husband, substantially built, with a conversational style given to declarations that brooked no comment, let alone contradiction.

"Mr. Sterling McGee," she announced, though no one had asked, "made this crossing in forty-nine with his brothers Asa and Ham. They came back by ship and over the Panama isthmus to get all the rest of them. He's the oldest of his family, a natural-born leader, and a fearless prohibitionist."

The "rest of them" consisted of the formidable Mrs. Sterling McGee; her thirteen-year-old daughter, Lettie, who had been married on the trail to a forty-year-old bachelor in her father's employ; Sterling's elderly parents; and the wives and children of Asa and Ham. Five other unrelated families made up the remainder of the party.

McGee and his brothers had proved masterful with wagons, hunting, and tracking, so the members of the train were well pleased with Sterling McGee as captain. There had been only two fatalities. A twelve-year-old boy was riding on a mule and leading a horse when the horse spooked. The boy got tangled in the rope and was dragged to death. A careless man—not a McGee—dropped a loaded pistol from his breast pocket when he leaned over. The gun discharged, blasting into his heart. His wife and five children were still with the party, determined to get on to California.

Mrs. Sterling, as she preferred to be called, hustled the Muller women to the front of the band of emigrants waiting apprehensively for the trial to begin, but not before she had shown off her fruit trees. Her wagon bed held two long, narrow boxes filled with manure, charcoal, and earth in which she had planted several saplings, each three to five feet tall.

"I've got me apple, pear, plum, cherry, and quince. And a grapevine, too," she said proudly. "Yes, ladies, you're looking at the future orchards of the Sacramento Valley."

Mrs. Sterling left the Muller children to Lettie, who settled them in a wagon with the canvas side rolled up so that they, too, could watch the trial.

It was a simple affair. The jury was made up of ten men from McGee's train, plus Henry and Roy. McGee appointed himself presiding officer, and Myers and his comrades were the witnesses. The witnesses agreed on the story, and the accused man, Lilburn Pratt, denied none of it, saying only that William Morgan, the victim, had been provoking him for weeks.

Henry listened carefully to the testimony, minimal and uncontested though it was. He did not like sitting judgment on another man, especially out here, where men's characters were so sorely tried. If he had to do this, he would make it as proper a proceeding as he could.

The twelve jurors retired to the end of the camp away from the spectators to deliberate. That the verdict would be guilty was not doubted by anyone. The question of punishment was the real issue.

"You've two choices," McGee addressed the men formally. He was obviously used to being in charge. "You can expel Pratt and leave him to make his way on his own to California or back to the states or wherever. Or you can vote to execute him."

"Murder's murder," said one man. "And there's only one fit punishment for it."

Mutters and nods showed several of the other men agreed.

"Ain't no trees for hanging," offered one man. It was not clear whether he was making the observation as a protest against execution or as a practical problem for carrying one out.

"We can run two wagon yokes up in the air and fasten them together for a gallows," suggested the first man. "Or shoot the devil."

"I heard he's got a wife and baby back in Kentucky," said someone else.

"That's of no account," another man pronounced.

"I'm for turning him out," Henry said. The thought of being associated with another death, particularly in this willful way, horrified him.

Henry's dissension emboldened other men to speak, and a lusty debate followed. Roy kept silent during the first round of exchanges among the jurors. Henry looked at him once or twice, and Roy seemed to be truthfully undecided, nodding thoughtfully in favor of first one side of the argument and then the other.

"Turning a man out to face the elements and the Indians on his own could be as sure a death sentence as anything," Roy finally said during a lapse in the debate.

"Not so sure as a noose around the neck," snorted a man who had been arguing for hanging. "Why should Pratt have more of a chance than he gave that man he shot? Say, he didn't even wait till the poor bastard was up out of his bedroll." This detail was one that had impressed several of the men as particularly gruesome.

"What do you think, Captain?" asked one of the men.

"I'm not on this jury," McGee answered.

"Still, you got an opinion," urged another man.

"Well, let me tell you a little story, boys."

Though Henry had never before served on a jury, he was sure this was irregular, even under these improvised circumstances. But no one protested. In fact, a number of the men nodded in anticipation, apparently used to McGee's stories and their relevance to decisions at hand. Henry remained silent, curious to hear what McGee would say.

"As most of you know, I am a prohibitionist. I always carry pledge cards in my pocket, and I'm proud to say I've convinced hundreds of men to sign the pledge.

"Well, my success has never been appreciated by saloon-keepers, and one time in Oregon City one of them sicced his dog on me as a reward for my efforts, which had been hurting his business considerable. The cur set his teeth in my leg good, as was his nature and his job—some might say his right, since his master had a grievance against me. But understandable or not, I couldn't subscribe to such goings-on. I choked that dog till he released his hold, and then I threw him down on a rock with all the force that was in me, which killed him outright. The saloon-keeper turned tail and never interfered with me again."

"You mean Pratt is like that dog?" someone asked.

"He means we got to set an example to others who might

choose to shoot someone they got an argument with," offered another man.

"Take it for what it's worth, boys," said McGee. "It's time to vote."

One by one, each man stated his choice. Henry was impressed by their solemnity. Despite the bravado with which some of the men had voiced their opinions during the heated banter earlier, they obviously regarded their task as one requiring the most sober consideration they could give it. Roy voted right after Henry, casting his ballot, as Henry had, for exile, though he still seemed unsure. Henry noticed that Roy was intensely studying the face of each speaker and checking on McGee's reactions as well, as if trying to determine whether he and Henry had placed themselves in good company or not by their vote. In the end, there were seven votes for execution, and five for exile.

"We'll have to take it to the whole company," McGee said, disgusted. It was plain he itched to make the decision on his own. "And they must vote without discussion. It'll be sundown in two hours."

McGee led the way back to the milling emigrants. The jurors followed, many of them almost shuffling behind him. It was as if, Henry thought, they were sons who had failed to live up to the high expectations of a powerful father. This notion annoyed Henry, who had been proud of the seriousness of his fellow jurors. He found himself glad the vote had gone as it had, not just because of his own convictions, but because McGee had been thwarted.

"What do you think it will turn out to be?" Roy asked Henry as they walked along.

"There's no telling," Henry said. "Though we all heard the same facts, I guess each man reaches his decision for his own reasons."

"Then you aim to stay with your vote?"

"Of course. What would change my mind?"

Roy shrugged. They had rejoined the main party. Roy strode to the other side of the crowd and climbed up on a barrel, which gave him a good vantage. Henry supposed he might be looking for Jerusha.

McGee laid the question out before the larger group as succinctly as he had before the jurors, adding that since they were deciding on a man's life, a strong majority was needed before they could act. Only the men were allowed to vote, but the women remained as audience. Indeed, no one present, not even the children, failed to feel a part of these weighty proceedings.

McGee called for a show of hands. At the last minute, while McGee was counting the arms raised in favor of death, Roy flung up his hand and joined them. The final tally was seven for exile, thirteen for execution.

"Lilburn Pratt," intoned Sterling McGee loudly, "the jury has found you guilty of murder. We sentence you to death by shooting at eight o'clock tonight. Make your peace with God."

The condemned man, flanked by two armed men and with his wrists bound behind his back, made no reaction to the verdict. Throughout the drumhead trial he had stood calmly and with soldierly erectness, as if he knew his fate and had already begun to take leave of the world. It was seeing this pitiable air of surrender, as much as his conscience, that had led Henry to argue for exile.

"What will happen now?" Alice said, coming up to Henry. Bailey was with her.

"Twelve men will be drawn by lot for the firing squad," he answered heavily. "Six rifles will be loaded with powder and ball, and six with powder only. That way, none will know who has made the fatal shot."

"And all twelve will be the killers," added Bailey scornfully.

Henry looked at her sharply.

"You may think of it that way, Miss Jeffers," he said. "The scheme is meant, however, to ease the cruel duty, not make it more onerous."

"Well, surely, Mr. Muller," Bailey said. "Your 'duty' here

is finished. We need not stay for the execution."

"Roy and I must cast our lots with the others."

It seemed Bailey was unprepared for this. She stared aghast at Henry for a moment, then turned and rapidly strode away.

"Henry," Alice said, laying her hand on his arm. "You voted against it."

"Yes, but the majority favored it, and we must go along with that. It's the rule of law."

"But if you're chosen . . ." Alice's voice quavered.

Henry looked at his wife. Despite the hot march along the Humboldt and all that had preceded it, she appeared vital and lovely. Faith's sharing of Hope had helped her tremendously, he knew, but there was something more, something he could not pin down, a new clarity and concentration about her, like honey that had seeped through three fine-sieved colanders from a comb melting in the strong July sun. He wished they could walk off right now, just the two of them, and lie down together in a meadow of timothy and black-eyed Susans. He wanted to kiss her, to drink from her, to forget every other tie except the one between them. But there was no such meadow within hundreds of miles of this place, and there were more claims on him than hers.

"If I am chosen," Henry finished her sentence, "I have a favor to ask of you."

"What?"

"I want you to witness it. To watch me do it."

He saw fear and aversion in her eyes. But he saw love, too, and resolve.

"If that will help you, Henry, of course I'll do it."

"It will save me."

WHEN THE LOTS were drawn, Henry was not among the shooters, but Roy was. Roy kept turning the little slip of paper around in his hand, as if the simple X on it were a code he could not decipher. Henry patted his shoulder compassionately.

"Well, Henry," Roy said nervously. "Isn't this something?"

"Royal," Jerusha said, "I don't want the children to see. Flinder's going to drive the wagon off over there, and we'll keep the young ones with us till it's over."

"This is nothing disgraceful, Jerusha," Roy said angrily. "It's got to be done."

"She's just concerned for the children," Henry said. "You want them spared this sight, too, don't you?"

"Yes, yes," Roy grumbled.

"Come to us right after, won't you?" Jerusha said, touching Roy's wrist tentatively, as if it were a hot flatiron. He brushed her hand away as he would a bloodsucking horsefly. She hesitated a moment, seeming about to say something more, then turned and left.

"You know, Henry," said Roy when they were alone, "I've never killed a man. Never even shot at one before. Not even an Indian."

"This isn't straight-out killing, Roy. It's like you're a tool. Like soldiers in a war."

Henry knew that in Roy's place, he wouldn't have been mollified by the comparison to a soldier, but it was all he could think of to say.

"I wonder what it will feel like," Roy continued, seeming not to have heard Henry. "I wish I'd know if my rifle is really loaded or not. Hell, they ought to load them all."

"Roy," Henry said, alarmed. "How can you wish such a thing? A man will be dead when this is over. A man just like you or me, who probably loves his life as well as anyone."

"It's only, Henry . . ." Roy said earnestly, floundering to express himself. "It's only that if they're going to ask a man to do a man's job, they ought to be square about it and let him take on the whole thing. If I'm going to have to kill someone, if it's all right, like they're saying it is here, then I want to do it pure like, not by halves."

Henry made no response. Awash in his own relief at being spared the ugly task, he was unable to understand Roy's train of reasoning. He'd thought Roy wanted consoling, and he was prepared to give him that as best he could. Now he did not know what Roy wanted from him, if anything. He wondered if he really knew Roy at all.

"Here's your weapon, Mr. Hall," said Sterling McGee, coming up to Roy and handing him a rifle. "It's time."

Roy left Henry and took his place in the line of men. Opposite them, Lilburn Pratt knelt on a blanket facing the river. His back was to the firing squad. It was how he wanted it. He'd also requested permission to give the order to shoot. Crazily, Henry noticed that Pratt's shirttail was half out of his waistband in back and that it was mud-stained; he wished someone had helped the man get more presentable.

Henry worked his way to the front of the small crowd of onlookers so that Roy would find a familiar face there. He had no more desire to see the execution than Bailey Jeffers did, but he felt he owed it to Roy. He'd grasped enough of what Roy was saying, he thought, to believe that Roy would want him to watch. Or maybe he owed it to God to watch, for sparing him from being on the firing squad.

The grim scene was rosily lit by the setting sun. It didn't seem right for the light just now to turn so soft and pretty. Henry felt a nudge and turned his head to discover Alice standing beside him. She slipped her arm under his and squeezed his hand hard. He thought of the time she had cut her foot open on a sharp rock in the creek back in Pennsylvania; she had squeezed his hand all during the doctor's sewing up and never uttered a cry of pain.

"Alice, you don't need to be here," Henry whispered.

"If you're here, I do," she said.

She answered him while keeping her gaze steadily on Pratt and the riflemen, and her tone was so no-nonsense, he did not dispute her further. Instead, he, too, turned his face to the drama before them.

"I'd like a prayer first," Pratt called.

Levi Myers, who had been one of Pratt's messmates and who was on the firing squad, set down his rifle, knelt on the ground, and recited the Lord's Prayer. His voice broke on "forgive us our trespasses," and he spoke more quickly after that, as if he were saying something shameful.

After the assembled company had echoed his amen, Myers stood up, picked up his rifle, and stepped back into line.

McGee commanded the twelve men to take aim, and they lifted their guns to their shoulders. A long, silent pause ensued during which could be heard here and there the scuffing of boots on the hard-packed sand and the muffled sobs of a couple of women. The men on the firing squad stood motionless, like a tableau, all eyes on Pratt's back, which moved visibly up and down with his deep breaths.

At last Pratt raised his right hand, which was the signal to shoot. The blast made Henry jump. He felt Alice start, too. But she had kept her gaze on Roy and had recoiled in response to the loud sound only. Henry had watched Pratt. The man's body jerked forward violently when the rifle balls struck him, his back arching sharply, his arms splayed out to the sides. For the briefest moment before he fell, he remained upright, illogically suspended, like a dancer poised to change his tempo. In that moment, Henry, too, felt suspended, held in a place that was no place, in a time that had no time. As from a great distance, he heard a child's single, shrill scream.

Then Pratt collapsed, and a world of dust and heat and rushing noises reclaimed Henry. Now Pratt lay facedown in the dirt beside a patch of prickly pear, blood soaking through his shirt in several places, spreading slowly like ink on a blotter.

Henry took Alice's hand and they went to Roy. Henry steered Alice carefully so that the corpse was at her back. McGee was collecting the rifles.

"Thanks for your help," McGee said to Roy and Henry. "It's a bad business, but it's part of what a man's got to do."

Henry did not answer him. Roy, looking shaken, gave McGee a quick handshake, then turned from him to peer out over the dispersing crowd.

"Say," McGee continued, unperturbed. "Why not come

have supper with us tonight? Put all this behind us." He waved his hand toward two men who were carrying Pratt's body away for burial.

"We'll be moving out," Henry said.

Roy and Alice both looked at him in surprise, but they didn't contradict him.

"Suit yourself," McGee said, walking away.

"Moving out?" Roy said when McGee was out of earshot.

"I don't care if it takes hours of travel in the dark," Henry said. "When we wake up tomorrow, we're not going to be looking out on this accursed spot."

September 10, 1852

Everyone has retired early tonight. It was a long day (we made twenty-two miles), and last night we got little sleep, as we traveled more than three hours after sundown in order to remove ourselves from the grisly events of yesterday evening.

Then, too, I believe everyone separated early tonight because we are not yet comfortable in one another's company after the part we played in Mr. Pratt's trial and death. Roy is the most marked, of course, and Henry, but we were all there, and so we each had a portion in it. We must sift and weigh what happened and our feelings about it and about one another and maybe forge some new places in ourselves to hold those feelings.

How still and regular life used to seem to me, like a well. All one had to do, I'd thought, was find a source of good water, build up a sturdy stone circle around it, and keep a tight-seamed bucket for dipping into it. Henry and our home and our children were my well. Now life seems more like a river, and I have seen on this journey the variety of rivers. They can be at flood tide or low and murky, wide or narrow, straight or serpentine. Beneath their reflecting surfaces, they hide quicksand and fish and eels; in California, the rivers run with gold. You can bring a bucket to a river, but you may not always pull up what you expect.

My thoughts are tangled. How is it that I can feel enlivened in the shadow of tragedy? What I shall remember most acutely about the affair of Mr. Pratt, I think, besides the awful explosion of the rifle barrage, is that Henry and I needed each other in equal measure. Is this too private a harvest? Is there really any other kind?

Chapter 19

ALICE SAT BESIDE the campfire with Hope newly asleep on her lap. Sarah sat on the ground beside the rocker and rested her head against her mother's knees.

Henry leaned against a wagon wheel just outside the fire's glow. Alice could smell the kinnikinnick tobacco. Occasionally he drew deeply enough on his pipe to illuminate his features. His bout with dysentery two weeks ago had thinned him. In quiet moments like this, he appeared drained, not only of robust strength but also of something more vague and more irreplaceable.

When Hope started to wriggle and whimper, Alice began humming Brahms's lullaby. After one stanza Sarah joined in, singing words Alice had invented.

"Go to sleep, little Hope. Close your bi-ig, brown ey-eyes," Sarah sang softly, her high, reedy notes a perfect counterpart to Alice's deep-toned humming.

Their coupled voices were the only sound in the vast quiet around them. The campfire was too small to crackle, made only of sagebrush and a few dry willow boughs.

The tune ended, Alice stroked her daughter's tangled hair.

"Off to bed with you now, Sarah," she said.

The girl rose wearily. She lifted the sleeping baby from her mother's lap.

"I'll set Hope in Aunt Faith's wagon first," she said.

Alice watched the slight figure move off into the darkness. The girl's head was bowed down over the baby in her arms. Alice could see the bones of the upper part of Sarah's spine pushing against her pale skin. How tall the child's grown, thought her mother.

A sudden vision came to Alice of Sarah in the yard on their last morning in Indiana, her face lit with excitement, her long hair blowing wantonly around her shoulder and cheek from one tawny braid that had come loose. Alice had noticed that day, as if for the first time, how the bodice of the girl's muslin dress pulled across her firm young breasts, still too small to bounce with her strides. Womanhood was beginning to interrupt childhood, and Sarah had seemed iridescent with the dual energies. Now the simple sight of Sarah's bones under her skin had made Alice realize that transformation was still at work. She felt a bittersweet mixture of pride, awe, and loss. Alice believed Sarah would never leave her as fully as Hank was bound to, but leave she would, and Alice's life would flap around her a little more loosely then, like a tight garment that's had the seams let out.

"Your song rang sweetly," said Henry, breaking into Alice's thoughts.

"I feel good tonight," Alice replied. "Full."

"You're a puzzlement. What's to feel good about in this desolation? I'm sure I'll not feel good until we're at this journey's end."

"We are nearing that, Henry," Alice said softly.

"Well, this day's done, anyway."

Henry arose more slowly than Sarah had. Alice almost expected to hear him creak. She was sorry to feel contentment, however fleeting it might prove to be, when he was so discouraged.

"I believe I'll just sit here a bit," she said.

Henry yawned, nodded, and climbed into the wagon.

Arms akimbo, Alice stood up and stretched, bending her torso and head back extravagantly until the skin of her throat was drawn tight.

The sky was densely black and swathed with stars. In the first sweep of Alice's gaze they all glittered whitely. Then as she continued looking at them, she picked out a few that burned with blue or green light.

Starting tomorrow, they planned to travel nights for a while to avoid the daytime's intense heat, which oppressed both humans and animals. One ox had dropped right in its yoke the day before yesterday.

Alice was glad they'd be moving during the cool night hours and resting by day. Still, despite the harsh sun, she found this sage-specked desert plain and its low, dusky hills strangely appealing. Henry saw the desert as barren and inhospitable. But Alice found Nature at work, harnessing beauty to hardiness in the fragile blooms of tiny, hairy-leafed plants, in the exact spacing of bushes that modulated their competition for water, in the scrawny, tight jackrabbits and coyotes. This land, once she was used to it, invited Alice to starings and long lapses of thought. There were no pretenses here. Death was out in the open, and so was survival. The desert warned that life cannot be absentminded, that it must be chosen, and planned for, and attended to.

Alice turned her back on the fire and the wagons and walked out into the desert a short distance. She knew she ought to turn around, but she was reluctant.

"I'll just go on to those big rocks and then come back," she said to herself, heading for a large formation several yards away. When she reached the rocks, she stopped and began turning slowly in a circle, peering off into the darkness as far as she could on every side. Halfway around she saw the faces.

Her heart leapt and she gasped. She did not move, and for a moment neither did they. Then the two Indians stepped away from the crevice in which they had been standing and presented themselves to her. That's what their movements reminded Alice of, a presentation, almost an introduction.

Her fear subsided, but only a little. McGee had warned them that the Diggers of the middle Humboldt were more aggressive than the other tribes they'd encountered so far. Just two days ago they'd passed a grave with the inscription that the man in it had been killed by Indians. Sticking upright in the dirt was an arrow with a card on it noting "This is the fatal arrow."

Now that the Indians were out of the crevice's shadow, Alice was able to see them more distinctly. They were women. Alice's anxiety ebbed a little more. Slowly, so that the Indians would not misinterpret her actions, Alice turned her hands palm up in front of her and shrugged her shoulders. She would have liked to be able to smile, but she couldn't manage it.

One of the women was standing slightly behind the other. The woman in back spoke to her companion in an Indian language; the woman in front moved a step closer to Alice and cleared her throat.

"I am not an Indian," she said hoarsely.

Alice stared at the two women in amazement. They were both dark-haired and dark-eyed and dressed alike in breech-cloths of cliff-rose bark, with rabbit-skin blankets over their shoulders and square-toed moccasins of woven bark. But as she looked more carefully, she realized that their features were structurally different and that the woman who had spoken to her was, indeed, not an Indian.

"Come to our camp," Alice said, gesturing towards the wagons and taking several steps in that direction.

The two women looked at each other and did not move.

"It's all right," Alice encouraged.

She began walking. They followed silently. Alice kept glancing over her shoulder to be sure they were still there.

The campfire was out and gave no light, but the strangers squatted beside it anyway. Alice sat down warily in her rocker. She felt as if any sudden movement would cause the women to evaporate before her eyes.

"I have not spoken my own language in three years," began the white woman. Her companion watched her intently, as if, by listening well enough, she would understand the words or as if she could read their meaning in the white woman's face, which to Alice appeared expressionless.

"Apaches killed my husband and our companions along

Santa Fe trail and took me prisoner. Later I was traded to Paiute for some blankets. Paiute and Shoshone are called Diggers by you."

She stopped speaking. With her arms around her knees, she rocked her body back and forth slightly. Her breaths came noisily through her flattened nose, which had obviously been broken sometime in the past and not well attended to. The Indian woman shifted her steady gaze to the few glowing embers among the campfire ashes and idly worked her fingers through her long hair, picking out bits of grass and sticks.

Alice had heard about the Diggers. Their environment offered them only roots, seeds, serviceberries, small animals, and insects to live on. Scantily clad and housed in simple brush shelters, they were not as impressive to look at as the Plains tribes or the eastern Iroquois nation. But they were said to be fearless in battle, and there were many tales of Diggers stealing emigrants' oxen and mules, which provided larger and more easily acquired meals than the rabbits, snakes, and rats they usually hunted.

"With Paiute, it was better," the white woman resumed. "I was wifed to only one man. Tinnemaha's husband." She cocked her head toward the Indian woman.

"What is your name?" asked Alice.

"I was Catherine Guthrie."

"How do you come to be here alone? You are alone, aren't you?"

Catherine nodded. "Alone. Except for the spirits. They are never far from Tinnemaha."

Alice ascribed this remark to the dire experiences Catherine Guthrie must have lived through. No doubt her mind was not as sound as it once had been. Nevertheless, Alice peered uneasily around the campsite. She half-expected to spot some hovering, wispy form. There were only the wagons and tents and the downtrodden animals.

"We went with some others to scout. We found two wagons and six graves. The men dug them up and took the clothes. All in our party sickened. All but we two died. Tinnemaha says we are marked to remind us of our dead." Catherine Guthrie pointed to several round scars on her cheek and forehead.

"Smallpox," said Alice.

Catherine nodded and stood up. Tinnemaha also rose.

"We will sleep here and be gone at sunup," Catherine said.

"But where will you go? Surely not back to the Indians. Mrs. Guthrie, you must come on with us."

"I will speak with Tinnemaha."

"But what can she have to say about it?"

Catherine's peculiar composure agitated Alice. Gone was her tranquillity of only an hour ago when she had sat humming with Sarah.

"Tinnemaha will say what she knows," Catherine said, as if that explained everything.

"Will you at least wait tomorrow until my husband and our friends can meet you? I'm sure together we can figure out something reasonable."

"Reason can be a part of it," Catherine answered in a soothing tone. "We will listen to some reason."

"Good," said Alice, feeling only slightly reassured.

Catherine and Tinnemaha walked away from her then without any gesture or word of good night. She watched them wrap their blankets more closely around themselves and lie down close together under the supply wagon.

Suddenly Alice felt chilled and very tired. She longed to fold herself against Henry's sleeping body. Walking quickly to their wagon, she heard a frantic scramble off in the darkness, where a catamount was killing a sage hen. It was the final sound of her day.

ALICE AWOKE just before dawn. Henry was still sound asleep. Taking care not to disturb him, she sat up to dress.

Outside the wagon, the air was damp with dew, the sky so

pale blue, it was nearly white. In the east, faint tints of pink and orange were being bleached out by the sun, which had yet to appear over the horizon.

Alice looked toward the rock formation where she had encountered Catherine Guthrie and Tinnemaha. Its curving folds and its color, a streaked rusty red like old blood, seemed most unrocklike. She wanted to see it more closely in the light, but she had only taken a few steps in its direction when Henry, slipping his suspenders up over his shoulders, emerged from the wagon.

"Henry," she said in confusion.

"Why, you look downright surprised to see me," he answered with a chuckle.

"I suppose I truly am," she laughed at herself. "I guess when a body is in the midst of strange occurrences so often, the familiar begins to look extraordinary."

"Well, this familiar man would be pleased to find an ordinary breakfast in the making."

Alice went to a box on the side of the wagon and took out coffee, bread, and the last of the dried beef. Henry started to go tend the animals.

"Henry, wait a moment, will you?"

He turned toward her with a questioning look.

"I took in two women last night, one that's been a captive of Indians and the other an Indian herself."

Now Henry looked surprised, unpleasantly so.

"Where are they?" he asked.

Alice pointed to the supply wagon.

"We must certainly give the white woman our protection, mustn't we?" Alice said.

"There'll be no place to leave her now until Ragtown, if we even pass that way. We can't be backtracking to Fort Hall," Henry said, rubbing the back of his neck. "Has she asked for our help?"

"No, but I believe it's only because her mind is a bit addled."

"As yours must have been last night. You should have waked me."

Henry looked around the small encampment, as if expecting to find an answer lying about somewhere like a forgotten pair of socks. When his gaze came back to Alice, his expression showed he regretted his harsh remark.

"I'll talk it over with Roy," he said more mildly.

Within the next half hour, everyone else was up, including the two newcomers, who squatted beside the supply wagon and seemed to take no notice of the curious stares aimed their way. They made no objection when Jerusha, aghast at their near-nakedness, brought them cotton shirts and muslin delaine skirts to put on. Alice's story was told and retold to the women and children while Roy and Henry stood conferring a short distance away from the wagons.

"I don't like it," Roy was saying. "How are we to know the Indians won't come after them?"

"Alice says they are all on their own. Probably won't be missed for weeks," Henry replied.

"That's just a woman's softness talking. There's no place for soft hearts and soft heads here."

Henry frowned at Roy but thought better of rebuking him for his oblique criticism of Alice. Her actions had first struck Henry, too, as burdensome and vexing.

"Roy, could you in good conscience abandon Mrs. Guthrie to the elements and the savages again? Think if it were Jerusha or Flinder who had been thrown thus on the mercy of strangers."

"And what of Flinder and your Sarah?" Roy countered. "Should young girls as they be in the company of a woman who's been passed over the prairie by who knows how many braves?"

"I doubt she'll speak to them of that. Or to anyone."

Roy fell silent. Henry could tell he was mulling over the situation, searching for more arguments. Henry was sure that in the end Roy would agree to taking along the stranded woman. There was really no other choice, which, Henry knew, was exactly what Roy disliked most about the predicament.

"You appear set, Henry," Roy said after several minutes.

"It's the Christian thing to do."

"Yes," Roy said heavily. "Only, after all we been through, a man gets to thinking first about himself. And his own, what's left of them."

Henry gave Roy a hearty clap on the back to show he understood Roy's feelings and appreciated his rising above them.

When the women saw the men approaching the supply wagon, they moved near enough to hear what would be said, but not so near as to seem to be intruding on men's business.

"Mrs. Guthrie," Henry said loudly, aware of the intent audience at his back.

The two squatting women stood up slowly. Catherine Guthrie looked Henry square in the face. Her expression was placid. He saw no hope or need in it, only a hint of curiosity in the slightly pushed-out lower lip. Henry did not know what he had been expecting from her, but he knew it was not this almost disinterested directness. Disconcerted, he glanced at the Indian woman, but she was looking past him to the group of women and children. Were neither of these two aware of the precariousness of their plight and the importance of the decision he was about to relate? He turned again to Catherine.

"Mrs. Guthrie," he repeated, "we are prepared to take you with us as far as the first settlement, which will be in California. We know you have suffered hardships. So, too, have we. I trust you will expect to be a working member of our group."

"As for her," Roy interjected, pointing his chin at Tinnemaha, "she can wait for her people to come fetch her. We can leave her some food, but we'll be sacrificing to do that much."

Alice hastened forward anxiously, then stopped as if she had changed her mind. She stood now between the two small groups of people, the men and the newcomers before her, the other women and the children behind her. Catherine Guthrie gave her a quick look, then addressed Roy.

"It is not wise to waste water in the desert. Tinnemaha is my water. I will not leave her."

"What foolishness is this?" said Roy angrily. "We offer you aid, and you talk like a crazy woman."

Henry laid a restraining hand on Roy's shoulder. He felt Alice come up beside him.

"Mrs. Guthrie," he said, "our resources are already strained. You ask too much."

"I have asked for nothing," Catherine replied evenly.

There was some shuffling and whispering from the rear group. Hope began to squall.

"Have you completely forgotten the ways of civilized folks?" Roy shouted at Catherine. "Where are your loyalties, woman, to say nothing of plain horse sense and common decency?"

"We thank you for the night's shelter," Catherine answered. "We will go now."

"Henry," Alice said urgently. He could not think what she expected him to do.

"Wait," Alice called to the two women, who had already begun to walk away. They stopped and turned. Alice went to stand beside them.

"Henry," she appealed, "are Mrs. Guthrie's feelings really so odd? These women had the same husband. They watched him die together. They nursed each other through smallpox."

"More damn foolishness," Roy scoffed.

Tinnemaha moved close to Alice and stared hard at her. She spoke at Alice's cheek. Catherine translated to the men.

"She says that this woman who walks in the shoes of her sister will soon walk in the shoes of her husband."

Roy made a guttural sound of disgust and waved his hand

dismissively at Catherine. Muttering something about dumb animals, he stomped off toward where the oxen and mules were picketed.

Alice moved away from Tinnemaha and reached out to touch Henry's arm. The lightness of her grasp, coming after the Indian's strange pronouncement, disturbed Henry. He pulled his arm roughly away from her.

"There's chores need doing around here," he said gruffly.

He turned halfway round away from Catherine and Tinnemaha, then turned back again more decisively. They hadn't moved.

"You will come with us," he said, as if giving an order. "Both of you."

He strode off in the same direction Roy had taken to herd the stock to the river to drink. At his approach, Jerusha called out a series of commands to the children, who scattered to their tasks. Henry felt as if he were a gust of wind dispersing them. There was an agitated rushing within him, too, which puzzled him. Usually when he had come to a decision in a muddied matter, he felt relief and calm. The rushing subsided as the day wore on. By the time they caught up the teams after supper and started to travel, it had reached a level he could almost ignore.

September 19, 1852

After a week of night travel, we have returned to moving by day. I shall miss the strange serenity of walking in the darkness. Meals were more congenial at midnight than in the baked heat of a sweltering day. But our daytime sleeps were never truly restful, hence the taking up of a more usual schedule.

The days are still hot, but more bearable, and the nights have been cold enough for frost. The river has been getting smaller and smaller, with fewer and fewer feeder streams. It is no more than a mud ditch now, and the water tastes bitter. We let the oxen wander to graze; one or two must be laboriously pulled out of the mire every morning. We will arrive at the Sink of the Humboldt tomorrow or the next day.

I wouldn't have thought it possible, but Catherine Guthrie and Tinnemaha have shown us how to glean some foodstuffs from this rough landscape. Yesterday they made a kind of cracker bread by crushing serviceberries into jam, mixing the jam with pulverized grasshoppers, and drying the mixture in the sun. Hank bravely tried it first, then urged the rest of us on. It had the flavor of fruitcake, minus the rum.

The children beleaguer Catherine with questions about Indian life. She will not talk of the Apaches, and the children have stopped asking because whenever they did, her face would darken and she'd become silent as a stone.

She does speak of the Paiutes, however, telling of how they grind pine nuts into mush and cook it with hot rocks, how they weave shoes and caps out of strips of bark, how they make flutes from reeds and baby carriers from willow shoots. She told the children that each person has a guardian spirit to give him strength, skill, and protection. When Gideon, wide-eyed, passed along this information, Jerusha said our Lord was a mighty enough protector and didn't need underlings to help Him, but I find it a comforting notion, even if it is not strictly true.

We are all quite used to Catherine and Tinnemaha already, though Roy mostly sidesteps them, and Henry is, at best, a mildly interested onlooker. I think we must have loosened or widened in some way to be able to plait these two women into our lives so smoothly. I wonder how we would have viewed them had they come down our farm lane in Indiana or even crossed our path earlier in the journey. It seems, looking back, that we were much weaker and more fearful then—we women, at least—or we believed ourselves so.

Perhaps, after all, it is not something new in us that they call to, but something overlooked.

Chapter 20

THEY REACHED THE Humboldt Sink at the hottest time of day. At this large, swampy area, the river, hardly worthy of that designation by now, disappeared into the sand.

One by one, the members of the Muller party walked to the lead wagon and looked out over the maze of small salt ponds, muddy sloughs, and stands of marsh grass. Beyond the Sink lay fifty-five miles of blank, forbidding desert where there was no grass and only one spring less than halfway across. The horizon all around was ringed by mountains. The mountains were divided into three sections by three gaps. They had traveled to the Sink through the gap to the north. Their goal, on the other side of the desert, was the gap to the west.

"We'll camp here," Henry said, turning to unhitch his oxen from the wagon's whiffletree.

Bailey, with Hank and Gideon following, walked to the edge of the nearest pond to inspect it more closely. Tinnemaha also approached the still, brackish water, but she went to a different spot some distance from Bailey and the boys.

Faith sat down in the shade of Henry's wagon. Alice handed Hope to her, and then began to help Jerusha, Catherine, and the girls unload what was needed to set up camp.

Roy stood beside Henry's team and fidgeted. Henry wondered why Roy had not gone to unpack the mules or to release the other oxen, some of which were almost too weak to move. Henry said nothing, however. He was so hot and weary that what would have been a quick and simple task in Indiana now cost him a great deal of effort and attention.

"How long you figure we should stop here?" Roy asked at last.

"The animals could use a week to fortify themselves for the desert crossing," Henry replied slowly.

He knew they could not afford a week, but the more days they could manage, he believed, the better off they'd be in the long run. There were still the Sierras to pass over, and it'd be helpful to have some reasonably healthy animals to start farming with in California.

"A week?" Roy exclaimed. "You must be mad, man. Or worse, fainthearted."

Henry felt fury surge up through his fatigue like vomit. He advanced close to Roy and stood silently before him for a long moment. Roy did not flinch.

"I'll not be slandered and I'll not be bullied, Royal Hall, by you or anyone."

"And I won't be cut out of decisions like I was a boy," Roy countered with equal vehemence.

"What reasons have you for pushing on except your own cockerel posing?" said Henry, each word like a satisfying bite of bitter tobacco.

Roy clenched his fists threateningly, but he stopped short of raising them.

"Another man in another place would fast find himself in the dirt after such a remark," he warned.

Out of the corner of his eye, Henry saw Faith leaving her seat in the shade. Strangely, he noticed that the hem of her skirt was down in back and had become curled and tattered from dragging on the ground for so long. His anger drained out of him in one swift slosh, as if he were a bucket that had just been upended.

"Roy," he said calmly, "we are in this place, not another, and we are who we are, tired farmers on a hard road. We must choose sense over pride. If you are discontented, tell it straight out."

"Talk don't matter. Actions do."

"What do you propose?"

"Stop only overnight. Cut grass for the crossing. Lighten up by leaving one or two wagons and some goods."

Henry looked toward the Sink while he considered Roy's suggestions. Haying and lightening their load were good ideas, though the women would fuss over the latter. But the animals needed rest, and only time could provide that.

He saw that Bailey and the boys were now beside Tinnemaha. Hank and Gideon were squatting, and Bailey was leaning forward to look at something Tinnemaha was pointing to on the ground.

Henry turned back to Roy.

"We'll do some haying and some unloading," he said, adding, "but we'll take two days here."

"Talk enough when horses fight," Roy answered, indicating his agreement.

"Pa," Hank called, trotting up to him. "Tinnemaha showed us antelope tracks in the wet sand, and geese and ducks and swans, too. Most likely on migration, Miss Jeffers said."

"Why not go hunting, Roy?" Henry suggested. "Some fresh meat would please all around. Hank and I'll tend to these." He slapped the bony haunch of the ox nearest him.

Roy hesitated. Both he and Henry knew Hank was really no substitute. Finally, however, he smiled and gave a nod.

"Set Flinder to work, too," he said. "I'll do my duty in good style on the hunt. And I'll see there's none of them thieving Diggers skulking about, neither."

IT WAS MIDNIGHT. The Muller party had decided to make a two-hour stop at the hot springs fifteen miles from the Sink before pushing on across the Forty-Mile Desert.

Roy had ridden ahead and dammed up the flow of one spring, so the water could cool enough for the animals to drink. Every water container had been filled before leaving the Sink, but there was enough only for the people.

The oasis was an eerie scene in the darkness. Jerusha de-

256

clared it an outpost of hell. A geyser of boiling water shot up
into the air several feet, and other springs murmured and
steamed around them. The night air was choked with the
smell of sulfur. Alice managed, however, to make a tolerable
pot of coffee with hot water from one of the springs.

They had left the Sink early in the morning, intending to
make the desert crossing in one long haul with only one or
two rest breaks. Though the way had been level, it was slow
going. The soft, sandy ground required the oxen to pull hard,
grueling labor in the baking heat. Between noon and nightfall, the sun had shone full in their faces.

There were only three wagons now, and fewer animals,
too, as the previous night Paiutes had slipped into the Sink
camp and stolen three mules, two oxen, and John's horse.
The supply wagon that Henry's family shared with the Halls
had been left at the Sink. All the oxen but one were in yoke,
four pairs to each wagon. It was a testament to the toll of the
journey on the animals that it needed eight of them to pull a
lighter wagon than six had pulled mere months ago. Only
Gideon rode, and then only when he was sleeping. The mules
were carrying less, too.

It had taken the women the better part of a day to settle on
what objects to jettison. Each person in the group, except
Catherine and Tinnemaha, who had no possessions, had
made sacrifices. Left in or near the deserted wagon were
clothes, scythes and other tools, books, Alice's rocker, Faith's
cedar chest, some cookware, Bailey's leather traveling case,
and a number of other things.

Though they were of negligible weight, Alice carefully laid
her white kid gloves in the seat of her rocker along with the
other things she had decided to abandon. The long-ago life in
Philadelphia that they represented was, she knew, irretrieva-
ble—had, in fact, never wholly existed outside of her daydreams. She found, stroking the supple leather, that she did
not feel the same pinched, secret need for either the gloves or
her daydreams that she once did.

Jerusha had introduced a comic note to the otherwise

dreary task of winnowing out when she theatrically unearthed from her wagon, to Roy's complete astonishment, a full-length mirror with an ornate frame of gilded gesso. Unmarred by its long sojourn, it had been wrapped so well that it wasn't even dusty.

Everyone took turns straightening their appearance or miming in front of it. Tinnemaha stood before it for a long time making various careful movements of face and body and occasionally extending one finger to touch the silvered glass. She led Catherine by the hand to the mirror and made her stay there beside her for a good ten minutes while she stared at their reflection, as enrapt as an art lover at a picture exhibition.

Later, when the Sink was far behind them, Alice looked back once and saw the bright gleam of the mirror reflecting the sunlight. She thought then of Lot's wife and her nostalgic backward glance. Sodom and Gomorrah must have gleamed in the distance, too. Alice decided God had been too harsh in his punishment of Lot's wife, who, after all, was not yearning after the sinful life of those cities but only, perhaps, fixing in her mind's eye the shape of a place that had been her home.

Lot's wife had shown her obedience by leaving as ordered. Had she to quell her memories and her rebellious heart as well? Apparently so. Wasn't that the lesson the story was meant to impart? It seemed to Alice that the Bible was hard on women for their most natural acts and feelings.

At two A.M. the men caught up the teams again, and the desert trek was resumed. The rest of the night was arduous. The sand now was almost as fine as dust. In some places, the wagon wheels sank hub-deep, and with each step, the animals dug in up to their knees. Two oxen and a mule died in their tracks, and three other oxen lay down from exhaustion and would not get up even when Roy beat them and set the dogs on them. There was nothing for it but to redistribute the oxen six to a wagon. The defeated oxen were dead before Henry and Roy called "giddap" to the newly formed teams.

Dawn revealed a flat, barren landscape, brilliantly white,

like a vast plain of ice. They were crossing the dry bed of an ancient brine lake. Not a single blade of green was growing from the salted earth. The wagon wheels crunched across the crusted surface.

They passed abandoned wagons and scattered equipment and scores of dead or dying draft animals, their lolling tongues swollen and cracked. The bleached bones of oxen, mules, cows, and horses from previous years lay on all sides, as numerous as feathers in a henhouse. It occurred to Alice that these loyal servants of man deserved their own heaven, an endless field of sweet clover with not a yoke or harness in sight. At least one owner must have shared Alice's sympathies, because one failing ox they passed had been compassionately covered with an old gum coat.

Several hours later, they were among sagebrush again, though the desolate, brittle plants stood barely a foot tall. The tired oxen, weakened by hunger and thirst, were moving ever more slowly. The sky was white with the sun's fiery glare, and every hour the heat grew stronger.

Finally, near noon, they crested a low rise and beheld ahead the welcome sight of cottonwood trees and green thickets along the shady bottomlands of the Truckee River. If the hot springs had been an outpost of hell, this place could surely claim to be an outpost of heaven.

As they neared the river, the thirsty animals, smelling water, began to walk faster and jostle one another impatiently. The mules trotted in spurts. Roy's horse neighed and tugged at the lead connecting it to a wagon.

Afraid the animals would run headlong into the river and topple the wagons and goods, Henry and Roy stopped to unhitch the horse and the oxen and unpack the mules. Freed, the sorry beasts did indeed rush on and plunge into the cold, clear water.

Later, the men drove the oxen and mules back to the stalled wagons to bring them and the packs to the trout-filled river, where they planned to camp for two nights.

CATHERINE GUTHRIE had let the Mullers use her Christian name in the beginning because she saw it reassured them. She let them keep on using it because then only Tinnemaha would call her by her Indian name. Catherine liked the notion that for the rest of her life she'd never hear that name in any other voice but Tinnemaha's.

It was strange to be among whites again, Catherine thought, noticing Bailey walking nearby, off to her right side. They were likable enough, what her father, a preacher, would have judged "good people." She understood them because she had once been one of them, but she knew they could never really understand her.

Catherine rarely thought about her past anymore. When she did, she framed it in her mind as her "other" life, though, in reality, it seemed to her more a life lived by another woman than a personal memory. The present woman, bound to Tinnemaha as she had never before been bound to another person, was who Catherine truly was, who, remarkably, she must have always been underneath.

The terrible weeks with the Apache braves stretched like a burning bridge between the two Catherines. She thought of that brutal time as a baptism that had lifted her from one state and deposited her in another. And, as was the case with baptism, the new state was the ordained one, the one God had meant her to inhabit all along.

Of course, Catherine had not seen this right away. The Paiute named her Yaxap, or Cry, she had been so mournful during her early days with them. Tau-gu, her Paiute husband, was much taken up with his duties as *niavi,* or chief, so he left it to Tinnemaha to teach Catherine their ways and gentle her into a place among them. It was not common for a Paiute man to have more than one wife, but it was not unheard-of. Sometimes, too, one woman would have two husbands, usually brothers.

Tinnemaha had spent many hours teaching Catherine how

to speak the language of their particular group of Paiutes; how to gather seeds, berries, and agave stalks; how to make piñon nut porridge; how to build the open-sided summer shelters and the bark and brush winter lodges. Tinnemaha did not teach Catherine how to fashion sumac, juniper, yucca, and redbud fibers into the fine, curved wedding baskets she was so well-known for, but she let her waterproof the everyday basketry jugs and bowls with pine pitch.

Catherine learned, too, how to greet the sun each morning with a handful of cornmeal or ashes, how to paint a corpse's face red, how to dance and gamble at festivals. And after several months of Tinnemaha's wise guidance and Tau-gu's infrequent and brief attentions, Catherine learned the last thing, encountering the most surprising and intricate change of all. When Tinnemaha pressed against her with the sureness of a man and touched her with the skillful diligence of a master weaver, Catherine learned pleasure.

In the wandering days before they chanced upon Alice Muller, Catherine and Tinnemaha had turned their situation over and over, and they had decided to find a way to live apart from both their peoples. California, vast and freewheeling, seemed a likely place in which to carry out their plan.

Catherine quickened her step to catch up with Tinnemaha, who was at the head of the short line of mules. She longed to slip her arm around the narrow waist and feel the heave of Tinnemaha's hips as she walked. Of course, she would not do that, but at least she could fall in step beside her and call her by her secret name, Tabuce, sweet-grass-nut-root, and talk again about the home they'd soon be making together on the other side of the mountains.

BAILEY COULD NOT SLEEP. Her insomnia annoyed her; she knew the next day would be unpleasant if she wasn't well rested. But she felt agitated for some reason, and though her limbs ached with weariness, she could not settle into an easy position.

Bailey's mind darted about, mostly in contemplation of her companions. Bailey was an inveterate observer. She had begun watching people as a child in order to ape behaviors that would let her fit in. As an adult, she had continued to feel like an outsider in every milieu of her life. Except this one. Very gradually, this little band of people, especially the women, had accepted Bailey, had even come, blessedly, to take her for granted, and in response, Bailey had relaxed and opened up like cut tulips in a warm room. But the longtime habit of observing others persisted.

When the going was rigorous, Bailey had noticed, the emigrants tended to be stoical. Differences in their natures faded before the work at hand. They became parts of the same animal. It was in the respites afforded by hospitable environments that peculiarities were expressed, that boundaries and special loyalties emerged.

For three days they had been traveling alongside the Truckee into the dry mountains. After the meager Humboldt, the forlorn Sink, and the slow desert, they valued the simple delights of clean water and greenery, though the track was a steady, demanding upgrade. This was the last river, the one that would bring them to the foot of the pass through the Sierras.

The young people had been livelier the past few days. They had made grass whistles and skipped stones over the water. When Faith relieved her of driving for short spells, Flinder walked with Sarah, their arms linked and their heads together in girlish conversation, as if they were passing down a country lane on a spring Sunday.

Catherine and Tinnemaha, herding the four mules, had positioned themselves at the head of the little party. They kept up a constant dialogue in Tinnemaha's language, all the while intermittently clucking at and cheering along the disgruntled animals. Bailey liked to walk beside them because of the musical pattern that formed from the lilting strings of sounds the women directed at each other and the drumming syllables they directed at the mules.

Faith was stronger in both body and spirit, though she still lapsed from time to time into states of inertia, almost as if she were sleeping while awake. The care of Hope had evolved into a shared activity between Faith and Alice. The two women passed the baby back and forth in wordless cooperation, somehow in perfect agreement on when each of them should take her. Hope truly had two mothers, for neither woman exercised primacy over the other. Bailey believed this arrangement was likely to persist in California, it was so obviously satisfying to all concerned.

Henry was still quiet and watchful, as he had been ever since Fort Laramie, but he had begun whittling in the evenings again. Bailey counted this as a sign that his mind was easier. He engaged Alice more than he used to in trail decisions, such as where to camp and when to take rest stops.

Indeed, Alice shuttled among all the members of the group like a spider delicately connecting the spokes of her web. And she did it with a spider's calm and a spider's invisible potency.

Roy remained on the edges of Alice's web, as wary as a mosquito. There was open tension between him and Jerusha. When Roy was around, that is. He often left his wagon for Flinder to drive while he rode away to scout out campsites or to hunt. Jerusha seemed equally displeased with his presence and his absence.

Once Bailey was near Jerusha when Roy came into view after a disappearance of several hours.

"There's a welcome sight," Bailey said, referring to the deer carcass she could see slung over Roy's horse.

"As welcome as water in your shoes," was Jerusha's unexpected reply.

Bunching the blankets at her neck, Bailey gave her meandering thoughts a mental shake and tried again to fall asleep. She drew into her mind the strains of "Long, Long Ago" in a woman's whispery voice. Bailey had never been able to elaborate on that voice, to conceive of it saying or singing anything else, but she was sure it was a memory of her mother's voice. Its power to pull her only failed when she did not give herself over to it fully, when she let herself feel foolish about it.

Bailey was just settling into the cocoon of presleep, where she often encountered the other scraps of the memory, the white blouse and the hazy face, when she heard footsteps outside.

The fear of Indians jerked her awake. She quickly dismissed that possibility, however, because she heard nothing stealthy in the footsteps. To reassure herself more firmly, she sat up and peeked through the tent flaps.

The moon had not yet set. Bailey felt as if she were looking at one of her own charcoal drawings, but with a much wider range of whites and grays than she had ever been able to create.

A movement fluttered at the edge of her vision. She turned her gaze in its direction and caught Roy just as he was swinging his leg up over his horse's back. His saddlebags were bulging, and Bailey thought she could make out a bedroll behind the saddle.

Roy leaned over the horse's head as if he were speaking into its ear, and the animal moved forward in a slow walk. A mule carrying a small pack followed, a length of rawhide reaching from the mule's bridle to Roy's saddle horn. Rouser and Old Smith trotted beside the horse. Roy often took the hounds hunting or scouting with him, but Bailey could not imagine what errand would require a pack mule and a midnight departure.

While Bailey continued to look out, her eyes grew accustomed to the darkness. Better able to distinguish objects in and around the camp, she noticed for the first time a figure in the shadow of the Halls' wagon. Jerusha, standing absolutely still with her back to Bailey, was also watching the departing rider.

The whole scene, drained of color and so silent, reminded Bailey of a dream. Besides the slow retreat of the little entourage, the only movements were an occasional swish of the horse's tail and the rhythmical rocking of the man's back, and these were getting harder to discern the farther away Roy got. Nevertheless, Bailey's overall impression was of animation and even noise.

Convinced she had blundered into a very private moment, Bailey withdrew into the tent.

September 29, 1852

We have made few miles today. Our departure was delayed by the discovery of Roy's desertion last night. The day has been a long and mute one, as each of us pondered this affront.

We are almost harder stricken by Roy's going than we were by the deaths we have had to bear. We are betrayed. Our anger and shock bind us more tightly to one another, but grief did that, too, and in a purer way.

Jerusha will not speak of it and only said that Roy will reap what he has sown and that though she may be bitten, she is not all eaten. Flinder confided to me that Jerusha told her Roy had taken with him the ruby earrings her mother left her, which wounded her greatly. He dug them from her portmanteau before she knew what he was about, and she could no more retrieve them from his pocket than she could dissuade him from his knavish course.

The Truckee's path through the mountains is narrowing, and the river winds sharply from side to side. We were forced today to cross it again and again, and in some places the banks were steep and the fords strewn with boulders. I fretted then for Henry and all the weight he feels he carries alone now, and as bitter as my fury with Roy is, I wished him among us again. At least until California, whereupon he may go hang himself in his own garters.

Chapter 21

THE MULLER PARTY was crossing the Truckee for the third time that day. Henry, driving the last wagon, was having some trouble directing the oxen. They insisted on picking their own way through the rocky streambed because their feet were sore. Repeated wetting from days of such crossings had softened their hooves and made them tender.

The oxen finally exited the river and began hauling the wagon out. Alice gripped the edges of the board seat and leaned forward as the wagon tilted on its way up the bank. A moment later she was grateful for her handhold. The wagon jolted backward suddenly. Over the clatter of objects knocking together inside the wagon, Alice heard a loud crack from the running gear.

"Is it bad?" she said to Henry, who had gone to investigate.

"Hind axle broke passing over a rock," he answered.

The other two wagons had been waiting a short distance ahead for the final wagon to clear the river before moving on. Now all the women and children walked back to the river and stood on the bank.

"What is it?" Sarah called.

"Broken axle," Alice replied when Henry failed to respond. He stood silently regarding the crippled wagon as if his stare alone could fix it.

Sarah squatted to get a better view under the wagon. The river was splashing around the back end of the wagon bed as merrily and indifferently as it did around boulders. Just seeing its dash discouraged her, especially when she stood up again and looked at Henry immobilized beside it and Alice sitting worriedly on the tilted seat. For the first time in her life, Sarah saw her parents as vulnerable. Blushing and swelled with a sad fear, she turned away.

"What's to be done?" Jerusha said to Henry after he had waded to shore.

"This running gear has a movable coupling pole, so I could cut the wagon down to a two-wheeled cart," Henry said without enthusiasm.

"Well begun is half-done," Jerusha said briskly, trying to bolster her brother's intention. "Gideon, go get your uncle's tools. You others stand ready to pass goods. We'll make a brigade."

Jerusha climbed onto the wagon to begin unloading. Alice moved to help her. Henry positioned himself to receive the things they passed down.

The work progressed quickly, as the wagon's load was light. Jerusha was surprised to see Henry stagger while carrying a sack that she had lifted easily. Assuming he had merely tripped on a stone, she said nothing. Alice, too, had seen Henry falter. She began watching him surreptitiously, but he made no other missteps.

When the wagon had been emptied and pulled ashore, Henry took up his saw and went to work. The others left to take the animals to graze on some rushes upriver.

When Alice returned with some pemmican and a cup of water into which she had mixed a little citric acid and a few drops of lemon essence for Henry, she found him leaning against the wagon with his eyes shut. The wagon bed was sawn one-third of the way across.

Henry opened his eyes when he heard Alice's footsteps. He turned smiling toward her, but not before she had noted the sallow cast to his skin and the tight set of his jaw. Plainly, his rest was not an easy one. She wondered when he had last been able to find an untroubled hour in which to feel the simple body fact of tiredness or to enjoy a still, empty mind.

"I'm right ready for a bite," Henry said, reaching for the food in Alice's hands. "Thanks."

"I'm afraid it's only felon's fare. We didn't figure we'd be stopped long enough to bother with a fire."

Henry ate rapidly, moistening each mouthful of pemmican with a swallow of the contrived lemonade. Handing Alice the empty cup, he turned back to the wagon and bent to pick up his saw. Instead of straightening up again, however, he fell to his knees. He only saved himself from sprawling out completely by dropping the saw and bracing his hands on the ground.

"Henry!" Alice cried in alarm. She leaned over him and grasped his shoulders.

"I'm all right," he said, still on his hands and knees. "Just dizzy."

Slowly he sat back on his heels.

"I must have turned too quick," he said.

He stretched out his arm for the saw, but Alice picked it up and held it away from him.

"Tell me what to do," she said.

"It would take me longer to lead you through it than to do it myself," argued Henry, shaking his head.

Henry had been staunchly ignoring the intermittent spells of weakness that had come over him in the past few days, and he was annoyed with himself that he had let Alice witness one. He didn't want her fussing about, trying to nurse him. There was nothing wrong with him, anyway, that wouldn't be cured by a few days of hearty food and decent sleeps. He just needed to get them all to California first.

"Let me sit here a bit, and I'll get back to work," Henry said, as if Alice had nagged him.

Still holding the saw, Alice looked thoughtfully at the goods piled on the bank. Three small sacks of flour leaned against a barrel of oats. Alice's medicine chest sat atop a firkin of lard. There were rolls of bedding and hampers of clothing, a spade and a pickax, a wagon bow, cooking utensils, and tins of compressed dried vegetables. Off to one side, as if it were too dainty to be found in such utilitarian company, stood a lady's writing desk of mahoghany with an inlaid burl top. It had been Alice's since she was fifteen and was one of the few "luxury" items to have survived the two load lightenings.

"Let's abandon the broken wagon," Alice said suddenly. "We could probably fit all those things in the other two wagons. And we'd free up the oxen, so even with putting eight oxen to each wagon, we'd have two spare instead of just one to work in and out of the teams."

"It would mean more unloading at night to make room for sleeping," Henry warned. "Or bedding outside no matter what the weather."

"You'll hear no objections."

Henry knew Alice would be true to her word. What's more, her suggestion was a practical one—it saved him time and work now, and it would allow Jerusha, Flinder, and him to spell one another driving. But something in him resisted the idea. Leaving unfinished the task of making a cart felt to him like a shameful failure. This was not how things were supposed to be. They were supposed to have all the wagons— and all the people—they had started out with.

Another mild wave of dizziness swept over Henry. If he had been standing, he probably would have swayed. When his head cleared, his objections to abandoning the wagon had slipped away from him, as if they were wily trout he had spied glimmering in the dark waters of a shaded lake and had not been quick enough with his line to catch. Miserable and confused, Henry knew only he was a man who needed relief, whether he liked it or not.

"Very well," he said. "Let's try it."

THE PINE-FORESTED upper canyon of the Truckee was even narrower than the lower canyon. Sometimes the wagons had to be hauled right up the riverbed, against the current. Henry, Jerusha, and Flinder waded hip-deep in the icy river beside the oxen, whose feet were so pained, they refused to walk at all unless they were led and goaded. For this work, Jerusha and Flinder wore pants that Roy had left behind.

The others struggled along the narrow space between the river and the canyon walls. Gideon fell repeatedly. Even the surefooted mules, who had been heavily burdened to lighten the wagons, trod with extra care. A few times two or three of the women had to wade into the river to help lift the wheels over large rocks. Faith, remembering John in the Elkhorn River, asked to be excused from the chore. To make up for this, she took on more mealtime and campground tasks.

Alice kept watching Henry for signs of illness. He would not reply to any direct questions about his health. He was fatigued, certainly, she could see that, and weaker than he had been at any other time, but because he did not give in to his fatigue and weakness, Alice could not ascertain if his condition was anything worse than the tiredness they all felt.

Finally, as days passed and Henry kept on with unflagging, though diluted, vigor, Alice banished worry from her mind. They had already managed so much. They would continue to persevere. She had struck a knot of vitality within herself so strong that even the cold river and the mountains ahead did not daunt her.

THEY HAD COME OUT of the canyon into mountain-ringed meadowlands and were traveling on level ground. The air was cold and damp, and after a few miles, it began to snow. Large, wet flakes came down thickly. In a half hour, the ground was covered enough for footprints to show, and the tree branches and rocks were collecting antimacassars of snow.

The Muller party had not seen another wagon along the Truckee, and except for an occasional deer, the meadows, too, were theirs alone. Tinnemaha told them there were no Indians in the area, either. Six roads, all new this season, competed with the old route for emigrants, each road leading to a different settlement in California and each vigorously promoted by boosters from those settlements. The Mullers had met agents at the Humboldt Sink who had tried to convince them to take Johnson's Cutoff to Placerville, and others who had talked up Noble's Road to Shasta City. Roy had been tempted, but Henry had not favored shifting their plans, reasoning that too little was known about the new roads, which were most likely no better than the old, anyway. Alice wondered if Roy was along one of those other roads right now. She hoped it turned out to be a toilsome one.

Alice had always liked falling snow, though she knew it could prove dangerous here. It would be a hard trial to have to winter in these mountains if the pass were blocked by early storms. Still, she was sure that even in that extreme she and her companions would not resort to murder and cannibalism as had some members of the Donner party, who had been trapped by blizzards on the eastern slopes of the Sierras six years ago.

But recalling the gruesome story did not block out Alice's contentedness with her surroundings. The troublesome river canyons were behind them. The way was clear, winding enchantingly among tall, widely spaced yellow pines and a few giant gray boulders. That certain silence that comes with falling snow called forth an answering silence and peace inside Alice. Though a foot might slide and unbalance her now and then, she marched ahead with a joyful rhythm to her step.

"WANT SOME RELIEF, MA?" Flinder asked, coming up to her mother. Jerusha was trudging along beside the rear wagon, driving the oxen.

Flinder herself had just been relieved by Faith, but Faith didn't like to drive too long. Flinger figured she might as well pass along the respite to her mother, who would never ask for one.

"I'm all right," Jerusha answered.

Flinder sighed. Since Roy's departure, Jerusha had been like a human fortress, barring all attempts at entry. Flinder had heard both Alice and Henry, on different occasions, bring up the subject of Roy, and each time Jerusha had flatly refused to talk. She seemed ashamed of what had happened, as if she and not her husband had been the wrongdoer. Flinder ached for her mother, so alone in her grief and rage. Flinder knew her well enough to know those sentiments were there.

"Ma," Flinder said, taking a deep breath, as if she were about to dive underwater, "why aren't you wearing your sapphires?"

Until the morning after Roy's departure, Flinder had never seen her mother without either the sapphire or the ruby earrings. Those tiny, sparkling jewels were all Flinder knew of her grandmother, except that she had died too young after being burdened with too many children. On the evidence of the lovely earrings, Flinder had long ago decided that her grandmother must have managed to hold on to an appreciation of beauty despite her hard life, and Flinder had resolved that she, too, would not let life's tribulations rob her of its pleasures.

"No need for vanity out here," Jerusha answered crisply.

"But I thought it was sentiment, not vanity, behind your wearing of those earrings."

Jerusha cracked the whip over the oxen's backs, though there was no need. They picked up their pace a bit, and Jerusha, too, walked briskly. It's as if she's trying to get away from me, Flinder thought, skipping to catch up.

The oxen soon slowed to their normal tread, placing their feet carefully on the slippery ground. Jerusha did not urge them on again. Flinder saw her stroke her earlobe as if it itched her.

"It don't seem the same with the one pair gone," Jerusha said at last.

"Anyway," she continued, anger curdling the dreaminess out of her voice, "now they remind me of him, not of her."

Flinder was gratified that her mother was finally letting out some of her feelings, but she was surprised to find that it also frightened her a little. Her own feelings about Roy were so jumbled, she was not sure now that she really wanted to know all that her mother felt. She wondered, too, what her mother expected from her.

"Should I hate him, Ma?" she asked, knowing the words were far more crude than the confusion they tried to express.

"He's still your father," Jerusha evaded.

"But he's been selfish and unfair."

"Do you hate him, girl?" Jerusha probed, restraining any inflection of emotion.

Flinder wiped away the tears that were filling her eyes and swallowed hard to drown the others waiting in her throat.

"I hate it that sometimes I feel sad on his account," she answered. "But other times I'm glad he's gone, if that's how little he cared for us."

"You'd do well to remember the smart of this injury, Flinder," Jerusha said solemnly. "It's the nature of most men to put themselves first. Like that Mr. Webster of yours."

Flinder's descent into her feelings about her father was pulled up short by this remark.

"Why, Jack Webster is nothing like Pa," she protested.

"He left you, didn't he?" Jerusha said.

"He's coming for me," Flinder insisted, her voice not as sure as she'd have liked it to be. The turn of the conversation had caught her off guard.

"Well, he shan't have you," Jerusha asserted. "I'll bear no daughter of mine to be under the thumb of an unreliable man. In fact, if I thought I could prevail, I'd see to it that you'd not give yourself to any man ever."

"You can't condemn them all!" Flinder said, truly shocked.

"They condemn themselves, every day on every side."

"I won't let you choose for me," Flinder declared hotly. "And I won't be poisoned by Pa's villainy or your bile."

Flinder flounced away from her mother, but Jerusha followed quickly after and stopped her by grabbing on to her wrist and jerking it. Furious, Flinder turned toward Jerusha. Still clutching her daughter's wrist tightly, Jerusha stepped in close to her so that their faces were only inches apart.

"Poison it may be," Jerusha said gruffly, "but it's our gift to you, my girl. Take it and use it."

Flinder felt torn between wanting to break free of her mother and wanting to embrace and comfort her.

"Oh, Ma," she said softly, "when Jack comes, I must make up my own mind."

The two women stood locked together as the wagon rolled past them. The faithful oxen were keeping on, uncritically following the wagon in front of them.

"Whoa!" came Henry's shout from up ahead.

Jerusha dropped Flinder's wrist. The girl stepped back from her mother, but she could not bring herself to leave. There was much about her mother she didn't know, Flinder realized, and much her mother would probably never know about her. Somehow they would each have to live with those limitations or they would lose the common ground they did share.

When Jerusha held out her hand to Flinder, the girl did not hesitate to take it. Wordlessly they walked together to the head wagon to inspect the campsite Henry had chosen for the night.

The snow had stopped. They were on the shore of a long, narrow lake that gleamed dark blue in the late afternoon sun. The deep color reminded Flinder again of Jerusha's sapphires. Across the lake loomed the final obstacle—the majestic Sierras and the seven-thousand-foot pass that would lead them across the summit.

October 4, 1852

Tomorrow we begin to ascend the mountains that stand between us and the aim of all our striving. I am fearful of the crossing, but when I look at the snow-topped granite range, I cannot but be struck by its beauty and magnificence. It saddens me that Henry does not lift his eyes in similar awe, even for a moment, but keeps them instead cast down on where the next footfall shall land. It was his spirit that drew him into this great trek. I do not want to think his spirit has been plundered by it.

We are all of us now drawing on our deepest reserves to sustain ourselves and one another. We meet each day, each hour, as we must, with full attention to its demands, pushing aside all thoughts of the dust that has settled behind us and the dawns that are yet to break.

Once in a Philadelphia shop window I watched pearl merchants picking carefully at rough pearls, peeling away layer after scarred layer, though some layers, to my untrained eye, seemed perfect. The white pearls shone pink or blue, sometimes ocher. It was as if the workers held beads of moonglow between their fingers. Their tools were as subtle as a lacemaker's. I have thought lately how we are like pearls, built in layers over the years, with, if we are lucky, somewhere among the layers, a perfect one, luminous and smooth. And if we are even luckier, someone or something will peel away what obscures that layer and bring it into the light.

Chapter 22

ALICE HANDED Henry a mug of coffee.

"I know it's weak, but it's hot," she said when she saw him frown after his first sip.

His frown remained in place, but he continued drinking. Jerusha, wrapped in a thick wool sweater, appeared from around the end of the wagon.

"There's a feel of snow," she said as greeting.

Alice looked at the sky. It was a bluish white, like the first yield from a cow before the fatty hind milk has let down. The mountains stood out darkly. They seemed impenetrable. Some thin clouds, which might signify snow, were snagged on the peaks.

"Let's start, then," Henry said.

Jerusha turned around and strode back to her wagon.

Henry handed Alice his cup and bent to straighten the doubletree, readying it for getting the oxen into yoke. The cup was still half-full of coffee.

"Henry, you haven't eaten yet," Alice objected, though breakfast consisted only of cold cornmeal cakes left from the previous night's dinner.

"Not hungry," he said. "I expect I've got a cold coming on. That always dampens my appetite."

"I wish I had some onion syrup for you."

"The best tonic for me will be getting across these mountains."

He left to get the oxen. Alice knew there was no arguing with him. She set Sarah to packing up the breakfast things while she nursed Hope inside the wagon.

THE WAGONS MOVED CAREFULLY along the lakeshore for a few miles, and at the head of the lake, they began to climb. The rising ground was covered with a foot of snow. Getting to the top of the pass would be the hardest test of the whole journey. Unlike the broad South Pass through the Rockies, this pass—like those on all the trans-Sierra routes—was as steep and rough as a mountain, earning the name "pass" only because of the higher, ragged peaks that towered around it.

The wagons moved more and more slowly, the oxen struggling up the grade from one short level spot to the next. Even with the advantage of the narrow ramps of packed dirt and rocks built by emigrants in earlier years, the going remained laborious. Shortly after noon, with the top of the pass in view, the front wagon rolled to a stop. Alice, trudging along right behind it, imagined she heard it shudder.

"The oxen are too weak to pull the loads up that steep pitch," Henry explained to Alice when she came up beside him.

Alice followed Henry's line of vision. They were facing a thirty-five-degree slope that rose 150 feet and was about 250 feet long.

"But they must go up," Alice said, as if her insistence would give the overburdened animals the extra strength they needed.

With snow covering the grass, the oxen and mules had had nothing to eat yesterday. The hungry animals bawled miserably through most of the night. Tinnemaha and the children had gathered pine needles to feed them in the morning, but it was sparse fortification for the work set before them today.

Jerusha, who had been driving the other wagon, joined her brother and his wife. Catherine, who was in charge of the mules, also came up to see what plans were being made.

"How about double-teaming?" Jerusha suggested. "Sixteen oxen might be able to do what eight can't."

"I was thinking of that," Henry said, surveying the terrain ahead. "Be hard to maneuver, though."

Eight yoke of oxen would stretch out to a length of eighty feet. If the slope crested sharply, which could not be seen from their current vantage point, the two front yoke of oxen would not be able to pull once they were over the crest, leaving more work for the other animals. Likewise, if the wagons needed to take a curving path, most of the pulling would fall to the wheel yoke.

"We'll have to put the strongest animals in the rear," Henry said at last.

"I think we could all use some hot food first," Alice offered.

Henry nodded, though he did not seem to really be listening. He was looking over the oxen, evaluating their relative conditions.

"I'll get the fire started," Catherine said.

They still had wood left from the wagon they'd abandoned at the Truckee. Flinder, Sarah, and Hank had taken turns splitting up most of the bed with an ax.

While the women prepared a simple meal, Henry and Flinder yoked sixteen of the strongest oxen together and hitched them to the front wagon.

Henry posted himself beside the lead yoke. Flinder stood next to the wheel yoke with a long whip. The rest of the party, their hands curled around bowls of hot oatmeal, watched anxiously.

On Henry's signal, Flinder cracked the whip and shouted "Giddyap!" Henry, too, shouted at the oxen and pushed hard against the wooden yoke of the first pair. The animals strained forward. Vapor clouds billowed from their wide nostrils. Some of them bawled and rolled their eyes back, as if appealing for mercy. The wagon moved only a few inches.

"All right, Flinder, that's enough," Henry called.

They all walked back to the small fire, no one wishing to be the first to speak. Faith filled two bowls with oatmeal laced liberally with heat-plumped raisins and shaved almonds. She handed the steaming bowls to Henry and Flinder. Sarah held out a plate of dried venison. Flinder took several strips of meat, but Henry waved the plate away.

"Must we abandon the wagons?" Bailey asked Henry.

Jerusha clacked her tongue, as if Bailey had spoken rudely, though the same question was in all their minds.

Henry ate a large spoonful of oatmeal. He did not look at Bailey, or at anyone. Squatting down, he put his bowl on the ground and extended his hands to warm them at the fire.

"We've lost so much already," Alice said.

"Necessities could be tied to the oxen's backs," Henry said, still staring into the fire. "We needn't take the wagons."

"Necessities?" Alice said.

"Food and bedding," Henry answered.

No one spoke. To leave the last two wagons and their few remaining belongings seemed a desperate measure, and they did not want to think of themselves as desperate.

Catherine watched Henry closely. He had picked up his bowl, but he was mostly just stirring the oatmeal around, taking half-spoonful bites now and then. He winced slightly when he swallowed, as if his throat were sore. Catherine saw that Henry had not really reached a decision about the wagons, but at the same time, his blank expression suggested he was not trying to think of alternatives, either.

Catherine remembered the council meetings the Paiute had held any time a serious decision was needed. Tau-gu, though he was *niavi,* was not expected to dictate matters on his own. In fact, his function was to carry out the wishes of the men and women of his band, not to rule them. Tau-gu had always been content with this limit to his power. Now, looking at Henry's heavy face, Catherine understood why.

She glanced across the fire to Tinnemaha. The Indian woman had also been watching Henry, but just then she looked up and met Catherine's gaze. Tinnemaha fumbled for a moment in the voluminous folds of her skirt; the garment was Jerusha's and was too full for Tinnemaha's slender build. A length of hemp rope around her waist bunched the skirt over her hips. Locating her pocket, Tinnemaha pulled out a small object which she kept hidden in her fist. Holding her fist straight out in front of her, she began speaking.

"She says her brothers run four days without food to trade with faraway peoples," Catherine translated. "And she says that what they once brought, she will carry back."

Tinnemaha turned her fist palm up and opened her fingers one by one. In her hand sat half an abalone shell the size of a large plum. Even in the muted light of the overcast day, its concave surface gleamed purple and green and silver. Tinnemaha offered the shell to Alice, who was standing beside her. Alice stroked its pearly inside and its dark, rough exterior. It was passed slowly around the circle until it got back to Tinnemaha.

"I suppose we may take that as a vote of confidence," Bailey said.

Henry smiled for the first time that day and stood up.

"We'll carry everything up on the mules and in our own arms. The oxen should be able to bring up empty wagons if we don't make them work on the slope, but take them to the top and let them pull from there," he said. "All right with everyone?"

Yeses tumbled over one another. A flinty energy quivered through the small group. Hope, lifting her head from Faith's shoulder, gave a squeal of delight at some unknown baby thought.

"So," Henry said. "Let's get a do on this job."

The rest of the day was spent toiling up the slippery mountainside with food and belongings. Everyone worked. Little Gideon was left to keep the fire alive and to answer any cries from Hope, who was bedded down in a wagon.

THE WEATHER CLEARED by late afternoon, though there was little heat left in the bright sun. After a supper of beans and rice and more dried venison, everyone went bone-weary to bed. The wagons were a little less than half-empty.

The whole next day was spent as the previous afternoon had been, with the added task of herding the oxen. The beasts lumbered reluctantly up the steep incline, slipping and complaining, and more than one of them left bloody trails in the snow when they lost their footing and struck their knees on rocks. They were rewarded at the top by a large stand of tall rushes growing above the snow. Unfortunately, two of the oxen ate so greedily, they died of surfeit.

The hard work spurred Henry's appetite a little. Alice took out time from hauling to boil up some trapper's fruit for him. She used dried apples and the last of the raisins and nuts, and lamented the lack of whipping cream. Henry dutifully finished it all, but his color was still waxen, and the cough deep in his chest persisted.

Getting the wagons up the following day was no light labor, in spite of their emptiness. There was room at the top for six pairs of oxen to line up, with forty feet of level ground to spare. The twelve fittest oxen were put in yoke and attached by chains to the wagon below. Henry did not have a long enough chain to reach the whole distance, so he had to fell and notch two small trees and connect them between the chains. He attached a drag to the rear axle to hold back the wagon in case a chain broke. Alice, Jerusha, Bailey, and Flinder were each assigned to a wheel as extra insurance.

When everything was ready, Henry led the oxen ahead the forty available feet and brought them to a stop. He waved down to Alice and Jerusha, who chocked the rear wheels of the wagon with small logs to keep it from rolling backwards. Next, Henry detached the chain from the oxen, and he and Faith backed the oxen up until the hind legs of the last yoke stood once more at the edge of the slope. Then Henry shortened the chain and reattached it and led the oxen ahead the same forty feet again. In this way, each wagon was hitched slowly up the slope to the top of the pass.

When the second wagon was at last up, Bailey looked down over the route they had climbed and shook her head.

"Seems more impossible from here than it did looking up

from below," she said to Flinder and Gideon, who were standing beside her.

" 'Tis God who brought us up safely, Miss Jeffers," Gideon said. "I prayed to Him."

Flinder laughed at her brother's seriousness.

"It was more our own hard work and stubbornness," she said, tousling his hair.

Annoyed, Gideon pulled away from her touch.

Bailey watched the small friction between the brother and sister with affection. It suddenly struck her that she was going to miss these people very much. They stood now at the summit of the pass through the Sierras. In another two weeks, they would all be parting company, setting themselves to engineer their new lives in California. Their separate lives. Bailey felt a catch of grief in her throat. It shocked her, but it also pleased her. These people were her comrades, the first she had ever had, and if that cost her some sadness, she decided, it was well worth it. She also decided, though she didn't yet know how exactly she would do it, that she would keep these people in her life somehow. Looking at the mountains around her, stately and silent in the waning daylight, Bailey thought that this was a fitting place in which to make such a pledge to herself.

She turned from the grand view to Gideon, who was kicking hard at a hummock of snow and still scowling.

"Now, Gideon," she consoled him. "One could answer that it is God who gives us our stubbornness."

"God and the roads He sets us on," Flinder added.

Gideon scrutinized the two women, as if trying to judge whether or not he had won any concessions from them. It was clear by the set of his face that he really didn't want to stay at odds with his cherished sister.

"Let's go to the fire," Bailey said.

Gideon fell in step beside Flinder. When she laid her arm across his shoulder, he drew closer, leaning his body against her hip and slipping his hand into her pocket to warm it.

"Where's Uncle Henry?" Flinder asked when they had entered the small encampment and she noticed he was the only one of the party not present at the fire.

"He's in bed," Alice answered.

"Before supper?" Flinder said, surprised.

Alice felt a hot anger flash through her. Flinder was only saying what she herself had said a little while ago, but hearing it from someone else exacerbated Alice's deep fears for Henry. His strength had persevered through the past three hard days, but now it seemed dangerously low. Trying to convince herself that he'd be set right by morning, she had no room for doubts, however slight.

"Hasn't he earned an early rest if he chooses it?" Alice snapped at Flinder.

"The girl meant no disrespect, I'm sure," Jerusha said.

"No, truly I didn't, Aunt Alice. Uncle Henry *should* rest, working full out as he has been while he's feeling poorly."

"I said nothing about him feeling poorly. Can't a man be weary?" Alice's tone was still sharp.

Flinder opened her mouth to reply, but behind Alice's back Jerusha motioned her daughter to silence. Just then Hope, bundled in rabbit skins and lying on a flour barrel near the fire, began to cry. Before either Alice or Faith could respond, Flinder went to the baby and picked her up. She crooned "Old Kentucky Home," and the child's crying subsided. Indeed, everyone around the fire was mesmerized by the nostalgic song.

For several minutes, the only sounds in the black-and-white landscape of snow, granite walls, and dark pines were Flinder's flutelike voice and the hiss of burning wood falling in upon itself.

October 7, 1852

We are at the top of the pass. In my mind's eye, I see the long road that brought us here from Indiana like a furrow rent in the earth. Sweat and tears and blood have dropped into that cleft. Seeds have been sown whose fruits we shall not know for some time yet, seeds from our old homes intermingled with strange seeds gathered along the way.

I must confess that I am grateful for this journey. The company of Bailey Jeffers and of Catherine Guthrie and Tinnemaha and the brushes up against Indians and other emigrants have shown me that there is not only one right course for a life, that any life requires choosings, however much we may shy from them or endeavor to attach reservations. I have learned, also, on this journey that I can do and endure more than I had thought I could. And I have learned that I can bring more to my husband and receive more from him. It's like the loaves and fishes in the Bible. The more freely I share, the more I find I possess.

Still, I anticipate the end of the journey with a fretful eagerness, like a child who has waited patiently all week for Sunday's pie and then hops about and whines when he smells it cooling on the windowsill.

I can hear wolves howling to one another from the higher crags. The fire has grown low. No one else is up, so I won't put on more wood. I go now to lie down beside Henry.

Chapter 23

THE WESTERN SLOPE of the Sierras was a maze of ridges and canyons that fell away from the pass as steeply as the eastern slope had approached it. Henry frequently had to fasten logs behind the wagons to keep them from making a wild downhill charge. On some inclines, these drags were not sufficient to control a wagon's descent. Then Henry would tie a rope to the rear of the wagon, snub the rope around a tree, and, with the help of the women, let the wagon down at a safe speed. None of the descents was as harrowing as the one at Goose Creek had been, but they could not banish that time from their minds, and after each successful lowering, the boys would whistle and shout and the girls and women would clap their hands or hug their nearest neighbor on the rope.

The trees they used for snubbing were usually pines. The ridges were thickly forested with them. The bark of Jeffrey pines scented the early autumn air with vanilla. Hank and Gideon scoured the ground each day for the huge cones from Coulter and sugar pines to use as kindling. When Alice kissed her son good-night, he smelled sharply of turpentine and woodsmoke.

Henry, on the other hand, smelled of the sickroom. Though he continued to push himself through the requirements of each day, he no longer hid his ailing condition, and he allowed Alice and Jerusha to doctor him without complaint. Each morning Alice rubbed his throat with a mixture of camphor and hartshorn to chase away his hacking cough. At night she wrapped his neck in a linen rag she had spread with a poultice of apple pulp and tobacco to soothe his sore throat and dosed him with sugared brandy to bring down the fever that had built up during the day. Jerusha tried one recipe after another to ease the dysentery—blackberry tea; fermented vinegar in hot water; spoonfuls of rum and molasses.

None of the remedies cured him, but Alice was encouraged that at least he was not getting worse. Still, she wondered, how long could he go on this way, doing the work of a healthy man without the strength of one? She knew it was his will as much as the medicines that kept him on his feet. He barely ate at all; his stomach was easily upset. Alice fixed him tapioca jelly and rye flour gruel, both of which he tolerated fairly well. Jerusha, insisting her brother needed the strengthening benefits of beef tea, made them stop early on the second day after crossing the pass so that she could butcher an ox.

By the fourth day on the western side of the mountains, they had lowered the wagons through Emigrant Gap and gained Bear Valley. The ground was free of snow, and grazing was good. The pleasant valley was scattered through with massive live oaks, the first the Mullers had seen since Missouri. They decided to rest two days here before pressing on to the Sacramento Valley, at least a week's travel ahead. Alice told herself that surely now Henry would regain both his health and his spirit. She pushed aside the memory of another pretty valley with a similar name, the valley of the Bear River, where she had lost Pilgrim.

ALICE WAS RIDING in the wagon with Henry, watching his pale, hollowed face and listening to his harsh breathing. He seemed far away from her. She struggled to remember how he had looked back home when he came in flushed and happy from an afternoon of plowing or splitting wood, bringing into the house on his clothing and on his skin the smells of sun-bright air and growing things.

The respite in Bear Valley had not had the effect Alice had hoped for. With no difficulties to goad him into action, Henry had lain back into his illness like a weary man collapsing onto a featherbed. During the two-day stop, he had gotten up only for meals. Now he rode in the wagon all day, something he would have been ashamed to do only a week earlier.

Alice had wanted to stay longer in the valley to spare Henry the jarring of the wagon, but she did not suggest it. To do so would have seemed to her an admission of the precariousness of his condition. Conflicting superstitions plucked at her. He would not die, she told herself, if she stayed constantly beside him. He would live if she behaved as if he would and left his side to do ordinary chores. He would live because he was the only man left. He would die because he was the only man left.

The first day back on the trail, Alice set little goals for herself as she walked along beside the wagon. She permitted herself to check on Henry only after counting the twentieth pine tree, after passing the big boulder at the fork of the creek, after exchanging a few words with at least four people.

Now, on the second day of Henry's confinement, Alice had given up such games. The need to sit beside him to catch the first sign of a change was too strong. Apprehension curled tensely in her womb like a dark fist. The press of it was undeniable. She turned her mind from it anyway.

Impulsively Alice reached for her journal and tore two pages from it. She began to write a letter to her husband.

Dear Henry,

You shall chuckle, I suppose, in a few days, when you are well, to think how I wrote you a letter while you lay in reach of my hand. I will not mind feeling foolish then, if only I can feel hopeful now.

So, truly, I am writing to you not for you, but for myself, to keep hold of a future wherein you still are.

We must be, at last, nearing the foothills today, the ground dips so gently. The wind bites, but there is no look of snow.

The wagon has stopped just now, and your sister is calling me. Perhaps when I come back, you will be awake. . . .

Alice put down her pen and paper and pulled the buffalo robe up to Henry's chin. The back of her hand touched his neck. It was moist with sweat. His fever was high again. Jerusha's calls grew more insistent.

When Alice climbed out of the wagon, she saw a large boulder beside the front wagon. The children were standing on top of it, the women beside it, their backs to her. She hesitated to join them, instead staying beside the wagon and listening to Henry's labored breathing.

Hank turned and saw his mother watching them. He leapt down from the boulder with the grace of a goat and ran to her.

"It's a valley, Ma, a beautiful golden valley below," he called as he ran. "It's California! It really is!"

Hank grasped Alice's wrist and pulled at her with the urgency of a toddler.

"Come see," the boy said.

"Alice," Henry rasped from the musty gloom within the wagon.

Hank let go of his mother and clambered up onto the back of the wagon.

"We can see the California valley, Pa. Do you want to come?"

Henry slowly propped himself up on one elbow. A coughing spasm seized him for several seconds. The sound of it was wet and harsh, the kind of sound, Alice imagined, a drowning man might make.

"Yes, son, I surely do want to come," Henry said hoarsely when the coughing had subsided.

"Henry, no," Alice objected, climbing past Hank and pushing Henry back down on his pallet. She didn't need to use much force. He looked up at her mournfully from his damp pillow.

"Please," he said. "One look."

Alice felt the knowing fist inside her tighten. Her belly ached as if it were her time of month.

"I'm afraid for you, Henry. It's too much."

Henry closed his eyes and sighed. Alice thought that he had lapsed into sleep. It unnerved her how smoothly he had been sliding into sleep the past few days, as if the difference between sleeping and waking were becoming more and more slight for him. But after a few quiet minutes, Henry reopened his eyes.

"You can help me get there," he said.

Henry coughed again and wiped his sleeve across his forehead, where beads of sweat had formed. He laid his hand over Alice's hands, which were clasped together in her lap.

"Now," he said. "While the wanting to still has ahold of me. Now."

Alice fought down an urge to scream. It was not clear to her what precisely she would scream, nor to whom, nor if her scream would be one of anger or anguish or both. She only knew she suddenly felt as if she were holding in a tremendous force and that its release would wear a terrible meaning.

"Sit up, then," she said to Henry, businesslike. "Hank, jump down so your father can lean on you as he comes out."

Henry sat up, moving stiffly, like an arthritic old man. Alice draped the buffalo robe over his shoulders. She followed behind as he shakily climbed down, ready to brace him if he fell backwards. Hank staggered a little under the weight of his father's hand on his shoulder, but he stiffened his legs resolutely and held up.

With the tottering steps of someone who has been lying down for three days and nights, Henry walked to the boulder between Alice and Hank. Jerusha cried out when she saw him and ran to meet them. She tried to shoo Hank away so that she could help support Henry, but the boy would not move, and when Alice took his part and told her to let him be, Jerusha had to content herself with walking beside them, chirring encouraging sounds at Henry as if she had lost the power of speech.

They led him around the boulder to its western side. He

leaned back against the cold, gray granite and looked down at the valley. Standing beside him, Alice looked at the valley, too.

It was golden, as Hank had said, the combined effect of the low, saffron position of the late afternoon sun, the tall, straw-colored grasses of summer's end, and new yellow-green shoots just sprouted after the autumn rains. There must have been a breeze down there, for the shaggy seed-heads of the dried grasses were undulating as if stroked by a giant hand. The view was one of unreal peace.

Alice turned from the valley to Henry. She noticed that the sharp mountain wind had raised tears in his eyes. He's seen the end, she thought; it's a good omen. He did not protest when she turned him back toward the wagon.

"Thank you," he whispered to her as she settled him among the bedclothes again.

"No thanking needed," she replied.

Alice looked into her husband's face, so familiar and, at the same time, so strange. It seemed, in the dimness of the wagon, that Henry had caught a little of the valley's golden light and was reflecting it to her, as the cool moon rephrases the energetic sun. Hold on to it, she wanted to say to him; save it for yourself; don't spill it out onto me.

"But thanking is needed," he insisted. "Thanking and so much more."

"Come to that, and I figure our tallies are even, Mr. Muller. Now rest."

She bent to kiss his cheek, but he turned his head suddenly and laid his mouth full on hers. Surprised, she returned his soft, slow kiss, then gently pulled away. Henry closed his eyes and rolled onto his side.

"Girlie," she thought she heard him say as she pulled the wagon canvas closed behind her. She looked in and answered him, but he said nothing. The regular rise and fall of his shoulder told her he was already asleep. She went to help the others with supper.

* ★ ★

THE NEXT MORNING Alice could not wake Henry. He lay immobile, still breathing, his skin waxy, a piece of mucus at the corner of his slightly parted lips.

When Jerusha came to see him, as she did every morning, she began crying. Alice let her sit with him while she breakfasted, then she sent her to drive.

Alice rode beside Henry's slack body and waited. Her back ached from the rigidity of her posture. Her feet fell asleep. She did not move until he did, and then she merely leaned over him, straining to catch some murmur. No words came. After two hours during which he only occasionally turned his head from side to side, Henry twitched convulsively three times through his whole body, as dogs do when they're dreaming. Then he lay still again.

Alice, immediately alert, knew right away that this stillness was different. She would not have believed he could be more still than he had been, but there he lay before her, lifeless.

Now that it was gone, she realized that earlier, despite his immobility, a vibration had yet clothed him, a hum, his soul, she supposed. Without it, he was no longer Henry. He was only a reminder of Henry, a Henry she could touch but could not reach.

A deep moan welled up in her, that dark fist unclenching at last. The sound was at once all of her existence and a being apart from her, pulling her along in its mad rush to nowhere. She dropped down beside Henry and gave birth to her wail.

"AUNT JERUSHA," Sarah said, approaching the fire. "Will you come see to Ma?"

Jerusha turned tired eyes on the girl. How like Henry she looks, Jerusha thought, especially wearing that worried frown. There weren't many days on this journey when Jerusha hadn't seen that expression on her dear brother's face.

"See to her?" Jerusha said.

"She's got herself in a state, and she won't listen to me." Sarah's voice trembled with sorrow and frustration.

Several hours had passed since Henry's death. One by one, the little party had climbed into the wagon to see him, Alice and her children standing outside as if in a receiving line. Catherine and Tinnemaha fixed an early supper. Bailey herded everyone to the fire to eat and pressed Jerusha and Alice to each swallow a bracing shot of whiskey.

A half hour ago, Alice and Sarah had gone to sit with Henry. Equally reluctant to speak their thoughts or to break the circle, the rest of them stayed silently around the fire.

"Do you want me to go?" Bailey said when Jerusha made no move to respond to Sarah's request.

"No," Jerusha said. "It's my place."

Sarah sat down beside Hank, who moved in closer to her and put his arm around her back.

Jerusha walked slowly to Henry's wagon. She did not want to have to see him again so soon. Tomorrow at the burying would be time enough. Of all the people in her life who had left her, none had shocked Jerusha in their going as much as Henry had. He was the only person she had ever let herself depend upon wholeheartedly. He had never let her down. Until now.

Jerusha paused outside the wagon and listened. She heard Alice moving around busily inside. It sounded as if she were crossing back and forth from front to back over and over.

"Alice," Jerusha ordered. "Alice, come out here."

Alice appeared at the rear of the wagon.

"Yes?" she said quietly to Jerusha, as if her sister-in-law were a peddler at her kitchen door.

"What are you doing in there?"

"I'm dousing Henry's clothes with camphor," she answered matter-of-factly.

"What for?"

"So we can take him to California."

Alice's voice remained soft and demure, as if her answer

were in no way extraordinary. Jerusha was stunned. Had she to deal with a madwoman now?

"You can't mean it," she sputtered. "Your grief has crazed you."

"I do mean it," Alice said, a steely quality dawning in her words. She smoothed her skirt and pushed some wisps of hair behind her ears, as if straightening her disheveled appearance would make her plan sound more reasonable.

"I have something to say in this," Jerusha declared. "He's my brother, after all. What you propose is not only impractical, it's indecent."

"You prefer to leave your brother for the wolves? How deep a grave do you suppose we could dig here in this cold, stony soil? Henry set out for California, and he will get there. I'll see to it no matter what any of you say."

With that, Alice withdrew into the wagon, leaving Jerusha agitated and confused and feeling as if a whirlwind had just whipped across her path, throwing everything around her into disarray.

Laboriously Jerusha hefted herself up onto the wagon and followed Alice inside. A candle set atop a barrel in the center of the wagon lit the interior with an orange glow. Tall shadows licked up the curving canvas walls and roof. The smell of camphor was intense, burning Jerusha's nostrils and throat with each breath and stinging her eyes, already sore from crying. When she looked at Henry, Jerusha saw that his face had been freshly washed and his hair slicked back with rose water. Alice sat beside him idly picking at a frayed edge of the blanket covering him.

"Alice, be sensible," Jerusha said kindly.

Alice dropped the blanket edge and glared at Jerusha. Jerusha was startled by the vehemence of the anger she saw in her eyes.

"Sensible? You can still ask for that?" she shouted.

Jerusha nodded helplessly.

"I must," she said. "A heart is too raw a thing to be set into the world unguarded."

Alice covered her face in the ends of her shawl and wept. When Jerusha encircled her with her arms, she sagged against her round shoulder and sobbed harder, great wrenching gulps of grief. It always sounds, Jerusha thought, as if such sobs can never end, and yet they always do.

"I know it's hard to leave him here," Jerusha said when Alice's weeping had grown more quiet. "Henry was the dearest person in my life."

Alice sat up. She calmed herself, wiping her eyes with a handkerchief and blowing her nose. She looked squarely at Jerusha and took a deep breath.

"I'm taking him," she said evenly.

Jerusha's eyebrows lifted in amazement and exasperation. She was just gathering herself together to argue again when Alice held up her hand to shush her before she could begin.

"It's only a few days more," she said. "If he's buried in the valley, we can send for him later to be laid nearby our new homes. We'll never get up here again."

Jerusha glanced from her determined sister-in-law to her neat, mute brother. She studied his gaunt face for a long time.

"I believe I have some camphor in my wagon," she said at last. "I'll send Gideon over with it."

"Oh, sister," Alice exclaimed, throwing her arms around Jerusha and hugging her hard.

"And I'll see if tomorrow Mrs. Guthrie and her friend and maybe my Flin will take the mules up to get some snow to pack around him. Should only take them a half day each way."

Alice nodded at the idea.

"Sensibleness does have its place, Jerusha, I know that," she said. "And I'm grateful you've turned yours so generously to help me in this."

"Yes, well," Jerusha said, embarrassed at the praise. "There's times, too, when a raw heart is the only proper guide through this world."

October 16, 1852

We have just finished packing the snow. Flinder, Catherine, and Tinnemaha brought down enough that we were able to cover Henry's body fully. I must mind to hold my pen and work it, as my fingers are numb from that hard task.

Soon the day's light will be gone, and I will need to turn to the tent where I shall sleep with Sarah and Flinder until our wagon is emptied of its doleful burden. But I delay. To be alone with my thoughts seems more fitting than to lie beside the girls and draw comfort from their warmth.

Sitting beside Henry on his last day, I was put in mind of the time he fell from the barn roof and how quiet he had lain in the dust of the yard for a few minutes. In that little time I had been visited with the pain of what losing him would be like. A tight fear had come on me and a quickening like's in the breast of a baby bird. How much broader is the feeling now it's here for true. My heart swells and swells to hold it all, and still it pours over until it is everywhere in me.

It has happened that after a passing thought, I say to myself, I must tell Henry that or I must see what Henry thinks. Or I have found myself sometimes turning at a sound, truly expecting to find him coming up behind me. Then, as quickly, I recall the impossibility of ever speaking with him again. Thus is the wound salted by the cruel mischief of my own disbelieving heart.

The Bible says there is a time to every purpose. I must trust it was Henry's time to die, as clearly as it was his time to move on from Indiana. My objections could not stop either one. Now, with him gone, I am dwelling solely in my own rhythms. I must learn my purposes and find their rightful times.

Chapter 24

I T TOOK THEM two days through the foothills to reach the Dutch Flat mining camp. The trail was dry and stony, but in some places, new shoots of green grass testified to recent rains. The slopes were timbered with large, widely spaced pine trees, clear, limpid turpentine oozing from their bark, and with tall cedar and spruce, manzanita, and groves of live oaks.

The women spoke little. This was not so unusual. Throughout the months of travel, there had been many quiet days, when people had walked alone or together, keeping their thoughts, whether of home or the land around them or one another, to themselves. There were times when the journey asked for silence, or when silence was all anyone could give beyond the work required of them. But this silence was different. There was a unity to it, as if everyone were harboring the same musings, and a tautness, like a bowstring about to be let go.

At least, it seemed so to Alice. She walked ahead of the first wagon, and she fancied she could feel the force of the others' thoughts pushing at her back like an east wind. No one, not even the children, had wondered aloud yet what the future would hold for them now that the journey's end was so close at hand, now that they were arriving under conditions so different from what they'd expected starting out. They had a goal—to reach the flat Sacramento Valley and bury Henry—and that was enough to keep them going for now. But questions hovered, waiting their turn for open attention.

Even the meal stops were without much conversation. Jerusha gave the children orders. Faith, her words high-pitched and songlike, talked aimlessly at Hope, simply to let the baby hear a soothing voice. Tinnemaha and Catherine exchanged a few sentences in the Paiute language. Flinder and Sarah spoke to each other as needed to get their chores done or to direct their brothers. Bailey sketched and ate, making a brief remark here and there.

Alice, taking Hope to nurse, sat on the ground and listened to it all—the sounds of meal making, eating, cleanup; the interweaving of the occasional voices, all so familiar; the throaty suckling of the baby at her breast; the wind brushing through the tops of the firs; birdcalls; the shuffling and snorts of the oxen and mules. And lurking underneath, like a cellar dug out beneath a house, was the dense hush of the cold wagon where Henry lay.

Midafternoon on the second day of travel, Hank spotted smoke tails from Dutch Flat, and soon after, the camp itself came into view, a jumble of tents, canvas-walled shacks, and log cabins nestled snugly up a pine-covered slope. When they got closer, the women and children could see that while some of the cabins had clapboard roofs, others had roofs of cloth or green cowhide. Mining tools lay about everywhere—picks and shovels, rockers, long toms, pans, and sluices. In one rock-strewn spot, a block and tackle had been built to remove large stones.

As the little party with its two wagons and its string of three skinny mules approached, man after man left off his digging or gravel washing to come and meet them. Alice, aware of what a sight they presented with their weather-reddened faces and their oft-mended clothing, quickly lost her self-consciousness. The men who stepped forward were so dirty, it was impossible to tell the color of their shirts, and not one was clean-shaven. In fact, most of their beards were so unruly, Alice wondered how they kept a path open to their mouths.

The number of men around them soon grew into a sizable crowd, and Flinder, walking beside the oxen pulling the front wagon, had to make the beasts halt. Her loud "whoa!"

echoed by Jerusha's "whoa!" to the ox team pulling the second wagon, were the first words uttered by either emigrants or miners.

For a long silent moment, both groups eyed each other with open fascination. Then one man separated himself from the others, and pulling off his soft flannel hat to reveal a greasy mat of dark hair, he nodded courteously at Alice.

"Pardon us for staring, ladies," he said to Alice, Faith, and Bailey, who had gathered together in front of the lead yoke of oxen. "But as most trains go by way of the old Johnson's Ranch savannah a bit north of here, some of us haven't seen a woman in six months or more—and I believe a few of them boys in the back there just might faint."

A loud guffaw arose from the men. It was a laugh so good-naturedly at the men's own expense that the women could not help but smile in answer, though Jerusha did come up to stand protectively beside Flinder.

The man who had made the joke squinted at the two wagons and then up towards the hills from which they had come.

"You got a little ahead of the others, now, didn't you?" he said.

"There are no others," Alice replied.

The man studied her more closely, clearly trying to determine what this meant.

"Where you from?" he said at last.

"Indiana."

"And you come all that way, over the mountains and the desert and all, alone? With no menfolk?"

There were murmurs of disbelief from the listening miners.

"The men in our party either died or deserted at different points along the way," Bailey explained.

"The best of them's here in this wagon," Jerusha called.

The murmurs grew louder.

"You mean you got a dead man in there?" someone shouted from the crowd.

"Was it cholera?" another put in.

Some of the men began to back away. Others covered their mouths and noses with their hands.

"No, we've seen cholera, and it wasn't that," Alice quickly put in. "It was some kind of mountain fever."

"Pushed along by plain discouragement," Jerusha added.

"How far is it to the valley?" Alice asked. "We want to bury him there."

"Well, it's a day or two down to Auburn, then another more days into the valley," the ragged spokesman said. "You could bury him here, though. We got a little graveyard. We even got a minister."

"When he's not drunk," a bystander yelled.

"Or playing cards," another shouted. More guffaws.

The spokesman frowned and waved his arm at the hecklers. Clearly he wanted the women to form a better impression of the rough little community. He shrugged at Alice.

"Better men than him has lost his morals in these gold fields," he said apologetically. "He's all right, really. Works hard when he's sober. Shall someone go fetch him?"

Alice turned to look at her wagon, which seemed to be waiting with almost human patience. Even the oxen were still, their thick heads held up, their large, sad eyes fixed straight ahead. Her gaze swept up from the wagon to the hills they had just descended and to the monumental, snowcapped mountains beyond them. Jerusha came up to her, and Alice turned to face her solemn sister-in-law.

"Alice, I think we should lay Henry here. It's a habitation, at least. The snow's nearly gone, anyway."

"Is the road to Auburn a good one?" Alice asked the miner.

"Passable," he said. "If it's not raining too hard."

"We'd want to come back and get him someday," she said.

"Well, ma'am, you could do that, I'd guess, without much trouble."

"All right, then," Alice decided. "If someone could find the minister and direct us to the graveyard?"

Two men peeled off from the group and walked briskly towards the collection of houses and tents, presumably to rout out the minister. Some of the other men, restless at simply standing and gawking, began circling the two wagons, as if expecting to find some strange difference about them that would explain how these women had managed to lose all their men.

"Hey, what's this?" one man cried out when he got back to where Catherine and Tinnemaha stood with the mules. "There's a squaw here. They got a goddamned redskin with them."

A few other men joined the speaker to see for themselves, as if the sight of an Indian were a novelty.

"Is it one of the ones from around here?" someone asked.

"Naw, she's got clothes on!" someone else answered, amid shouts of laughter.

"Well, I'm from Oregon," growled a man with no teeth in his upper gum, "and in Oregon, we'd rather shoot an Indian than a deer any day."

Catherine moved quickly to stand in front of Tinnemaha, who watched the faces of the nearby men intently. Though she didn't understand their words, Tinnemaha could read the tone of their voices and the set of their bodies, and even before Catherine had taken up her defensive posture, Tinnemaha knew to keep alert. Catherine and Tinnemaha had no weapons, but neither did the men. Yet.

"She's one of our party," Alice called. "A friend."

Sarah began to cry. Jerusha shushed at her. Flinder put a consoling arm around Sarah's shoulder.

"It's this girl's father that lies dead in that wagon," Flinder shouted to the men near the mules. "If you won't help us, if your only thought is to frighten us, then I say he's too good to lie in your ground. I wouldn't want a one of you to touch the shovel that would dig his grave or hold the hammer that would build his box. And someday when you're needing aid and comfort, I hope you meet up with men whose hearts are a match to your own."

Sarah was crying harder now, and in order to embrace her cousin more completely, Flinder turned her back on the men who had threatened Tinnemaha. Alice wrapped her arms around Sarah from behind and laid her cheek on her daughter's head. Her heart ached with the knowledge that no embrace, no words, could save Sarah from cleaving her own way through grief.

Whether it was the sight of the three intertwined females, the impact of Flinder's angry speech, or their own consciences, several men stepped forward and hustled away the offenders, who, for their part, put up no real resistance.

Slowly, in groups of two and three, the others turned away and headed back to their work, with some mumbled apologies and much looking back over their shoulders at the women. The original spokesman and two other men stayed behind talking quietly together off to one side. After several moments, the three returned to where Alice and her party stood. Sarah had calmed down, and Alice and Flinder had disengaged from her.

"I'm Plutarch Baker," the spokesman said. "And this is my brother Plato and our partner, Jed Disharoon. We'd like to offer you all the use of our cabin while you're here. It's a good, strong one—not like some of these you see."

"Thank you, Mr. Baker," Alice said, "but we're used to our wagons and tents and the bare ground. There's no need to put yourselves out."

"You know, ma'am, we've all got wives and children back in the states—me and Plato in Virginia, Jed in New York—and we worry about them and how they're getting along, and somehow helping you ladies and your young ones would kind of make us feel like we was doing something for them, too. Guess that sounds funny."

"Not at all," said Bailey.

"To tell the truth, ladies," said Jed Disharoon, a man with the build of a young bear and almost as much hair, "Dutch Flat can get a mite wild sometimes, and you'd keep safer in a good, solid house with us sleeping outside than you would in your wagons."

"Very well," said Alice. "As you seem to wish it so much, and to ease our own minds about our friend Tinnemaha, we accept your kind offer, though I think we'll only be here for tonight and maybe one other. And since we are to be your guests, let us introduce ourselves. I don't know what I was thinking not to have done it sooner."

Everyone gathered around and gave their names. The men made much fuss over Hope; a baby was an even more rare sight than a woman. When Plato, teary-eyed, declared that his wife had been expecting when he'd left a year and a half ago and had since given him a daughter he'd yet to see, Faith forgave him his rough appearance and let him hold Hope. Indeed, Plato was so delighted at being granted this privilege that he carried the baby all the way to the cabin. Plutarch took charge of the wagon carrying Henry and turned the oxen toward the graveyard. Jed went to check on the progress being made in finding the minister.

The log cabin was sixteen by twenty feet. It had an earthen floor and a door of hewn cedar, but no windows. Backlogs were burning in a large fireplace at one end of the cabin; when they entered, Plato relinquished Hope to her mother and added more logs to build up the blaze. Three rifles hung over the fireplace.

At the opposite end of the cabin were the bunks, framed into the wall. On top of a barrel that was serving as a table Alice saw several sheets of illustrated stationery showing California scenes—the Sacramento City waterfront, Chinese miners, a flume under construction in the bed of the Feather River. In a rough cupboard sat a few wooden and tin dishes, bottles, flatware, a tin frying pan, and a coffeepot. Three large sacks of flour and several cakes of tallow were propped under the bunks. Dried beef and suet hung in a line along the point of the roof.

"We'll bring in some dry breaks to make mattresses on the floor," said Plato. "If you've got blankets or buffalo skins to lay on top, why, it's almost like a featherbed."

"Thank you." Alice smiled at him.

It was strange to be inside a house again, even so rude a one as this. Alice kept circling the one room, noticing every detail—the scattered articles of clothing, the bunch of onions beside the fireplace, the spiderweb in the far corner. How could they bear to be without windows? In my house, she thought, I'll have windows on every side, if I have to use fruit jars for window glass.

In my house. The phrase had come so naturally to mind, it was not until it was formed that the gravity of it struck her. Where would her house be? And what would it be, now that it was no longer to be the home of her husband? Alice realized that during the journey she had given little thought to the specific details of their California home, except to know that as soon as possible, after she'd got the family vegetable garden well in, she'd put in flowers. She'd begun collecting wild-flower seeds along the Platte and had found some, too, beside the Sweetwater and in South Pass.

Henry had said that after wintering near Sacramento City in a tent or in a quickly thrown-up cabin, they would go wherever in the Sacramento or San Joaquin valleys good land was available. The state government was selling to settlers at $1.25 an acre, and for another $1.25-per-acre payment to a ditch company, land could be irrigated. Just by squatting and putting a small amount of money down, they could get up to 160 acres, more if they put some acreage in Alice's name.

Henry had planned to put in wheat at first; it gave a high, quick yield and only required shallow plowing, and he'd read that the hard white California wheat was selling well in England and Ireland because it didn't rot on board ship. With wheat, they might clear the expenses of buying the farm with the first crop. Later, Henry had dreamed, they'd have orange, almond, and olive orchards and livestock, sheep maybe.

Alice wondered if she could manage any of that on her own. Were all the men in California gold-crazy? Could she find reliable hands to help her? Shockingly, the idea of a new husband flew across her mind, but it seemed as unlikely and undesirable an occurrence as growing a tail.

Alice's ruminations were interrupted by the arrival of Jed Disharoon with the Reverend Thatcher, a thin, nervous man whose left eyelid twitched every few seconds. He was cleaner than the other men they'd encountered, and he was sober, though he appeared to be not entirely at ease with the state. He spoke rapidly and at length, saying little of any substance, trotting out platitudes about death and marriage, about the overland migration and the great promise of California.

Thatcher was not only a stranger, but a man of such a different type from Henry that Alice could not imagine him officiating over the burial, so she said she'd be pleased to have him there, but that she would prefer to give the remarks herself. Jerusha, slightly scandalized, suggested that the reverend should at least read from Scripture at the graveside. Alice agreed to this, and the burial was set for the following morning.

THE DAY WAS as sharp and perfect an autumn day as anyone could wish for, even a poet. The sun was as bright as truth, the shadows were deep and cool, the air smelled of moss and woodsmoke and pines.

The Muller party, following their three hosts and Reverend Thatcher, mounted the rise to the small graveyard. There they found their wagon, a freshly dug hole in the ground, and an open pine coffin with the lid propped against it ready to be nailed on.

Alice knelt beside the coffin and looked at Henry, whose cheeks and hands had a grayish cast to them. His hair and beard gleamed wetly, whether from morning dew or the remains of the snow, she did not know. A faint odor of decay hung over him, but it was mostly obliterated by the scent of the newly cut wood and a lingering aroma of camphor. Reaching in, Alice opened Henry's vest and slipped into his shirt pocket the letter she had begun in the wagon up on the mountain, the letter she had never finished and he had never read.

Alice stood up and faced her companions. Slowly she studied each one in turn. They had all dredged out the most presentable clothes they could find for the occasion. Their faces were scrubbed and their hair neatly smoothed. Jerusha presented the grandest appearance in a wrinkled bombazine dress that had somehow survived the discardings done each time they'd had to lighten their loads. The black twilled silk gleamed in the bright October sunshine. How earnest and strong they all looked, Alice thought, despite the evidence of their hollow-eyed faces and their thin, chapped hands, and how glad she was to have them with her at this moment.

"We're come to this hillside today," she said, her voice tentative at first, then sure, "to take our leave of Henry Muller, my beloved husband. To the strangers here, I declare that he was a man possessed of a generous and tolerant heart, to which each in our party can bear witness."

"Amen," Jerusha interjected.

"I never wanted this journey," Alice continued, "but I undertook it. To keep my family together. I failed in that. Yet these last months have been the truest of my time with Henry, and they might not have come to pass otherwise. I tell this private thing to you, my companions, because I cannot say it to him. If God has any part of tenderness, Henry knew it was so."

"May he rest in peace," said Jerusha.

The Bakers fixed the lid to Henry's coffin and, with the help of Thatcher and Disharoon, lowered it by ropes into the ground. Then the reverend cleared his throat and carefully recited the opening words of the Twenty-third Psalm in a rich baritone that must have sounded fine in some small church back home. He held his head high, a worn Bible clasped tightly against his chest as if he thought someone might snatch it from him. Gideon joined in at "he restoreth my soul," his childish piping an almost musical counterfoil to Thatcher's low tones. After the man and the boy had spoken a few lines, the others added their voices, advancing toward the end of the Psalm like rowers pulling together to a much longed-for shore, Thatcher and Gideon marking cadence, making them go slowly enough to really listen to the well-known words.

Alice, Jerusha, Sarah, and Hank stayed on the hill until the men had completely filled in the grave. The first few shovels of dirt were the hardest to bear, they fell so smartly against the coffin. By the end, though, the only sound was the metallic slide of the shovels dipping into the pile of loose dirt.

The rest of the party returned to the cabin to prepare a lunch to thank the miners who had helped them and to console the chief mourners. They had put on a stew of bear meat, potatoes, onions, chili beans, and peas early that morning, and Faith and Flinder had readied pecan pies for baking. Beets were stowed in the hot embers to cook. But the finest treats of the meal for the women and children were the Mexican oranges and the Swiss cheese.

"Enough gold dust will buy you just about anything you could want to eat," Plato declared.

"It can't buy you the know-how to put it all together right, though," said Jed. "I've gotten passable good with bread, when I get the time to do it, but pies and cakes and such have just defeated me."

Alice marked this comment with interest. Perhaps there was another way than farming to provide for herself and her family, by which she now meant Faith and Hope as well as Sarah and Hank. Faith had decided not to return to Indiana. Alice thought of Bailey's plan to run a boardinghouse in one of the small cities of the mining counties. She and Faith could probably manage something like that. Jerusha might want to work with them, too. By the looks of the men here, a laundry or a bakery would likely turn a handy profit as well.

Once more Alice surveyed her companions, who were sitting in an approximate circle on plank benches or on the ground in front of the Baker cabin. Food was being passed and exclaimed over, stories of the trail and of California were being swapped. There were smiles, nods of recognition, frowns and clucks of sympathy, some exaggerations and some omissions. How quickly and smoothly, Alice thought, both we and these miners are able to take up again the handiwork of society and shape it afresh. She felt stir within her a stubborn, nourishing certainty that she and her friends would find their way in this new place, would make a way if one could not be found.

November 10, 1852

We are fully into our cabin today on the outskirts of Auburn. It's a bit crowded with Faith, Jerusha, and myself and all the children, but it's only for the winter and far roomier, in any case, than a wagon. The rest have gone into Auburn for supplies and to see Bailey off south to Murphys, a prospering town by what the miners tell of it. I am left here with Hope and the remains of the settling in. Despite the crisp air, I have set Hope, well wrapped, outside to nap. She's that used to living in the open, she makes an awful hurrah at being indoors, as if we'd tied her up and closed her in a cage.

In the unpacking, I came upon this battered journal, neglected in past weeks, and sat down to leaf through it. I find pages wrinkled from the rains along the Platte, whole words rinsed away in places, and other pages smudged with dirt or campfire ashes. My thumb follows the torn edges of the pages that made my dear Henry's letter. When I read what I wrote over all the weeks on the trail, I am transported to the places I saw, I hear the people, I feel again what I felt.

Bailey had said I should keep up my writing and should harvest pieces from my journal for a book that she might illustrate. I put the idea aside almost before she had spoken it all. There is the bakery business to launch first, to get us through the winter, and in the spring, the making of a true home. The notion of land grows stronger in me; I am lured by the way the turn of the months carries meaning on a farm and by the opportunity for solitude my own place will afford me. But with this book in my lap, cramping my writing to fit all my thoughts onto the final few empty pages, I begin to imagine what it would be like to sift through it efficiently, as one sorts lima beans, discarding the blighted ones and the little tooth-breaking stones and rinsing the dust from the good ones so that the cooking water will make a clean, tasty broth. And Bailey's suggestion does not seem so outlandish after all.

The men said we made our journey to start anew and to be part of great events. But as I consider taking up my pen again as a regular task, I find that I am drawn to set down not wide, impersonal glories, but the common little bits that go on day by day, the chores and smells and songs and aches brought forth in each season of Nature and each season of man. The faithful rendering of such things seems to me no mean accomplishment. What are great events, anyway, but scrap quilts of many lives pieced together with common thread of homely cotton?